Into the Fire

Also by David Wiltse

Into the Fire

David Wiltse

G. P. Putnam's Sons

New York

G. P. Putnam's Sons
Publishers Since 1838
200 Madison Avenue
New York, NY 10016

LIBRARY OF CONGRESS CATALOGING-IN-PUBLICATION DATA
Wiltse, David.
Into the fire / David Wiltse.
p.   cm.
ISBN 0-399-13969-9
1. Private investigators—United States—Fiction.   I. Title.
PS3578.I478I58   1994
813'.54—dc20   94-25352   CIP

Printed in the United States of America
1 2 3 4 5 6 7 8 9 10

To D. G. Selbst,
whose courage and talent continue to inspire

Chapter 1

After setting fire to Harold Kershaw, Aural decided it was wise to leave town, the better part of a display of independence being the surviving of it. Harold was a vindictive man when he had a score to settle, not to say just plain stone mean when he was in a good mood. Aural decided to scoot on out of Asheville while the score still read plus one in her favor.

She caught the bus to Richmond, paying full price for the ticket—she had taken the prudent measure of emptying Harold's wallet into her pockets before adding it to the conflagration—but got off in Statesville and hitched her way to Elkin. In Elkin she boarded a bus to Galax, Virginia. Harold was certain to come after her. Aural was afraid of being caught, but she didn't think that Harold had a real chance of actually catching her since sleuthing was not at all in his line of work. In the first place, Harold would be required to ask strangers for information. In her experience, Harold didn't talk all that much or all that well. Certainly not to her. What he excelled at was grunting and opening beer bottles with his teeth—the advent of screw-on caps had done nothing to discourage this propensity—and, when the mood was on him, chewing glass. He was also good at pissing contests, or so he claimed. Aural had been forced to witness only a few and declined further invitations to watch. It was one of those pastimes like golf, she figured: fun for the participants, maybe, but of less than nominal interest to spectators. But Harold was so proud of his urinating skills that he contrived to demonstrate them without the excuse of a contest. His favorite display was to stand in the back of his pickup as it raced through a neighboring village such as Swannanoa and pee for the entire length of the main street. Aural liked those stunts better than the contests—at least she got to drive. Once or twice—towards the end of her relationship with Harold—she had tried to bounce him out of the truck bed, but he had surprisingly good balance for a man who was drunk enough to piss his way through town. She had succeeded only in making him wet himself which was hardly lethal. The one time made him mad and the other time made him laugh.

After spending the night in Galax, Aural engaged the motel owner in an elaborate conversation she knew he was going to remember—coming as it did from a pretty young thing such as herself. Even then, Aural had taken the precaution of leaving her blouse about half unbuttoned to insure she got the man's attention. She let it drop that she was heading for Kentucky, where she had kin. No sooner had she left that dump than she took the first ride she could flag down that was heading for West Virginia, where she didn't know a soul.

That was enough covering of tracks to throw off Harold. Someone who knew what he was doing could probably find her, but Harold didn't and he was too dumb to think of hiring a detective. He certainly wasn't going to go to the police. She knew that setting him alight was probably against the law in some circles, but to Harold it would seem more like a breach of faith. A matter to be dealt with personally. His dealings with the law had always been on the wrong end of it, and he would not turn to them for succor now.

Hitching a ride was no problem, not for a woman who looked like Aural. At twenty-eight, she looked more like eighteen. She had the type of face that bespoke perpetual innocence with the kind of virginal glow that belied her experience, which, she thought, was beginning to tote up rather weightily. Her body, however, had the kind of lithe loose-jointedness that cried out to men like a foghorn at dusk. Standing beside the road, a hand on one denim-clad hip, the other thrust jauntily outwards in a model's pose, her whole form seemed to be saying, "Go ahead and try." It was only when the cars and pickups ground to a halt and the drivers got a closer look at the face as pure as a girl's in her white Confirmation dress that confusion set in. Aural played on the confusion for as long as the drive took.

She was not particularly worried about the alleged dangers of hitchhiking. She was an expert at manipulating men, especially men of a certain brutish stripe—which, in her experience, included most of them—and if she couldn't keep them in control with her wits, there was always the utility knife secured inside the top of her boot by a strip of Velcro. The knife was her idea, a sort of primordial legacy from a long line of McKessons who had never been without a weapon. Aural had had a blade on her since she was ten. The Velcro strip was a refinement she got from Jarrell Robeaux, a Cajun of intemperate inclinations whom she had spent a few months with in Biloxi. It was the only thing worth keeping that she got from him if you didn't count the little scar just behind her right ear where he had clipped her with his metallic Stanley Powerlock tape measure.

On route 52 in Welch, West Virginia, Aural caught a ride with a fat man who didn't want to talk but kept one eye turned on her the whole ride as if he had just seen something on television about the dangers of picking up hitchhikers. It didn't take her long to realize that he was not being paranoid, he was simply ogling, and with that knowledge Aural relaxed—she was more than comfortable being ogled, she had been ogled by the best of them for years—and took advantage of the silence to reflect on her latest adventure.

It was Harold's boots that had been the death of the relationship, she mused. He had taken to slinging them at her as a matter of course, almost absently, the way he might pick up a stick and keep tossing it for a dog to retrieve. The insouciance of the gesture bothered Aural. She didn't particularly mind if her mate slung something her way now and then—she'd never had one who didn't—but it seemed to her the throw ought to at least be done out of anger. She could understand anger, she had hurled the odd object at Harold, too, not always in self-defense. One time, she remembered, she had flung a soup pot at him; it wasn't exactly full of hot soup at the time, but it wasn't precisely empty, either. Harold had done nothing particularly egregious to deserve it, as far as Aural could remember. She had simply looked over at him where he sat at the kitchen table, his features blurry with hangover, his belly swelling over his belt with the beginnings of a paunch, his hair sticking out from his head at all angles like he'd been sitting in front of a fan while applying mousse. He was picking his back teeth with his finger and coughing as if about to throw up. He was unwashed, unclean, and generally unsavory, and Aural had had the penetrating insight that her standards had fallen to an unacceptable level. Also, it was hot as hell and so humid they might have been underwater. They were fixing to eat soup because it was all that was in the house and so Aural had let fly with the pot, hoping, perhaps, that it might lead to Harold's self-improvement.

So it was not exactly the fact that he tossed his boots at her so much that towards the end he had taken to slinging them at her head. Her face was her fortune, her mother had always told her, and Aural believed it although she had yet to see a penny from it. Rather than have her fortune damaged by size eleven Dan Perkins, Aural had taken her incendiary leave.

Harold was the sixth man she had lived with in the last eight years, each one worse than the other, as far as she could tell. The embarrassing part was that no one had forced her to associate with any of them. Aural never lacked for options when it came to the male population. She had chosen the selection of roughnecks and shit kickers all on her own. It was enough to make her wonder if she actually liked being cuffed and sworn at and kicked around. Not that she didn't usually give as good as she got. Aural would never consider herself abused. She was free to leave at any time, and eventually she always did. She was capable of defending herself, too. It was more a question of lying down with swine, as her father would have put it. He used to have a quote he would offer in that line, but then he had a quote for every line of disappointing behavior Aural could come up with. She couldn't remember most of them. Could it be, she wondered as they pulled into a burg called Bald Nob and the fat man made signs of making his move after all, could it be that she actually liked men who were mean and stupid and no earthly good for her? Now that was just plain sad.

When the fat man reached for her thigh she caught his hand and bent his fingers back until he screamed. He managed to use his good hand to swerve to the side of the road and slow down just enough for Aural to hop out of the vehicle. She was left standing on the dusty road on the far side of Bald Nob, looking back towards a tent they had passed just moments ago when the fat man overreached himself. It looked to Aural like a fine place for a preacher's daughter to find herself on a summer's day.

Chapter 2

Nimble as a goat, lithe as green willow, his body not much longer than the coil of rope strapped to his pack, the boy scampered up a rock face with the insouciance of youth. He never thought of danger, had no fear of falling, indeed had only the fuzziest grasp of the concept of mortality as it applied to himself. Standing above on belay, his hands taking in slack, his leg braced to absorb the shock of any fall, John Becker watched young Jack climb with a mixture of envy and apprehension. A good climber had no fear—or at least he never thought of it as fear—but he always had a healthy respect for the perils presented by any ascent. At ten, Jack was simply too young to recognize the hazard presented by the unremitting, unbreakable law of gravity.

Jack attained the ledge where Becker stood, virtually springing up on it, his face beaming with accomplishment. Becker remembered his own labored breathing as he had hauled himself up after the long pitch. Jack looked fresher than when he had stood at the base of the rock. Galileo had it wrong, Becker thought. Gravity does pull harder on some bodies than on others.

"Well done," Becker said.

Jack's smile split his face. "It was easy."

"Uh-huh."

Jack turned and looked back down the rock. Becker resisted an instinct to grab him by his belt. "That wasn't very high."

"Yeah, well, we'll work up to Everest gradually. Not till next week at the earliest."

The boy waved at his mother who stood at the base, looking anxiously upwards.

"Your turn," Becker said, wiggling the rope.

Jack laid out the line as he had been taught, took a braced position, then called out, "On belay!" Becker smiled at the seriousness in his attitude.

"Christ, I hope so," his mother muttered to herself. She stared upwards but could no longer see his face over the ledge.

"Climbing!" she called and took her first foothold on the rock. She could feel the rope tauten subtly, allowing her freedom of movement while still suggesting security.

Behind Jack's back, Becker took his own anchored position, ready to serve as instantaneous backup if the boy should fail.

Karen climbed slowly but steadily, with a workmanlike approach. She had come to climbing only recently, under Becker's tutelage, and although her body was strong and her reflexes as sharp as any other trained FBI agent's, her mind was reluctant to surrender to the arcane pleasure of embracing stone.

The problem with opting to spend your life in a primarily male society, she thought, was proving that you could do it. And proving it and proving it and proving it. The testing never stopped. As Associate Deputy Director of Kidnapping, she was as high as any woman had ever been in the Bureau, and she had gotten there a lot younger, too. But even so there was the constant nag of having to demonstrate again and again that she deserved to be there, that she could be as macho as any of them if the occasion demanded. And somehow or other, the occasions seemed to be always cropping up. Not that Becker doubted her, she knew that. He had no desire to turn her into a man with softer parts. He liked the femininity of her mind, was as fascinated by it as he seemed to be fascinated by so many things that were not his by nature. Of all the men she knew, Becker was the only one that she was certain accepted her just the way she was . . . Still, here she was, pressing her nose against the stone and cracking what few fingernails she could allow herself to cultivate just because Becker's former wife had been a rock climber. Showing off for her man and her son. Why was it, she wondered, not for the first time, that they never felt inclined to knit *her* a sweater for Christmas to impress *her?*

Karen's ascent to the ledge was somewhat less impressive than Jack's. She hoisted herself just high enough to sit, then leaned back, her feet dangling into space.

"Well done," said Becker.

"Pretty good," said Jack. She caught the note of condescension in his tone, but she wasn't sure if the rest of his thought was, *for a woman,* or *for my mom.* At ten, her son was already a confirmed sexist, although Becker had assured her he might grow out of it.

"Next vacation we go somewhere I can wear a skirt," she said. Becker sat beside her, snuggling his thigh against hers.

"I promise," he said. "Fair enough, Jack?"

At his silence, both adults turned to look at him. The boy was staring upwards, his attitude suddenly frozen into one of apprehension.

"What's that?" he asked, pointing.

"It's called a chimney," Becker said. "I told you about them."

"You didn't say they were so *small*," Jack said.

The chimney was actually a vertical seam in the rock, a narrow split a few feet wide that extended upwards as if the stone had been torn by giant hands. The technique of climbing it was for the climber to use his body like a wedge, forcing his legs against one side of the chimney wall, his back against the other, and inching up as if his shoulders and buttocks were hands. Like so much of rock-climbing technique, it required a certain faith in addition to mindless resolve.

Becker had selected this stretch of mountain because although it was tiring it was not dangerous and there was a wide variety of techniques available within a small range.

"Do we have to go *inside* it?" Jack asked nervously.

Becker studied the boy carefully. "Not if you don't want to—" he started.

"I think you should, Jack," Karen interrupted.

"It's all right to be afraid of something," Becker said to Karen.

"I know it's *all right*," Karen said with annoyance. She was caught again in the conflict between wanting to protect her child and fearing she would injure him by isolating him from all of the risks and challenges that made boys into men. She wondered if single mothers produced the most macho of sons out of a dread of creating weaklings. "But I think he should do it. It's why we came."

"I think he should decide," Becker said patiently. Karen's eyes flashed angrily for a second.

"I think he should do it," she said.

Jack looked back and forth between the two adults.

"Couldn't I just go straight up that way?" Jack asked, pointing out a route that avoided the chimney.

"Sure," said Becker.

"But then you'd never learn how to do *that*," Karen pointed at the rip in the stone face. "You'll have to learn it sometime."

"Why?"

"Because life is like that, Jack," she said. "It never lets you off easy."

"We're all afraid of something," Becker said softly. "There's nothing wrong with it."

"*You're* not afraid of anything," Jack said.

"Sure I am. I'm afraid of lots of things," Becker said.

"Like what?"

"Right now I'm most afraid of climbing that chimney," Becker said.

"Huhn-uh."

"Trust me, Jack. I'll break into a sweat the minute I get inside it."

"Then how come you want to do it?"

Becker shrugged. "Do you know what 'counterphobic' means, Jack?"

"No."

"It means I'm more afraid of being afraid of something than I am afraid of it." Becker chuckled. "Let me try again. It means I do the things I'm afraid of. I don't want the fear to win."

"Are you really afraid of going into that chimney?"

"Honest to God. I'm scared even thinking about it."

"I'm not," Jack said. He stood and started towards the chimney.

"Nice psychology," Karen said, getting to her feet.

"That wasn't psychology," Becker said, "it was the truth. I'm scared shitless."

Karen looked at him closely. His face was ashen and sweat had broken out on his forehead. Karen started to say something but Becker rose quickly and started after Jack, heading towards the chimney.

Chapter 3

Lights out in the cellblock was like sun down in the jungle, time for the predators to emerge and for the vulnerable to hunker in hiding. But unlike the jungle where the hunters moved in stealth and silence, within the cement walls of Springville prison it was the predators who made most of the noise. And there was no place for anyone to hide.

Three cells away, the new punk was being introduced to the pleasures of prison life, and his screams excited the inmates. Cries of support rang out from the length of block as his fellow predators urged on the aggressor. Some of the habitual victims raised their voices, too, eager to have someone else degraded. And of course a few of the victims had come to love their victimization, some to adore their tormentors. Their response was to coo sympathetically or to eye their cellmates seductively. Not that much seduction was required. The prison population is primarily young, and most of the prisoners already have too much testosterone for their own good or that of society. Sex pervades the prison like the overheated summer humidity, clinging to the skin, freighting the air.

"Get used to it, honey," said a weary voice, offering the only advice applicable to the situation. Once a punk was initiated, there was no turning back, no reversing of roles. For the rest of his term he would remain what he had become.

Cooper lay on his bunk, listening to the uproar, a slow grin building on his lips.

"Hear that, punk?"

The shape on the bunk above him did not stir.

"I'm talking to you," Cooper said. He kicked upwards and slammed his foot into base of the upper bunk.

"What?"

"Don't pretend you don't hear me," Cooper said. "You hear me."

"What is it?"

Cooper's grin broadened. He enjoyed it when his punk tried to out-smart him because, in here, in the cell, there was no way anyone could outwit Cooper. In the world, intelligence counted for something. Every two-bit clerk who could subtract well enough to make change for a ten was intimidating to Cooper. They could disrespect him and live be-cause there were too many of them to kill. Everyone seemed to sense the awkward and clumsy movements of his mind and to dance around him like hyenas around a shackled lion. They were legion and he was just one. There was nothing he could do but let them cheat and bully and mock him. The world belonged to the agile; but here, in this cell, the universe belonged to the strong. Cooper's power was rooted neither in wit nor cunning but in raw strength.

"What is it?" Cooper said in mincing tones, mocking the convict above him. "What is it?"

"Honestly," Swann said. "I don't know what you want."

" 'Honestly.' "

Cooper waited for Swann to respond, then kicked the bunk again.

"Now," he said.

Swann leaned his head over the edge of the bunk. He had the look on his face that Cooper loved to see. The placating look of someone trying to hide his fear while calming a menacing dog.

"I don't feel very well," Swann said.

"Shit," said Cooper dismissively. "I want it now."

"No, truthfully, Cooper. I think I have an infection. It might put you in jeopardy. I wouldn't want that."

Cooper laughed. He recognized the tone even if he didn't grasp all of the substance. It was the same bullshit that they all tried on him in the world, scooting around him with their words, twisting things so he didn't know what to think.

He didn't have to put up with it here.

"Time for your nightlies," Cooper said.

"You know I want to . . ."

"I know you do."

"Anything you want. Normally. But tonight . . ."

Cooper grabbed the smaller man by the ear and pulled until he came off the bunk, yelping in pain.

"Old Coop's going ridin'," called out a neighboring inmate who heard Swann's groans.

"Coop's ridin'," Cooper called back happily, delighted to be recognized. He was a respected man on the block, people spoke to him, called out his name in admiration. If not the strongest man on the block of strong men, he was close.

Three cells away, the new punk's initiation came to a climax with the exultant scream of his tormentor. Between catcalls from the kibitzers the punk could be heard weeping. If he didn't stop soon, the predator would beat him until he couldn't. Cooper hated weepers, particularly crying women—or anyone that reminded him of them.

His punk didn't cry. His punk loved him. Not just because Cooper protected him from the other cons who might want to abuse him. He loved him because he loved him, because Cooper was lovable, because he was a good man, and a stud and a nice guy—or at least in as much as circumstances allowed him to be a nice guy. Niceness was not a highly valued characteristic in the jungle.

Cooper tightened his fingers around Swann's throat, feeling the cords of muscle that held the little man's head to his body. It would be so easy to yank it right off. Just one good tug, Cooper thought. He was strong enough, he could pop it off like he was snapping string. Cooper wondered if Swann would flap around like a chicken, or would he just die, collapsing like a poleaxed steer. Cooper had seen the way cattle died in a slaughterhouse, falling as if a hole had opened beneath them, finished without a twitch. He had never seen a human being die that quickly, there was always some fuss, usually noise, too. But then he'd never seen anyone die because his head was pulled off, either. He tightened his grip on Swann's neck until the punk began to cough.

Cooper felt the throbbing begin.

"You love me, don't you?" he demanded, his voice husky now and low so no one else could hear.

"I love you," said Swann.

Cooper thrust harder, beginning to lose control.

"I love you, too," Cooper said, each word tortured from his frantic breathing, and for the moment he truly did. He wanted to squeeze his punk in his arms although the position did not allow it. He wanted to be wrapped in another person's embrace, to feel the warmth of another body, his beloved's body, against his skin.

Cooper finished with the orgasmic scream of a cat, announcing his dominance as he had learned to do in prison, letting the listeners know of his triumph. Quiet passion was for the prey, not the predators.

He slumped across Swann's back as the last of the tremors shook him, then, as always, was almost immediately filled with guilt. He thrust the punk away from him, pushing him with his foot against the wall.

The punk hit his head and moaned.

"Shut up," Cooper said.

"That hurt."

"You're lucky I don't kill you," Cooper said. "If I didn't have to live with you, I'd kill you."

Swann was silent, a shape in the dark, huddled against the wall. Cooper wanted to kick him again. Like a cowering dog, he thought. Just asking for the boot.

"You know that, don't you?" Cooper asked.

"I know that."

"If I didn't have to live with you, I'd probably pull your head right off. You know I could."

"I know it."

"I killed a faggot once."

"I'm not a faggot, Coop."

"You'd better not be."

"I just do it because I love you."

"God damn if I'd share a cell with a faggot. If I ever find out you are one, I'll kill you anyway, I don't care if I never get out. I'll kill you just like I did the other one."

There was a silence and for a moment Cooper thought it would be a bad night, the punk would be moody and difficult, perhaps he really was sick, maybe Cooper had injured him after all. He was always such a little shit when he felt abused and, although Cooper could force him to cooperate, he didn't do it with the same ego-satisfying sincerity. Who knew what went on in his mind, crouching over there in the shadows? Fucking little clerk, Cooper thought, little snot-nose behind the cash register. Cooper had stuck his .38 into the face of dozens of them, seen their smugness change to fear in a second. Seen the color drain out of their faces as if the gun was a siphon and Coop a vampire. Little shit-fuck, dirty little shit-fuck, hiding in the dark, sniveling.

Then Swann broke the silence.

"How did you kill him?"

Cooper relaxed. The tone of voice was just right, the punk was in the proper mood. He would ask the questions and Cooper could say the things he loved to say. It was the part of the evening he liked best, the part after sex when he talked about himself and the things he had done and the things he was going to do. Cooper had forgotten many of the details, but the punk remembered, he coached Cooper when things slipped his mind. Cooper never felt stupid when telling his stories to Swann.

"I kicked him to death," Cooper said.

"Why?"

"I told you, he was a faggot."

"When did you do this, Coop?"

"At night. He come up to the car and said could he do anything for me and I said, yeah, faggot, you can do something for me. You can eat my boot."

"I meant how long ago did you do this?"

"Why didn't you say so?"

"I didn't make myself clear, I'm sorry . . . Was it just before you came to prison, or longer, or . . . ?"

"It was . . . uh . . ."

"Was it five years ago, when you were in Nashville?"

"That's right."

"Did the police know about it?"

"I don't know. I didn't tell them. I don't suppose he did, do you?"

"Was that before you killed the girls, or after?"

"Before."

"How did the girls happen?"

"You like that one, don't you?" Cooper said.

"I like whatever you like, Coop. Your favorites are my favorites."

"They're all my favorites. I wouldn't have killed them if I didn't like it, would I?"

"Would you rather tell me about another one? Do you want to talk about the Mexican?"

"Which Mexican? I done more than one Mexican. I done lots of them. I hate Mexicans."

"The one when you were picking oranges?"

"I done lots of Mexicans," Cooper repeated vaguely, trying to remember.

"You said he got in your face because of his wife."

"Oh, yeah." Cooper waited for further reminders. There had been so many, how could he be expected to recall the details? That's what the punk was good for. Cooper told about them when they occurred to him; it was up to Swann to remember what he said.

''She was coming on to you . . . She was sticking her ass in your face when she was on a ladder.''

Cooper chuckled. ''I remember. Wiggling her ass around in my face like it itched.''

''And she wanted you to scratch it.''

''Wanted me to fuck it, is what she wanted.''

''That's what I meant . . . Did you, Coop?''

''Did I what?''

''Did you fuck her?''

''What do you think?''

''Did you make her scream?''

''I always make them scream.''

''Is that the best part?''

''What?''

''Making them scream? Is that the part you like best?''

''I like seeing their faces when I put the gun in their mouth.''

''You don't do that to the women, do you?''

''I wasn't talking about the women.''

''Okay.''

''Stick to the point,'' Cooper said. ''We're talking about the Mexican.''

''I'm sorry. I get confused sometimes,'' the punk said.

Cooper smiled in the darkness. The shit-fuck clerks were smart only about what they were smart about. They weren't smart about what Coop was smart about. They didn't know shit about the things Cooper knew.

''There's a lot of them to remember,'' Cooper said magnanimously. ''I lose track myself sometimes.''

''There are an awful lot of them. You must have done more people than anybody on this block.''

''I done more than any con in the whole damned prison, and don't you forget it. I probably done more than anybody anywhere. What's the record?''

''I don't know, Coop. Seventeen, eighteen?''

''Shee—it, that's nothing. Is that all? I must have done thirty. More probably.'

''Do the police know about them?''

''Who cares?''

''They're the ones who count, they keep track.''

''They do?''

"They're the scorekeepers, sort of. If they don't know, it doesn't count."

"Bullshit. If I done them, they're dead."

"Just a manner of speaking."

"Bullshit."

"You're right, Coop."

"I'm trying to tell you about the Mexican."

"I want to hear about it."

"Then quit confusing me with all this other shit."

"Sorry."

"I could rip your head off if I wanted to, you know."

"I know you could . . . Did you rip the Mexican's head off?"

Cooper chuckled. "Naw . . . I gutted him. He come at me with his knife—you know all them Mexicans got knives, they're fucking born with them. I stuck my gun in his face and took the knife away and then I gutted him with his own blade. You should have heard him gurgle in Mexican."

"Spanish."

"What?"

"What did you do with the body?"

"I stuck it in a culvert."

"Do you suppose the police have ever found it?"

"I don't know, you little shit. Do police usually go looking in culverts?"

"I don't know that much about the police, Coop."

"You're in here, ain't you? I guess the police know about you, all right, you little dickhead."

"That was different. I made a mistake, I didn't kill anybody."

"You tried though, didn't you? You just couldn't pull it off."

"I didn't try, I was just defending myself. She attacked me, I was just defending myself."

"Assault with a deadly weapon, right? The judge didn't think you was 'defending' yourself. He thought you was trying to kill your landlady with a meat cleaver."

"She attacked me, the woman was deranged."

Cooper turned his back to the other man. He didn't understand what "deranged" meant and he was tired of talking about someone other than himself.

"You're so innocent, I guess they ought to let you go, then," Cooper said, trying to think how to get the conversation back to him.

"I know everyone says they're innocent, Coop, but I really am."

"You just couldn't manage it. If you'd killed the bitch the way you should have, maybe you wouldn't be here now, did you ever think of that? Kill them and who's going to report it? Who's going to testify if they're dead? You just didn't have the balls for it. And not everyone says they're innocent. I ain't innocent. I just ain't been caught for what I done, they don't know the half of what I done, nobody does, not even you. But I'm not telling them, let them find out for themselves."

"They'll never find out about you, Coop. You're too good at it. You must have bodies hidden all over the country."

"Uh-huh."

"You put the Mexican in the culvert . . ."

"Yeah."

"And what else?"

"What else what?"

"What other bodies did you hide?"

Cooper tried to think. He knew the answer, he just couldn't come up with it right away. That was how his mind worked, it always got there eventually, but sometimes not as fast as others thought it should. Well, fuck them.

"Them girls," he said triumphantly. "I hid them girls."

"Are those the ones you burned to death?"

"Hell, no. I burned them alive," Cooper said, laughing.

"That was in Pennsylvania?"

"Yeah . . . No. Not Pennsylvania. Can't you remember anything, you little fruiter? It was in West Virginia."

"I'm not a fruit," Swann said.

Cooper was paying no attention. For once the facts sprang clearly to mind. Some memories were fuzzy and some clear and some so vague he didn't know if he dreamed them or lived them. But this time the pictures sprang vividly to mind.

"I did 'em in an old coal mine in West Virginia," he said proudly. "Just outside a town called Hendricks."

"Why a coal mine?"

"I needed somewhere—what do you call it?—someplace alone."

"Secluded."

"That's it."

"Why did you need a secluded place? You never did any other time, did you?"

"Because they were going to make a lot of noise."

"Why didn't you gag them?"

Cooper grinned in the darkness. He knew all the answers this time.

"Because I wanted to hear them."

"How come you did two at a time, Coop?"

"Did I say that? Did I say I did two at a time?"

"I just thought . . ."

"Don't think, you might hurt yourself," Cooper said. Damn, he knew so much more about this stuff than any goddamned clerk. It was a wonder anybody so stupid was allowed to live. "I did 'em six months apart. I planned it good, too. I got together enough food and shit to last me a week. And a couple cartons of cigarettes. And a lantern. And some candles. It's dark in a mine, you know, you got to have some light."

"You took a week killing them?" Swann was horrified.

"What's wrong with that?"

Swann was silent.

"Anything wrong with a week?"

"No," Swann said quietly. "I wasn't criticizing."

"I could pull your head off if I wanted."

"I wasn't criticizing."

"I hope to shit not. Ask me something else."

"Where did you find them?"

"Who?"

"The girls you took to the abandoned mine."

"It was a coal mine."

"Nobody was using it anymore, were they?"

"Of course not. I told you. It was an old mine."

"Where did you find the girls you took there?"

Cooper brayed. This was the best part. He loved this part because of the reaction it got from Swann. Every time.

"I picked them up at church."

He could hear the little punk gasp. Every time. He had never seen such a religious nut. Cooper knew what was coming next. He heard Swann shuffling off his ass and onto his knees.

"Could we pray now?" Swann asked although it wasn't really a question. Cooper knew that Swann would pray now no matter what Cooper said or did, short of bashing his head against the wall.

"Sure. Pray," Cooper said. He rose from the bunk and knelt beside Swann, facing the crucifix that was barely visible in the gloom. Cooper didn't see what harm could come of humoring the little man now and then. It made him play his part more eagerly if he knew he got his reward at the end. And, besides, Cooper figured the praying couldn't hurt, especially since it was mostly about him.

"Dear Lord, Sweet Jesus, Angel of Mercy," Swann intoned, "look down on our beloved brother Cooper and bring the spirit of redemption to his soul. Pierce his hardened heart with your love, Sweet Jesus, and let him know the joy of loving his fellow man . . ."

Swann enthused onward and Cooper's focus soon drifted off. Cooper had heard the little punk keep at it for hours at a time, so there wasn't any need for him to try to keep up with it all. He paid little attention to the words of the prayer, they often confused him anyway, but he liked the rhythm, the singsongy way the phrases were punctuated by "Sweet Jesus" and "Darling Lord," as if Swann were calling out to his sweetheart in the next cell and wanted to make sure he was being heard. The specific message wasn't important, anyway. It was the concern that Swann showed for his cellmate that touched Cooper. The punk cared for him; he really did love him. Somewhere in the midst of all the blabbing to god, Swann would get around to the fact that Cooper was being released soon and would need all the help the darling lord could spare when he reentered the world. He would ask sweet Jesus to walk hand in hand with old Coop and keep him out of trouble. Cooper liked that image and in his mind sweet Jesus looked a lot like Swann himself, but with a scraggly beard. Swann already had the messianic hair down to his shoulders and some nights Cooper would remove the rubber band that held it in a ponytail and run his hands through it. There was comfort in the idea of a Christ-like Swann, short and weak but smart in a lot of ways that were valued in the world, walking down some long dirt road with his hand in Cooper's. And, in truth, Cooper had some need for comfort. The prospect of freedom after five years of confinement filled him with trepidation. Not that he would ever admit to such anxiety to Swann or anyone else. If they saw the slightest sign of fear or even uncertainty, they would take it for weakness and swarm all over him, prying and pulling at whatever slightest chink they could find until they ripped him open and fed on his insides. But the fear was real, however well he hid it. In truth, Cooper had never done well in the world. It bewildered him with its complex rules and escalating demands. Even his pleasures had to be circumscribed or the police would be on him. In prison the rules were clear and quickly learned and if you were strong enough and vicious enough, you could make your own. And here, at least, someone loved him and cared about his welfare.

Cooper put an arm around Swann's shoulders, feeling the knobby bones through the mottled skin. In full light, Swann's torso and legs were covered with freckles. For some reason only his face had been spared the spots. Cooper had learned to love them. His punk leaned his head against the big man's chest and continued to pray.

"Sweet Jesus," Swann implored, "bring your divine love to the heart of Darnell Cooper the way he has brought love to mine. Let the light of your great goodness shine upon him. Deliver him from the pit. Cause him to dwell no more in the valley of the shadow, darling Lord, but lift him up to your mountaintop of light!"

"Amen," said Cooper, prematurely.

"And, sweet Jesus, cleanse his mind of those thoughts which torment him. Lift from him, Lord, those obscene fantasies that haunt his soul. Raise up his eyes so that they might dwell forever on your sweet goodness and look no more into the abyss of the evil pit."

Swann shivered and Cooper did not know if he was cold or frightened. He himself was getting excited again. When the punk got through praying, he was usually very receptive. Sometimes he thought up new ways to do it. His punk had a lot of imagination.

Chapter 4

Karen had placed the envelope on the kitchen table for him and Becker left it there amid the crumpled napkins and the spilled remainders of Jack's breakfast cereal while he did the dishes and straightened the kitchen. Giving the table a swipe with the sponge, he worked around the letter as if afraid to soil his hands by touching it. Kitchen duty was a chore that Becker had assumed on his own; Karen had never mentioned it, he had never volunteered. On the first few mornings he had spent at her house, she had gotten Jack off to school, then departed for work herself while he was still reading the newspaper at the table. "Just leave it," she had said, referring to the general litter while bending to give him a kiss. "I'll do it when I get home." Becker had not left it and it did not take long for her to stop urging him to do so. The same process was at work when he gradually assumed the duties of dinner chef. He cooked the first few times because it seemed unfair for her to have to launch into meal preparations as soon as she walked in the door. He cooked the next few times because he didn't like the frozen entrées and slapjack concoctions that Karen tossed together on her own. After that he cooked because he realized he liked to, and because no one had ever told him he had to. Now, after living together for a year, Karen still remembered every so often to say thank you, which Becker considered a surprise bonus. Jack never thought to voice his gratitude without prompting, but then Jack was ten and assumed that service was his due.

With the dishes rinsed and stacked in the dishwasher and the counters and tabletop cleaned and straightened, Becker was forced to regard the letter once more. It was addressed in typescript to "Agent John Becker" in care of "FBI, Washington, D.C." The envelope was plain white, ordinary stationery as unremarkable as the typewriting. With a sigh, Becker lifted the envelope by its edges. Whomever it was from, Becker didn't want to hear from him. FBI agents didn't receive friendly letters addressed to headquarters. They got angry letters, they got plead-

ing letters, they got threatening letters from attorneys insinuating law-
suits, they got paranoid letters from screwballs concerned about UFOs.
And, in Becker's case, there were letters from psychopaths.

More than one of the serial killers whom Becker had tracked and apprehended tried to stay in touch with him, as if their relationship had not
been severed by incarceration. They wrote to him as if they knew him,
as if they shared something in common, some deep affliction of the soul
that had empowered Becker to find them—that had allowed them to be
caught by one of their own. For these correspondents the twisted
growth within their souls that made them the way they were was a
source of exultation. They loved their mania, clutched it gleefully, protected it fanatically. He could sense their caged but unaltered joy like
the cackle of the demented in every line they wrote. They crooned to
him from their prison cells and mental wards like wolves howling for a
caged brother to join them. For Becker, his understanding of their de-
mentia was a sickness that he had quit the Bureau in a vain attempt to
expunge. If he was no more capable of reforming his soul than they
were, at least he could avoid the exercise of his failings. He was like a
man with allergies that medicine could not control. Unable to live
cleanly in a certain place, Becker had taken himself elsewhere, out of
the FBI, away from the antigens that plagued him.

But the crazies would not let him go, they called to him, singing their
siren songs of mutuality through the mail, and the Bureau, conscientious good citizen that it was, acted as middleman, running him down
with the messages of lunacy.

He slipped a paring knife under the flap and opened the envelope,
then turned it over to shake out its contents, still reluctant to come into
contact with it. The masthead of *The New York Times* floated to the
table. Scissors had cut away the newspaper's motto, "All the News
That's Fit to Print," on one side, and the weather information on the
other, leaving intact only the name of the paper and the date immediately underneath. The edition was two years old.

Becker flipped the paper to its other side. There was the name CAR-
TIER in large letters, part of an advertisement which had been cut away,
a portion of a female model's face that was part of an adjoining ad, and
the word "News," the second half of "News Summary" having also
been excised. Pinching just the tip of the paper, Becker held it up to the
light, half expecting to see an "invisible" message scrawled in some
lunatic's urine.

What he saw were tiny dots of light bleeding through the paper, poked with caution through the letters of the masthead by a pin. Above the masthead was another series of dots. On the reverse side of the paper, the holes in the masthead fell in the empty space of the illustrations used for the advertisements.

A game player, he thought. Someone wants me to cooperate so he can jerk me off at the same time he does himself.

But despite his annoyance, Becker rummaged through the extra bedroom that they called a family room until he found an old Scrabble set. For each letter in the masthead with a hole in it, Becker selected a lettered square from the Scrabble set and placed it on the table. The *o* and the *w* each had two holes, so he added an extra of each letter to his little pile. Taken in order from the masthead, the letters spelled "hNwwooki." Placing the capitalized *n* first and following it with a vowel, Becker came up with "Now i howk." Nothing more intelligible presented itself immediately, so he shuffled the tiles and tried again. At the first random casting the letters formed the word "wowikhno."

With rising exasperation, he reshuffled the letters, then again and yet again, trying to find words that made sense. After ten minutes of effort his hands froze over the tiles. His message was on the table before him.

"i kNow who."

"So you know who," Becker said aloud, his voice sounding strange in the empty house. "Who what? Or who cares?"

The dots that ran above the masthead took a bit longer to decipher. They were neatly, almost meticulously placed, as if they had been ruled off with a caliper. Applying a tape measure, Becker determined that they were precisely one eighth of an inch apart. In some cases two dots ran vertically and in some cases one stood alone. The vertical holes were also precisely one eighth of an inch from those below them. However, they were not systematically aligned with any of the letters in the masthead that ran below them. The dots were a message by themselves:

$$\cdot \quad \cdot \cdot$$
$$\cdot \quad \cdot \quad \cdot \quad \cdot$$

At first glance they looked to Becker like a broken box kite, and then like an old-fashioned door key. He played with the idea for a moment before deciding that the pattern didn't look much like a key after all. Leaving the tiles and their message on the table, he paced the kitchen, wondering why he was taking the trouble in the first place. Whoever had sent him the message had been smart enough, or knew Becker well enough, to make it a puzzle. He knows my weakness, Becker thought. Or one of them at least. If the message had been straightforward, Becker might well have dismissed it out-of-hand, throwing it out with the morning's trash. Now here I am, he thought, joining this jerkoff in his activity.

Disgusted with his correspondent, and with himself for accommodating the faceless ghoul, Becker reached out to crumble the bit of newsprint and its cryptic holes when he stopped, arrested suddenly by the date on the newspaper. There was nothing special about the date itself; it rang no bells; Becker could recall nothing unusual about the day; but its very presence was strange. The man had cut away everything else from the paper that was irrelevant. Why had he left the date? The obvious answer was that the date was not irrelevant.

''i kNow who'' meant he knew something about someone who did something on that date. And in that newspaper? *The New York Times* was a large newspaper; where was Becker supposed to find the ''who''? The dots had to be a page number. The correspondent wanted Becker to solve this code, after all. He was trying to say something and he wanted to be heard, even if his listener had to work a bit first. He is confident that I will take the trouble, Becker reasoned, so he must be equally confident that I can break the code. It can't be that much of a mystery. The punctured letters didn't amount to much of a code after all, just enough to avoid a cursory inspection. Whatever the writer was trying to hide, he wasn't trying so hard that someone of average intelligence couldn't find it, Becker thought. The code was meant to be a puzzle, not a mystery, and puzzles, by their nature, can be solved.

Becker walked the mile and a half to the library, a stroll he took frequently to clarify his thoughts. He had replaced the masthead in its envelope and carried it with him in his pocket, feeling as if he were transporting something smarmy and indecent. Traveling the clean, tree-lined sidewalks of Clamden, Connecticut, Becker felt like a dirty old man with pornography in his possession, as out-of-place in this verdant patch of suburbia as a flasher in his trench coat.

Don't pursue this, he berated himself. Whatever it is, it's no good for you, no matter how little you involve yourself. Alcoholics don't sip wines just to determine the source of the grapes. It's a quagmire, your entire association with that past life. Put a toe in to test the surface and you'll get sucked in again, right up to the neck.

Becker removed the envelope from his pocket and dropped it on the ground, then turned abruptly and walked back home, quickly, as if someone were after him. He had gone only a few hundred yards before he realized he was brushing his hand against his pant leg as if to cleanse it of something clinging to his fingers, like the slime trail of a garden slug.

At home Becker swept the Scrabble tiles into the box with his cupped hand and forearm and replaced the game in the family room. He straightened the kitchen once again, took out his well-worn copy of *The Chinese Cookbook* by Craig Claiborne and Virginia Lee and leafed through it in search of a recipe for the evening's meal. He felt clean, he felt virtuous, like a former addict who has passed up a fix; he had been tested and found strong.

Ten minutes later Becker found the envelope where he had dropped it. He picked it up and continued his walk to the library, where he found a primer on computers and refreshed himself on binary code.

Counting with a base of two rather than civilization's customary ten was simple enough once the method was understood. Becker remembered it from the years when he had devoted himself to computers, but felt it wise to check his calculations against the book.

Assuming the two dots aligned vertically meant 1 and the dots that stood alone represented zero, the number in binary code was:

10011

In the decimal system, the ones and zeros translated to the number 19.

The librarian at the information desk, identified by the brass plate in front of her as June Atchinson, showed Becker how to operate the microfilm machine and where to find the files of film of back copies of *The New York Times*.

She knew Becker—most people in Clamden knew him or knew of him—but only a few were able to differentiate between the man they saw and the man they had heard about. To June he seemed a pleasant, unfailingly polite and frequent visitor to the library, but when she looked at him it was impossible for her to dismiss the stories she had heard. The FBI agent with too many deaths to his credit—if credit was the right word. A man whose talents were too much like the predilections of those he hunted. It was all rumor, of course, but it stuck to his image all the stronger because of that. June chided herself for crediting the rumors—she liked to think of herself as a better person than that— but the stories were too persistent to ignore. He was a good-looking man, virile, with the appearance of strength despite middle age, but with nothing about him to suggest a hidden and rapacious bloodlust.

She watched him with open curiosity as he worked the microfilm machine. Becker was aware of her attention as he was normally aware of most of what went on about him, the habit of watchfulness never having left him. The FBI had taught him a form of reasonable paranoia, and Becker had refined it with an attention to nuance that had made him extraordinarly effective. He was also conscious of his reputation and was glad the real story was not known. The truth was worse than the rumors and was known only by his therapist, and then only in part. Even Becker did not know the whole truth about himself, although he worked at it with a diligence made possible only by his high tolerance for psychic pain.

He found the *Times* that matched the date on the masthead and turned the knob of the machine, watching the blurred catalogue of the day's events flash by until he reached page 19.

There were stories about the apple industry and the suicide doctor, but the item sought by Becker leaped at him from a tiny box in the lower left corner, a throwaway story sent over the AP wire and beloved by editors because it was just the right size to fill small holes in the page's layout. The headline read, "Body Found in Coal Mine."

The dateline was Hendricks, West Virginia, and the story told in terse journalistic prose of the discovery of the body of a twenty-year-old woman in a branch shaft of an abandoned mine. The woman had been identified by her dental records as a local girl who had been reported missing nearly three years earlier. No details were given concerning the cause of death, and Becker could imagine that after three years in a mineshaft there would be little soft tissue remaining on which to perform an autopsy. The story went on to say that foul play was suspected—although no reason was given for the conclusion—and that a broader search of the mine was to be undertaken.

Becker lifted his head from the black and white of the microfilm and widened his eyes as if trying to awaken from a sleep. He did not know how long he had been staring at the newspaper article, but his mind had leaped through the machine and into the darkness of the West Virginia mine where a girl's body lay on the gouged and routed floor of rock. He did not see her as she must have been found, a pile of bones encased in rags, but as she must have died, a living person, fearful, panicked, in pain. In his imagination she had just been killed and Becker was there beside her, feeling the last warmth of her body, her final breath still hanging above her, still distinct amid the chilly ambient air of the mine. The sound of her final cry faded away in the vastness of her grave and over it Becker could hear another, frightening sound. It was her killer's breathing, rapid, excited, orgasmic. Becker could sense the man behind him, looking at the girl over Becker's shoulder, leaning in close, as close as Becker himself, savoring the death. Becker was aware of the man's leering smile, his dancing eyes, his nostrils flared in the effort to suck in the girl's last breath. Without turning to look, Becker knew the light was already fading from the killer's eyes, the climactic feeling passing from his soul. Whatever he had done to her, however long it had taken, however much trouble it had caused him, it had been worth it. The killer had what he wanted and Becker could feel his final trembling sighs of satisfaction ruffle the air around them both. The purr of a monster.

Becker returned to the present with a shudder and saw the librarian quickly dipping her eyes back to her own desk. The colors of the day swept back to him, the relaxed quiet of the library replaced the deathly stillness of the mine, the humid cold of underground gave way to the gentle warmth of the building. He was among the living, sitting among the ordinary, surrounded by the comfortably mundane. There were no monsters in the library. Except himself.

The librarian looked at him quizzically, then rose and crossed towards him. Becker realized he had been staring blankly in her direction.

"Everything all right?" she asked.

Becker regarded her quizzically for a moment before he understood that she was referring to his use of the microfilm viewer.

"Oh, yes, fine."

"It's kind of an old system now," she said. "But it still works."

"Is it common?" Becker asked. "I mean, storing *The New York Times*. Do most libraries do it?"

"I don't know about most," June said. "Certainly a lot of them. It is the newspaper of record in the country, after all. We only go back twenty years, but I'm sure some larger libraries go back much farther. Was there a particular year you wanted?"

"I was just wondering where I would find a two-year-old copy of the *Times,* the actual newspaper."

"We keep them, the actual papers that is, until they send out the latest microfilm. That's at least eighteen months. I suppose it could be two years in some libraries if they aren't too quick about getting rid of the old copies. Space is a problem here, we're just too small until we get our new addition built.''

"So some libraries might have them?"

"Oh, surely some would, somewhere. Or of course people save them, individuals, I mean. In attics and garages. I don't know why."

"Sentimental value?" Becker asked ironically.

"I suppose. Or neurosis. There are an awful lot of screwballs around.''

"Yes," said Becker. "I know."

"Oh, don't bother with that," she said as Becker started to remove the film from the machine. "I'll take care of that."

When he was safely out the door, June sat down at the microfilm machine and read the page that had caused Becker to blanch and stare as though at an apparition. For a moment, as she had watched him from across the room, he had become so inert, so preternaturally absorbed, that she wondered if something might have happened to him. When he finally came out of it she had the fleeting impression of a man bursting to the surface of the water, gasping for breath.

There was no trouble finding the story, Becker had turned the focus onto it until it filled most of the screen. It caused no reaction in her. Just another dreadful story in a world that had become replete with mayhem. And West Virginia seemed so far away from the suburban comforts of Fairfield County, Connecticut. She wondered what it could have to do with Becker. From all she had heard, he was retired.

It's none of my business, Becker told himself angrily. I didn't want it, didn't ask for it. I am no more responsible for it than the woman who picks up a phone and hears a heavy breather panting in her ear. *I* am the victim, he thought. I am being defiled by this obscenity sent through the mail. And forwarded to me by the Bureau. They don't want to protect my privacy, of course. What they want is to get me involved. They would like nothing better than for me to get stirred up by some random lunatic and come back to work to solve a case that would lead to another case and another and another until he was back in their clutches again, their leash around his neck, their specialized ferret to be sent down into every vile-smelling hole they could find in a nation burgeoning with homicidal madmen.

To hell with it, Becker said, to hell with the Bureau, to hell with his correspondent. He put everything back in the manila envelope and tossed into the pile of old tax returns Karen kept in the closet of the family room. Out of sight, out of mind, he told himself, knowing it wasn't true.

Chapter 5

As the Apostolic Choir of the Holy Ghost whipped itself into its nightly frenzy of syncopated devotion, The Reverend Tommy R. Walker peered through the curtain to view his congregation to see how well they were responding to the Apostolic's enthusiasm. To his dismay, they appeared to be the usual collection of deadheads, whiners, and malcontents come to witness a miracle or two and not about to be diverted by a mixed dozen of black-and-maroon-robed overweight men and women singing their tonsils out. They could get *that* sort of thing at regular church. What they had come for tonight was something out of your ordinary run-of-the-mill preaching and spiritualizing. They had come to see the wonders of the Lord as performed personally and with that special panache that was the trademark of the good reverend himself. They wanted curing, they wanted laying on of hands, they damned well expected to witness the lame walking and the blind seeing again, not to mention the cleansing of souls and soothing of troubled spirits and the odd elimination of tumorous growths and palsied afflictions. They had come to Bald Nob on this particular night anticipating just about every miracle and living proof of the Holy Spirit that man could conjure up from a cooperative divinity, short of finding them all permanent employment.

All of which Reverend Tommy would deliver, of course, because that's what he was good at. Still, it wouldn't hurt his efforts if they got off their hands and *enthused* a bit ahead of time instead of sitting there, staring at the Apostolics as if all that melodic yelling was nothing more than a collective reaction to seeing a mouse. Expecting Reverend Tommy to do all the work. As per usual.

Having sized them up in general as the normal bunch of small-town, farm-country, tight-assed pinchpennies, Tommy turned his attention to his congregants in particular, seeking out the diseased and dim-witted whom he would heal that night. Down front, where Rae had positioned her in one of Tommy's three wheelchairs—he needed more but they were surprisingly expensive—was the lady with the bad shoulder whom he would cause to rise from her wheelchair and walk again. Next to her, looking as if he really needed the wheelchair, sat an elderly man with a portable oxygen tank and tubes feeding into his nose. Tommy figured the man could get along without the oxygen long enough for him to remove the tubes and praise the Lord for a moment or two. They almost always could unless they were in a hospital bed under an oxygen tent. But then the Reverend Tommy R. Walker didn't heal in hospitals.

What Tommy was looking for more specifically were the members of the audience whom he could not cure, that is to say, in whom he could not reliably muster a manifestation of the Holy Spirit. Rae had pointed out the mean-faced farmer with the fiery rash running down his face and under his shirt. He was the kind of man who would clutch at the Reverend Tommy, strong enough not to be pushed off with Tommy's patented forehead thrust, angry enough to demand proof of his cure, loud enough to protest when the rash didn't vanish. And an affliction like that was so damnably *visible* that there was no way to fake its removal. At least Tommy had not yet devised a way to fake it. The farmer would continue to glow strawberry red clear to the back of the tent unless Rae pulled the switch and killed the lights entirely. It was much easier to avoid the man in the first place. Let him be dealt with in the general heal-off when Tommy went down the line, thrusting Satan from foreheads with the speed and impersonality of an athlete administering high-fives following a winning play.

The Apostolic Choir had groaned their final notes to an unenthusiastic round of applause, the deacon/director taking too many bows, as usual, so that he was still bobbing his head in false modesty several seconds after the crowd had slumped back again into silence. Rae took the stage and began her warm-up, extolling the virtues of Jesus and the Reverend Tommy R. Walker in more or less equal parts and doing her damndest to lather the people up a bit in anticipation. The problem was, Rae's damndest was no damned good. She was no public speaker, and that was a fact. The Reverend Tommy did not wish to be unchristian about it, but Rae had no more charisma than a dead sheep. She was good working the audience as they came in—her simple country manner put them at ease and her naturally sympathetic response allowed them to confide in her like a friend—but a friend was not what you wanted up onstage. What you wanted up onstage was somebody who could tie a knot in their tails and make them like it, and tail-knotting was not something people took to from a woman who usually reminded them of their plain-looking cousin who was such a good listener. Rae was a hard worker, sincere, loyal as a tick hound but not much smarter and consequently not too demanding in a variety of ways. In a not to-tally unrelated matter, her breasts had begun to droop unappetizingly. That was a deficit that could be corrected easily enough onstage when she had the benefit of undergarments, but not in the Reverend Tommy's bed, where he liked his women naked and sweating and loud and young. Rae was never very loud, either, come to that.

When Rae reached the part about Jesus raising Lazarus from the dead and implying—though never claiming outright—that the Reverend Walker was very nearly up to such a feat himself, a latecomer slipped into the back of the tent. She was wearing faded denims and a man's workshirt and sporting a face that Tommy thought looked like an angel. Or, if there were such things as angels, that's what Tommy thought they ought to look like. At least that's how they should look if they wanted to recruit any male souls.

He would have liked to study her more, but Rae had come to the conclusion of her introduction, straining up on her toes—the only way she knew to indicate total enthusiasm—and the choir was bursting into ecstatic noises and the electric piano was playing and the tambourines were ringing and Tommy checked to be sure his fly was zipped and clutched his golden Bible in his hand and hurled himself through the curtain and onto the stage, shouting praises to the Lord.

The Reverend Tommy was a quick and prolific sweater, a curse dur-ing his teenaged years, particularly when in pursuit of girls, but turned nicely into an asset in his Bible-thumping, crowd-working career. An average man could prowl the stage and wave his arms and testify for the Lord for a good long while before he began to perspire, but Tommy would break into a sweat within the first few minutes and it would pour off his face and under his arms and down his back so that his shirt would stick to him and his hair would turn as stringy and lank as if he had just been in the river. He looked, he would sometimes joke, as if he had baptized himself right there onstage without the aid of anybody else's water. The audiences responded to the effect because it made it look as if he was wrestling with the devil in a mighty and powerful way, and they figured that any man with that much natural internal heat could surely spare some healing warmth for them.

A sallow man, his complexion looked even whiter when contrasted with the coal blackness of his hair and massively bushy eyebrows that met in the middle atop the the bridge of his nose. His hair had always been as black as tar and Tommy took some cosmetic pains to keep it that way now that nature wanted to sprinkle it with gray. The combination of light and dark was even more pronounced under the dim lights within the tent—it was easier to perform miracles in the gloom than in broad daylight—and at times, to the more devoted and imaginative of his audience, he seemed to be lit by an inner light. Others, if they could have articulated their perceptions, would have said the combination looked more satanic than holy, but who was ungrateful enough to question the source of healing?

Tonight neither sweating nor his complexion nor his tireless thumping and pounding and exhorting and top-of-the-register prayer were having the desired effect. The citizens of Bald Nob just weren't sensing the presence of the holy spirit among them, and Tommy was feeling a bit of panic. Lately, audiences had been getting worse, although he didn't remember any of them being quite this moribund. He blamed the perfidious influence of television. They could find a good shouting and praying and healing just about every week on the tube, and with altogether better production values than Tommy could muster. The television ministers would even heal long distance—all one had to do was huddle up close to that TV set and feel the medicinal touch coming right at them through the airwaves. For a donation of suitable size, the evangelist would even mention the viewer's name and affliction during his broadcast, offering personalized service in the privacy of his own living room but within earshot of millions. That sort of thing made audiences entirely too passive, yet too demanding. There was no substitute for the actual contact with a human hand as offered by the Reverend Tommy R. Walker, but it had become increasingly difficult to convince an audience of that. Tommy would have killed for a chance to go on television himself, of course, but in the meantime, television was killing him.

From the corner of his eye he saw the girl with the angel's face start to move. He had kept track of her during his orating, staring at her as much as he could allow himself while still turning his charms and attentions on the whole crowd. She had seemed from a distance to be smirking at him, but the lights were at their dimmest in the back of the tent and Tommy could not be sure. He was trying to devise a way of meeting her after the show and wiping that smirk off her face at the same time he relieved her of her clothing, and it might well be that his split focus accounted in part for his lack of success with the rest of the audience. Spellbinding required a good deal of attention to the business at hand as well as great energy.

For a second he feared that she was moving towards the exit, but then he realized that she was coming down the aisle towards him. He had not called for the afflicted to come forth yet, and her movement caught the attention of the audience. Now they were looking at her, their interest caught more by the beautiful girl than by his spellbinding, and, damn it, that was just the kind of thing that could make him have to start all over again.

She stopped right at the edge of the stage, standing next to the wheelchair of the lady with the bad shoulder.

"Reverend Tommy," she said.

Tommy tried to ignore her and kept right on preaching as if she didn't exist, weren't there right in front of him, the cynosure of the whole damned crowd of gawking rubes.

"Reverend Tommy," she cried again, this time louder, and with her arms reaching out to him. There was no ignoring her now and, God help him, this time he had heard her voice, the garbled noise of a severe speech impediment. Vocal problems were the *worst*. You could get a cripple to stand for a second or two and you could sometimes induce a flash of light for the blind if you pushed on the eyeball—or you could make him think you did—but there was no way someone with a cleft palate was going to shout "Praise the lord" in tones that were suddenly round and intelligible. The whole damned audience could hear the afflicted was still afflicted, no matter what the afflicted thought about himself.

"Heal me," the beautiful girl was saying, or at least Tommy guessed that was what she was saying. Even as he was trying to figure a way out of this, Tommy could not help but feel anger that such a lovely woman would be given such a hardship to bear. She was young, looked to be no more than eighteen, with her whole life to face with a mouth that could never pronounce her thoughts.

Tommy looked around for help but Rae was frozen in the wings, as surprised as he was, and the choir, who doubled as security and general calmer-downers as well as the catchers of his healing thrusts, were standing there mesmerized, their tambourines dangling. The deacon was only now beginning to stir, but it would take him far too long to get to the girl and get her out of the way. This creature was just too pretty for the audience to dismiss and forget about. They wanted her by God *cured* and no nonsense, and Tommy could feel the force of their demand as he crossed to the edge of the stage.

She held her arms up to him as if offering herself to a saint. Tommy started to kneel down to her, hoping to work something out of sight of most of the audience, but she grabbed his arm and pulled herself up onstage, giving him no choice but to make it look as if that was what he wanted. Short of kicking her back into the audience, there was no way out but to deal with her.

"Heal me, Reverend Tommy, I know you can. I know you can," she said, or some such garble. Tommy could hear the audience "awwing" in sympathy with her defect. The poor young thing, they thought, and so pretty, too.

"I am going to heal you, sister," Tommy said loudly.

She started to make some more noise, but Tommy clamped his hands on her face, closing her jaw to shut her up. She was just as beautiful up close, and even in the midst of his panic Tommy wondered if he couldn't just kiss her back to health right here and now.

The Reverend Tommy was about to say that he was more than willing to heal her once he got to the healing portion of the show when she winked at him.

Startled, Tommy reflexively yelled, "Satan be gone!" and pushed the girl away from him and off the stage, forgetting in his astonishment that his catchers were not yet in place.

The girl was nimble and landed on her feet but staggered a bit and doubled over as if caught in a seizure of some sort. Her body quivered a bit and for a second Tommy wondered if he had done her some sort of neurological damage. But it was her fault, scaring him that way. What was she thinking of?

Amid a great hush, the girl slowly straightened up. Tommy thought of leaping back into his preaching to cover up whatever devilment came out of her mouth now, but he knew the audience would not forgive him if he did.

She looked up at Tommy, this time half-lifting her arms in a pose reminiscent of the Pope, her eyes gazing worshipfully at him on the stage. Her face was flushed with the spirit in a way that Tommy had not seen in years, and when she spoke, her voice was filled with awe.

"Thank you, Reverend Tommy," she said. Her tones were soft but clear as a diction teacher's, every syllable precise.

"Thank God," said Tommy, half in wonder himself at the transformation.

"Praise be," she agreed, then, in a voice filled with tears but resonating with all the joy the Apostolic Choir strove for but never achieved, "Praise Jesus!"

Tommy stared at her in amazement as the audience erupted.

"His wonders to perform," she cried.

The audience was on its feet, yelling and screaming in appreciation.

"And his servant, Tommy R. Walk-er!"

Oh, they loved him then, but they loved her even more. Nothing like seeing perfection restored. Tommy watched her hold them, lift them and shake them. At that moment she could have had their wallets just for the asking and they would have blessed her for taking them. She was the best he had ever seen.

And it was the best night he had had in months.

Chapter 6

His punk was crying again, trying to hide it, as if you could hide anything in a cell. He was in his bunk over Cooper's head, weeping and sniffing and answering "nothing" whenever Cooper asked what was wrong. Cooper knew what was wrong, though. The punk was crying because Cooper was leaving in the morning.

"You'll be all right," Cooper said, not at all certain that it was true. Swann's new cellmate might turn to be someone not as nice as Cooper. Or, worse, he might turn out to be someone like Swann himself, someone who could offer Swann no protection against the other predators. His punk could turn out to be free meat. Cooper had seen others in that position ripped apart, torn into bits like a piece of steak thrown in among the lions. They wouldn't show him the kind of consideration Cooper had, they wouldn't talk to him and make him feel like a human being the way Cooper had always strived to do.

But it was not just fear for his well-being that made Cooper's punk cry. It was love, too.

"You'll forget me, won't you?" Swann asked.

"Naw."

"Yes, you will," Swann said bitterly. "You'll forget all about me as soon as you leave, I don't give it a day. You won't ever think about me again."

"Sure I will," said Cooper.

"No, you won't. I know how your mind works."

"I said I would," Cooper said, getting annoyed at the line of the conversation.

"Promise?"

"What?"

"Promise you won't forget me?"

Cooper sighed wearily. The emotional demands of the punk sometimes made it not worth the effort, but tonight he could afford to be magnanimous. Tomorrow he was getting out of stir. Tomorrow he was going back to the world.

"I promise," Cooper said.

"What do you promise?"

"Whatever you want."

The punk was quiet for a moment and Cooper considered kicking him. Cooper wasn't through talking yet, but he didn't want to talk about the punk, he wanted to talk about himself. He had his own concerns about his impending release, but he did not know how to bring them up without giving the punk an advantage over him. Even the weakest of them could find a way to exploit a vulnerability, even someone whom Cooper had treated as well as Swann, even now with only hours left to go.

When Swann spoke again it was in his babyish, wheedling tone of voice.

"Can I come down there?" Swann asked.

He didn't really feel like it, but Cooper grunted permission. If the punk only knew how decent Cooper was to him.

Swann slipped into Cooper's bunk and cuddled against the big man.

"Will I ever see you again?" he asked. He sounded like he was going to start crying again.

"Sure," said Cooper.

"When?"

"Well, not till you get out, because I ain't coming back here."

"I won't be out for three years. If I can live that long without you."

"You'll be fine," Cooper lied. "They know you're my punk. They wouldn't dare mess with old Coop's punk."

Swann didn't bother to refute such arrant nonsense. For all he knew, Cooper believed it.

"I wonder if you'll even remember what I look like after three years."

"I remember everything," Cooper said. "There's nothing wrong with my memory."

"I didn't mean that."

"Ask me anything. Ask me about the Mexican."

"I know you know about the Mexican and the girls and all the rest of them . . ."

"And the faggot, don't forget."

"I know. I know you'll remember all of that. I'm worried you'll forget about *me*. Can I write you sometimes?"

"I don't write letters," Cooper said.

"No, I'd write to you. You wouldn't have to answer. And I could call you, too, if you'd like that."

Cooper was silent.

"I could say things to you," Swann whispered. "I could talk the way you like sometimes."

"All right," Cooper said uncertainly. He was never comfortable on the phone, the other voices got annoyed with him, they wanted him to answer them back too quickly when he needed time to think.

The punk caught the uncertainty in his voice. "Everything's going to be fine," he said. "I know you're a little . . ." He groped for the right word. "Afraid" was not what Cooper wanted to hear. ". . . concerned about how it's going to go in the world."

Cooper grunted noncommitally.

"But everything is going to be just fine."

The punk began to stroke Cooper's chest as if he were petting a large beast.

"Just remember, you have two friends that you never had before when you were in the world."

"Who?"

"And you can ask both of them for help and they will always be there for you."

"Who?"

"Jesus, you have Jesus for a friend now, don't you?"

"Oh, yeah."

"You can always ask Jesus for help. You know that, don't you?"

"I know that."

"He will always answer you if you ask him, but it may not always be in a way you understand."

Cooper snorted. Fat lot of good that would do him.

"You said two friends," Cooper demanded.

"And me," the punk said. His hand slipped lower and stroked Cooper on the abdomen.

"Uh-huh."

"You can always ask me for help, you know. You do know that, don't you? If you're in trouble, or if you're confused, you can always get in touch with me."

"I know," said Cooper, although it had never occurred to him. What good could the punk do while languishing in prison? Chances were he couldn't even help himself.

"I'll give you postcards with a stamp and my address already on them. You can write a message if you want to, but you don't even have to. If I get the card I'll now you're thinking of me—and I'll pray for you right then. That would be good, wouldn't it?"

Cooper grunted again.

" 'Cause Jesus and I have one thing in common," Swann continued. His fingers were now brushing Cooper's pubic hair. "Do you know that is?"

Cooper was no longer attending the punk's words. His entire focus was on the other man's hand.

"We both love you," the punk said.

Cooper arched his back, trying to draw Swann's fingers closer. If the punk continued to tease, Cooper would kill him.

"Shall we pray together?" Swann asked, his voice cajoling.

"After," Cooper said. He pushed the little man lower.

I could snap his head off, Cooper thought as he felt the tension rising in his body. I could squeeze hard enough so his head popped right off like a doll's. Not this time he wouldn't. He'd be caught. But starting tomorrow he could pull off all the heads he could find.

Just before he cried out with release he imagined doing it to dozens of clerks and foremen and schoolteachers, one after the other. He saw their faces, men and women, looking so surprised as their necks broke and their heads rolled away.

Chapter 7

Karen arrived home to find neither Becker nor Jack there. A lamb stew sat on the stove, ready to be reheated for dinner. As was Becker's preference, she could detect the heavy presence of scallions and peppers and the usual concoction of Indian spices. The meal would be delicious and the house would smell for several days afterward of cardamom and coriander. This time a thick mat of dark green permeated the stew, giving it the appearance of something skimmed from atop a stagnant pond. With a fingertip, Karen determined that the algaé-like substance was spinach cooked to the point of disintegration, and, yes, delicious. Becker's cooking was a fair model for the man himself, she thought: unusual, exotic, and ultimately very savory. But strange, always a little strange.

Passing through the gap in the backyard hedge, Karen walked across the tiny center of six shops and the branch office of a bank that passed for the commercial hub of Clamden. Three years after moving to Clamden, Karen was still amazed that a town so determinedly semirural could exist within an hour's commute of New York City. Clamden's small-town flavor and undemanding pace was a tribute to the power of its zoning laws. Heavily if not predominantly peopled by refugees from Manhattan who still made their living there, the town nonetheless acted as if it were sealed off from the rest of America in a time capsule, a happy remnant of the 1950s. There actually were still stay-at-home mothers, Karen marveled. She encountered them at evening meetings for parents at the school when she swept in, always a bit late, always a bit harried, the cloud of concerns from her job still buzzing around her head like a swarm of gnats. They would be there in their slacks and Laura Ashley print dresses, chatting amiably about team suppers for the gymnasts and bake sales at the church while Karen sat uneasily in her business suit, a snub-nosed .38 automatic in her purse, her FBI badge tucked in her vest pocket. It was an incongruity that troubled her at times but at others was strangely soothing. Again, a fair description of her life with John Becker.

She found Becker and Jack on one of the three elementary school playgrounds, kicking a soccer ball in the gathering dusk. Becker's friend Tee, the Clamden police chief, was with them, cheering for Jack and occasionally taking a big-footed swat at the ball himself. As was usually the case, it was Tee's voice that carried above the other two, full of self-mocking bluster and general good spirits. Jack was noisy, too, cheering himself and working hard at a sport that did not come naturally. Becker was mostly silent, parrying Jack's attempts to pass him with the ball, yet still quietly encouraging. He moved with an ease and athletic grace that seemed to be a part of everything he did.

Karen thought of the incident with Jack during their climb. The patience that Becker seemed to demonstrate in everything he did, the careful explanation, the genuine understanding of Jack's fear. And yet the odd tilt of his perspective. The insistence on embracing one's fear. Karen was delighted that Jack had the influence of a man in his life and Jack adored Becker. She loved him herself, she thought. Or at least she did at times, and maybe a sporadic love was all anyone could hope for short of starry-eyed lunacy. It was better than no love at all, and Karen had decided to settle for it, especially as it was interlaced with a very real physical passion that had shown no signs of diminishing. His touch still made her shiver with anticipation and his kiss weakened her knees . . . And yet . . .

Karen slipped back into the shadow of the forsythia hedge that bordered the playground and continued to watch, unseen . . . And yet there were those moments, those odd, unsettling moments when Karen was not sure who or what she was living with. Nights when she would be aware of his lying wide awake beside her until daybreak, not tossing and turning in a fight with insomnia, but lying there, poised, as if listening for the sound of something that stalked him in the dark. As if only his constant vigilance kept the beasts away.

In her experience all men wrestled with their particular demons, usually urges to infidelity, or drink, or general irresponsibility, but those demons were nothing more than imps compared with the devils that struggled for possession of Becker's soul. He had explained his fears to her, of course, and that had only made them the more frightening because, despite her resistance, she had known what he was talking about, she had recognized some of his demons as her own.

Karen walked back to the house she shared with Becker and waited for her family to return. In her purse she held the instrument that might free Becker's demon and allow it to control him once again. He had made no mention of the previous letter that she had brought to him, but his reaction of silent dread had told her how deeply it had touched him. She recognized the same postmark, the same typewritten address. Whatever it was, it continued.

She thought of keeping the letter from him but knew that it was pointless. If the demon was stirring in Becker's soul, only Becker could deal with it. The letter writer would get to him some way eventually, and Becker would have to wrestle with the devil by himself.

At first Becker ignored the letter, leaving it where Karen had dropped it on the coffee table. They went through the evening as if the missive did not exist, sitting like excrement in the middle of the living room. It was only at night, when he heard the slightly labored breath that signaled Karen's deeper sleep, that Becker rose quietly from the bed and returned to the living room. The stationery caught the moonlight from the window and glowed, taunting him to continue to ignore it.

The correspondent's device was the same as the first time, the masthead of *The New York Times* pricked with pinholes. Sitting in the spare bedroom that doubled as an office for both Karen and Becker, he deciphered the message with the Scrabble tiles.

"i kNow whY."

The code at the top of the page was:

$$\cdot \quad \cdot \ \cdot \ \cdot$$
$$\cdot \ \cdot \ \cdot \ \cdot$$

—another box kite. Becker wrote down 10111, then translated it to the number 23.

There was nothing to do but wait until the next day, when he could look up the relevant page and date at the library, so Becker sat in the den pondering the meaning of the code.

His correspondent had chosen to encrypt his message, but why? Not to keep the contents secret from Becker, that much was obvious. Therefore he must have been concerned about interception when he wrote it or when he mailed it. Was he creating his message in the presence of someone who was involved, someone dangerous? Or was his mail read by someone before being sent?

Becker tried to imagine a sequence in which his correspondent sat in the presence of a witness and poked pinholes in a carefully scissored masthead of a three-year-old copy of *The New York Times*—without attracting attention. It seemed unlikely. The advantage of course would be that the observer would not easily decipher the message, but would that not make the correspondent's actions all the more suspicious?

A second alternative was that the correspondent was fearful of the message being found once it was created. Which would seem to mean that there was no good place to hide it. How much space would be needed to secrete a few square inches of paper? But an addressed envelope would be harder to hide. Which might mean that the correspondent had no quick access to a mailbox. His message might have to sit around for some time before being mailed—if the correspondent was a shut-in, for instance. Or if the correspondent lived in some remote area far from the nearest mailbox.

Becker studied the postmark again. Decatur, Alabama. Not exactly the middle of Alaska, but not New York City, either. Alabama was rural enough that mailing a letter could easily be a bit of a problem, and the postmark was never a very accurate indication of where a piece of mail had actually originated. Becker knew that his own mail frequently bore the imprint of a Stamford post office, and Stamford was thirty miles and at least four intervening towns away from Clamden and had an entirely different zip code. Decatur, Alabama, could be the funneling junction for outgoing mail for a surrounding area of hundreds of square miles.

A third possibility was that someone read the correspondent's mail before it went out. Becker had seen Karen do it with Jack's letters to his school pen pals. And she had actually made him make corrections in thank-you letters to grandparents. But then Jack never had a stamp and usually neglected to seal the envelope as well. Becker knew that his correspondent was not a child. He wished that were the case. He wished that he was on the receiving end of a prank, some more sophisticated version of eight-year-olds calling strangers and giggling through their hands as they asked if the hapless adult on the other end of the line had Prince Albert in the can, and if so to please let him out.

What Becker had on the other end of his line was an adult, an intelligent one who was afraid of something, or someone, and trying, probably at some risk to himself, to get help. If he or she was attempting to give Becker information about a long-dead girl who had been found three years ago in an abandoned mine, then the most obvious conclusion was that the correspondent was hiding his actions from someone who had some reason for the information not to come out.

But why me? he wondered. Why not just the FBI in general? Any of the agents could have decoded the message and gotten onto the case immediately. Why select an agent who is no longer active?

He knew the answer without thinking about it. Because he was known. The correspondent had either heard about Becker, or, worse, had encountered him. If he was one of the latter, Becker thought, if he was one of the psychopaths whom Becker had stalked and captured . . .

He had never caught one easily. They were all too clever to be tracked down by traditional police work, that was why the cases were given to Becker. It was never a case of just finding a fingerprint or a laundry mark or a dropped match book with the name of the bar where the killer worked. Old-fashioned police work was necessary, and it helped, but there was any number of cops and agents who could do it and ultimately it was never enough. Ultimately it was Becker who immersed himself in the case in a way few others could—or would allow themselves to do. He put himself in the killer's skin and sank into the killer's mind, forcing himself to think his thoughts and dream his fevered dreams. There was nothing mystical about it as many of his colleagues thought. There was no ESP at work. His therapist understood the way it worked—and the price Becker paid. No one understood a thief better than another thief. An arsonist understood an arsonist. And men who killed because of the incomparable thrill it gave them were best comprehended by . . .

Becker left the den and walked quietly through the darkened house, pacing and cursing in his mind the intrusion of the correspondent. I was clean, he thought. I was out of it and away. Part of a family. Building a life. Then the tentacle of his own insatiable beast reached out for him, slithering through the cracks of his jerry-built security. He could feel the slimy touch on his leg, tugging him downward even as its coils reached upwards for his throat.

He eased open the door to Jack's room and saw the boy in the moonlight, one arm thrown above his head as if he slept hanging from a branch. Becker loved to catch the boy unawares, the look of innocence radiating from him. Becker was in awe of the cleanness of Jack's life, the purity and the simplicity. He was a boy, doing boy things, thinking boy thoughts, and feeling only those emotions that a boy of ten should feel. At his age Becker had already been put through the terrors of abuse that had shaped him and brought him to his present crisis. He regarded it as a small miracle that he was able to share Jack's youth, and almost as much as he feared for himself, Becker feared that his own past might in some way taint Jack's future.

In the darkness of the living room, Becker forced himself to sit quietly and to contain his anxieties within his own center. If his was an addiction over which he had attained a certain amount of control, he had done it without the twelve-step self-help groups that existed for every other type of addiction. There were no meetings for people with his affliction. Others who shared his problem were shifting silently through the shadows of the outside world, preying on the innocent. They did not come forth for treatment. Unlike drunks and druggees who might seek counseling when they hit bottom, the creatures in whom Becker specialized yearned for the bottom. It was what they had sought all their lives, and it was there and only there that they found the release that they needed, even as they sank ever farther in the ooze. For them there was no limit to how far they could sink, because each successful kill only increased their depravity and furthered their need. There was no bottom. All that limited them was time. How long could they go on before they were caught? Becker had no doubts that there were many who were never caught, who killed and killed until their own hearts gave out with the sheer excess of joy of it all.

Becker's self-help group could only meet in prison, where he had personally put many of them. Or in a cemetery, where he had put even more. It was after planting his first victim underground that Becker had discovered what he had in common with the men he hunted. He was, he felt, the same as they, except that he had a license to hunt. His victims were loathed by society and he was applauded, but in Becker's mind he was merely performing a kind of socially accepted cannibalism. The big fish in the pond eating all the smaller ones, he thought with self-disgust.

But there was something else that set him apart from his fellows, of course, besides his FBI badge and official connivance, and it was the cause of his pain. Unlike them, Becker wanted desperately to stop. He did not believe that an actual cure was possible; he would always be who he was in the deepest recesses of his soul, and no amount of therapy had convinced him otherwise, but he was convinced that by an exercise of sheer will he could alter his behavior. He could *stop*.

And he had done so although it took a resignation for the Bureau to accomplish it. They had not accepted his resignation, delegating him instead to a status known in bureaucratese as "inderterminate medical extension," which meant that they could reach out for him when they needed to and not worry about him otherwise. For his part, he was not obliged to respond when they called. But they knew he would. A ferret did not refuse to go down a hole. It was what he had been bred to do. It was where it lived.

At the library the next morning Becker settled in front of the now familiar microfilm screen and quickly located the date and page of the message. Once again the story was at the bottom of the page, nothing more than a bit of filler taken from the AP wire. A second body had been found in the same mine in Hendricks, West Virginia. Another young woman who had been missing for months. Her remains had been found as a result of the discovery of the body of the first young woman, and officials indicated that they would continue to search the mine.

There was even less information than there had been about the first body, but less was needed. One woman might have somehow gotten lost and died from exposure. Not two. Not in different shafts of the tunnel. The second girl had been reported missing three months after the first.

He found something that works, Becker thought. The killer had discovered a method that he liked, a means of abduction, a means of disposal. Why wouldn't he repeat himself? If it works, use it.

Serial killers always stumbled a bit at first, learning by trial and error what worked best for them. The first attempts were usually clumsy and less than perfectly satisfying, reliant more upon dumb luck than careful planning. Many of them were caught in the beginnings of their careers because they didn't know what they were doing yet, they made crucial mistakes before refining their methods. But those who survived the early times learned quickly and soon mastered their grisly craft.

This one had begun his mastery, Becker realized. The newspaper was two years old, the girls' bodies had not been discovered for three years. The cave could be stuffed with corpses. Becker could be receiving documentary evidence from his correspondent for weeks—but he knew he would not. His correspondent had said "i kNow whY" this time. He knew who and he knew why and he was eager to tell Becker or he wouldn't take the risk of the coded messages.

Becker took an atlas of the United States from the library shelf and opened it on a table. Decatur, Alabama, was a long way from Hendricks, West Virginia. More than four hundred miles by road. Not that distance made much difference. The letters were arriving years after the fact. A beast could slither a thousand miles in that length of time. And of course he would have had to abandon the coal mine as soon as the first body was found. He would have located a new hole long since. Another hole in the ground crammed with the decaying remains of someone's daughter.

You do have another hole, don't you, you son of a bitch, Becker thought. No reason to give up, not while you're enjoying yourself, not while your heart is pumping fast enough to leap through your chest when you do whatever it is you do to them. Only now you've got a witness, don't you. Someone close to you who knows what you're up to and is almost too scared to stop you. Almost.

For the first time Becker perceived his correspondent not as another scum dweller trying to entice him into the swamp, but as a friend. A decent human being who knew what he saw and hated it and wanted to stop it. Despite risk to himself, he was signaling Becker from afar, alerting him to the existence of a man-eater.

Using the length from his fingertip to the first knuckle for a measure, Becker approximated a radius of 30 miles and drew an imaginary circle with Decatur as the center. He started to write down the names of the towns within the circle but stopped when he noticed Springville. There was no need to look further. Springville was the location of the Alabama state prison.

Becker leaned back in the chair and studied the ceiling for a moment. Behind the information desk, June Hutchinson watched with interest.

Write again, my friend, Becker thought. Prison is a big place, help me find you. Help me find him.

Chapter 8

Aural could sing a lick, too, damned if she couldn't, voice like a Southern angel, just enough twang to put everyone in the audience at ease. She didn't have what could be called a strong voice, but the Reverend Tommy R. Walker's Apostolic Revival didn't require an Ethel Merman. They had microphones for power, all Aural had to do was hit the notes in that sweet, breathy soprano and electricity would take care of the volume. In Aural's case, it even seemed that less was better. If she was hard to hear, the audience would just learn forward and listen all the harder, like hummingbirds straining for that last taste of nectar. No one ever strained to hear Rae, that was for sure; they didn't care.

The Reverend Tommy might have been amazed at Aural's command over the audience, at how easily she slipped into Rae's role and delivered an audience to him not only primed but panting for more spiritual uplift if it looked and sounded anything like Aural. It might have astounded him how quickly and easily Aural understood what the business was all about and how to work the crowd until they were so lathered up with a zest for redemption at Tommy's sweaty hands that they fought their way to the front, clashing crutches and all. Even more important—and most becoming in a woman, Tommy thought—was her grasp of the financial side of religious labor. They opened their wallets wider when Aural was around, no question about it—and what kind of a pissant peckerwood back-country farmer could refuse to give generously when the angel Aural was holding the plate, especially now that Tommy had her wearing the black-and-crimson robe during the offering. Might as well plead poverty to Gabriel, whatever the hell *he* looked like. Archangel or not, he sure didn't have anything over Aural in the looks department, except maybe the wings.

And, as if anything else were needed, she didn't cost much. All she asked for was a widow's mite to live on, and since she lived in one of the trailers with all the rest of the show, that was a mighty small mite at that. The Reverend Tommy could not have been happier—well, there was one little thing that troubled him, but he planned to take care of that soon enough if he could just find the opportunity without Rae sulking around in the background.

But if Tommy was amazed at Aural's skills with an audience, she herself was only mildly surprised at how quickly it had all come back to her after a hiatus of a decade or more. Her father had been a straight evangelist, content to merely get the sinners to their knees, crying tears of relief and redemption, and not striving for actual medical marvels, but the process was much the same. And it was still a rinky-dink operation, doomed to the smallest of communities and remotest of backwaters by the lack of charisma of the man in charge. Her father had never been very good at it, an assessment Aural reached in her early teens, and neither was the Reverend Tommy R. Walker. He could dream of going national on satellite television, but it was a dream he was having for himself; Aural wasn't joining in. There was more to religious healing than prolific sweating and a loud voice, and the sad part was that the Rev didn't know what it was.

"Funny name, Aural," Rae said after Aural had been with the show a week. Rae had already been eased off the stage and Tommy had relegated her to befriending the audience as they filtered in for the show. Rae didn't mind giving up her spot on the stage, she had never been comfortable doing it in the first place, but she did mind being shoved to the back of Tommy's attentions offstage, and that was clearly what was happening whether the new girl was aware of it or not. And of course she had to be aware of it—she was a woman, after all.

"I've heard of 'Oral' like in Oral Roberts, of course," Rae continued. "But 'Aural' is a new one."

"It's my own," Aural said. "My given name was Aura Lee, like in the song," she said, pronouncing it as one word, Auralee. "I never liked it, so I just kept the part I did like."

Rae smiled. Aural knew the woman was trying to be friendly. They always tried to be friendly when their men were attracted to her, and Aural was always willing to be friends back, but it never worked out in the long run. The men always got in the way and the women ended up hating her even when she had not wanted the men. Sometimes, she thought, it was *because* she had not wanted their men. Most of the time her friendships with other women had been brief and frustratingly truncated. She could still laugh easily with them and share secrets immediately in the way that women have, but Aural had found in general that it was easier for her to get along with men. At least, with them, she had no unrealistic expectations. Even when they pretended that they just wanted to be friends, Aural knew better. There was something comfortable about the predictability of men, and they were so much easier to manipulate. Women used their brains too much. Aural had never known another woman who wasn't always trying to figure out how to get what it was she wanted from a man while making him believe it was his idea. Men, in Aural's experience, didn't think with their brains at all, and they sure as hell didn't waste any of their TV time pondering the nature of their relationships. Aural flat-out *knew* she was smarter than any man she was ever going to meet.

"With all your talent," Rae was continuing, "I'm surprised you didn't ever go into show business. You sing just as good as some of the girls you hear in Nashville."

"Why, thank you, that's sweet," said Aural. "I did think of a career like that one time—when I was younger. My daddy was particularly excited about it . . . 'Course my daddy tended to get excited. He was a man of—enthusiasms. He was fixin' to bring some agents and record people and such to come take a look at me."

"My goodness. How exciting."

"Well, I guess so. I was only sixteen at the time so I just sort of took it for granted—you know, the way kids do."

"Darling, you can't be but two years past sixteen now," Rae said with less than perfect honesty.

"Bless you," said Aural with equal candor. "But I'm *way* past those teenage years, and thank goodness, too. It seemed to me I was so horny I just itched. Didn't you feel like that, just itching all over and dying to find some young buck to scratch you?"

"I never thought of it quite that way," said Rae demurely. She placed her hand at her throat as if to ward off such thoughts.

"Oh, I did. 'Course the thing about that is it's never very hard to find a man who's willing to help you out. Fact, it's nearly impossible to find one who ain't."

Rae remained silent. Her experience had not been the same at all. Platonic friendships seemed to be what men offered her most. Aural continued volubly and Rae realized the young woman had reached a topic that interested her.

"I realize now that at that age a lot of that was just plain old curiosity, you know. I mean, I just flat wanted to *know* what this sex business was all about. People make a mistake keeping it a secret from little kids, don't you think? That just makes it a mystery, and everybody loves a mystery. Once you've seen a few men with their pants down you realize there ain't going to be no real surprises, they're all pretty much alike except for those who are worse, but by then I guess it's too late to worry about the mystery anymore. You've already got the habit.''

''I'm sure you're right,'' Rae said, secretly lamenting the fact that she didn't have enough experience to be certain if Aural's assessment of men was right or not. But it did have an intuitive correctness to it.

''The thing is, I wish I had some other bad habit instead of men. I'd rather chew tobacco if it was up to me, but I guess we don't get to pick our bad habits, do we?''

Rae wondered how Aural managed to keep a complexion as smooth and pink with all of this worldly experience going on. She herself had a tendency to spot up whenever she needed to look nice, and stress of even the mildest sort caused cold sores on her lip.

''What happened with the record people and all?'' Rae asked.

''Oh, yeah. Well, Daddy had them all set to come to one of his shows, and I guess they did, but the night before that I ran off with Earl Hockfuss who was this boy with the cutest strand of hair that fell across his forehead in a certain way that made you just want to cry or scream or grab hold of something soft and squeeze real tight. When Earl would reach up and push that hair away, I used to tighten up my butt and press my thighs together, you know what I mean, Rae? 'Course, I was only sixteen, remember. I must have thought hair made the man in those days. Probably from hearing Daddy preach about Samson and Delilah or something.'' Aural laughed. ''I was given to easy impressions back then.''

''You ran off and got married?''

''No, honey, I just ran off. Earl and me went to a motel in Black Ridge and stayed there for three days until Earl decided he was too sore to continue.''

''My goodness.''

''I know. But it was educational. At least it was for me. If old Earl learned anything in them three days, he never let on, except maybe who was the stronger sex when it came to sex. But I learned a lot, most of it disappointing.'' Aural grinned in a way that made Rae feel that she ought to blush. ''But not all of it, honey. Not all of it.''

''What did your daddy do when you ran off?''

"I don't know. I ain't seen him since. He prayed, I imagine, then looked around for someone to beat up on. That's how I know he missed me. I wasn't there for him to beat up on."

"But he was a minister," Rae said.

"Hon," Aural said, touching Rae's arm. "Hon."

The Reverend Tommy R. Walker found himself alone in his trailer with Aural, a blessing to be savored and consumed. The Apostolics were striking the tent and Rae had taken herself off to town to buy groceries, which usually took quite a while because Rae was an ardent coupon clipper and comparison shopper. Rae could turn a half hour in the supermarket into a half-day excursion, and for once, Tommy R. was grateful for it.

Aural was looking exceptionally good. She had dropped the beatific pose that worked so well onstage, and was showing excitement and agitation. Tommy assumed it was about him until he realized she was asking for more money.

"You know I'm worth it," she said. "You clean doubled your receipts since I been in the show."

"Now . . . doubled . . ." Tommy hated money discussions—with employees. It was enough to dampen a man's ardor.

"Easy. I can judge a collection plate good as you, and they just keep getting fuller, don't they? You don't supposed it's because your miracles are getting better, do you?"

"That's why they come, missy. To see the power of the Lord revealed through my hands."

"Them people had glue in their pockets before I showed up. I seen you work alone, remember?"

"That was a bad night. That happens."

"It ain't happened lately, though, has it?"

"Lookit here," said Tommy. "It's not like you wasn't appreciated. Didn't I put your picture on the poster right next to mine?"

"Right under yours."

"Under, over, alongside, what difference does it make? I'm making you a star, honey, you ought to be grateful. You got your beautiful face on every telephone pole and shop window in Pikeville."

"I didn't ask to have my picture on no poster. What I'm asking for is a cut of the cash."

"The Apostolics don't get a cut, and they been with me five years, give or take a member. Rae's been with me seven, she don't get a cut."

"I'm not studying Rae. I assume you got your own deal with her."

Tommy rose and crossed the trailer in three steps to stand beside her.

"I got one deal with Rae that could easy be yours," he said, looking down at her. She was such a little thing, once you stood next to her. It was just her pep that made her seem bigger. Tommy greatly admired pep. As long as it was properly channeled.

"Let's stick to business," she said.

The Reverend Tommy put his arms around her. He was no giant, but she barely came up to his chest. It made a man want to protect her.

"This could be business, if you want to look at it that way," Tommy said. She turned so that her back was to him, but she didn't push him away.

"What kind of business you call this?"

Tommy pressed his groin against her back. His arms slid round her waist.

"The best kind," he said, his voice growing husky.

"I'm talking about money, Reverend. I didn't come in here for no salami."

"That's all part of the service," Tommy said. He thought he felt her push back against him, thought she wiggled her ass just a little bit for him. "I offer salvation and salami at no extra charge."

Aural slipped her hand behind her and touched his fly. Tommy leaned his face onto the top of her head.

"Shit, Rev, that ain't no salami."

"You guessed."

"That's more like one of them cocktail sausages you eat with a toothpick."

Aural tapped him once sharply with her knuckles and Tommy released her, jumping back.

"You forget who you're talking to," he said, drawing himself up and trying to reclaim his dignity.

"And you don't even *know* who you're talking to," Aural said. "I ain't one of them starry-eyed little things who comes up to you after a show, her little mind all whirly with the thought of sin, 'Oh, save me, Reverend Tommy, save me,' and you slip 'em salvation standing up against the back of the trailer."

"You ain't, huh? The way I heard it, you been boasting about how you can wear a man out."

"I told Rae that in private," she said, her face suddenly hot with betrayal.

"And that's how she told me," he said. "In private."

Tommy read the emotions on her face and realized he had found a weakness.

"She oughtn't a done you like that," he continued. "That was a mean thing to do. You didn't deserve that."

"I guess I'll survive it."

"You could get right back at her, you know."

"With you?"

"No better revenge, honey. And I promise you, I know a whole lot more than that teenager with the funny hair. I can please you good and at the same time you'll be having your revenge."

Aural smiled. For just a second it seemed almost inviting. She looked into his face, where the eyebrow rode across his forehead like a fuzzy black caterpillar. When he squinted his eyes with his seductive look, the caterpillar appeared to crawl.

She wasn't that hard-up, Aural thought, not nearly that hard-up. But the fact that she'd even considered it indicated that she had better find herself a man, quick, while she still was calm enough to do the choosing herself. If it turned out that the man picked you, God knows what you'd end up with.

Tommy put a hand on her cheek. His palm was already sweaty.

"Come on, sweet thing," he said, his voice husky again. "You know you want it."

"But what do I want?" Aural asked, still smiling sweetly.

"Well, suppose we experiment till we get it right?"

Tommy put his other hand on her breast and watched her eyelids quiver. He knew it. Some of them just had to say no first, that was all. There was nothing like persistence, it beat charm all to hell.

She put one of her hands atop his hand that was on her breast and he felt her fingers delicately intertwining with his own. Her other hand slid down to his zipper and Tommy smiled as she pulled it slowly open. He liked the languid approach, nothing hurried, she knew what she was doing. He tried to knead her breast but she held that hand firmly so he just relaxed as he felt her fingers groping into his pants. If she wanted to do all the work, that was fine with him.

Her fingers snaked into his shorts and tickled his scrotum. They slipped smoothly around his testicles and squeezed.

Tommy moaned with pleasure.

"Oh, yeah," he said, his eyes closed.

She squeezed. And squeezed. And squeezed.

''Hey.'' His eyes shot open to see her smiling up at him.

Tommy tried to pull her hand away, but she held on firmly and the pain was worse. Her other hand still gripped his fingers and would not release him. He had no leverage and nothing to work with. Meanwhile, she just kept squeezing harder.

''You're hurting me!''

''Well, sure,'' she said matter-of-factly. ''Funny how something can feel so nice, and then so bad, ain't it? Just too much of a good thing sometimes.''

''You're breaking my balls!''

''You can heal them, sugar,'' she said. She was still smiling. That was the oddest thing to the Reverend Tommy, that she just kept smiling, not maliciously, but with the suggestion of real pleasure.

When he thought sure he'd end up a eunuch if she didn't stop, he hit her.

She reeled back, shaking her head from the force of the blow that had struck her on the forehead. But she released his balls. Tommy cradled his crotch with both hands, keeping an eye on Aural all the time as if he expected her to grab at him again.

But she didn't look aggressive anymore. She didn't look particularly injured, either. What she looked more than anything was gratified. As if she had known all along that he was going to hit her, had expected it, and was glad that he had finally gotten around to it.

Chapter 9

The manager told him to wait a minute and Cooper moved off to one side of the counter, eyeing the customers as they got their hamburgers and chicken bits and french fries. Cooper didn't like most of them, he didn't like what he saw in their faces when they glanced at him then looked hurriedly away as if they had just seen something that polite people didn't stare at. He preferred the open gawking of the little kids, the ones too young to care about manners. They usually got their arms jerked for looking at him too long, and sometimes their parents would kneel down beside them and explain things in urgent but instructive tones. Cooper wanted to squash those parents, wanted to step on them right where they knelt and jump up and down.

The manager was a shifty-eyed bastard himself. Cooper had told him he wanted a job and was not afraid of hard work, just the way he had been coached in the class on readjustment to society that they gave in Springville. He had been polite, said please, called the man sir even though he was a scrawny bastard that Cooper could have snapped into pieces with one hand. He had been told to wait and he was waiting but that didn't mean he wasn't aware of what the manager was up to. Cooper saw him say something to one of the employees in the back of the kitchen, saw the employee laugh. How some pimple-faced kid wearing a paper hat thought he could afford to laugh at Cooper was a mystery the big man would like to solve by squeezing pimple-face's head until it popped open.

After making Cooper stand there long enough to show that he was the boss, the manager returned with an application form.

"Just fill this out," the manager said, offering Cooper a pen.

Cooper stared blankly at the paper.

"It's just a formality," the man said. "We can always use someone who's willing to work."

"I'm willing to work," Cooper said. He held the paper back to the man as if the transaction had been completed.

"You still have to fill it out," the manager said.

"I can do dishes," Cooper said.

"Good."

Cooper looked into the open kitchen, seeking the dishwasher or the sink.

"We use mostly disposable dinnerware here," the manager said.

Cooper wondered what he was talking about: dinnerware. Cooper knew how to do dishes, he had been trained to do that in Huntsville, he knew how to work the machines.

"Why don't you just fill it out and return it to me when you're finished. No hurry, take your time."

The manager walked away and Cooper sat at one of the plastic tables, his big legs folding uncomfortably under the surface. He saw the place to put his name and printed it there in block letters. A few more of the questions were easy enough, but some of the rest of them confused him. They had taught him at Springville how to fill out a form like this but he had forgotten some of it. He wished that his punk were there. The punk could read like nobody's business.

A male employee swabbed at the table in front of Cooper's with a sponge. Cooper wrinkled his nose at the scent of the astringent cleanser. He growled menacingly; it was hard enough to concentrate without somebody sticking ammonia in his nose. Cooper glowered at the employee. The man heard the sound and turned to look. He had the big eyes and swollen head of Down's Syndrome, and his face was wreathed with a beatific smile.

"Hi," the man said sweetly.

Startled by the sweetness, Cooper said "hi" in return, then studied the application form again. A fucking retard could get a job here, Cooper thought. Did the ree have to fill out a form, too? They couldn't keep him from having a job now, there was no way they could deny him, he could work rings around that guy.

He glanced at the worker again and the man was still smiling, his eyes so happy he looked as if he and Cooper were long-lost friends. I don't know you, Cooper thought. Don't look at me like you know me, I'll bust your fat head wide open for you.

The employee worked his way across the room, blissfully unaware of the malice in Cooper's darting looks. Cooper glanced around for the

manager, wondering if the man was aware of the caliber of his employees. Maybe Cooper would have to point it out to him if the manager
gave him any static about this bullshit application. Cooper knew how to
work in a *kitchen,* goddamn it! He wasn't just some table swabber, he
had worked in a kitchen that served over a thousand men three meals a
day. He could do the work if they'd just let him!

His eyes began to burn and the application swam before him, taunt-
ing him with stupid-ass clerk questions and words as tangled as knots. I
ain't no goddamned ree, he thought. Give me a test, something to see
can I do the work, not an application for a ree. He started to crumple the
form in frustration, then stopped, the readjustment counselor's words
droning over and over in his ears. "Just remember, none of it is directed
at you personally, it's just the way society works. Be patient, take a
deep breath, try again. Keep trying. Keep trying."

The readjustment counselor had been a woman with silver hair and a
big mole right beside her upper lip. Sometimes she had reminded
Cooper of his mother. Sometimes he had wanted her to come to his cell
and keep explaining things, everything and everything until he understood. Sometimes he thought he might like to kill her. He wished
she were here now to see the kind of shit they tried to make him do in
the world. He wished the punk were here so he could help him with the
form. The punk had said to call him if he ever needed help. Cooper
thought of doing it now, but then he would have to read the words
on the form into the phone and he didn't like the phone in the first
place . . .

Now the form was wrinkled. He thought of asking for a new one so
that the manager wouldn't think he didn't take care of things—and
maybe a new one would be easier to read, maybe he had been given the
wrong one in the first place—but he didn't want the manager to think he
was responsible . . . he could say the retard had messed up the paper
when he was wiping the tables. He could show the manager how it had
happened and in the process he could demonstrate how well he could
clean a table himself and then the form wouldn't be necessary at all, and
if the ree tried to deny that he had messed up the form, Cooper would
mess him up in a way he'd never forget.

He smoothed the paper as best he could, looking around to see if the
ree was watching him, possibly anticipating his ploy. He noticed the
girl looking at him, her face lowered to suck milk shake from a straw,
her eyes peering out from under her brows. When he returned her look,
daring her to keep staring, she smiled and didn't turn away the way

everyone else did. What the hell was her problem? If she didn't stop gawking at him, *he* would be her problem pretty damned fast.

The bitch stood up and crossed towards him, still sucking on the straw. She looked about eighteen, old enough to be legal, anyway, and not bad looking but if she didn't stop staring at him, he'd gouge her eyes out.

"How ya doin'?" she asked, releasing the straw at last. A drop of chocolate shake rode her lower lip. She thrust out the tip of her tongue and licked it away.

"What?" Cooper thought she was referring to the application and he smoothed it again.

"Said 'hi'," she said. "Forget your glasses?"

"What?"

"I see you're having a little trouble with the form there, I figured you forgot your glasses. Want me to read it to you?"

Before Cooper could figure out what the trick was, she had slipped into the booth opposite him and swiveled the paper to face her.

"It's wrinkled . . ."

"I don't imagine that matters," the girl said. " 'They just want the facts, ma'am.' " She grinned as if she had made a joke and Cooper squinted at her, trying to figure out what she was up to.

"Well, now," she continued, "let's see what they want from you. Name; well, you got that one right. Hello, Darnell Cooper. Are you really thirty-three? You don't look it, you look much younger."

"What are you studying me for?" Cooper asked.

"You're what they call well-preserved, I guess," she said. There was a smile in her voice even when she wasn't smiling. "Now here where it says previous employment . . . have you ever worked before?"

"Sure."

". . . Want to tell me where?"

"The kitchen."

"Well, now, Coop, I think they want more information than that."

Cooper was confused by the use of his nickname. "You don't know me," he said, almost certain it was true.

"Have you forgotten so soon?" she asked, then laughed. "No, I don't know you, and I'd remember somebody like you, believe me. God, you look strong."

"I'm stronger than just about anybody," Cooper said.

"I believe it. Where'd you get that tattoo?"

"Somewhere."

"I like tattoos."

"Uh-huh."

"I have one, you know."

Cooper was silent. How was he supposed to know that?

"But it's in a place I can't show you until I know you better." She laughed at herself again. "They tell me I'm shameless. Do you think I'm shameless?"

"I don't think about you at all," Cooper said.

"We'll have to get you over *that* . . . you're not one of *them,* are you?" She flopped her wrist at him.

Cooper stared at her. He could see part of her cleavage. She had it showing like that so he could reach his hand in there, he knew that. That's why women dressed the way they did, to make it easier for you.

"You're not an old fagalorum, are you? There's an awful lot of *that* going around these days, and it's always the best-looking ones. Why is that? . . . They say a lot of body builders are like that . . . Just my luck . . . It's not that I have anything against it, it just seems like such a waste, that's all . . . Are you?"

"What?"

"They say Stallone is, but I don't believe it. Are you?"

"What?"

"A fag."

Was she asking if he was a faggot? Cooper could not believe it.

"I killed one once," he said, immediately regretting it. But she didn't seem to mind.

"Well, you look like you could, easy enough."

"I could. I did."

"I'll bet you did . . . Are you as strong everywhere as you are with them arms?" She looked like she was blushing all of a sudden, but Cooper couldn't imagine she had suddenly turned shy.

"Yeah," said Cooper.

"Tell you what, why don't I fill this thing out for you . . . you know, since you lost your glasses. And then you could take me out for a milk shake."

"You just had a milk shake."

She grinned. "You don't miss a trick, do you? Maybe we could find me another one. I'm insatiable."

She put her hand atop his for a moment, still grinning like they were sharing a joke. Cooper grinned back at her and looked at her cleavage. She took the pen from his fingers.

When she bent over the tabletop to do the form, she showed even more of her breasts.

I could kill you so fast you wouldn't believe it, he thought. I could kill you just like that. Then he remembered the girls in the coal mine. Or I could kill you real slow. I could take forever.

She seemed to know he was thinking about her because she looked up at him and smiled again.

"I'm fudging things just a little bit," she said. "When I'm finished they'll put you in charge of the place . . . 'Cause we want to keep a great big hunk like you around town, don't we?"

"Have you ever been in a coal mine?" Cooper asked.

"Darling," she said, "I'll try anything once."

Chapter 10

The third letter was different. It didn't exist.

The envelope was the same, addressed to Becker in care of the FBI, and the postmark was still Decatur, Alabama, but Becker opened it to find nothing inside. No letter, no message written in the envelope itself, nothing, not so much as lint.

Had his correspondent simply forgotten to put the clipping from *The Times* into the envelope? Or was he under sudden pressure and unable to do so for reasons of his own safety? Or had someone taken it out? If the correspondent was dependent on someone else posting his mail, as Becker suspected, then it was possible the man had been caught. And if he had been caught, what had become of him?

Becker held the envelope to the light to see if it was the medium for the message itself. There was no imprint of something having been written without ink. There were no holes in the envelope.

Feeling foolish, Becker lit a match and held the envelope over it to bring out any invisible ink. There was none. Searching through Jack's room, he came up with a magnifying glass and perused the envelope inside and out. Again, nothing that he could find. There were vastly more sophisticated ways to hide a message, and to discover it, but Becker was certain his correspondent did not expect him to take the stationery to the FBI lab. Both messages had been sent to him, not the Bureau. Whatever message there was, the correspondent expected Becker to find it by himself, and that meant without elaborate scientific help.

And the longer he thought of it, the more convinced Becker became that there was a message there somewhere. If, as he had first suspected, someone had intercepted the message, why mail just the envelope? Why alert the recipient that something had gone wrong? Especially when the recipient of the letter was someone in the FBI? Much safer, and much more likely, that whoever removed the message would have withheld the envelope as well.

Therefore, the message was in the envelope, on the envelope, or the envelope itself and not impossible to decipher because the writer expected Becker to do it. Closing his eyes, Becker ran his fingers across the surface of the stationery, thinking to find some pattern of bumps, perhaps in the address, a primitive Braille that Becker could comprehend. The envelope was perfectly smooth except for the address and the stamp. He gently rubbed the address again and again. It was rougher than the surrounding paper, which indicated that it had been typed and not laser printed, but if there was any meaning in the roughness, Becker could not detect it. Perhaps a blind man could, but Becker was not blind and did not have that kind of touch and the correspondent must have known it.

The only true relief on the front surface of the envelope was at the stamp, where the glue had failed to adhere in one small spot, raising up the perforated edge enough for Becker's fingers to detect it. He studied the stamp itself under Jack's magnifying glass and found nothing unusual.

Feeling like an amateur detective, Becker turned on the flame under the teakettle. Hercule Poirot would not have done it like this, he thought. Agatha Christie would have found a way for her prissy, abstemious sleuth to have solved it through sheer deduction. But I'm not as smart as old Hercule, he admitted, I usually have to get my hands dirty.

When the kettle whistled, Becker held the envelope over the spout and steamed the stamp until it curled. Underneath the stamp and slightly smudged by the steam was a series of dots, another number in binary code. This time the dots had not been made by a pin, so they could not be detected from the inside of the envelope. They were as small as pinpricks, however, and looked as if they could have been made using a pin as a stylus, but this time with ink. Or a substance substituted for ink.

It was a reddish brown, the color of iodine, and Becker guessed that it was blood. Perhaps as a touch of melodrama, or perhaps a matter of convenience. It was almost impossible to find a bottle of ink lying around the house—or around the prison—these days, and blood, one's own blood, was always readily available, especially in small amounts and when the writing instrument was a pin. A jab or two in the finger would provide enough to write a number in dots, Becker thought.

The number this time was a longer one. Becker drew a series of boxes and labeled them underneath from right to left, advancing by an order of 2, 4, 8, 16 and so on until the boxes had crossed the page. He placed a dot in each box that corresponded to a mark on the envelope, then toted up his result with a pocket calculator. The number was 15113054.

Karen found him sitting in the den, staring into space. There was a pizza box on the kitchen table, evidently to serve as dinner, but no plates, no napkins. Becker was certainly not fussy about the niceties of dining, but in the past months he had become increasingly conscientious about the small things and this sudden neglect served Karen as a warning that something was wrong. Not that she needed much warning. She had noted his increasing withdrawal since the arrival of the first letter, and his current fugue left no doubt about his mood.

"The latest letter?"

Becker did not look up at her.

"The final letter," he said.

She moved behind him and rubbed his neck and shoulders. He took the massage like so much stone and she quickly stopped.

"How do you know it's the final one?"

"He won't write again."

"Well, then, good. Now you can forget about it, whatever it is."

"He has summoned me," Becker said sarcastically.

Karen paused, hoping she would not have to pump every single answer from him.

"How do you mean, 'summoned you'?" she asked at last.

"He's told me where he is and who he is and he can't very well come to me."

He continued to stare at a spot on the wall; he had not looked at her since she entered the room.

"So I'll have to go to him."

"What is it, really?" she asked.

"I'm scared," he said.

"Then don't do it."

He chuckled humorlessly.

"If I didn't do things I was afraid of, I wouldn't get much done."

"You've got nothing left to prove, to yourself or to anyone else. Certainly not to the Bureau."

"Maybe to myself, though . . . You know what it's like, Karen. You know how seductive it is."

Karen was silent. On a case with Becker she had killed one person while allowing another to die of self-inflicted wounds. Both had deserved to die—they had killed many times—but it was not the morality of her choices that had bothered Karen. It was her reaction. She had felt, for the first and only time, the savage thrill of killing, the thrill that Becker feared would consume him. Horrified and exhilarated, she had confessed to him that she understood and shared his passion. But she had denied it ever since, and her strongest denial was to herself. She had transferred to Kidnapping to decrease her possible exposure to temptation and had been grateful for each promotion that took her higher up the ladder and farther from the dangers of the field.

"Not really," she said. "I know that it troubles you."

He looked at her searchingly for a second. He never pressed her on the subject. Becker knew what he knew but respected her desire to forget. He wished that he could do the same.

"Yes. It 'troubles' me."

"You're out of it, John. Stay out if that's what you want."

"I kept solving the puzzles of the letters, didn't I? I knew it was trouble from the first, but I kept solving them. Maybe it's what I want to do."

"They're just letters—you didn't solicit them—they aren't forcing you to get involved."

"I know."

"If there's a problem, let the Bureau handle it."

"They are handling it," he said. "With me."

She stopped massaging his shoulders and slipped her chin to his head, her hands to his chest.

"Just don't do it. Stay out of it. It costs you far too much."

"I need to get into a prison to talk to an inmate," he said. "Can you arrange it for me?"

Karen hesitated. "You can visit without any help."

"I need to be alone with him. We can't do it through Plexiglas with cameras on us and a guard standing ten feet away."

"John . . ."

"I don't want Hatcher involved in this. If he is, I won't go near it. You have the authority to arrange it."

"John—I can't."

"Does Hatcher have a marker on me?" A marker was a directive that Deputy Director Hatcher was to be informed of any Bureau action involving a subject agent.

"You know this is touchy," Karen said.

"Restricted information, right? Okay, I understand. But it wouldn't be restricted if he didn't have a marker on me, would it? You could answer the question then."

"No comment."

"So I am marked, which means I can't do anything without Hatcher being involved, at least as a silent observer, and since I won't do anything if Hatcher is involved, it means I can't do anything. Great. So I'm off the hook. I'm doing nothing."

He stood and took her in his arms. "I got sausage and mushrooms on the pizza. Okay?"

Chapter 11

In Washington, the center of American democracy, a city that thrives on secret meetings and private agendas, a clandestine meeting was held between Congressman Quincy Beggs and FBI Associate Director Thurston Hatcher in the Congressional Office Building. There was no pressing need for the meeting to be a secret save for the natural predilections of both men. Both knew there was a time to go public, a time to share the results of their public-spirited efforts with the public itself, and there was a much longer time to keep quiet about their activities lest the public actually come to expect something from them. There was no point in sharing things with the populace, both men would argue, until there was actually something to share.

Beggs was a short man, going to fat, which spread unattractively across his neck, crowding his collar and bunching up under his chin. It gave him the look of a man who was unused to shirt and tie, a working-man forced into the suit by the demands of his office. In truth, the Congressman was a lawyer by training, a politician by inclination and ambition, and wore a look of perpetual discomfort only because his neck size continued to expand no matter what size collar he wore. If his spreading girth made him appear to be a man of the people, however, Beggs was astute enough to avoid dieting. His very appearance became a prop in his political act, and he was above all else an actor. In fact, Biggs was never more comfortable than when acting a part in front of large groups of people—unless it was now, when he was acting a part in front of an audience of one.

Associate Director Hatcher was a perfect audience. Having entered the Bureau during the sartorially imperious reign of J. Edgar Hoover, Hatcher never felt fully dressed without a suit and tie and a crease in his pants leg. He would have appeared as out-of-costume in leisure wear as Richard Nixon. The resemblance, many of those under him would say, did not end there. Hatcher's dissembling of sincerity was particularly awkward, an equal in duplicity, his critics said, to the former President's assertions of honesty. One had to be seriously predisposed to the man—or have a vested interest in his success—to believe him. It was part of his skill as a director, and manipulator, however, that Hatcher was able to predispose those in authority towards him. He offered them what they wanted and presented it with all the deference of a born sycophant.

"It seems possible, Congressman Beggs," Hatcher was saying, tugging at the crease in his blue serge, "just possible, that I may have a lead in finding the man you are after. Pardon me, I misspoke when I said 'I.' I meant *we,* of course. There are many good men and women involved in all of the work of the Bureau."

"Certainly. Excellent people," Beggs agreed.

"I consider myself just part of the organization."

"You're too modest, Mr. Hatcher. There is no need in this office. Your contributions to the Bureau are well known."

"Well, thank you. I confess that I do have a special interest in this case—because, of course, I am deeply aware of how it affects you personally, Congressman."

"When might you expect some results in this line of investigation, Mr. Hatcher? Not that I mean to influence your management of the case."

"Of course not . . . If I supervise the matter directly myself—which of course I intend to do—I should think we might expect some substantial results by summer."

"Early summer or late summer?" Beggs asked. His biennial election was in November.

"That's impossible to predict," said Hatcher. "But naturally I will expedite matters as much as possible. In a case this old, there are always difficulties—but then the satisfaction of a solution is that much greater."

"Indeed it would be. I think I can safely say that the people of my constituency would be very impressed. As would I, Mr. Hatcher. As would I."

Hatcher smiled demurely and tended to his pants.

It was a perfect Washington deal. No whisper was made of promotion for Hatcher, no mention of Beggs' need for a shot in the arm in the coming election. None was necessary, all was understood. Neither man had any personal feeling for the other at all, but they had just become staunch allies.

Hatcher left the Congressional Office Building feeling very pleased with himself. For him, it was a no-lose situation. If he delivered, then Beggs was in his pocket and deeply in his debt. If Hatcher failed to deliver, it was very likely that Beggs would not be reelected and would no longer be of any consequence to Hatcher anyway. He would then have to curry favor with the new member of the Oversight Committee who replaced Beggs, of course, but with the resources of the investigative arm of the Bureau at his disposal, that was never very difficult.

The only problem that remained was Becker. Becker was always a problem, it was in the man's nature, but it was also equally in his nature to be a solution. Hatcher merely needed to tighten a few screws.

Chapter 12

"What you mean you burned him? Like at the stake?"

The questioner was the Deacon of the Apostolics. He sat with his choir in the front row of seats in the tent prior to the Reverend Tommy R. Walker's Miraculous Faith and Healing Revival in a fallow soybean field just outside of Pikeville, Kentucky. Aural sat perched on the stage in front of the choir, her feet dangling over the stage like a schoolgirl on a wall.

"No, he wasn't a *witch*," she said. "He was just an ordinary son of a bitch."

Rae tittered and Aural gave her a mildly baleful look. Once again Rae had revealed something Aural told her in presumed confidence. It wasn't the worst habit in the world since nothing Aural had confided was anything she was particularly trying to keep secret, but it did suggest a certain surprising defect in Rae's character. Aural would never have taken her for a blabbermouth. But then maybe she'd never had as interesting a friend as Aural to blab about before.

"You can't burn every son of a bitch," muttered a female member of the choir. There was a note of regret to her voice.

"Ain't no bonfire big enough," chimed in another female. The men seemed discomfited.

"How did he happen to allow you to do this?" the Deacon asked Aural directly.

"I wouldn't say he actually *allowed* me to do it, Deacon. He was registering his protests, you might say."

Hebron James, the basso profundo of the group, a surprisingly small man considering the depth of his voice, looked at Aural in horror.

"You burned him *alive?*" he rumbled. "With the poor man pleading for mercy?"

"Just 'cause he shucked his boot at you?" the Deacon joined in. "Girl, that ain't Christian."

"Not *just* 'cause of the boot," Aural said defensively. "The boot was the last straw, so to say."

One of the women murmured sympathetically.

"Comes a time when you had enough," Aural said. "Comes a time when you had too damned much."

"Amen," offered the woman, a particularly heavy soprano who had taken Aural's side from the beginning.

"Damn, I don't care what he done," Hebron continued. "To burn a man *alive . . .*"

"You know he deserved it," said the soprano, offering a meaningful glance at the bass. "You know he had it coming to him."

"No man's got that coming to him," Hebron insisted. "I don't care what he done."

"I know you don't care," the soprano said. "That's pretty clear."

"Man's got his troubles, too," Hebron said, directing himself to his shoes. "Ain't just the women's got problems. Man's got his reasons for what he does."

"Now that's surely true," offered the Deacon. "These things ain't never one-sided. What did you do to provoke him, honey?"

The other women caught their breath in outrage, but Aural only laughed. "Everything I could," she said. "About the only way to get the damned fool's attention was something painful upside the head. I had to ring his skull like a bell every now and then just to let him know I was still around."

Rae spoke with the conviction of a woman who had just recently seen a talk show on the subject. "That was an abusive relationship," she declared.

"Ain't they all," said Aural. "Ain't they all."

The crowd waiting outside the tent after the show had grown to almost a quarter of the one that had been inside earlier. Everyone seemed to want to talk personally to the performers, like fans at a rock concert. Many of them were for the Reverend Tommy, of course, eager to touch the hands that had healed so many, but more of them, and an ever increasing number, were for Aural. They clustered around her so thickly she could scarcely move, thrusting things for her to sign, speaking her name, some in whispers, some in chants as if invoking it. The men crowded in for a nearer look, hardly believing that the beauty they had perceived from a distance could withstand closer scrutiny, then lingered, amazed. The women came to see if that sweetness, that aura of holiness and divine self-assurance, could survive removal from the stage, the lighting of the tent, the spirituality of the show. If the girl was truly inclined to sainthood, they wanted to be next to her, and if she was sham, they all of them, men and women, hoped to be relieved of the unexpected hopes she had given rise to.

Aural disappointed none of them, smiling indefatigably, murmuring words of encouragement and humble thanks. She signed their autographs, suffered their questions, allowed them to touch her velvet robe and, occasionally, stroke her long hair. She took credit for none of the miracles of the evening, directing them all to the Reverend Tommy, who stood amid his own coterie only a few yards away, straining to hear what was being said by Aural and her admirers while still nodding sympathetically to the sufferers clustered around him. It had not escaped his notice that her following grew and grew. Some of the faces had become recognizable, coming to show after show even though Tommy was careful about holding performances in towns at least fifty miles apart from each other. They had begun to follow her like groupies, and Tommy's awareness of the potential for gain in the situation was offset by his increasing envy.

He was going to have to do something about it, that much was for sure. It was rapidly becoming the Aural McKesson Show, featuring the Reverend Tommy R. Walker, instead of the other way around and if he wasn't careful, Aural might wake up to the fact that it could just as easily be the Aural McKesson Show, featuring herself as saint and singer, and to hell with the Reverend Tommy altogether. The girl had shown no aptitude for curing folks as yet, and as far as he knew she hadn't even tried, but she certainly understood the technique, and Tommy was not so far gone in self-esteem not to know that she could do it just as well as he could if she put her mind to it. Probably a lot better because, damn it, she had that look of sanctity about her when she was up on that stage, wearing that robe he gave her, that no amount of thumping and sweating by Tommy would ever overcome. If her followers could ever see her the way she really was, a foulmouthed, ungrateful, irreverent, greedy, sacrilegious little tease of a tramp—the way Tommy knew her to be—but then the trick was always to keep your public life and your private life separate, and Aural had seemed to understand that from the start.

He was going to have to deal with things pretty soon, because to hear Rae tell it Aural could walk away with the Apostolic just by crooking her finger. And with Rae, too, he suspected, even though she would never admit it. Rae had become more fascinated with Aural than she was with Tommy. And growing rebellious and uppity in little ways under the girl's influence, too. The Apostolics sure weren't the Mormon Tabernacle Choir, but they were trained and docile and worked cheap and without them and without Rae to do the hundred little things she did, Tommy would be without a show, without a livelihood, without a goddamned prayer. He was too old to start over again with nothing more than a gold Bible and a winning way and ten thousand feet of patched canvas tent.

Tommy looked over to where Aural stood amid her fans. She was smiling that little smile she used when she was being saintly, nothing big enough to show actual mirth. It was the kind of smile a mother used when watching her child do something endearing for the umpteenth time, patient, knowing, ever tolerant of her beloved. The people around her were lapping it up. He saw Rae standing at the edge of the crowd, studying Aural with the same devotion as all the others, as if she actually *believed* the act, as if she didn't have access to the real Aural whenever she wanted it. The flock attending Tommy had dispersed, many of them gravitating towards Aural's crowd, so that Tommy stood alone, watching the phenomenon he had helped to create.

Either he had to harness Aural in a way she couldn't get loose from him . . . or he had to get rid of her, quick.

He didn't have any idea of a way to harness her—she could shrug him off and walk off with his show anytime she wanted to—and it wouldn't be long before she realized that as well as Tommy.

But he did know how to get rid of her.

Chapter 13

Cooper had to walk three miles to work because there was no public transportation to the restaurant and he did not have a car, but the walk did not bother him. On the way to work it gave him a chance to run over in his mind his course of action for the day, and on the return trip, when it was dark outside except for the headlights of cars going past on the road, he used the time to pore over the day's events and see where he had done right and where he had gone wrong. It wasn't like the life in prison; there were so many ways to make a mistake here in the world. Nobody yelled at him at the job when he made a mistake—Cooper was not the kind of man to raise your voice to—but they had other ways of letting him know. Ways that made him feel much worse. He knew they were all talking about him behind his back, mocking him, laughing at his incompetence, smirking at his slowness.

But he had ways of getting back at them. That was what he considered on his walk to work, the methods he would use to get even with all the snickering, condescending shitass little clerks who worked in the restaurant with him. A different way for each one. He could just squeeze them all together and punish them at once, but that wouldn't be any fun. He wanted to get them one at a time and do it leisurely so they knew why they were being punished, and he wanted to do each one in a different way—because that would be fun.

He didn't know exactly when he would start repaying his fellow employees, but he knew he would have to have a car first, for two reasons. If he had a car he could transport them somewhere away from the restaurant. Finding a place wouldn't be hard—the road was lined by scruffy, piney woods on both sides and there was nothing in there but trees and bushes and snakes. Cooper knew that because he had gone exploring. The land was no good for farming, too close to the road for living. It was junk land and Cooper was thinking of ways of putting a whole lot of junk on it. Or under it.

The other reason he'd need a car was to go away in when he was finished. He'd have to be stupid to just stick around, still walking to and from the restaurant when there was nobody left to work in it but him. And Cooper wasn't stupid. Sometimes it took him a while to figure out exactly what he wanted to do, but that didn't make him stupid. The clerks at the restaurant would find out just how smart he was, soon enough. As soon as he got a car.

And he wasn't going to steal one, either. He knew better than that, that was the way to have every cop in the state pulling you over and asking for your registration. It would be his own car, it would belong to him, he would pay for it with his own money. Or at least he'd make the down payment. He could see himself doing that, walking into the used-car lot, pointing to the car he wanted, then wiping that smug smile off the salesman's face by pulling a wad of bills from his pocket and counting them off. He could see himself taking the keys from the hands of the clerk who *would* be impressed now, getting behind the wheel, and driving right out of there with the registration in his pocket. After that Cooper couldn't see any more about the car; that was the only picture he had in his mind. But it was enough. It would be fun, and he knew what he'd do once he got the car. That part was a little fuzzy, too, but not because he couldn't see it clearly. Rather, because he could see too many possibilities.

Meanwhile, the walk was fine with Cooper. Once in a while some stranger would slow down and offer him a ride. Cooper liked that, as long as they didn't try to talk to him too much. He liked sitting in a different car, he liked studying the driver from the corner of his eye, he liked imagining what he'd do to the driver if he tried any funny stuff. Sometimes they would ask him what he was grinning about. He hadn't told any of them yet—but he might.

He remembered the girl. Her car was old, but big, with lots of room, even up front. It had a muffler problem, but what Cooper remembered best was that she let him drive and got him onto the highway and then urged him on until he was going fast, so fast he couldn't do anything but drive. She kept telling him to go faster and faster and that's when she did the amazing thing and slipped down on that big front seat and told him to pay attention to his driving or he'd kill them both. But it was very hard to pay attention to his driving with her doing that to him, and she wasn't just teasing about it either. She went at him like she was starved, with all kinds of moans and sloppy noises which he thought were probably words but he couldn't make them out because of what she was doing and he didn't know why she'd bother talking then anyway. But she was very good at it. And fast, so fast he hardly got to the part where he thought about how easy it would be to kill her before he was finished. Cooper tried to watch the road, but he swerved badly a couple of times towards the end and nearly put them into the ditch. When he howled and cried out at the finish, she lifted up from the seat, wiping her face and laughing.

"I gather you liked that," she said, still laughing. "Either that or you got it caught in the zipper."

She was slouched against her door now, looking real pleased with herself. Her blouse was open and he saw her reach her hand inside.

"Keep driving," she said.

"Where?" he asked.

"See, that part's easy," she said. "You just point the car and the road'll take you where it's going."

Cooper didn't like her tone of voice now, but after a minute she slid her naked foot across the seat and started playing with his leg with her toes. He didn't remember seeing her ever take her boots off.

She was kind of purring now and her hand was working under her blouse but Cooper didn't like being touched so soon after and he felt like kicking her out of the car while they were speeding along.

"I could kill you, you know," he said.

"You're about to get your chance, sugar," she said. Her foot was now in his lap, but what she thought she was going to accomplish with her heel was a mystery to Cooper. Grinding it around like that now just annoyed him.

"Uh huh," he said.

"My turn," she said.

Cooper looked at her askance. If she thought he was going to do what she had just done, she must be even crazier than she was acting.

"Keep your eyes on the road," she said. "I'll show you where to turn off."

He pulled the car onto a dirt lane that wasn't much wider than the car itself and that was the first time Cooper explored the piney woods.

Walking to work, he grinned at the memory.

The retard with the bug eyes was all right, Cooper liked him, he decided. He just smiled a lot and said friendly things and never tried to give Cooper advice and never made comments on how he was doing. But the guy who hung around the french-fry vat, Lyle, Kyle, whatever his name was, was beginning to be a real pain in the ass. Cooper had seen his kind before. He was scared shitless of Cooper—the only sign that he had any sense at all—but was trying like crazy to be friends with him. Cooper just knew he was going to have to hurt him some, if only to stop him trying to be a buddy. Cooper didn't want Kyle for a buddy, he didn't need some pimple-faced teenager for a pal, the kid didn't know his ass from a sandwich bun. If Cooper hurt him some, the kid would stop trying to be so chummy, and it would also serve to make him realize that Cooper really was dangerous. Once they thought he wasn't dangerous, they would think they could do and say anything, make fun of him any way they liked.

"Where's that girl I saw you with?" he was saying now, winking at Cooper like they shared a secret.

"Who?"

"The one I saw you with," Kyle said.

"You never saw me with a girl," Cooper said.

"Yeah, I did," Kyle insisted. "You drove off in her car. An Oldsmobile about a hundred years old."

Cooper did not think anyone had seen him with the girl.

Kyle slipped an order of frozen potato slices into the simmering fat, which convulsed briefly with a subdued hiss.

"What was her name?" Kyle asked.

"I don't know," Cooper said, honestly.

"Sure you do. Mayvis, ain't it? I see her around here a lot. She's a real beaut, ain't she?"

Cooper pulled the rubber garbage can from under the counter and dragged it towards the door. It wasn't really his job, it belonged to the ree, but Coop needed to get out of that kitchen. How come he hadn't noticed Kyle watching him when he drove off with the girl?

"She's okay," Cooper said.

"What did you do with her?" Kyle asked, his voice insinuating all kinds of things.

Cooper looked up from the garbage to stare at the kid. He wondered if he shoved the boy's hand into the boiling fat if that would shut him up.

"Something," Cooper said.

"I just bet you did," the kid said, and winked again. Then, to anyone else in the kitchen who wanted to hear, he said, "I just bet old Coop did something mighty interesting with Mayvis."

Somebody grunted something which Kyle took as encouragement to continue.

"He did it so good she hasn't come back," Kyle said. "Ain't that right, Coop?"

Cooper thought of shoving the boy's whole head into the french-fry vat, but instead he lifted the garbage can in his arms and backed out the door.

"Where'd you leave her?" Kyle persisted. "Some of the rest of us would like to find her."

"Somewhere," said Cooper. The screen door was yanked shut by its hinges, but Cooper could still hear them talking about him.

Chapter 14

Clamden's chief of police loped heavily after the soccer ball, holding on to his holster with one hand while the rest of the paraphernalia on his belt—radio, baton, keys, cuffs—slapped against his hips and butt.

"You destroy the myth of the graceful fat man," Becker said.

Tee swung mightily at the ball, catching it glancingly off the side of his boot so that it dribbled ineffectively in the general direction of Becker.

"Not fat," Tee puffed. "That's a paunch. It's a sign of respectability."

"You're getting awfully respectable," Becker said. He got to the ball in a few quick steps and rerouted it towards Jack.

Tee patted his stomach affectionately. "Think of it as a symbol of authority," he said. "Underneath all this flesh and equipment, I'm lean as a whippet. The uniform is very misleading. Right, Jack?"

Jack grunted something that could have been agreement as he concentrated on the ball, his mouth open with the effort. He and Tee had basically the same skill level, and each had been kicking a ball about the same amount of time.

"Your basic criminal type is skinny," Tee was explaining. "Righteous bulk just naturally intimidates him."

Jack kicked the ball to Becker and once again Becker deflected it to Tee with apparent ease. The guy was like one of those flippers in a pinball machine, Tee thought. He barely touched the ball, hardly kissed it, and it seemed to go exactly where he wanted and with speed and power. Tee was, once again, impressed by the easy athleticism of his friend.

Tee kicked another errant shot and laughed at himself.

"I'm more of a football player," he said. "This is a damned European game. Whoever heard of not using your hands? It's unnatural."

"Most popular sport in the world," Becker said, dancing to the ball and flicking it over to Jack.

"Oh, sure, the world. What do *they* know?"

"Speaking of your basic criminal type—" Becker said.

"Now you're talking," Tee said. "I know him well. I can pick him out of a crowd by the dishonest way he looks and moves."

"Nice talent," Becker said. "Must have its uses."

"It's why they made me chief of police," Tee said. "The old unerring eye. I can not only pick out your malefactor—that's police talk, Jack, very sophisticated—" Jack nodded to indicate that he was listening. "I can even tell you his criminal specialty."

"How is that done, exactly? That specialty thing?"

Tee picked the ball up and placed it on his hip.

"You know how pets and their owners start to resemble each other after a while? It's the same with your average perpetrator. After a few years, he looks like what he does. Your burglar develops big ears and shifty eyes, for instance."

"Pay no attention to him, Jack," Becker said.

"A sex fiend grows hair on his palms, just like they warned us."

"I was told you'd go blind," Becker said.

Jack took the ball from Tee's hands and the big man seemed hardly to notice. Jack recognized this tone in their voices; when the two men teased each other like this, Jack was better off playing by himself until the mood passed.

"You'll notice I do not wear glasses," said Tee.

"I hadn't noticed, but then I can't see too well."

"I feared as much. Always sad to see a good man go bad."

"Well, now, given your expertise in these matters . . ."

"I am, after all, the *chief* of police."

"And have the paunch to prove it," Becker said. "So, as the expert, what can you tell me about the man watching us from the hedge?"

Tee studied the forsythia hedge surrounding the playing field. It took him a moment to discern the shape of a man standing amid the foliage. He shook his head, acknowledging Becker's ability to see things without seeming to look. The man was behind Becker's back, and Tee could not remember that Becker had ever so much as turned around.

"What do you do, smell them?"

"This one is a little riper than most," Becker said.

The man was at least forty yards away. Tee had been joking; he was not sure that Becker was. He had asked Becker once how he did it, how he appeared to notice everything without paying attention. Becker's answer had only increased the mystery. "The way a deer does it," Becker had said. "He notices everything because everything is a threat. He's afraid." Tee could see nothing deerlike about his friend, nor could he detect any fear. The man he knew was not a passive prey animal, cringing at shadows. He was the shape within the shadow; he was a carnivore.

"He could be a scout," Tee ventured of the man in the bushes. "My legend may have spread. Or Jack's perhaps."

"Could be, I suppose," Becker said.

"You sound dubious. I'd say a soccer scout or a fan. Or he could be lost."

"Waiting for a bus?"

"Or a prevert."

"That's a fan of sorts," Becker said. "Maybe your legend *has* spread."

"Don't look at me. I don't attract that kind of attention. I have my admirers, of course."

"Being the chief, you would."

"Can't be helped. But they're all manly men and womanly women."

"I've heard about the women. Are you still chasing Mimi at the doughnut shop?"

"We're just good friends," Tee said, his voice temporarily serious. He cast a look at Jack to see if the boy was listening. "I want that understood."

"I believe you, but then I'm gullible."

"Do you think I should walk over there and intimidate the guy?"

"I wouldn't bother."

"I could beat him senseless for loitering. The chief is allowed to do that, you know."

"Or you could just shoot him from here and save yourself the walk."

"Not the worst idea. Then again, I have a radio on my hip, you'll notice."

"Let's have some music then," said Becker.

"I could summon help, provided there are any batteries in it."

"Actually, I wouldn't bother with any of that," Becker said. He signaled for Jack to kick him the ball. Becker scooped it up with his toe and caught it midair on his ankle, bouncing it to his knee. "He'll be coming to visit us pretty soon. You can pound him senseless when he arrives."

"Oh, good."

As if on cue, the man stepped out of the hedge and started towards them. How does he know these things? Tee asked himself.

Associate Director Hatcher of the Federal Bureau of Investigation, the man in charge of the various Violent Crime Divisions on the East Coast, stood in the bushes and watched John Becker kick a ball. He hated the way Becker kicked a ball, hated the way the man moved, the way he seemed to do everything with an effortless grace that mocked the clumsy efforts of those around him. It was one of the reasons that Becker was the most effective agent Hatcher had ever seen. One of several reasons, and Hatcher envied him all of them. Except one. Hatcher, for whom most things came only with practice and diligent effort, had one consummate skill that Becker couldn't touch. Hatcher knew that he wasn't the brightest agent around, nor the bravest, nor the best organized. He certainly had no natural talent for sleuthing, no instinct for the profession, no insight into the criminal mind beyond what he had been taught in class. What Hatcher had, what Becker lacked totally, was the ability to manipulate people. They didn't usually give awards and medals for such a skill—they gave promotions. It was not a talent that others would praise or envy, and other men did not yearn to be close to it as they did to athleticism or humor. In fact, it made many people dislike the possessor. Many, but not all. It was recognized by others who had the skill, and they manipulated Hatcher to manipulate others, and it would work that way until he rose to the top and did all the manipulating himself. That was how it was with power.

Most men in the Bureau would not have made this trip to see Becker in person, they would have thought it belittled someone as highly placed as Hatcher. But that was because they viewed status as the important thing, and there they were wrong. The important thing was to get the results that would solidify his position and increase his grip on the power his office offered him. Becker could not be manipulated by telephone, nor could he be summoned to Hatcher's office as if he were still employed by the Bureau. He could not be ordered to take an assignment; he could not be soft-soaped into it either. The secret to manipulating anyone was to know his weaknesses, and Hatcher knew Becker's.

Becker's first weakness was that he hated Hatcher, hated him openly and defiantly and made no attempt to hide it. This made him a biased reporter and immediately discounted Becker's account of things with his superiors. Hatcher hated Becker, too, but knew better than to ever reveal it to anyone. Publicly, he praised Becker's undisputed courage and skill, bending over backwards to give the impression of fairness. This gave credibility to the slightest and grudging suggestion of any deficiency.

Becker vented his hatred of Hatcher to anyone who would listen. Hatcher used his hatred of Becker only in the places where it would do the most good, and that was one of the differences between them. Not that he ever wanted to do Becker too much harm. The man had his uses. Properly directed and sparingly employed, Becker could be used to carry another's career. He could be saddled and ridden. Hatcher had managed to make Becker's successes his own triumphs in the past and he felt confident that he could do it again.

The big cop was staring at Hatcher now and talking to Becker, who didn't bother to turn to look. He had been spotted, which did not surprise him. Hatcher had not performed well in surveillance technique in training, and even if he had, it would have been hoping for too much to spy on Becker for very long without being detected.

As Hatcher stepped out of the bushes and started across the field, Becker finally deigned to look in his direction. He said something to the cop and they both laughed. The forty yards across empty field seemed like an eternity with their eyes on him. It was like walking into a sniper's scope with Becker looking at him and Hatcher had difficulty with the simple process of walking now that he was so conscious of it. He stumbled once and looked back to find the vengeful bit of turf that had tripped him, hearing the laughter of the cop floating towards him. Simple acts of coordination had always been troublesome for Hatcher—he never knew where to put his hands when talking to someone, and matters of rhythm eluded him entirely. He was used to these embarrassments and quite accustomed to the amusement his discomfort gave to others. He no longer minded when they snickered up their sleeves at him; while they were having such a good time at his expense, they never noticed that he was outmaneuvering them.

Becker would be reveling in his humiliation, of course, but Hatcher knew he could turn this to his own advantage. He would not waste energy worrying about his pride.

Becker was bouncing the ball with his whole body now, keeping it in the air off his knees, feet, shoulders, chest, and head. It was an impressive display of control and agility and gave Hatcher another twinge of hatred. A man that age had no business looking as agile as a tap dancer.

When he got within twenty yards, Hatcher began to smile. It always took him a while to conjure one up, but once he had it securely on his face, he could keep it there for as long as needed.

"What does your unerring eye tell you about this one?" Becker asked as Hatcher stepped into the open.

"Definitely a villain," Tee said.

"Absolutely."

"A brown suit, black shoes. Looks like a fashion felon at the very least."

"There's more."

"Christ, is he stiff! He moves like Nixon." Tee laughed when Hatcher stumbled. "Definitely not a cat burglar."

"So? Your expert opinion?"

"As chief of police—you want the official verdict?"

"Please."

"There's a snake in the grass approaching us."

"Close," Becker said. "But a snake at least has the conviction to get right down on its belly. Hatcher does not have that much courage. He's more of a lizard."

"Friend of yours, is he?"

"Of long standing," Becker said.

Hatcher mistimed his approach and stuck out his hand to shake far too soon. He had to walk fifteen yards with his hand thrust forward, a smile fixed on his face.

"Associate Director Hatcher, FBI," he said, moving first towards Tee. "Nice to meet you, officer."

"Chief," said Becker.

"I beg your pardon, Chief . . . ?"

"Terhune. Thomas Tee Terhune. How are you?"

"A pleasure." Hatcher turned to face Becker as if just noticing him for the first time. "John. How have you been?"

Becker did not take Hatcher's offered hand.

"I don't feel like it," Becker said.

"Pardon me?"

"I don't feel like doing it. I don't want the case. You can go back."

Hatcher widened his smile and tipped his face skyward for a second as if overcome by a laugh.

"Actually . . ." he started, then Jack joined the company, easing the ball from Becker's hand. "And who is this? You must be Special Agent Crist's little boy. Jack, isn't it?"

"You know it is," Becker said. "You boned up on Karen's file on the way here from New York."

"You're certainly getting to be a strong-looking young man, Jack. Do you want to be an agent like your mom when you grow up?"

"He's going into proctology instead. The work's the same but it pays better." Becker stepped between Hatcher and the boy as if to protect Jack from contamination. "Go home with Tee," he said. "I'll be there in a few minutes."

Becker took the ball back from the boy's hands and dropped it to the ground, imprisoning it with a foot.

"You're looking well, John," Hatcher said as Tee and the boy walked away. His cheeks were burning with humiliation, but his smile was firmly in place. He knew his eyes revealed his hatred, but Becker was not looking in his eyes. He was not looking directly at Hatcher at all.

"Go down to Springville and talk to the man yourself," Becker said. "You don't need me. You've probably already identified him by his prints on the envelope or the DNA in his saliva on the stamp, for all I know."

"I'm not sure who you mean."

"Look, Hatcher, I know honesty is a difficult concept for you, and I don't want you to break a habit of a lifetime and start dealing in it wholesale, but at least fake it for the purposes of this conversation or else this conversation is over. You've been reading my mail, right?"

Hatcher dropped the smile and assumed his forthright look.

"Naturally we screen anything that comes in addressed to an agent, for your own safety."

"I'm not an agent. I'm out."

Becker got the ball in the air, using only his feet, and suddenly Hatcher was confronted with a maze of black-and-white checks sailing between himself and Becker, each flight a tightly controlled arc coming off Becker's knees and feet. Finally he caught the ball on the top of his foot and held it there like a juggler waiting for applause.

"Very impressive, John."

With another flick, Becker aimed the ball in a lazy arc towards Hatcher, who stepped back, startled, trying to catch it with his hands. The ball fell to the ground and Hatcher stared at it for a moment, as if making sure it was dead before picking it up.

"Well, technically, the U.S. government considers you to be on indeterminate medical extension. Naturally we all still consider you a part of the team."

"I quit. I'm not going to do it anymore. I've told that to half a dozen people." Becker wiggled his fingers, calling for the ball.

"I do see that, but technically—and I hate to be technical, but there are those times when it matters—technically you were put on medical extension before you—uh—announced your dissatisfactions, and just as we cannot dismiss an agent when he is on extension because of stress or other psychological reasons, so, too, we cannot accept a resignation under those circumstances. It might be stress-induced, you see. It wouldn't be right for us to do so."

"I should have had Tee shoot you. It would have been so much simpler."

Hatcher tossed the ball to Becker's insistent fingers, throwing it underhanded. To Hatcher's intense annoyance, Becker deflected it off his knee, tapped it with his forehead, and put it into Hatcher's chest. This time Hatcher managed to hold on to it.

"We do think we know who has been sending you the letters," Hatcher said, struggling against an urge to hurl the ball into Becker's face.

"Of course you know. That last number was his prison identification number, wasn't it?"

Becker wiggled his fingers again, calling for the ball.

"I am told it may have been. I wonder, John, could we go to your house? Agent Crist should be back from work soon and it would be good for her to take part in this discussion."

This time he handed the ball to Becker.

"Is this a discussion? I've already given you my answer."

"Inasmuch as it concerns her, too."

Becker stuck the ball on his hip.

"How does it concern her?"

"In her work, I mean."

"Karen is in Kidnapping. Are you treating this as a kidnapping?"

"Actually, I'm moving Special Agent Crist to Serial Killings."

"Why?"

"Why not? She's an excellent agent and a very competent administrator. It's the usual procedure for grooming people for advancement to move them around, get them familiar with as much of our scope of operations as possible."

"You can't do that."

"Why is that, John?"

"I don't want her involved in Serial Killing."

"Uh-huh."

"Don't do it, that's all."

"It's the proper career move for her, John."

"It wouldn't be good for her."

"Would you care to elaborate? It might help if I understood just why."

"No, I wouldn't care to elaborate. She was in Serial once; she has enough experience with it."

"We do have certain procedures. If it were up to me—"

"It is up to you, Hatcher. It's all up to you. I'm telling you, I don't want her transferred to Serial."

"I see. Well, it is a little unorthodox. However, you're right, she was in Serial briefly as a very junior agent. Just one case, as I recall, before she transferred out. I don't recall the case in detail."

"Sure, you do. It was my case. It was your case, too, as a matter of fact."

"Oh, that's right, John. I'd forgotten . . . There were some deaths, as I recall."

Becker glared at him, but Hatcher's bland tone never wavered.

"Well, I suppose we could fudge things a bit under the circumstances. I could make it a temporary posting for her, just for this one case, then she would be through with Serial for the rest of her career. I don't think it would affect her overall performance rating."

"Who gives her that performance rating? Not you, by any chance?"

Hatcher tightened his smile another notch. "Naturally, the quicker the case is closed, the less Special Agent Crist will be exposed to Serial."

"Meaning if I don't take the case, I'm responsible."

"There's no connection, John. You and Agent Crist are separate entities—who just happen to live together."

Becker took a step towards Hatcher and dropped the ball, bringing his right foot into it with a massive blow.

"No!" Hatcher yelled and fell to the ground, cradling his head in his hands. Even as he dropped he realized that Becker was not aiming the ball directly at him. Close, but not at him. If he had wanted to, he could have decapitated Hatcher with the ball.

Hatcher got to his feet, cheeks blazing with humiliation, but he didn't mind the embarrasment. He had what he wanted.

He had Becker back at work.

Chapter 15

The Reverend Tommy R. Walker lay on his back on the bed with Rae astride him, naked for a change. Normally she would be wearing her nightgown shoved up to her hips, or a t-shirt that she slept in during the warmer months. Often as not she was wearing her socks, too, complaining about cold toes even in the warmest weather. A shy girl, old Rae, Tommy thought, and after the first year or so he didn't much mind if she stayed covered up or not, there not being that much to look at anyway. Lately, however, since Aural's arrival, she'd been shedding clothes like a Christmas tree dropping pine needles. First went the socks, and then the shirt, and lately she'd taken to slipping into bed every night with nothing on at all, primed and ready to go. Tommy had been getting quite a workout, which was another surprise because normally Rae was not one to initiate anything. Now all of a sudden the last few days she was like a bitch in heat, presenting herself to him every time he turned around, naked as a jay and in the full light of day. She had always been a lights-out, curtains-drawn kind of girl before this.

"Oh, Tommy, you great big—hunk," she said, searching slightly for the word. It wasn't exactly talking dirty, but it was talking, which was more than she ever did before unless he told her exactly what to say. It didn't matter that it seemed awkward coming from her and was never the right thing—the very fact of vocalizing was interesting.

He knew it was all about Aural, of course. He had but to mention the younger woman's name and Rae would be sliding up and down against him as if the thought of her was as exciting to Rae as it was to Tommy. The last few times they had talked about Aural while Rae was riding him, him asking questions about what she'd done and said lately and Rae gasping out answers between her little puffs and pants. This whole business of sitting on him was Aural's idea, he bet. He was fairly certain she'd been giving Rae tips on what to do, because Rae sure as hell had shown no natural gift for the sport before this. Rae seemed to like the position, too, once she got used to being exposed the way it made her.

"Oh, Reverend," she moaned. "You are so large."

Tommy told himself not to laugh. The girl was trying and should be encouraged.

"Thank you," he said.

"You're like a whole big piece of—ummmm!"

She closed her eyes and waggled her head from side to side.

"Like what? A whole big piece of what?"

"Ummm!"

He grabbed her hips, holding her still for the moment, which was the last thing she wanted.

"A big piece of what?"

She struggled with him, trying to think of something but having trouble with the concept.

"Salami," she gasped at last, pushing his hands away and pumping now for all she was worth.

Tommy knew what the plan was, of course. Rae was hoping to fuck him senseless so that he wouldn't have the strength to think about chasing after Aural. Aural, who was undoubtedly egging her on, was probably hoping the same. But they were wrong on two counts, Tommy thought. One, frequent sex didn't make you want less, it made you want more. Sex was the greatest aphrodisiac in the world, and Rae could bang him three times a day after every meal and he'd still find a way to lust after Aural if he was of a mind. And second, he wasn't any longer of a mind. He was still obsessed about Aural, all right, but not to get in her pants. He'd had a taste of what kind of a painful mess that would be. What he wanted now was to get rid of her. Quickly, cleanly, neatly. And as they were always saying these days, information is power.

"Oh, Reverend," Rae was sighing as she collapsed on his chest. "You are the best."

"How would you know?"

"You make me so happy, sugar," she said.

"How would you know I'm the best? You ain't had but a handful of men in your whole life. Least that's what you told me. You weren't lying to me, were you?"

"No, honey. A woman just knows these things, that's all."

"Well, as it happens, you're right. I am the best, but how you would know it is beyond me. Someone like your friend Aural might know, of course. Maybe she took one look at me and told you."

"I don't need any help to know a good thing when I got it," she said, not wishing to be drawn in. Tommy was frequently a little cruel after sex, but then Tommy was frequently a little cruel anyway.

"What was you saying about her burning her boyfriend?" Tommy asked, pushing her off him and rolling onto his side.

"Did I say anything about that?"

"Well, yes, Rae, you did. Just about the time you was tugging down my shorts. I guess you forgot about it because you found the salami."

Rae giggled and slapped his shoulder. In the past she would have blushed like a beet and hidden her head. Old Rae was blossoming all around.

"A good salami makes a hungry woman forget all kinds of things," he said.

"You," she said, prodding him again.

"So how did this boyfriend take to being burned alive is what I want to know."

"I don't think he appreciated it much."

"I wouldn't think so. How come Aural ain't afraid of him coming after her and tying her to a stake with a can of lighter fluid and a bag of briquettes?"

"Aural says he's too dumb."

"Too dumb to want to get even?"

"Too dumb to find her," said Rae.

"Uh-huh."

"Although why you'd want to be with a man who was that dumb in the first place . . . heavens."

"Not all women have your intellectual interests in salami, Rae," he said.

Rae tittered and reached between his legs.

"It ain't *all* intellectual," she said.

He removed her hand. Did she think he was a machine?

"Even if her boyfriend can't find her, ain't she worried that the cops might?" he asked.

"Why would the cops find her?"

"Why? Well, Rae, I may be wrong, but it seems to me that setting a human being on fire is probably a felony of some kind."

"In North Carolina."

"Hell, anywhere."

"I mean, she did it in North Carolina. She's in West Virginia now. Doesn't it have to be an interstate crime or something like that?"

"What the hell is an interstate crime?"

"Honey, I don't know, but I don't think North Carolina police can just drive up here and arrest her for something she did down there unless it's a *federal* crime, and then it ain't their job."

"Whose job is it?"

"A federal crime? Well, that would be for the FBI, wouldn't it?"

"Would it?" asked Tommy. He got up on his knees so he was over her for a change. "A case for the FBI, huh?"

"I think so," Rae said. She toyed with the hair on his chest, twisting it into strands. If he didn't stop her he would end up looking like he was wearing corn rows.

"You know what?" he asked.

"What?"

"I think Aural had better be careful who she tells her stories to because somebody might take it into their mind that she should be reported."

"Who would do that?"

"You never know," said the Reverend. "Human nature is a very curious thing. Very curious."

Chapter 16

A truck passed Cooper as he walked along the highway, its brake lights on as it decelerated rapidly. A heavy mist had lifted only minutes ago, leaving the pines coated with moisture that sparkled in the early morning sun as it broke through. At times the reflection was blinding, and drivers heading east drove with their visors down and sunglasses on. Cooper watched them, some shading their eyes with their hands and squinting against the glare. Ahead of him, a slight bend in the road coincided with the solar angle in such a way that drivers were blinded for several hundred yards and the traffic there had slowed to a crawl. As Cooper approached, the sun's angle changed enough of a fraction of an arc that the glare was even worse and people were actually stopping their cars, a few of them pulling to the side. Cooper walked beside them, marveling at the sight of dozens of cars behaving as if a stop sign had suddenly materialized in the center of the highway.

The drivers looked so stupid to him, immobilized by the sun, blindly creeping after the rear ends of the cars in front of them like elephants in the circus linked trunk to tail, while the traffic in the westbound lane raced by at normal speed.

"Idiots!" Cooper yelled. Those closest looked around, gawking, trying to find the source of the voice. Some of them insisted on putting their heads out their windows and looking up, staring into the sun, as if they had heard the voice of God.

"Dummies!"

A man two cars away leaned out, his necktie dangling outside the car. "What?" he asked. "What is it?" The man was looking in the direction of Cooper, but not at him. Cooper thought about grabbing that necktie—one of the currently fashionable eyesores with a flock of herons against a background of green and orange—and yanking on it until the man's head fell off.

"You're a dumb shit," Cooper said.

The man just kept squinting, looking more puzzled than threatened.

"What?" he asked again, as if the sun were affecting his hearing as well as his sight. "What?"

It was then that Cooper realized the extent of his invisibility. Nobody could see him. Which meant nobody could stop him, nobody could report him. He felt suddenly omnipotent. He could do anything he wanted to any one of these people in any of these cars and no one could stop him. No one would even know that he was the one who did it.

Walking farther, Cooper passed a young woman who glanced up at him as he came abreast of her, then away, towards the backseat. Cooper got to her blind spot and turned and studied her. She looked good, small and clean and neat, and there was something about her mouth that reminded him of that other girl. Her hair was cut close to her head, which made her look like a girl pretending to be a boy. He didn't know why, but Cooper liked that, he felt his excitement growing. He could reach right in there and grab her, he thought, and no one would know. Right in the middle of a crowd and no one would see because he was invisible. He could do what he wanted—he could make *her* do what he wanted— surrounded by dozens of cars and people and no one would know anything about it.

Cooper laughed in anticipation and the woman lifted her eyes in his direction. She had been studying the floor of her car, trying to avoid the sun, but now she looked up, shielding her eyes with her hand.

She looked stupid, too, squinting at him that way and not seeing him. They were all stupid, Cooper realized with a surge of superiority, stupid as a herd of cows. Only he could see where he was going, only he was invisible.

The doorlatch on her car was up, so Cooper yanked the door open and pushed into the car, propelling her into the passenger seat.

At first she was too frightened to speak and her mouth moved open and shut as silently as a fish. Stupid, Cooper thought.

"What . . ." she finally sputtered. "Who are you?"

"I'm Invisible Man," Cooper said. He grabbed her by the arm and she gasped and tried to pull away, but of course it wasn't possible to pull away from Cooper.

"Please," she said, "Please," and she thrust her purse at him.

She wasn't trying to get out the other door as he had thought she would. The woman seemed to be trying to climb into the backseat instead. Cooper glanced back and saw the infant in the car seat for the first time. The baby stared back at Cooper, its big blue eyes as curious as Cooper's own.

The mother was panicking, but her fear hadn't transmitted itself to the baby yet and it studied Cooper calmly.

"Hi," Cooper said, reaching his finger towards the child.

The mother tried to pull Cooper's hand away from the baby, so he jerked her back onto the front seat. She bit into the hand that held her, sinking her teeth as hard as she could. The infant was reaching for Cooper's finger, but he had to snatch his free hand away in order to club the woman.

The baby seemed to sense that something was wrong and its face wrinkled in preparation for a scream. Cooper wiggled his finger before the baby again but it was too late and the child let out an anguished cry.

The woman had slumped onto the seat, so Cooper was free to reach for the infant with both hands, but the crossbar on the car seat confused him temporarily. Suddenly horns were blaring and Cooper heard someone yell, "Hey, asshole!"

The sun had moved and traffic in front of him was already receding into the distance. The man behind him, the one with the necktie, was honking and yelling, in a great rush to move on, and Cooper realized that he was visible again. The woman moaned, her eyes fluttering open and shut and open again, and the baby screamed.

Cooper took the purse that the woman had offered him and left the car. He ran into the woods, with the man with the necktie yelling at him, and he ran until he could hear no more sounds from the highway.

Cooper crouched behind the empty propane gas tanks that crowded the fence at the back of the restaurant. Kyle came out the back, dragging the garbage towards the dumpster. He passed the police car that was parked close to the dumpster, its front light pulsing on and off the high beam and the front door still open as if someone had arrived and jumped out in a hurry. Glancing around to see if he was observed, Kyle peered into the cop car. Cooper could almost feel the boy's temptation to slip inside the automobile, to sit where the cop sat, to speak into the radio, to fondle the shotgun clipped to the dashboard. Kyle was grinning with nervous excitement, his freckled skin flushed.

Red on the head like the dick on a dog, Cooper thought and laughed silently.

Kyle resisted the temptation of the police car and hoisted the garbage can with some trouble into the dumpster. Cooper wanted to take the can away from Kyle and lift it with one hand, just to show him how he could do it. Instead, he hissed.

Kyle looked around, startled, as if he had heard a snake. It took him a moment to locate Cooper, who was waving from behind the propane tanks. He hurried over, glancing back at the restaurant.

"Was it you? I figured it had to be you, but I didn't know."

"What?"

"The cops said somebody wearing one of our uniforms grabbed a lady's purse in broad daylight on the highway."

"That wasn't me," Cooper said.

"Right in broad daylight. I said, Jeez, that sucker's got balls. I figured it was you."

Cooper shook his head without conviction.

"They said he was a great big guy, that's all the lady remembers. But about eight different people saw him in his uniform. He was even wearing his hat."

Cooper took the striped paper hat off his head.

"It was you, wasn't it?"

"No," Cooper said. "Are they looking for me now?"

"Of course they're looking for you, duh. What do you think the cop car is doing here?"

"You didn't tell him where I was?"

"I didn't know where you were. I just saw you right now."

"Uh-huh."

Cooper laid his hand on Kyle's shoulder.

"And I wouldn't have told him anyway, I swear," the boy said, suddenly talking much faster. "I wouldn't tell him no matter what, but I *didn't* tell him anyway because I didn't know."

"I didn't do it," Cooper said.

Kyle tried to back away, but Cooper's grip tightened on his shoulder.

"I knew that. I believe you. You wouldn't be that stupid."

"It wasn't stupid," Cooper said.

"*I* know that, it's the cops who said it was stupid, not me. I knew you wouldn't do anything stupid. We're friends, Coop. We work together. I know you."

"You don't know me."

"Well . . ."

"You're not my friend."

"Sure I am, sure I am."

"I've got two friends," Cooper said.

"And me. I'm your friend. You can count on me." Kyle tried to twist his head to see if there was any activity at the back of the restaurant, but Cooper's grip continued to grow in pressure. The boy felt tears coming to his eyes.

Cooper tried to remember who his two friends were.

"My punk," he said, not aware he was speaking aloud, "and somebody else . . ."

Two cops came out of the back of the restaurant, each holding a cup of coffee. Kyle started to speak, but Cooper reacted quicker, yanking the boy behind the tanks and clamping a hand on his mouth so fast that the boy's neck snapped back as if he had been hit.

When the cop car drove off, Cooper looked at the boy's struggling form as if had just noticed it for the first time. He removed his hand from Kyle's mouth and the boy gasped and sputtered and looked for a second as if he were going to speak again, but Cooper didn't want to hear from him, he knew the kind of thing he'd hear, so he closed his hand on the boy's throat and used that grip to beat his head against the propane tank.

The tank made a dull, hollow sound, like the biggest drum that Cooper had ever heard. When the boy stopped squirming after the fourth or fifth hit, Cooper carried him to the dumpster and tossed him in. He laughed about that as he ran through the back lots. He laughed until he reached the safety of the pines. He didn't know why, it just struck him as funny.

After his second day of walking, Cooper emerged from the woods to follow the sound of a tolling bell. He found himself on a dirt road and he walked towards the bell, drawn by not only by the sound but by its promise of human community. He was tired of sleeping on the ground and talking only to squirrels and he was hungry. There was money in his pocket that he had taken from the woman's purse, so he could buy food. He had counted the money many times; he didn't think it was enough to buy a car, any kind of car, but he was certain it was enough to buy a meal. There was also her credit card, and Cooper knew there were ways to get money and food and cars and anything you wanted with somebody else's credit card, but he had never understood how it was done. He knew his punk would know. Even if the punk didn't know something like that right away, he could sit down and figure it out, just by thinking about it. And if that didn't work, he wasn't afraid to ask someone else.

Cooper never felt comfortable asking people questions when he didn't already know the answers. It was just asking to be ridiculed, but somehow it never bothered the punk. Swann. He had said Cooper wouldn't even remember his name, but, there, he did remember. He said it aloud, "Swann," and found himself suddenly close to tears. Cooper shook his head, angry at himself. He didn't know what the hell *that* was all about, crying over a punk.

Cooper's hand hurt where the woman in the car had bitten him and it was turning a very angry looking red around the tooth marks. As he walked, he put the sore hand to his mouth and sucked on it a little, which made it feel better. The sound of the bell kept getting louder and even though there was no way to see very far through all the trees that lined both sides of the road, he could tell he was getting closer.

Suddenly there was a wider spot that spread and spread and sitting there right beside the dirt road was a one-story, one-room clapboard church. An old man stood in the yard, pulling on a bell that looked more like a dinner bell than a church chime, and a fat-faced man dressed in a shiny black suit, white shirt, and black bow tie stood by the doorway, clasping a black book to his bosom. He looked to Cooper like the preachers he had seen in Western movies, except that his skin was the color of dusty shoe leather. Cooper had also seen undertakers dressed like that, usually in the same movies. Lots of people got shot in movies like that; there was plenty of work for both the preachers and the undertakers.

Cooper's sudden appearance startled both men, and the old one missed several beats on the bell rope.

"Are you sure you're in the right place, sir?" the preacher asked as Cooper headed straight for the front door. The preacher was smiling but he didn't look very welcoming nonetheless. Cooper stopped next to the man, looking at his face and then at the interior of the church. He towered over the minister, whose size was more lateral than vertical.

"What?"

The minister smelled of very old sweat and bourbon and some kind of perfume. Cooper wrinkled his nose in distaste and the minister moved back a step.

"You're welcome, of course," the minister said. "All sinners are welcome."

"Uh-huh," Cooper said.

"Did you walk all the way from Wycliffe?" the minister asked, trying to strike up a conversation.

"What?"

"Your uniform," the minister said. "The nearest one of them is in Wycliffe. I wonder, did you walk all the way from there, because I see you got no car."

Cooper looked at his striped shirt. He had lost the hat somewhere in the woods.

"Which way is Wycliffe?"

"That way," the minister said, pointing in the direction in which Cooper had been going before he stopped at the church.

"How far?"

"Walking or riding?"

Cooper squinted at him, suspecting a trick.

"About seven miles by car," the minister said.

"Uh-huh . . . Do you think I could get a job there?"

"Yes, sir, I bet you could. You already got the clothes."

Cooper debated whether to keep walking towards the restaurant in Wycliffe or to go inside the church. He poked the black book the minister clasped to his chest and the heavy man staggered back a step.

"I know what that is," Cooper said.

"Hallelujah," said the minister.

"Jesus is my friend," Cooper said, laughing slightly with pleasure at remembering who his second friend was. He wanted to tell Swann that he had remembered a great many things. He searched his pockets until he found a postcard.

"Amen to that," said the minister.

The old man gave up on the bell and shuffled past both Cooper and the minister and into the church. He had recovered from his initial shock and now had no curiosity about the sudden appearance of the candy-striped giant at all.

"You can go on in, if you like," the minister said to Cooper. "You just about the first. The womens will be along directly."

"Womens?"

"Well, it's mostly womens, now isn't it. Womens takes to the spirit better than men. I don't know why."

"Uh-huh."

"Maybe they is just better and cleaner spirits altogether. Take away the womens and I wouldn't have hardly no congregation whatsoever."

"I like women," Cooper said.

"Bless you," said the minister and smiled with real warmth for the first time. "I know what you mean. I do know what you mean." He chuckled conspiratorially.

The minister seemed friendly and Cooper thought of telling him about the woman who had helped him with the questionnaire and then took him out in her car, but then thought he'd better not. He walked into the church instead.

Cooper sat on a bench in the third row from the front and thought about his friend Jesus and his friend Swann and realized that he knew Swann a lot better than he knew Jesus. Jesus was really Swann's friend and had become Cooper's friend, too, mainly from being talked about so much.

He stayed there when the congregation filtered in, nearly filling the church with their heavy, gaily clothed bodies, but giving him a wide berth on either side as if he emitted a repellent force field.

He liked the singing, which certainly wasn't pretty, but it was loud and enthusiastic and one of the women in front of him seemed to keep fainting and waking up and yelling something about Jesus and then fainting again. He liked that part, too, even though the preacher, who must have seen it, didn't pay any attention to it at all.

When it was all over and everyone else was leaving, Cooper started walking towards Wycliffe. No one offered him a ride. When he came at last to a postal box he took the postcard from his pocket and studied the address that carried his punk's name. He thought for a moment about writing a message but remembered Swann had said it wasn't necessary. He would know automatically that Ol' Coop was thinking about him and would start praying right away. Cooper mailed the postcard, proud that he had remembered. It wasn't until he had walked several miles farther that he recalled that he was hungry.

Chapter 17

Becker was met at the Nashville airport and driven to Springville by car. The Birmingham airport was actually about twenty-three miles closer to the prison, but the airfare was cheaper to Nashville so the Bureau travel agents had booked him that way. The agent-in-charge in Birmingham was alerted that Becker was on his way and to stand by for assistance if necessary, but inasmuch as Becker came escorted by a special agent from Nashville, the Birmingham agency was more than happy to maintain a healthy distance and let Nashville cope with it. Becker's visits had a way of turning into a lot of trouble for anyone close enough to get involved.

Nashville had complained briefly about having Becker routed through their office since his ultimate destination was really on Birmingham's turf, but there was very little real point in arguing with the pencil heads in Procurement, the department that dealt with such niceties as paying for airline tickets. The recent wave of cost accounting had made them, if not the tail that wags the dog, at least the hand that jerks the tail that yanks the whole animal around. Several expensive and disastrous operations in recent years—the most notable belonging to a sister organization, the Bureau of Alcohol, Tobacco and Firearms—all widely publicized much to the involved bureaucrats' chagrin—had everyone pulling in his fiscal horns. The fact that ATF was subsequently nearly subsumed into the DEA, although not entirely related to the Waco fiasco, was a message not lost on anyone in the Bureau above the rank of foot soldier. Small, cheap, discreet operations had become the order of the day, ones that could reap public-relations triumphs with a minimum of expense. Tales of the FBI thwarting kidnappers, for instance, were just the ticket. Or of serial killers rooted out and apprehended. Not only were the headlines immense in such cases, but the publicity was all positive. And, in an increasingly accountable age, such cases were eminently cost-effective. Becker's trip, in Hatcher's estimation, was perfect for the current mood. If it was a success, those who mattered would know who had initiated the success—Hatcher would make sure they knew. And if nothing came of it, the Bureau was out only the cost of a business-class seat to Nashville and miscellaneous—but monitored—expenses. Since Becker did not even require a salary because of his medical extension status, his price was perfect for the spirit of the times.

Desiring no more involvement in a Becker investigation than his Birmingham counterpart, the Nashville agent-in-charge sent his most dispensable operative to escort him.

Her name was Pegeen, a nod to her Irish heritage, which should have long since petered out but refused to die. Her great-grandfather, Sean Murphy, was the only Celt in her family tree for the last seventy-five years, and he had fathered daughters with a Danish wife. Her grandmother had married a man of German ancestry and her mother had married a man so thoroughly Americanized that he could trace six different national skeins to his present status, none of them Irish. Pegeen's father's last name was the only relic, several generations old, of a single male ancestor called Haddad, the first, last, and only Lebanese member of the family. And yet, despite the countercurrents over the years, the Gaelic stream had remained the dominant one in the minds of the women in Pegeen's family. Pegeen Haddad, with no disrespect intended towards her father or anyone else on her multifarious family tree, considered herself to be Irish.

Thanks to the determined, perhaps even pugnacious genes of Sean Murphy, Pegeen's hair was the color of a raw carrot, her eyes blue-green, and her skin, when seen in contrast to her hair, the white of a sheet of good rag writing paper.

When Becker first saw her at the airport, holding a cardboard sign bearing his name and perusing the incoming passengers as if any one of them might be concealing a bomb, he thought she was an unfortunate-looking specimen. With her hair tucked under a baseball cap that rode too low on her head, her ears stuck out, giving her an almost goonish appearance, a sort of female version of Huck Finn, complete to the sprinkling of freckles across her nose.

She wore faded blue jeans with a rip across one knee, a red t-shirt that did nothing for her complexion, a navy blue blazer, and a pair of clunky black shoes that looked as if they had been borrowed from her father. All in all she looked like a college kid on standby for a flight home at Thanksgiving, one of those who didn't get invited to spend the holiday with a boyfriend. The blazer was to conceal her weapon, Becker knew, since she didn't carry a purse and the jeans were too tight to hide anything bulkier than a credit card. He couldn't imagine what the baseball cap was for, except perhaps as a fashion accessory. The ubiquitous cap, which did no one any aesthetic favors at the best of times, looked particularly incongrous on a young woman trying to masquerade as an FBI agent, he thought.

"You expecting terrorists on this flight?" he asked.

"Sir?" If he had doubted that she was an agent before, the ever-present, distinctively pronounced "sir" would have dispelled them. Drilled into them during training, it was a form of address that was used as much for distancing as for respect. The young ones were even more lethal with it than their elders because with them it carried an added heft of ageism. The one word, diligently applied, could hurt a man concerned about aging worse than a volley of curses.

"You're checking out the passengers as if you expect them be carrying Uzis," he said.

"Do you know anything about terrorists on this flight, sir?"

"Just joking."

"Terrorism is not a funny business."

"No. Sorry." Becker pointed to the card bearing his name. "I'm your man."

"You would be Special Agent Becker?"

"I wouldn't be if I could help it, but I am."

"Sir, I wonder if you'd oblige me with some form of identification?"

"Why? Are you going to arrest me?"

"No, sir. Just a precaution. A driver's license would be good enough if you don't have your Bureau ID."

"Do you mean anyone would seriously want to pretend to be me if they didn't have to?"

"I think a lot of people pretend a lot of things, sir."

Becker handed her his driver's license.

"Well, if you hear of any volunteers to walk around in my skin, be sure to let me know, will you?" he said.

"Something wrong with your skin?" she asked.

"It's too damned tight," he said.

She scrutinized him carefully as if looking for places where he might be bursting through his seams.

"You look fit," she said finally.

"So do you."

She studied him a moment longer, examining his comment for sexist content.

"I try," she said finally. She extended her right hand to shake while her left extended her FBI identification.

"Special Agent Haddad," she said.

"Hi."

"Do you have luggage, sir?"

Becker hefted his overnight bag. "I'm ready to go. This shouldn't take long."

"Very good. Just follow me, then, sir."

"One stop first," Becker said.

In the gift shop Becker bought a carton of cigarettes, discarded the box, and distributed the packs in his various pockets.

He opened one of the packs, stripping off the cellophane and peeling away the tin foil. He breathed deeply of the cigarettes, then offered the pack to Pegeen.

"It's the only time they smell good," he said. "Before they start to kill you."

"You're not a smoker," she said, her tone sounding more accusatory than she had wanted it to.

"Why not?"

"No stains on your hands or teeth."

"You've got quick eyes," he said. "Very good."

"Thank you, sir," she said dryly. She found herself bridling at what she took to be the condescension in his remark. They praised her too much for the little things, as if she were a child, all the older men of the Bureau. And they all were older, even the young ones, especially the ones close to her own age. They acted in her presence as if they were veterans of the Trojan Wars who loved to impart hoary words of wisdom earned through the ages. As if she were not only a child, and a girl, but a project, an experiment in pedagogy. Could they possibly teach this amazing dog to talk? Could they convert this woman into a man? is what they really wanted to know, Pegeen was convinced. She told herself to calm down and not start any fights. They had a long way yet to go.

"I haven't smoked in twenty years. They're bribes. Very small bribes."

"Cigarettes as prison currency. Yes, sir, I do know that. Shall we go then? . . . If you're ready?"

When they reached the parking lot Becker asked about the cap.

"Do you always wear it?"

"It was my day off when I got the call to pick you up, but since I'm going to be a chauffeur, I might as well look the part. It's the closest I could come . . . You don't like it?"

"I think it looks silly enough on baseball players."

After a pause she said, "I can change it when we get to the car."

"You always wear a hat?"

"I'm very fair," she said.

"A nice quality."

"I mean my skin. I burn easily."

"I see that."

"What does that mean . . . sir?"

"I see that you have fair skin," Becker said carefully. He was getting the feeling that Special Agent Haddad wasn't carrying a chip on her shoulder, she was sporting a whole brick. "I can tell that by looking at you."

"Do you have a problem with that?"

"No. Fair skin is fine with me."

"Thank you."

"I'm making no judgments on your skin, Haddad. It's not my skin."

"That's right," she said. "My skin is fair and yours is too tight."

"Did I come in the middle of something here?" Becker asked. "You haven't known me long enough to be mad at me."

She looked at him, surprised.

"I'm not mad at you, sir. I thought you were attempting to make conversation by those comments about my hat and my complexion, so I was conversing back."

"Ah," said Becker. "You thought I was criticizing you."

"Why would I think that, sir? As you pointed out, you hardly know me well enough to do that."

"Sorry," he said.

"Not at all. You have nothing to apologize for."

She yanked open the car door. "I'm just here to drive," she said, some of the words lost in the sound of doors opening and closing.

"Sorry to ruin your day off."

Pegeen shrugged.

"Happy in your work?" Becker asked.

"Just fine, thank you," she said. She tossed her baseball cap into the backseat and put on a soft brown felt hat with a large floppy brim that slouched over most of her face.

"Very nice," he said.

Pegeen maneuvered the Ford out of the parking lot.

"What do you call that hat?" Becker asked pleasantly.

"Ethel," Pegeen said. She laughed abruptly, as if she had caught herself by surprise.

Becker paused long enough to show he recognized the joke. "I meant the style. Does it have a name?"

"It's called a Trilby," she said.

"I like it," Becker said.

"Oh, good."

Pegeen got a receipt for the parking charges, then turned towards I-65, which would take them to Springville.

"Do you need anything before we begin? Any bladder problems to take care of?"

"Just that prostate thing, but nothing I can do about it here," Becker said.

Pegeen turned and looked him directly. Becker grinned in what he hoped was a winning manner.

"Special Agent Becker, we have a two-hour drive to Springville. Sir, I think it will go more smoothly for both of us if we don't try to be pleasant."

"Yikes," said Becker.

"Sir?"

"Step on it," he said.

Perhaps it was the silence, or perhaps it was the lulling of the road, but after about an hour of driving Becker thought he detected a slight easing in Agent Haddad's posture. Her knuckles, which never left the proper ten-minutes-to-two position, had relaxed enough so that blood was flowing back into them.

"I hope I wasn't rude," she said without preamble.

Becker thought for a moment before answering. "No. You could call it direct, but not rude. I'm sure I deserved it in some way. I usually do."

"It wasn't you," she said. "Not really—well, some—but mostly it was just me. I thought maybe you don't drive, but you do have a license."

"Have we just changed the topic?"

"It's just that it seems more efficient for you to rent a car and drive to

Springville by yourself. That would allow me to do the kind of work I'm trained for.''

"How long are you in the service?''

"A year and a half.''

"It doesn't surprise you that the newest agents always get the shit work, does it?''

"The youngest *female* agents do, I have noticed, yes.''

"Ah,'' said Becker. "Double discrimination. And then you have to put up with me to boot. No wonder you're pissed off.''

"I'm just a little curious why they want to take a college graduate, a woman who has passed the Bureau's rather rigorous training—you would agree it is rather rigorous, wouldn't you?''

"Rigorous,'' Becker said.

"I have a master's degree, for that matter. And nearly sixteen months of active service to my credit. Why would they want to make me a taxi driver for a straightforward delivery? It wastes my whole day.''

"Shoots the hell out of mine, too,'' Becker said.

"Yes, but you're going to Springville for some purpose, presumably, not just along for the ride.''

"You really don't know why they assigned an agent to drive me there?''

"No.''

"What do you know about me?''

"Nothing. Should I? Did you used to be famous?''

Becker laughed.

"You're not shitting me, are you, Special Agent Haddad? You didn't bone up on my file? You didn't ask around?''

"No. Should I have?''

"So you really don't know why you're here. No wonder you're mad.''

"Why am I here?''

"To keep an eye on me,'' Becker said.

"Why do I need to do that?''

"Because I'm the big bad wolf,'' Becker said.

Pegeen looked at him to see how to read his remark. His voice had been flat and serious, and she studied his face for any clues that he was joking. He was faintly smiling but it looked to Pegeen like a very rueful smile, an expression of deep regret.

"You don't look like one to me,'' she said.

"I'm wearing my sheepskin,'' Becker said. He turned to her and his smile widened but she thought his eyes the most mournful she had ever seen. "I told you it was too tight . . . And I'm about to pop out of it."

Pegeen tried to laugh, not knowing what else to do.

By the time they reached the prison Becker was sunk so deeply within himself that Pegeen wondered if he was still with her at all. She parked the car in a slot reserved for prison personnel and waited for Becker to get out. From her vantage point behind the wheel she was too close to the prison to see much but stone. A parking lot stretched away on one side, a well-tended lawn on the other. It could have been an industrial plant, a factory, a warehouse.

"This is it, sir," Pegeen said.

Becker was slouched, staring straight ahead as if reading patterns in the stone that faced their car. His arms were crossed tightly on his chest, as if he were cold. Or something else . . . No longer distracted by the driving, Pegeen took a long look at his face. He seemed oblivious to her presence. There was a darkness in his visage that Pegeen knew but refused to recognize at first. She cleared her throat, moved about on her seat, hoping to bring him out of it, but he was sunk into the emotion. Eventually she had to admit that he looked like nothing else so much as frightened.

"We're here, sir," she said finally.

"I know," Becker said, still facing forward. "We've been here a long time."

Pegeen considering asking him what he meant, then decided to let it go.

"Is—uh—is everything all right?"

"I'm just scared," he said, matter-of-factly.

Pegeen did not know how to respond. She could not remember an adult male who had ever admitted to fearing anything. Instinctively she wanted to reach out to comfort him, but this was the FBI, they were both agents, they were on duty, Becker was a grown man . . . she touched his shoulder.

"I'm sure it will be all right," she said.

"Promise?" His tone was boyish, but with a note of humor that said he was aware of how he sounded.

Still not turning to face her, Becker took hold of the hand that rested on his shoulder.

"Do you want to talk about it?" she asked.

Becker shook his head, continuing to stare at the stones in front of them. Resisting the urge to draw him closer and comfort him with an embrace, Pegeen sat perfectly still, letting him hold her hand.

Slowly Becker seemed to change, or rather his hand seemed to change. He did not move it, there was no more pressure in his grip, no alteration in the position of his fingers or his palm, but gradually Pegeen became aware of a growing heat. It was as if he were transferring energy to his hand by just thinking about it. Or perhaps she was doing it, Pegeen thought. It was possible. It was equally possible that nothing whatsoever was happening, that she was just imagining it. He certainly gave no sign that anything was happening; he had not moved since enwrapping her hand in his.

It wasn't sexual, she was almost sure of that. Almost. But she didn't know what else it was. Well, maybe compassion, fellow feeling, something like that. Maybe he just had a higher body thermostat than most, or she did, or something about the two of them in combination caused it. All she was certain of was that she could not stop thinking about the sensation of their two hands together. And the equal certainty that he must be also aware of it.

She tried to think what she would tell the agent-in-charge if he did quiz her about her trip as Becker seemed to think he might. Would she tell him that nothing happened, but she sat holding hands with another agent for—how long had it been? It seemed a very long time. Pegeen remembered going to a movie with a boy in her early teens and feeling his hand resting upon her leg throughout the film. She had been so surprised, and nervous, and excited, that she had sat still as a statue for the whole feature, and he, for his part, had not moved an inch. It was only when the lights came on and the hand still did not move that Pegeen had looked to see that she had been pressing her leg against the armrest the whole time.

She stole a glance at the clock on the dashboard. On arrival, she had noted the time to include in her trip report. She had not been holding his hand for more than a minute. Or was *he* holding *her* hand? She had forgotten.

He turned to her at last and there was real warmth in his smile this time. He squeezed her hand, then let it go.

''Thanks,'' he said.

Pegeen felt her ears burning. She knew they would be fiery red, but he didn't seem to notice.

''Did you want me to accompany you or shall I wait in the car?''

''Have you ever been in one of these?'' he asked.

"A prison?"

"A cage," he corrected.

"I've been to plenty of jails."

"It's not like a jail, a jail is just a holding pen, there's still hope they'll get out. This is a cage. It's different."

"As part of our training we were shown—"

"I don't mean a tour," Becker said. "Have you ever been in one after the warder leaves? When the animals are hungry and feel like turning on each other?"

"No, sir. I haven't. Have you?"

"Do you know the worst part of a place like this?"

"No, sir, I don't," she said. Continuing to call him sir seemed silly now, but she didn't know how to get out of it. Nor did she know that he would want her to. It's not as if anything happened, she reminded herself, not as if anything really passed between them. That parting squeeze of the hand had been a gesture of camaraderie, nothing more. It was even somewhat condescending, as if *she* needed the comfort and encouragement. She should have given *him* the heartening squeeze.

She had paused, expecting him to continue. When he didn't, she asked, "What is the worst part of a place like this?"

"The smell," he said.

"The smell?"

"If you ever have a chance, smell it. Deeply. See if you can tell what it is. It will teach you something about what we keep in these cages. And why."

He opened the door and cooler air rushed into the car. Pegeen did not realize how warm it had become in there.

"Do you want me to come with you?"

He turned back, leaned in the open door.

"Do you remember what kills a werewolf?" he asked.

"A stake through the heart?"

"That's a vampire," Becker said, grinning. "We're talking werewolves here."

"I forgot," she said.

"That's okay," he said. "It doesn't come up that often—but when it does, it helps to know. You kill a werewolf with a silver bullet."

He continued to grin but Pegeen could find no humor in his eyes.

"So when I come out," he continued, "if you notice tufts of hair growing on my hands and face, go straight home and melt down the silverware your grandmother gave you."

He brushed her cheek very lightly with the tip of his finger as if removing a speck of dirt, then turned and walked into the prison. To Pegeen the spot where he touched her burned as if his finger were a match. She felt her ears. Like ovens, two fiery betrayers.

Pegeen remembered everything that had passed between them since Becker got off the airplane. She had registered it all without effort, without conscious thought, the way she did with any exchange, particularly with a man, and she drew it up again now and examined it, probing it for meaning, turning every word and every look in her mind to reveal facets that might hold the clues to what it really meant. It was easy enough to do, she recalled their conversations verbatim. After a moment she put her hand to her cheek once more, gently covering the spot where his finger had grazed her. Amazingly, she could still feel the fire. She held her hand against it to keep it there.

Chapter 18

A guard led Becker to the room to be used for the interview, then left him there while he went to fetch the prisoner. The room was not much bigger than a cell and had the same cinderblock walls, the same sickly green paint. Instead of a bunk, there was a small table and two chairs, no window except a small opening at eye level in the door. The overhead light bulb was controlled by a switch on the outside of the room. Becker could only guess at the uses to which the room was put customarily. It was certainly not for ordinary interviews, which were conducted under strict scrutiny with television security cameras, guards within earshot and bulletproof glass separating the prisoner and his visitor. Becker would be alone with his prisoner, free to do what he liked. Hatcher had seen to it, of course. It would have taken someone of his level to arrange this amount of privacy. Becker wondered what Hatcher thought he was going to do with the prisoner that would require this much seclusion. But he didn't spent much time on the idea, he didn't want to waste his energy on the way Hatcher's mind worked.

He stood behind the chair facing the door, trying at first to keep the awful claustrophobic dread of the prison from affecting him, then giving in to it as he would give himself to the surge of the ocean or the silence of the night. There was no point in fighting it, it was too vast, the trick was to survive it.

As always happened when he was in a prison, a spate of self-loathing overtook him. Never far from the surface, the prison smell brought out his guilt, the claustrophobia sucked it forth like a poultice. I belong here, he thought. I should be in a cage like the rest of them, only the good fortune of my circumstances keeps me out. My impulses are the same, my needs same as those I put in here. It's only because I'm useful to them that they don't throw me in, too. I've done things, been awarded citations for things that would put others on death row. Only my position as a Bureau agent has kept me out and free.

His ruminations were disturbed when the guard returned with a prisoner in tow. The guard withdrew, leaving Becker alone with the prisoner, who stood just inside the door, looking quickly at Becker, then at the room, as if seeking a means of escape.

"Hello," Becker said.

The man nodded uncertainly, continuing to look nervously around the room. Becker realized that the man half expected Becker to jump on him. He was a small man, his long hair flowing to his shoulders like a woman's, his prison work shirt opened to his sternum. Some form of mascara and shadow had been applied to his eyes.

"Becker," Becker said. He indicated the other chair. "I got your letter."

"You're Becker?" The man seemed genuinely surprised.

"I know, I don't look the part."

"No, no, it's . . . No, you're right, you're not what I expected."

"What were you hoping for, Dick Tracy?"

"They said you were . . . I thought you'd be . . . I don't now. Bigger."

"No, just life-size. Sorry."

"I didn't think you would come at all. I'm Swann."

"I know."

Swann started to offer his hand, then quickly withdrew it and sat in the chair opposite Becker. He looked up at Becker from under lowered brows. It's meant to be either seductive or a parody of shyness, Becker thought.

"I really didn't think you would come."

"I would have said you were counting on it."

"I hoped . . . well, I mean, I hoped . . . I prayed. I prayed a great deal."

Becker smiled ruefully. "I'm not the answer to anyone's prayers, believe me."

Swann's face darkened. "I believe in prayer, Mr. Becker. I truly do believe in it. It's the only thing that's kept me sane."

"Why me?" Becker asked. "Why not just contact the FBI and tell them you have some information for them?"

"I couldn't just contact anybody. Our mail is censored, you must know that. And even if it wasn't, I couldn't risk having anybody find out what I was doing. Do you know what they do to stoolies in this place? . . . Even now, a meeting like this, what if they find out?"

"The guard thinks I'm an attorney reviewing your case for civil rights violations. I don't know what the warden has been told. If anyone finds out what we talk about, it's because you told them."

"Me? I would be killed."

"Why me, Swann? Why specifically me?"

"I heard about you."

"Heard what?"

"They talk about you in here. Lots of them seem to know you or to know about you. You have a rep."

"I'll bet."

"I hear you climb, you climb mountains. You're a rock climber, right?"

Becker said nothing. Swann smiled at him, knowing his information was correct.

"You'd be surprised how much they know about you."

"You a climber, Swann?"

"Well . . . not really. I worked with ropes a little bit, I know what's involved. That's scary work."

"Not so scary if you know the safe way. You ever try it?"

"I believe in gravity. If it tells me to go down, I go down. It was just interesting that they say that about you. Someone who would do that, take that kind of risk for no reason. It's unusual. I don't really understand it."

"You're surrounded by risk takers in here."

Swann shivered. "I don't understand them, either. Please don't lump me with them."

"The judge already did that. You pleaded to three counts of manslaughter and aggravated assault."

"My lawyer told me to do that. My landlady attacked me, she went crazy and just came at me, I was defending myself . . ."

"You misunderstood me, Swann. I said the guard thinks I'm an attorney, you don't. Spare me the bullshit."

"My innocence is not bullshit to me, Mr. Becker."

"Uh-huh. Well, innocence is a relative thing. You did slit the landlady's gullet, after all. Or at least you said you did when you pleaded guilty."

"It was a horrible time, she was coming at me, I struggled with her, she tried to stab me—you don't know, you just don't know. How could you understand what it was like?"

"You'd be surprised at my imagination," Becker said. "Why me, Swann? I can't think I have a lot of fans in here."

"Oh, they don't hate you, isn't that odd? They think they know you. It's like—I don't know—like wolves from different packs will kill each other sometimes, they don't like each other maybe, they've got to defend their turf, but they understand each other. They understand each other better than they understand the sheep."

Becker took the open pack of cigarettes from his pocket and inhaled the scent of tobacco again. Swann's analogy linking him to the people he pursued in a commonality of understanding was too close to the bone. It was as if the prisoner had read his thoughts of only moments ago. Becker tapped a cigarette loose, paying great attention to the work as he tried to settle his mind.

Swann accepted the cigarette gratefully and Becker shoved the whole package across the table to him. Swann's hand covered it and it was suddenly gone.

"They say you're fair," Swann said and Becker thought briefly of Pegeen's use of the word earlier. "They say you'll treat people right if they're straight with you."

Becker laughed. "Nobody in here ever told you I was fair. But maybe they told you I was an idiot who would believe whatever you said."

Swann laced his fingers in front of him, then studied them for a moment, pouting.

"They said you can tell." He said, his tone lower, more sincere. "They say you can look at a man and know if he's telling the truth. They say you can see it in his eyes."

Becker snorted. "Who am I supposed to be, the truth fairy? You can't tell anything by looking into a man's eyes. Any good liar can control his eyes. I look at his hands."

Becker chuckled as Swann predictably stopped moving his hands and folded them on the table in front of him. Becker knew he would be unable to treat them naturally for the rest of the interview. They were strong hands, unusually large for a man Swann's size, with thick wrists. In truth, Becker never paid much attention to a person's hands, either, but he liked making the prisoner uncomfortable. Nothing valuable was ever learned when the person being interviewed was too comfortable.

"Men don't look each other straight in the eyes, anyway, don't you know that, Swann? It makes them uncomfortable, it's an unnatural act. We look women straight in the eyes, not other men. You sure as hell must have learned it in here. If a man looks you straight in the eyes when he tells you something, it means one of two things. Either he's lying to you or he wants to fuck you.''

Swann twisted uneasily on his chair.

''I know about that part,'' he said.

''I imagine you do,'' said Becker.

''That's why I wrote to you.''

''Okay.''

''I want revenge on an animal.''

''I didn't think it was your civic duty.''

''I'm a man,'' Swann hissed. ''A man. He called me his punk, he called me his wife—and he used me like his whore. He nearly killed me. Many times. Many times. He threatened to snap my head off, and he would have, anywhere else he would have. He wouldn't regret it, he wouldn't even think about it . . . No, that's not true, he thinks about them, all of them, he loves to think about them, brag about them, go over and over how he did it and where he did it and who they were. He kills them again, every night. Probably even in his sleep. And he'll keep doing it, there's no doubt about it. I could find a record of only two of the killings, but he talked about dozens of them. I found the two girls in the coal mine in the paper—I work in the library, I searched everything I could find, but most of them wouldn't have been in the paper—he killed migrants and fringe people, they wouldn't be in the *Times* and that's the only newspaper we have that goes back . . .''

''He's killed while in here?''

''No. But he's gone, he's out. He got out three weeks ago.''

''Why didn't you tell us about him when he was in here?''

''I did. Look at the dates on the letters. He was still in here . . . He was still with me. Living with me. Talking about them. Using me . . . And they cheer, did you know that, Mr. Becker? The other prisoners cheer like it's a sport. I felt like a Christian—I am a Christian—being thrown to the lions and everyone was cheering for the lion.''

''Revenge isn't a very Christian sentiment,'' Becker said.

Swann had been edging closer to Becker, leaning in across the table, propelled forward by his intensity. Now he sighed audibly and leaned back in his chair.

''I have thought of that,'' Swann said. ''I wish my heart were without hate. I have prayed for that . . . But it hasn't been given.''

''You can always keep praying,'' Becker said.

''I always do, Mr. Becker. I always pray. I think that Jesus understands me. I know he does.''

"You're not that hard to understand. Even I can do it."

"But Jesus not only understands. He forgives."

"Does he forgive the man you're turning in, too? Does he forgive all those killings?"

"He might," Swann said. "I don't."

"What's his name?"

Once more, Swann looked nervously around the room. He opened his mouth to speak, then changed his mind, shaking his head.

"That doesn't seem like a lot to ask," Becker said.

"You don't understand how dangerous it is in here," Swann said. "If I give you a name, even if they don't know it, I will know it. If anybody asks me if I gave somebody up and I know I've given you his name—I'm such a bad liar, I get so frightened—they can smell it on you, I swear some of them can smell if you're lying, if you're scared. And he may have friends still in here, I don't think so, I don't think he had any friends but me, but you can't be sure. Isn't there another way? You'll figure it out, you can look at the prison records—if you could find me you can certainly figure out who he is. Just don't make me say his name. I've got to be able to say I didn't tell you anybody's name and believe it myself."

"So what are you giving me? What am I here for?"

"Him, I'm giving you him. Those bodies in the newspaper, the girls in the coal mine, he killed them, he admitted it to me, he bragged about it. He's never been tried for those. There are dozens of others. He'll confess to all of them, I think he would have confessed to anyone, anytime, because he's proud of all the killings. He thinks they make him a man. But nobody ever asked him, the cops never knew anything about him because he just drifts, he's done things in states that don't even know he's alive. I can tell you what to ask him."

"You're willing to testify against him? I thought you wouldn't even tell us his name."

"If I'm safe, I'll do whatever you want. You can't ask me to risk my life by testifying while I'm still in here."

"I didn't ask for anything from you, Swann, you sought me out. I was just as happy not knowing anything about this."

"You don't want to know about this? He's a killer, a serial killer, a mass murderer. I thought you would want to know. What kind of a cop are you?"

"Ex."

"Then why are you here?"

"Why am I here? I'm here because some shit-faced little con got tired of being buggered every night by the ape who shared his cage and thought he'd be real clever and write secret little notes in code to me. As if I gave a shit. As if I had nothing better to do than get involved in a lovers' spat. What am I supposed to be, your trained dog, you can sic me on anyone you want?"

"Lovers' spat? He's a killer!"

"The country's full of killers. There are more of them outside the walls than in—do you think I want to hunt them all down? There are fourteen-year-old killers in every gang in every housing project in the country. There are people killing their parents and parents throwing their babies out of windows and guys driving by with Uzis and spraying a crowd and lunatics strapping bombs to themselves and wiping out the local McDonald's and there are assholes blowing people away in traffic jams. There are killings on the goddamned sports page. And I haven't even gotten to the ones who kill with a fucking motive. What do I care if the guy who was fucking you is dusting a few? He's your problem, not mine. You work in the library? Take those scissors you used to cut out my cute little code and plant them in his intestines next time he bends you over, that's how it's done in here, haven't you figured that out? Take care of yourself, you little shit, don't try to get me to do it, I'm not your big brother."

Swann slumped in the chair, crestfallen.

"You don't believe me about him?"

"What's to believe? There's a guy in prison who's killed somebody? I have no trouble believing that. I just don't give a shit."

"You're going to betray me, aren't you?" Swann said, his face suddenly terrified. "You're going to give me to them, you're going to tell them what I've said."

"Who did you tell?" Becker asked.

"Tell what?"

"Who did you tell about your clever little scheme to get hold of me? How many did you tell?"

"I didn't tell anyone—do you think I'm crazy?"

Becker was on his feet. He jerked the front leg of Swann's chair off the floor with his foot, held the neck of the chair to keep it from falling so that Swann was on his neck, off-balance, halfway to the floor.

"Who did you confide in, who helped you, who were you whispering to about this, Swann?"

"Nobody. It was all my idea."

"You're not smart enough."

"The hell I'm not."

"You're a halfwit who got caught slicing up his landlady. How smart can you be?"

"Smarter than you think."

"That's not hard. Who taught you the binary code?"

"Nobody. I learned it in the library."

"Do some."

"What?"

Becker righted the chair and pushed Swann against the table so that he was pinned against his chest. Becker dropped a pen in front of Swann.

"Show me the binary code for 99."

"Now?"

"No, mail it to me, you little shit. Of course now. Do it there, do it on the table, just the way you sent it to me."

"You think I can't?"

"Do it."

"I told you, don't lump me with the rest of these people in here. I'm different."

"Uh-huh. Do the code."

Swann was silent for a moment, his hands folded in front of him.

"Do it," Becker said.

"I'm praying," Swann said. "I'm praying for Jesus to change your heart."

"Pray for him to teach you binary code real quick."

"I don't need to pray for that, Mr. Becker. I already know the code. You want 99?"

With speed and certainty, Swann marked a series of dots on the table:

· · ·
· · · ·

"It's not really a mystery, you know," Swann said. "Anybody who's computer literate can do it. Does that prove I wrote the messages by myself?"

Becker sat opposite Swann once more.

"I'm going to say this very calmly," Becker said, "because I want you to hear the specifics of what I have to say and not just the emotion. But if you have half as much sense as you seem to think you do, and if

you believe any part of the stories you've heard about me, you'll realize
that I mean exactly what I say. All right?''

"Of course.''

"I never want to hear from you again. I do not want communication
of any kind, in any form. What's more, if I receive communication from
anyone else in this place, I will assume that it came from you. Is that
clear?''

"That's not fair, you can't hold me responsible . . .''

"Fuck fair. Is it clear?''

"Yes.''

"Good. If you are stupid enough to disregard what I've just told you,
if I ever even hear your name again, I will personally deliver you to that
pack of howling hard-ons in there and I will tell them what you have
done. Is that clear?''

"They would kill me.''

"Is it clear?''

"Yes.''

"Good.''

Becker stood and shoved his chair neatly in place under the table.

"Is that all?'' Swann asked.

"That's all I wanted to say.''

"What about what I told you? Aren't you going to do anything about
it?''

"What is there to do? He's out, he's gone.''

"You can find him, I can help you find him.''

"How?''

"I know where he said he was going. I know where he is now.''

"How?''

Swann looked around the room once more, craning his neck to see
that the window in the door was empty.

"I need to be safe. I have to be safe before I can talk freely. Can you
promise me I'll be safe, Mr. Becker?''

"Me? I just made my promise to you. You didn't seem to like it.''

"He's a homocidal maniac. He kills people, he tortures and kills
them. I can give him to you, isn't that worth something?''

"It might be to some people. What's it worth to you?''

Swann closed his eyes and clasped his hands in front of himself
again.

"Will you please help me, Mr. Becker?'' he asked, his eyes still
closed. "I am dying in here. I don't deserve to die, Christ has forgiven

me for my sins, I've served three years . . . if no one helps me, I will never survive until my parole. Am I so loathsome that I deserve to die in this place?'' He fell to his knees in front of Becker. "Do you know what it's like in here? The monsters are fighting over me. They put their hands on you, you hate it, it disgusts you—and then you feel yourself getting aroused. You hate yourself for it, but they won't let you just receive, they want you to participate, they want you to cooperate. They want you to make up things to do, things that will make them feel good. And you know what you do? You remember what feels good to you, you remember what you liked to have your girlfriend do to you, and you do it to them, you remember how it feels on yourself and you get excited as they're getting excited. They don't care about you, they don't even know who you are, but they still make you act as if you like it . . . and you get so you do.''

Swann put his hands on Becker's knees and Becker stood abruptly, stepping away from the man.

"What do you want, Swann?''

"Will you at least tell someone at the FBI what I have to offer? Will you tell them you met with me and you know that I have valuable information?'' He reached again for Becker's knee and again Becker stepped away.

More than anything, Becker wanted to leave. He felt the oppression of the prison clinging like a film to his skin and he wanted to run from the room and hurl himself into sunlight and water, to stand under a waterfall and have the obscenity of the prison scoured and flushed from his body. Swann's supplications held him back as surely as if the man were clinging to his leg.

"All right,'' he said.

"Bless you!'' Swann cried. He reached for Becker's hand. Becker stepped around him and pounded on the door for the guard.

"Praise Jesus,'' Swann said, rising to his feet.

Swann stood next to Becker at the door, his body nearly touching Becker's. Becker could feel the heat of the other man's presence. He turned his head away.

"You've saved me,'' Swann said. "You've saved my life.''

Swann touched Becker's arm and Becker jerked away but Swann held on to his shirt. "I can't thank you, I can never thank you.''

"Stand away,'' Becker said. He felt the closeness of the man like a great weight pressing down on him.

Swann slid his hands down Becker's arm until he was clutching

Becker's wrist. Becker tried to pull away as Swann raised his hand to kiss it. Swann's grip was surprisingly strong and Becker could not wrest his hand free as Swann placed his lips on Becker's palm.

"No," Becker said. Swann muttered something into Becker's skin, and it sounded like more prayer, but Becker was unsure if the man was praying to Jesus or to him.

"Let go of me, damn it."

Swann was kissing Becker's hand, peppering it with little pecks of his lips, working down the length of it to the fingers. His lips touched a fingertip and opened and took one of Becker's fingers into his mouth. He rolled his eyes up to look Becker in the face.

With a cry of disgust, Becker yanked his hand away at the same time that Swann released his wrist. His knuckles flew upwards, hitting Swann in the mouth and the nose.

"I only wanted to thank you," Swann said reproachfully.

Becker did not look at him as he pounded again on the door.

Despite the blow to the face, Swann had still not backed away. He stood too close, so that Becker put a hand on his chest and pushed him back. Swann's fingers touched Becker's hand again before Becker yanked it away.

"Keep your hands off me," Becker said.

"You didn't have to hit me," Swann said.

"Sorry," Becker muttered. He stared anxiously out the window in the door, looking for the guard. Surely he wasn't locked in here; he didn't have to stay in here any longer with this man. The air seemed heavier still, as if weighed down on him; the walls seemed unbearably close.

"I was only thanking you."

"Just keep your distance," Becker said.

"Are you frightened of me?" Swann asked softly. There was a taunt-ing in his voice, the first recognition by a chronic victim who suddenly realizes he has an advantage. "You seem frightened. You don't need to be." His voice became softer, gentler with each sentence as his sense of control grew. "I'm your friend, you know. I want to be your friend."

Becker turned and looked at him for the first time since he had hit him. Swann's face was wet with tears, and blood trickled from his nose onto his lips. He had not wiped it since Becker's blow. When he caught Becker's eye he parted his lips and smiled. His teeth were red with blood and his eyes twinkled with a sense of victory.

* * *

Pegeen stood at the guard control room, just outside the first-level cellblock, and, trying not to let the guards know what she was doing, she smelled deeply of the air. At first there was just the odor of cleaning liquid, heavily ammoniated with a scent of lemon, but as her nose grew used to that, Pegeen began to detect the deeper, pervasive smell, the true, identifying smell of the prison. It seemed to hover on the other side of the control room like a column of heat in a furnace, rising from the ground to the fourth-level cellblock, containing itself within its own shimmering boundaries inside the vessel of the cauldron, betraying its presence only with occasional puffs just as the heat outside a furnace gives only the slightest clue of the fury of the inferno blazing within.

The stench was of sex, old sex. Sex dried and crusted and worn on the body, but with something else, a sort of grace note of emotion, a commingling of old sweat and new perspiration, both of them caused not by exercise nor heat, but by fear. The prison smelled of sex and fright. The smell was rape.

Pegeen waited by the car for Becker's return. After leaving the prison she had called a colleague in Nashville and asked what he knew about John Becker, a former agent, now on indefinite medical extension. The colleague, a fifteen-year veteran, had laughed at her naiveté but seemed eager to fill her in on Becker's career as he perceived it. He hit the highlights, most of which seemed to be Bureau legend.

"One ba-aaad dude," he had concluded gleefully, bleating like a sheep. "And you say you're with him?"

"I'm with him," she said.

"What are you doing, holding his hand?"

"Something like that," Pegeen had said, feeling herself blush.

"Well, when you get it back, check your hand for blood," he had said, laughing. "Becker never comes out of a case without blood on his hands." Then his tone had become very serious. "Now, no shit, Pegeen, this is the straight stuff, okay?"

"Okay."

"Be careful, be very careful . . ."

"I'm just the chauffeur."

"Great. Let's hope it stays that way. What I'm telling you, kiddo, is first of all, forget his record, the man is the best. I mean the best, nobody else comes close. But things have a way of happening around him. I'm not saying it's his fault—or maybe it is, I don't know. Just keep your eyes open and your wits about you."

"He seems nice, actually."

"Did I say he wasn't nice? He's nice." She heard his chortle of condescension distantly, as if he were trying to hide it, but not too hard. "Nice. Jesus, Pegeen, you're such a girl."

"I'm not going to respond to that."

"Now don't get upset. I don't mean it as an insult . . ."

"Thank you so much. It's not."

"It's just that 'nice' is what makes you a girl, thinking about people that way, assuming things like that."

Pegeen began to regret having made the call. "I don't think *you're* nice," she said. "That should be good for something."

"But I actually am nice."

"I'll have to refine the definition, then."

"The point is, you're like a little kid who wants to run up and pet every dog she sees. Well, some of them are pettable, and some of them bite . . . And some of them aren't even dogs. They can take your arm off at the shoulder; they can tear your throat out when you bend over."

Pegeen hung up the phone. What had Becker called himself? A werewolf. Not the man who had needed to hold her hand before he entered the prison. That was not a dangerous man, it was a sweet, troubled, sensitive man. What, she wondered, would he be when he came back out? To her surprise, she felt a thrill of anticipation.

Back in the car, Becker was agitated and distracted, answering Pegeen's questions only with grunts. When they returned to the highway he kept his eyes on the road, searching for something.

"There," he said finally, pointing a finger. "Pull over there."

"Where?"

"The motel."

"Why are we going to a motel?" Pegeen asked, dutifully steering into the motel courtyard.

Becker didn't answer but bolted from the car and into the office. He returned quickly, holding a key, and he strode to a motel room and entered. Pegeen followed reluctantly, puzzled. There had been no mention during training about agents darting into motel rooms in the middle of the day.

The door of the room was ajar, but Pegeen knocked first. What if he was lying naked on the bed? What if he was . . . She stopped trying to imagine and admitted to herself that she had no idea. She knocked again, spoke his name, then eased the door open.

She saw his shoes and socks where he had discarded them outside of the bathroom. The bathroom door was open and she heard the sound of the shower running.

She said, "Hello?" feeling foolish. She waited for several minutes, uncertain what he was doing or what she should do in response. Finally she sat on the edge of the bed, waiting. Would he emerge from the shower with fangs and fur like the werewolf of the movies? she wondered. Would he come out wearing a towel? Without a towel? Should she go wait in the car? Steam billowed out from the bathroom door. She decided to just sit tight and see what happened next. Whether or not he was the "ba-aaad dude" she had been warned to be careful of, he was a damned sight more interesting and less predictable than any of the agents at the office. Or than any other man she knew, for that matter. The steam filled the entire motel room. Pegeen threw her feet up on the bed and relaxed into the pillow. The spot on her cheek where he had touched her still burned, but she knew that was just her imagination.

Chapter 19

In the speckled shade of a dying fir, Cooper squatted and studied the restaurant across the highway. The tree was a victim of acid rain, and half of its needles had turned brown and sere, mottling the canopy with scrofulous patches like a dog with mange. Cooper eyed the restaurant, his fingers idly toying with the dead needles that littered the ground around him, raking them into little piles while his mind raced, trying to figure out his situation. They had given him another application, even though Cooper said he'd already filled one out in the other town, even though he was wearing the striped uniform jacket of the restaurant chain to prove he'd worked there. Still, they wanted another application, as if they didn't believe him, or were trying to trick him, trying to make him look stupid. Cooper had glanced at the application and then at the manager who handed it to him. His name tag said he was Ted. Cooper thought of saying, here Ted, here's your head, then breaking the little clerk's neck for him and stuffing the application in the hole.

Instead, he had taken the application across the street, where he could be in the shade and think what to do. Last time, of course, he had made that girl fill out the form for him. Cooper had forgotten exactly how he had made her do it, but he remembered that it worked, he had gotten the job. He remembered other things about the girl, too. He remembered how she had let him drive her car and how she had surprised him while he was driving and then how she had taken him into the woods and surprised him some more. She had liked him, he knew that. She told him so and she certainly acted like it, or at least as if she liked part of him. She had told him she loved the way he howled.

"Most men don't say nothing, they don't make a sound, not a peep. You just throw your head back and hoot like an Indian on the warpath. That's a nice thing, Coop. Men aren't usually very good at enjoying themselves."

He remembered that he had howled a lot in the woods, maybe exaggerating it a little bit for her sake. She laughed every time he did, but not a mean laugh; she wasn't making fun of him.

He wished he could see her now. He would trick her into filling out the application again and this time, afterward, when they got in her car, maybe he'd surprise her.

There was something about her he had forgotten, he knew that, something important. He lifted a pile of dead needles in his hand and let them out like grains of sand. They sparkled like shards of copper when the sunlight hit them, like a lively shining living stream of copper, but lying on the ground, in the shade once more, they were as dull and drab as dirt. A few of the needles were stuck in his hand, pasted there by perspiration. Cooper brushed them off, dried his hand on his pants, then rubbed the sweat from his forehead, wetting it again. It was very hot, even in the shade.

Mayvis, that was her name. Cooper stood up, pleased with himself for recalling it. Her name was Mayvis and she had written it down for him so he could remember it. Cooper looked in his wallet; he remembered she had tucked the paper with her name on it in his wallet, which had disturbed him at first—he didn't like people handling his personal property—but she kept talking to him the whole time, explaining that he could call her anytime he wanted to have some more fun or if he needed anything at all.

"You can even call if you just want to talk," she said, then laughed—he wasn't sure if he liked that particular laugh—"but I don't guess you'd want to do that. Hell, I don't care, just call if you want to howl into the phone. 'Course, if you want me to make you howl, that's even better."

"Uh-huh," Cooper had said.

"Are you going to remember me at all, Cooper?"

"Sure," he said.

"I'll bet. If you do, you'll be one of the first. Anyway, here," and she had tucked the paper with her name on it into his wallet and slipped the wallet back into his pocket, pausing back there long enough to give him a squeeze.

"Ooohhh," she said, pretending that just touching him made her shiver.

Cooper found the paper in the little plastic pouch where some people carried pictures. Mayvis Tway, it said, then underneath it, a telephone number. Cooper left the shade and crossed to the restaurant to make a phone call.

*   *   *

"I'll be goddamned," she said. "Sure I remember you. I never thought I'd hear from you again, though."

"You said to call you," Cooper said.

"I know I did, honey, but not everybody pays real close attention to what I say the way you do. They're mostly shitheads."

"Uh-huh," Cooper said. "Shitheads."

"This going to be kind of a one-sided conversation, ain't it?" she asked and Cooper did not answer because he wasn't sure what she meant.

"Well, where the hell are you?" she asked, her voice tinkling into his ear. She was pleased to hear from him, just as she had said she would be. Cooper decided he liked her.

"I'm at the restaurant," he said.

"Which one? . . . The one where I found you?"

"Yeah. But not there."

"What does that mean?"

"I'm at the one in . . ." He struggled to remember the name of the town that the preacher had told him. "Wycliffe," he said at last.

"Sugar, that's a sixty miles from here. How'd you get over to Wycliffe?"

"I walked," he said.

"Walked? You couldn'ta walked all the way to Wycliffe."

Cooper didn't answer.

"Well, never mind," she said. "What did you want?"

"You said to call," Cooper said.

"Well, that was nice of you."

She sounded like she was going to hang up. Cooper hated the telephone.

"They give me another paper," Cooper said.

"What do you mean, honey?"

He struggled to say it right.

"Let's have some fun," he said.

She laughed again, sounding the way she did when she was with him in person. "Well, why didn't you say so? Do you want me to come get you?"

"Uh-huh," he said.

"In Wycliffe?"

"Uh-huh."

"It'll take me an hour, you know. You think you can wait that long for Mayvis?"

"Uh-huh."

"I don't want you to think this means I don't have an active social life now," she said. "Wouldn't want you to take me for granted or anything." She laughed again, so merrily that Cooper laughed too.

"Now, tell me again, what's your name?"

"Cooper."

"That's right," she said. "And, Cooper . . . you're which one? The one that howls?"

Cooper howled into the phone. She was still laughing when she hung up.

It's not that I'm hard up, Mayvis said to herself, I'm just sentimental. She told herself a lot of shit like that, and amused herself most times with it. It had taken her more than an hour to get to Wycliffe and she wasn't sure that Cooper would be there when she finally arrived. She wasn't sure he had been there in the first place—he might have been playing a trick on her. They did that often enough, taking advantage of her good nature and her willingness to go halfway to accommodate a man. Cooper, if she remembered him clearly, didn't seem the type for cruel jokes, but you could never be sure with a man, cruelty was always just a scratch or two under the surface. She didn't recall ever driving sixty miles for a man before, at least not for one with whom she had no relationship other than one rather active and sweaty afternoon, but she'd done dumber things for sex, there was no question about that; even if Cooper turned out not to be there, she'd engaged in wilder-goose chases and had exposed herself to greater humiliation just to get laid. She did have that little problem of wanting it. Wanting it a lot. Often. And with new partners, if partnership was the right concept for the way most men went about it. It seemed a pretty solitary pursuit for most of them, something they did for themselves with Mayvis just happening to be conveniently in the way.

She had to do something about her sexual habits, of course, she knew that. She had promised she would, promised her friends and her parents and even herself. She should start going to those meetings again, but frankly, what no one had ever explained to her satisfaction was why it was okay for all the men to fuck everything they possibly could and nobody telling them they needed help, and why it wasn't okay for her to do the same. If nothing else, it was a kind of interesting activity. You met all kinds of people that way. If she acted coy and waited until the men made a move on her, first of all the shy ones never would and consequently she would only get to meet the aggressive ones, which would drastically reduce her experience. Mayvis saw no reason to limit herself to just one kind of man. She had tried being faithful to just one man, tried pretty hard for a while, but it just hadn't worked out for her. She was too gregarious. She was too friendly. He became too boring. The truth was, it wasn't really the sex Mayvis was after, it was the attention. And in seeking the attention she had also become addicted to the excitement. All of this had been explained to her in the group her parents had sent her to. She wasn't really having fun at all with all those men, they told her. She was seeking something which she could never find from strangers, and in the process she was exposing herself to great dangers. One didn't have to be a genius to know what those dangers were, but Mayvis was getting a thrill out of her own peril, they had explained. The people at the meetings had been very educational, they had loved explaining things, they knew so much jargon that it was as if they didn't even have to think about what they said, they just kept repeating key phrases, expecting her to agree with them. After a while it had seemed easier to agree than to argue.

Roger, one of the men in the group, spent part of every meeting talking about how his sexual fantasies had ruined his life. He read pornography, he confessed. He sought women other than his wife. He masturbated daily. Although he announced his failings in the prescribed manner, bewailing his misery and praising his higher power for allowing him to attend the meetings and take charge of his life, he always sounded a little proud to Mayvis. Roger sounded as if he were determined to make his sexual hyperfunction a bit more hyper than anyone else's. At the last meeting she had attended, Mayvis had called him on it.

"If pounding your pud makes you so unhappy, why don't you just quit it?" she asked.

He had smirked at her with the superiority born of true understanding. "And why don't you quit balling guys you pick up in convenience stores?" he demanded.

"Because it doesn't make me unhappy," she said. "I like it."

"You are in denial," he said. They always said that to anyone who didn't agree with them.

"Maybe," Mayvis replied. "But I'm not whacking off in gas station toilets."

He managed to look pained and smug at the same time. After the meeting, when Mayvis apologized for her comments, Roger asked if she wanted to sleep with him to see what she had been missing. She had not been back to the meetings since.

She wasn't certain that she would recognize him—there had been an awful lot of faces to remember—but when she saw him standing outside the restaurant, looking like a tree with muscles, she remembered, all right. He was standing there holding a piece of paper in his huge hand. He was wearing a candy-striped uniform jacket that looked as if it had been slept in it for weeks. His face and arms were covered with dust and streaked with sweat trails. He looked at Mayvis as if he really had walked the sixty miles from Hazard.

It's come to this, she thought. I'm picking up goons. I'm sleeping with halfwits. Maybe I should go back to those meetings after all. I could sleep with the jerk-off Roger, who isn't very nice but changes his clothes once a week.

Then Cooper saw her and smiled hugely and she remembered that he really was kind of cute, in a mammoth sort of way, the way a bear can be cute.

Mayvis consoled herself with the thought that if nothing else, she could spot the loonies, the really dangerous ones, from a mile off. Cooper looked menacing because of his size—his great size was also part of his attraction—but she knew from experience that he was as malleable as mud. She knew how to handle him.

Cooper didn't volunteer why he had left Hazard and walked sixty miles to find the same job again, and Mayvis didn't ask. In all honesty, she didn't care. She wasn't planning to adopt the big guy—she doubted very much that she would ever see him again after today—or that she would want to. She had just been so touched that he had called. Men in Hazard seldom called her; only strangers did. Men who had been given her name or read it scrawled on a wall somewhere, they called. She knew why they were calling, of course. Sometimes, if she felt like it, she went out with them, but she always made them take her somewhere first, out to eat or to a movie, somewhere they would be seen with her. It was the price she made them pay for calling her. If she selected them, that was different—no charge, and the front seat of the car was good enough.

She wasn't about to make Cooper take her out to dinner, however, even assuming he could pay for it in the first place. She didn't particularly want to be seen with him, not even in a town where no one knew her. She wasn't going to do anything with him, either, not even in her car, until he got cleaned up.

"Now pay attention this time," she said, filling out the application. "Next time you'll be able to do it for yourself."

"You do it," Cooper said.

"I am doing it, but I'm not always going to be around for you."

"I'll call you," Cooper said.

"Listen, sugar, I'm not your traveling secretary. Just watch and learn."

"Let me drive," Cooper said. Mayvis was still behind the wheel, resting the application form on the horn button.

"Just hold on."

"Let me," Cooper said.

He reached across the seat and lifted and dragged her to the passenger side, then slid behind the wheel himself. The speed and ease with which he accomplished it startled Mayvis. She had never been handled with such strength.

"Hey, now, listen. You go on in that washroom and clean up first."

"No."

"I mean it. You don't clean up, that's it, I'm going home." She returned her attention to the application, deliberately not looking at him. If you acted as if you expected to be behaved, you usually got your way, she had found. When they were horny, they'd do whatever you said. It was only afterward that they got difficult. She could feel him staring at her but she kept her eyes on the paper.

"Go on now, honey, while I finish this for you. Then you can drive, okay?" She patted his leg for encouragement, still averting her eyes.

Cooper took hold of her wrist. She turned to look at him for the first time. His eyes were flat and expressionless. Big and brown but unreadable, like the eyes in a mask. Mayvis realized suddenly that she was very frightened.

She tried very gently to pull her hand away; she didn't want to make it a contest of strength.

"The sooner you go, the sooner you'll get to drive," she said. He kept looking at her, nothing showing in his face. Mayvis smiled as friendly as she could make it, while her eyes flicked rapidly around her. They were in a fast-food-restaurant parking lot, for God's sake. There were people everywhere. Nothing could happen here, she thought. Relax, relax and talk to him. "You want me to finish your application, don't you, hon? I can't do that with just one hand."

She waited, looking for some flicker of recognition in his eyes. They looked like two buttons sewn on a doll's face. For the first time she realized how stupid the man was. She had thought he was reticent, like most men she knew, uncommunicative and clearly a little slow, but not really stupid. She had assumed he had a reading disability which accounted for his application problems, not that he was too dumb to understand the words.

"Coop?" she said softly.

"What?"

"Why don't you let go my arm now?"

Cooper looked down at her arm as if seeing it for the first time, as if puzzled to find it clasped in his hand. He studied it for a moment.

"Did you want to let it go, hon?" Mayvis asked.

Cooper released her and she pulled her arm back slowly, as calmly as she could.

"Wasn't you going to wash up now, Coop?"

"Huh?"

"Remember, you said you was going to go into the washroom in there and clean up so we could take a ride together. With you driving. And here, sugar, you can give them the application form, too. All done up good so you'll get that job again."

"Okay," Cooper said. He got out of the car, and Mayvis breathed deeply in relief, but then he reached back in and took the keys from the ignition.

She watched him walk across the parking lot, the keys dangling from his massive hand. Her instinct was to run, to abandon the car, give it up, and run to safety, wherever that might be. There was no denying her fear, she had been flat scared there for a minute, and if a man made you feel like that, then get the hell away from him.

Then reason took over. First of all, nothing had happened, she told herself. She had handled him, controlled him very easily, as a matter of fact, once she realized the situation. He was stupid, not dangerous. Secondly, she wasn't about to give up her car. For what? It wasn't the first time a man had held on to her too long. She trusted him a whole lot more where she could see and control him than she did driving her car around alone. If nothing else, he was apt to get lost. Was she so scared that she was going to give a man a possession worth thousands of dollars and just walk away? Nothing could scare her that much. The idea of calling the police came to her and was dismissed in a second. She knew how the police would treat her. With her reputation, they would assume the worst, always. It was like a hooker calling rape. Who would believe her? And about what? He held my wrist? I was scared? What's a cop going to do for me? Haven't you already fucked this man, Mayvis? they would ask. Now he can't touch your arm? It wouldn't be any better reporting a stolen car to them, either. It would just be giving them an opportunity for all the dirty-minded comments they could come up with. It would be even worse back home in Hazard. She had slept with two of the cops on the force there, and three others were mad at her that she hadn't done them, too. She could just see herself calling the cops.

Cooper returned to the car and they drove off. The front of his face had been splashed with water, but Mayvis could still see the dust on his neck and his ears. His wrists were speckled like a dirt patch after a brief shower.

"I'm going fast," he said when they hit the highway.

"Well, slow down," she said.

He turned to face her, looking away from the road entirely.

"Come on," he said. "I'm going fast."

When Mayvis didn't move he grabbed her hair and yanked her face into his lap. She got the idea then.

Cooper howled and pulled the car off the road onto an access path not much wider than the car. Pine boughs whipped at the windshield, and dust rose up behind them in a reddish-brown cloud.

"Now put your foot here," Cooper said.

"What?"

"Put your foot here and play with yourself like before," he said. He grabbed her leg and dropped it into his lap. "Put your hand in your shirt," he said.

"Coop, let's just give it a rest for a minute, okay?"

"Put your hand in your shirt," he said, reaching for her arm. He slapped her hand against her breast to remind her of what to do. "Like last time," he said.

"It doesn't have to be just like last time," she said. "Let's be spontaneous."

"Do it like last time," Cooper said.

He pulled the car off the path and onto a ridge of weeds and scrub brush.

She put her hand under her blouse, moving slowly, keeping her eyes fixed on his.

"Now, listen, honey, I think you forgot something about last time that was different."

"No," he said.

"Yes, you did. Don't you remember what was different last time? . . . I told you what to do last time. Remember? That way you didn't have to think about it, you just got all the fun."

"Then we got out," Cooper said as if he didn't hear her. Grabbing the foot that rested in his crotch, Cooper got out of the car and dragged Mayvis across the seat and stood her up. "In there," he said, pointing to the woods.

He held her by the arm and walked into the woods. Mayvis told herself to stay calm. All she had to do was try to repeat the sequence of their last time together and everything would be all right. Nothing was going to happen to her that hadn't happened before.

In a wider opening among the trees Cooper pushed her down and undid his belt while standing over her.

"Like last time," he said.

"Sugar, I don't really recall exactly—"

"No," Cooper said, shaking his head impatiently. "Not like that." He maneuvered her until he had her where he wanted her then entered her with a grunt.

"I could kill you," he said, his breath coming faster.

"No, sugar."

"I could pop your head right off."

He put his hand on her throat, but it was no good with her looking at him. He didn't like anybody looking at him, even though she had done so last time. But last time was different because it was so surprising; this time he could have his way. Cooper turned her over and pulled her back to him to take her the way he had taken the punk.

"No, sugar," she said. "Not that way. That will hurt. No, sugar."

"Time for your nightlies," he said.

Cooper pulled her back firmly against him and drove into her. She screamed and Cooper smiled, expecting to hear the encouraging calls from the other prisoners, but the only sounds were made by Mayvis.

"No!" she cried. She was wriggling, trying to get free, and her motions excited Cooper. He put his hand around her throat and squeezed.

"I could pull your head right off," he said. "I've done it before."

She kept screaming and Cooper tightened his grip until he could no longer hear her cries, and when she fell silent he began to fill the woods with his own noises.

He thought he heard the chorus of approval echoing through the trees, the cons yelling and growling in appreciation of Old Coop. The punk was just lying there and Cooper gave him a push with his foot to get him away. The punk groaned but didn't move. Cooper thought of just kicking the shit out of him, just for the fun of it. But then a squirrel moved in one of the trees and Cooper watched it for a moment, fascinated by the way it moved around and around the trunk of the tree, always so nervous and skittery as if it were looking over its shoulder all the time.

After a time Cooper realized something was missing and he put his arm around the punk's waist and pulled him to his knees.

"Let us pray," Cooper said. The punk hung limply in his arm, so Cooper slapped him on the head. "Let us pray," he said again, prompting him.

"Sweet Jesus . . ." the punk whispered.

The punk's hair was longer and the freckles were gone and Cooper realized it was the woman, not the punk, but he had known that all along, of course he had. There was nothing wrong with pretending, he assured himself.

But he wished it was Swann. He could tell Cooper what to do now. Swann had been a bitch sometimes, but he was Cooper's bitch and he always came around for him in the end. And he seldom cried afterward. This bitch better not cry, either. Cooper hated a crying woman worse than anything.

Cooper rested his back against a tree and pulled Mayvis back onto his chest. He ran his fingers through her hair.

"Tell me you love me," he said.

"I love you," Mayvis said.

"I love you too, Swann," Cooper said. But it didn't sound right and it didn't feel right and Cooper felt an anger growing. He didn't want this woman on his chest, he didn't want her saying she loved him.

He continued to run his fingers through her hair because it felt good even though a rage was building in his throat, and gradually her body relaxed against his. Cooper watched the squirrel and a blue jay that seemed to be scolding it. When the bird finally shut up, Cooper became aware of a sound closer to him. Very softly, as if she knew she shouldn't do it, the woman was crying.

She turned her face to him suddenly, rising off his chest.

"You hurt me," she said. Tears ran down her cheeks.

Cooper's rage was too great to contain any longer—he felt it bursting from his throat into his head so that he was filled with it, his eyes, his ears, his skull crammed with rage. I'm going to kill her, Cooper thought. There seemed no other way to quell his anger.

Chapter 20

When they returned to the Nashville airport, Becker and Pegeen were met by an airline official who asked them to follow her. The official led them to a door marked personnel only, unlocked the door, and ushered them in, then quietly withdrew, leaving Becker and Pegeen to confront their greeting committee. Hatcher was the first to his feet, all smiles and cordiality, as if he had just happened to run into them by chance.

"John, how good to see you," he said, and then, as if knowing better, he did not try to shake hands but turned instead to Pegeen. "Special Agent Haddad? I'm Associate Director Hatcher. Pegeen, isn't it? Nice to meet you."

Pegeen winced involuntarily at Hatcher's name, or, more specifically, at his title, which he pronounced with great clarity. She noted the other man and the angry-looking woman behind Hatcher, but there was no doubt that he was the power in the room.

"How do you do, sir," she managed haltingly, but Hatcher had already turned from her, his interest nothing more than a social twitch.

The other man rose from his seat behind the conference table. Pegeen thought he looked too soft to be an agent. She was right.

"Hello, John," the man said.

"Gold."

"It's been a while."

"That was the idea," Becker said. "To make it as long as possible." Then to Pegeen Becker said, "My shrink. Or rather one of the Bureau's shrinks, the one who specializes in me."

Gold shook Pegeen's hand and murmured his name so diffidently that Pegeen wasn't sure if it was Murray, Maury, or Mary. Becker walked to the woman and kissed her. She seemed to accept the kiss without qualms but she did not bother to rise from her seat. She kept her eyes fixed on Pegeen, and Pegeen knew she was in trouble.

"This is Assistant Director Crist," Becker explained to Pegeen. "I call her Karen because I live with her."

The woman nodded cooly at Pegeen, and Pegeen understood the reason for the woman's hostility. She dismissed the small sense of betrayal as unwarranted and irrelevant. He had no reason to tell me he was married or living with someone or anything else, she thought, we were just working. I didn't mention my marital situation with him, either. But then I had nothing of any interest to mention. He did, but he didn't so much as hint at it. And what did that indicate? Pegeen warned herself to pay attention to the business at hand. She had heard of Karen Crist, of course. There were very few women in the Bureau who outranked her, and none had risen so far so fast; all of the younger women in the organization watched her every move with fascination and inspiration. But she was not only a phenom and a role model, Pegeen realized. She was also a jealous woman. Which meant a potentially dangerous one. Pegeen resolved to walk very lightly.

"I just thought we'd take this opportunity to see how things went," Hatcher said.

"What opportunity is that?" Becker asked. "The fact that we all happen to be here in the Nashville airport? You're right, that is a pretty good opportunity."

Hatcher leaned back in his chair, the smile still fixed on his face. He was prepared to let the others run the meeting, had instructed them to do so if Becker was resistant to Hatcher's methods.

Karen leaned forward slightly. "What happened in the meeting with Swann, John?"

Becker scanned the three across the table from him very carefully before speaking. Pegeen thought he had the look of a hunted animal who was deciding which of his pursuers to attack first.

He decided on Gold.

"What's going on, Gold?"

"Well . . ." Gold looked at Hatcher, then Karen. He shrugged. "I'm here basically to talk to you in case you . . . in case you want to talk to me."

"I don't want to talk to you."

"Well . . ."

"We listened to the meeting, John," Karen said.

"You had the prison room bugged?"

Hatcher, still smiling, studied his fingernails.

"That decision was taken," Karen said.

"And I wonder who took it?" Becker asked. Hatcher did not look up. "A new low, Hatcher."

"There are some things about the meeting we'd like you to explain," Karen said.

Becker ignored her, directing himself to Hatcher. "Not because you taped me without letting me know," he said. "Because you're making my wife run this interrogation."

"I didn't know you were married," Hatcher said. "Congratulations."

"We're not . . ." Karen said.

"I call her my wife," Becker said.

"I have no problem running this interview," Karen said. "If you feel uncomfortable, John, then—"

"You don't refer to agent Becker as your husband, do you?" Hatcher asked blandly.

"No," she said.

"You see why I was confused," Hatcher said, lifting his hands slightly as if to show they were sparkling clean. "Apologies all around."

"None necessary, sir," Karen said. She turned to Becker. "We had a wire in the prison interview room. We didn't have a camera. Some of the conversation seems rather ambivalent and we thought it best to clarify any ambiguities."

"You sound rather hostile to the man Swann," Gold prompted. "Was there something going on that we couldn't pick up on tape?"

Becker glared at Gold. Pegeen could see the psychologist visibly wilt under the stare.

"Perhaps we'd better talk about it in private," Gold said.

"Was there a delay coming back from Springville?" Karen asked.

"You had a stopwatch on me, too?"

"Perhaps agent Haddad can help us out here," Hatcher said, his smile widening. He arched his eyebrows in silent question.

"We, uh, did make an unscheduled stop, sir."

"Oh, really?"

Pegeen glanced at Becker for a clue on how to proceed. He kept his eyes boring holes into Hatcher. For his part, the Associate Director seemed unaware of anything but Pegeen.

You don't lie to an Associate Director, Pegeen thought. Whatever else you do, don't be that stupid. Then here goes your career.

"We stopped at the Hi-Ho Motel," she said, feeling as if she had just walked into the room and put her foot in a cow turd. She had their attention now.

"The Hi-Ho Motel," Karen repeated without inflection.

"It's a—uh—motor lodge. Just outside of Springville."

"I wanted to take a shower," Becker said.

"I understand," Hatcher said.

"No, you don't."

"And what did you do while Agent Becker took a shower?" Hatcher asked.

"I waited for him, sir."

"Where?" Karen asked.

Since I'm already dead, this will bury me, Pegeen thought.

"Pardon me?"

" 'Where did you wait,' I think is what Assistant Director Crist is asking," Hatcher volunteered.

"In the motel room, sir . . . It seemed best." Her ears felt tinged with fire. Betrayed by her complexion again.

"I understand," Hatcher said, nodding.

"That was my assignment," Pegeen said, making matters worse, she realized.

"What was?" asked Karen.

"To keep an eye on Agent Becker."

"You were assigned to drive him," Karen said.

"I was also told to assist him with anything he needed," Pegeen said.

"Did you feel he needed assistance in the shower?" Hatcher asked. He's enjoying it, Pegeen realized. He likes seeing me squirm. "Not specifically the shower, sir, no."

"I told her to come in," Becker said. "Leave her alone—she doesn't have anything to do with it."

"Why did you think he needed assistance?" Gold said. His tone was genuinely sympathetic, and Pegeen liked him immediately. "Was he upset?"

"Yeah, I was upset," Becker said. "She did the right thing, I was upset and she wanted to make sure I was all right."

"I understand," said Hatcher.

"You don't have a clue," said Becker.

"What were you upset about?" Karen asked.

"I was upset that I was working for Hatcher," Becker said. "I'd sworn to myself, never again, but there I was, sitting in prison with a sick little puppy licking my hand, and I felt so dirty I couldn't stand it, so I took a shower. Now, if you don't leave agent Haddad out of this, Hatcher, I won't tell you what you want to know. Do you understand that?''

Hatcher turned to Pegeen, smiling, if possible, even more insincerely than before.

"I think that will be all for now. And thank you so much."

Pegeen felt all of their eyes on her back as she walked out the room, but she thought she could distinguish those of Karen Crist. They were the ones with the daggers on the end.

Gold cleared his throat, but it was Hatcher who spoke.

"So, John. You have your way; you have what you asked for. I wonder now if you could tell us what it is you think I want to know."

"You heard the tapes, what do you think?"

"I wasn't there, John. I didn't see the man."

"Why not go there? He'll be happy to see you. I don't think he gets nearly enough visitors."

"But I don't need to go, John. You've already gone, you're the expert in this particular area, so you tell me. Are we on to the killer of those girls in the coal mine? Can this man Swann help us find him?"

"If you give him what he wants, this man Swann will help you find Jimmy Hoffa."

"You recommend that we work with him, then?"

"I recommend that *you* work with him. I don't want anything else to do with him."

"You seem to have had an—uncomfortable—experience. I regret that. I had hoped you might like to come back to work full time."

Before Becker could retort, Karen interrupted. "We just want you to assess Swan as a source, John. It's important."

"Why?"

In the silence, Karen and Hatcher exchanged glances. Gold moved uncomfortably in his chair.

"Well, naturally, some of us don't share your view of the importance of murder that you expressed to Mr. Swann. What was it? Everyone is killing everyone else, so what do a few more matter? That's a paraphrase, of course. A very curious attitude for a law officer, John, although I know you will hasten to tell me that you are no longer an officer. Nonetheless, this man Cooper seems to have murdered a good many people and may be about to do many more, and I for one would like to stop him.''

''Cooper is the cellmate?''

''Darnell Cooper,'' Karen said. ''He did five years of hard time for assault with intent, never requested parole, wouldn't have got it if he had, got out three weeks ago. Never showed up to meet with the parole officer.''

''Gone?''

''Without a trace so far. But we haven't been looking very long.''

''Just since my meeting with Swann, or did you have a head start?''

''Just since your meeting.''

Becker nodded. ''Well, good luck to you.''

''Thank you, John,'' said Hatcher. ''You've been most cooperative, as always—in your own way. I have matters to tend to, so I'll leave you now, but I'm sure you'll have things to discuss with Dr. Gold and Assistant Deputy Crist . . . Actually, Deputy Crist, if you could accompany me for just a moment. You have more access to Agent Becker than the rest of us, and I expect there are one or two things you'll want to clear up with him, but if you'll just come with me now . . . So nice to see you again, John.''

Becker leaned over in his chair and studied the floor after Hatcher and Karen had gone.

''What is it?'' Gold asked.

''I'm looking to see if he leaves an actual slime trail.''

''He's my superior, John. Karen's too, which is more to the point. What do you accomplish by treating him that way?''

''It gets some of the venom out. Isn't that what you shrinks like us to do? Ventilate the venom?''

''It makes Karen's job a good deal harder. If you won't behave when she's in the room—''

''When will I behave? Is that the rest of that sentence? Karen's a big girl, Gold. She's far better at the politics of all this than you or me. And can you imagine what would happen if I were nice and docile and, God help me, polite to Hatcher if she were around? Do you know what that would do for her? It would make Hatcher think she was my keeper. He'd have her there every time anybody talked to me, he'd have her supervising my every move. And when I did rebel, and we both know I would before long, it would look like her failure. She's a lot better off if I make it clear to Hatcher that she can't control me either.''

"It's an interesting approach. You maintain your freedom, Karen maintains hers. Does Karen see it that way, too?"

"Why are you here, Gold?"

"I was told to come, John. By Hatcher directly."

"Before or after you listened to the tapes?"

"After."

"Why? What's so important about this case?"

"You know they don't tell me—I'm just a shrink. I don't deal with casework. I'm just here for you because of our relationship."

"What does that mean?"

"In case you needed to talk to me. You did sound rather upset on the tape."

"So Hatcher hurried you to Nashville to check on my state of mind? Just out of the goodness of his heart?"

"I don't know about the goodness of his heart. You're very valuable to him."

"What a terrifying thought."

"Do you want to talk, John? About the interview?"

"Not particularly."

"But then you never particularly want to talk to me, do you?"

Becker laughed. "You've noticed?"

"You've dropped a hint here and there . . . Swann got to you some way, didn't he?"

"The place got to me. The situation. Him, too, maybe. I felt—I felt like I couldn't get away."

Gold nodded. "I don't know what it's like. I've never had to go into a prison."

"Keep it that way."

"Yes, please God . . . What sort of a man is he?"

"Small."

"You know what I mean."

"But you don't. Listen, Gold, don't ask me to appraise anybody in prison. They play a role the whole time they're there, all of them, every single one. They don't dare to let their guard down or let the mask slip for a second. One wrong word, one sideways glance, and someone will see it, because believe me, everyone is watching. Everywhere. There's nothing but eyes, all around you. You know how vultures work? They don't come down to see a healthy animal walking along—they don't waste their energy. If you're crossing a desert, it doesn't matter if you're actually dying—if you can act like a healthy human, they won't come near you. But if you limp or stumble or wilt, they'll see it from miles away. The important thing in prison is to be what they expect you to be. You'll find your role in the first week, and you'd better play it to the hilt or you're a goner. So don't expect to get a true picture of any con. He's playing a part.''

Gold was silent for a moment. Not for the first time he wondered about his wisdom in electing to work with men with whom he had little affinity, who labored under dangers with which he was unfamiliar. Every one of them knew more about peril and fear and overcoming anxiety than he would ever know, no matter how long he listened to them. And Becker, of course, for all the time they had spent together, knew demons and devils and shades of hell that Gold was grateful he had never even dreamed of. And yet, even though they seemed to have nothing in common, Gold felt an affection for Becker that transcended the doctor/patient relationship. He thought Becker liked him, too.

''Did it come back to you at the interview, John?''

''Did what come back?''

''The . . . feeling you get sometimes. What we've worked on.''

''Is that what we've been working on, Gold? That old-time feeling?''

''It did, didn't it? You wanted to hurt him, didn't you? Isn't that what upset you? Isn't that what the shower was about—he brought back that feeling? Or rather, the prison did, the circumstances, the claustrophobia . . .''

''Wrong on two counts, but otherwise, dead-on.''

''Which two?''

''One, the interview, the claustrophobia, whatever it was—it didn't bring the feeling back, because the feeling was never really gone, *is* never really gone. You should attend more twelve-step programs, Gold. You'd realize that old habits don't go away, they just get under control.''

''And?''

''Wrong on count two. I didn't have the feeling that I wanted to hurt him . . . I had the feeling that I wanted to kill him . . . But you knew that, didn't you?''

''Yes, I knew,'' said Gold.

Becker twisted a corner of his mouth ironically. ''So nice to be understood,'' he said.

Karen wrapped herself in silence for half the flight to New York, burying her face in files and typing memos on her laptop computer.

Becker was grateful for the interlude of peace. He knew that in time he would have to account for his stop in the motel with Pegeen. Karen was not suspicious, nor had he ever given her cause to be, but trust beyond a certain point veered toward indifference, and he knew that Karen was not indifferent to him. She had based her career on a mastery of details, and she would want to know all the particulars of his motel visit when she got around to asking.

Becker pretended to sleep and then slept. Karen woke him as they approached New York.

"You'll be pleased to know that Hatcher has taken you off the case."

"Oh?"

"That's what you wanted, isn't it? That's why you behaved that way with Swann."

"What way?"

"Hitting him."

"I didn't hit him."

"He says you did. He requested medical treatment after you left."

"The little shit."

"No doubt. But he is also considering a lawsuit. I don't think he'll go through with it—Hatcher will mollify him one way or another."

"Why is he so involved, Karen? What does Hatcher want with this case? It can't do him any particular good, can it? He's operating on too lofty a scale to benefit from the capture of one man."

"If you're a black hole of ambition like Hatcher, ultimately you suck in everything to your benefit, but in this case it wasn't very hard. One of those two girls who was found in the coal mine—her uncle was Quincy Beggs."

"Never heard of him."

"No one else had when his niece disappeared—what, ten years ago? As a result, he ran on a fiercely aggressive law-and-order platform and got elected as a congressman from West Virginia."

"I've still never heard of him."

"But Hatcher has. Now four-term Congressman Beggs is on the Oversight Committee, the congressional committee that deals with our budget and, not indirectly, some of our top-level promotions. You have heard of that one—haven't you?"

"So Hatcher has a chance to deliver to Beggs the man who killed his niece. No wonder he's so involved."

"Just thought you'd be pleased to know you're off the hook," Karen said.

"And you're still on it."

Karen shrugged.

"I really am sorry," he said.

"I'll manage."

"I'm sorry you have to."

Karen returned her attention to the computer. Becker put his hand on her arm. "It really was just a shower . . ."

"I believe that. I do."

"Good . . . Nothing went on at all. She's just an agent."

Karen smiled patiently. "The sorry thing is, you probably believe that, too . . . Men . . ."

"What does that mean?"

"Something 'went on' with her whether you noticed it or not. I saw the way she looked at you. And she knows I saw it."

"There wasn't anything special in the way she looked at me or the way I looked at her or the way Hatcher looked at you or any combination thereof," Becker said.

Karen shook her head patronizingly. "John, you're a very sweet man in your special way, but you don't understand women at all."

"I was there, Karen. Nothing happened, nothing was said, nothing was intimated. I did nothing to lead her on, she did nothing to lead me on. I bent over backwards to treat her like another agent. I wouldn't have made a man sit in the car—"

"You really don't get it, do you?"

"There's nothing to get."

"You didn't take a shower because you have a fetish for cleanliness. You took a shower because you felt deeply soiled by your encounter with Swann, isn't that right?"

"Yes."

"And you let her see that about you. You showed her how vulnerable you are underneath the superagent exterior. Don't you realize how attractive that is, John? If you share your vulnerabilities with a woman, we read that as intimacy. To her, you had a very intimate moment together. Not because she was in the next room when you took a shower, but because you allowed her to know you needed it in the first place."

"It doesn't really work that way, does it?" Becker asked.

"It worked with me," she said. She took his hand and held it until they landed.

Chapter 21

Nahir Patel had reached the fourth chapter of *The Satanic Verses* when the battered Oldsmobile pulled into the station. Nahir didn't consider himself much of a Moslem. His mother had dragged him to Episcopal Sunday school until he was in his mid-teens and was able to mount an effective rebellion, and his father seemed to have no religion whatsoever beyond an abhorrence of pork sausage. As a family they attended a mosque—which required a trip to Memphis—only when relatives visited. Nahir himself had drifted into a vague belief in an essentially indifferent creator to whom one applied for relief in emergencies but otherwise ignored. With mild variations, he discovered, it was the basic American concept of the deity, based primarily on convenience, with no thought required. Best of all, it was a maintenance-free credo, plastic enough to cover a variety of permutations—he knew one girl who thought God was revealing herself through the animals—while demanding absolutely nothing of the believer. Islam, on the other hand, had some rigorous requirements, the hardest one being, for Patel, belief.

However, thoroughly non-Muslim though he was, Patel could not help feeling an illicit, not to say mildly dangerous thrill when reading the work of a man condemned to death for heresy by a large segment of Islam. It seemed akin to deliberately walking under a ladder or breaking a mirror just to prove one was not superstitious. Rationally, there was no danger, yet one did not take such unnecessary chances without the sense of tempting retribution.

A man seemingly larger than the car itself got out of the Oldsmobile and puzzled for a moment at the gas pump. Nahir watched him with half an eye, wondering briefly that there were some people in this day and age who still did not understand that one must pay before receiving the gasoline. The instructions were writ large, but somehow some people never managed to see them. The big man stuck the hose in his tank and squeezed and looked at the pump and squeezed some more.

Nahir returned to his book. He had been working the five-to-midnight shift for six months now and had seen all manner of dummies in that time. They all caught on eventually and came to visit him in his Plexiglas booth. He had a microphone at his disposal if he had wanted to help the customer, but he chose not to use it. He would be off duty shortly and he wanted to read a bit more. At home, he kept the book out of sight, not wanting to risk stirring up any atavistic orthodoxy in either parent. He thought they were enlightened—for parents—but there seemed no reason to press the point. He had time enough to read while on the job, after all.

The big man had finally noticed Nahir in the booth.

"I want gas," he said.

Duh, thought Nahir. No kidding. Although schooled in politeness at home, he found that the insulation of the booth led one towards a degree of insolence that only absolute security could nurture. No one could touch him in his little booth. The glass was even bulletproof. There seemed little need for civility when the worst that could happen as a result of rudeness was a dirty look and a nasty remark. What were they going to do, drive away without gas? A few did, but if any had ever reported him to the manager, he had never heard about it.

"You have to pay me first," Nahir said, making no effort to conceal his contempt.

The man seemed bewildered by the statement.

"I want gas," the man said, and then, as if clarifying things, he added, "For my car."

Nahir made a big display of seeing the car for the first time. "Oh, for your *car!* Why didn't you say so?"

The man nodded. "Gas for my car."

Nahir could not believe this moron.

"Pay first," he said. He turned back to his book. Let the goon figure it out, or not.

The man scowled at him. "I don't like that," he said.

Nahir sighed deeply and looked away from his book, letting the man know how tired he was of the whole conversation. He turned the microphone on so that his words were issued into the night.

"You don't like what? Paying? Sorry, chief, that's the way the system works. Pay now, gas later."

"I don't like the way you talk to me," the man said.

Nahir leaned his face right against the glass, grinning contemptuously.

"I'm not here to talk to you. I'm here to throw a switch that allows you to pump gas, *after* you pay for it. Got it? Too hard? You. Money. Give me. I. Gas. Give you."

"I could kill you," the man said.

Nahir smirked.

"Ooo," he said. "Oooo."

The man smashed his fist into the Plexiglas in front of Nahir's face. Nahir jerked back, startled, and the man struck the glass shield again and again, hitting it with the power of a club.

"Hey," Nahir cried. "Hey, calm down." He looked out into the night for help. The station was lighted in the unreal sodium light, but outside that oasis was a desert of blackness.

The man kicked the cage in the metal siding below the glass. Nahir heard the thuds as if he were on the inside of a drum. People had hit the glass before, but no one had ever attacked the metal. He did not know how strong it was; he *hoped* it was strong enough, they wouldn't have built it that way if it wasn't strong enough, would they?

The man was hurling his whole body at the shack now, slamming with his back and shoulders with his full weight behind the blows. The booth groaned and shuddered. Nahir thought he heard the whine of bolts giving way. He was being attacked by a hurricane of rage, and the storm had worked its way to the door of the booth. The door was held by a dead bolt, but that was secured only by screws. The door bucked and crashed as the man alternately yanked on the handle, then threw himself against it. Nahir could picture the screws popping and the giant catapulting into the booth.

"I'll give you gas," Nahir shouted. "Please stop! I'll give you gas. Fill it up, fill it up!"

It was not until Nahir remembered to use the microphone and his voice reverberated through the empty Chattanooga night that the man seemed to hear him.

"Free gas!" Nahir shouted, crying with fear now. "Free gas!"

The giant stopped and nodded once as if he found the notion reasonable, then returned to his car and turned on the nozzle. He watched the pump rather than Nahir.

With the giant looking away, Nahir dialed 911 and whispered frantically for help. The huge moron returned to the booth and Nahir quickly hung up.

"No charge, no charge," Nahir said, waving the man away.

"I want some money," the man said. His voice was perfectly calm, as if it were the most ordinary request.

"Yes, sir, how much would you like?"

Oh, no, I confused him, Nahir thought. The giant was actually considering sums.

"Why don't I give you all of it?" Nahir asked.

"Yes." The man nodded.

Nahir opened the cash drawer and took out half the money. It occurred to him that he could pocket the rest and report all of it as stolen. The giant was certainly too dumb to know the difference. Nahir was proud of himself for recovering his wits so quickly despite the incredible stress. He had turned a bad situation into something positive for himself.

He put the giant's share of the money into the revolving drawer and slid it out.

"That's all I have," Nahir said.

"That's okay. Thank you."

"No, I thank you." For a moment Nahir thought the comment was too much, that the moron might react again, but he walked to his car and started it up. "Y'all come back now, you hear?" Nahir said, doing his best cracker twang.

Nahir waggled his fingers in a parody of a wave, then froze as he realized the man had put the car in reverse and was driving backwards straight at the booth, and very fast.

Cooper thought he had to do something about the Oldsmobile. The rear end was badly smashed after driving over the snooty clerk at the gas station, and it sounded as if it was scraping against the tire. He could steal one from somebody else, but not this late at night, not unless he got real lucky and saw someone just getting into or out of a car. He had never learned how to steal a car without a key. Somebody had tried to explain it to him once, but Cooper found it confusing and far too much trouble when all you really had to do was take somebody's key away from him. He decided to wait until morning when lots of people were getting in and out of cars, then he would drive back to that Dairy Queen where he had seen that girl. She was a cute little girl with her hair all braided like that. She didn't look anything like Mayvis, but she smiled when she took his order and seemed real helpful. He wondered if he couldn't get her to help him the way Mayvis did and then maybe she'd do some of the other things Mayvis did for him. He had already found a good place in the woods where he could take her.

Chapter 22

The Reverend Tommy was more agitated than usual when he finally returned to the trailer after the show and the increasingly extended meeting with fans and converts that succeeded the revival meeting itself. He should never have let Aural do any actual healing. Now that she helped him out by laying on hands, the people could not get enough of her.

"Did you see her tonight?" Rae did not need to be told that he was referring to Aural.

"During the show? Of course."

"No, not during the show. Afterwards—did you see her afterwards?"

"No, darling, I hurried back here to get ready for you." Rae was wearing a new magenta teddy and she touched it with both hands, hoping for a reaction. She didn't think the color was the best for her complexion, but Aural had helped her to find one that was cut long enough to hide the thickest part of her thighs and it was available only in magenta.

"Well, you won't believe what she's up to now," he said, paying no notice to her lingerie.

"What is it?" Rae asked cautiously. Tommy expected Rae to share his outrage over Aural's ever-rising stature, but Rae not only liked Aural, she was becoming increasingly indebted to her for her tips on how to make Tommy her sex slave. His bondage was a long way from complete, but Rae felt she was making progress. He hadn't noticed the teddy yet, but he might later when he took if off her.

"She was standing on a *box*," Tommy said. "Can you believe that? A goddamned *box*."

"She was standing on a box?"

"Don't you get it? The box makes her taller, taller than anybody. There she is, her head above everyone's, her goddamned little face shining like she's an angel. She does enough of that *on*stage. The last thing I need is for her to be carrying a box around so everyone can gawk at her offstage, too."

"You think it was her box?"

"Of course it was *her* box, Rae. You normally see any boxes outside the tent after a show? Boxes don't just grow out of the ground, they don't just materialize. She put it there, she planted the damned thing so she'd be taller than me."

"Maybe someone brought it for her? One of her fans?"

"None of *my* fans come equipped with boxes, do they, Rae? That just isn't the kind of thing people bring with them to a show. We're not crating oranges here, you know. How come you take her side, how come you're always defending her?"

"I'm not defending her, Tommy. She certainly shouldn't have brought a box, that's for sure."

"You're on her side, ain't you?"

" 'Course not . . .' "

"Why not? Everybody's on the side of the angel—hah-hah, some pun. You might's well team up with her, too."

"I'm on your side, darling." Rae fumbled with his belt with one hand while rubbing him with the other.

"For Christ's sake, lay off, Rae. Can't you see I'm upset here? I'm too mad to fuck."

"I'm just trying to comfort you, Tommy."

Rae continued to work on his belt. Aural had told her of the value of discreet insistence. Any healthy man, according to Aural, could be diverted from just about anything else in life by his erect organ if a woman went about it in the right way.

"Well, I've got a little surprise coming for our sweet angel-face," Tommy said. He allowed Rae to pull his pants to his ankles, scarcely noticing. "She's going to have a visitor pretty soon."

"Who's that, honey?"

"Let's just say he ain't her biggest fan," Tommy said, laughing. "You might call him her *anti*-fan."

Rae slipped her hand down the back of the Reverend Tommy's shorts with a conviction taught to her by Aural. It was not a move she would ever have thought of making on her own. She wiggled her finger a few times, then thrust. That got Tommy's attention.

"Whoa!" he said, but he didn't mean stop. As it turned out, Tommy wasn't too mad to fuck after all.

*   *   *

The next morning, after the Reverend had gone out and she and
Aural were sharing coffee in her trailer, Rae told her what Tommy had
said about her *anti*-fan. Aural had shrugged.

"What is that suppose to mean?"

"He said it like it was the anti-Christ or something," Rae explained.

"He's siccing the devil on me, is that it? The man's been preaching
too long—he's beginning to believe it himself."

"It didn't sound good, Aural," Rae said. "He laughed when he said
it, but he wasn't joking. I think he's up to something. You best be careful."

"My *anti*-fan? Sugar, I don't know what that means, but unless it's
got a couple of heads, I'm not too worried." Aural patted her boot, and
when Rae wrinkled her brow in puzzlement, Aural showed her the knife
for the first time. She pulled it loose from the Velcro strip and held it in
her palm.

"Honey, what is that *for?*" Rae asked, shocked.

"Whatever is necessary," Aural said. "You can imagine."

"Well, no, I can't."

"What world have you been living in?" Aural demanded. "You
mean to say you don't carry anything to defend yourself with?"

"Defend myself from what?"

"Well, the Reverend Tommy, for starters."

"Honey, the Reverend and I are getting on real well, thanks to you."

"Sure—now. That don't never last. What do you expect to do if he
takes it into his mind to beat on you?"

Rae paused, considering her loyalties in the matter. It was not a fierce
struggle. "He has done that from time to time. But only when he was
upset."

"Figures. And what did you do about it?"

"What was I supposed to do?"

"There's lots of options. What did you do, Rae?"

"Nothing."

"Nothing? Just let him beat on you?"

"I asked him to stop."

"Rae, in my opinion doing nothing is not an option." She held up the
knife. *"This* is an option."

"I couldn't."

"He don't have to know that. Make him wonder. You never know, it
might just add a little spice."

"He's so much stronger . . ."

"He's got to sleep sometimes, don't he? Just remind him about the lady who cut her husband's dick off and threw it in the vacant lot."

"She *didn't*."

"Bless her heart, she did. It was all over the papers and teevee. You didn't see that? It just naturally perked up every woman I know. I tell you what, the good Reverend has heard about it even if you ain't. You can just bet them old boys is whispering to each other all across the country, 'Guard your pecker at night—and for God's sake don't get 'em mad!' "

Rae tittered. "Aural, you sure do have your very own outlook on life."

"I know men," Aural said. She returned the knife to her boot and closed the Velcro strap over it. "Bring on this anti-fan. If he has balls, I know how to deal with him."

Chapter 23

Cooper awoke to barking. A savage-looking dog, part Doberman, part mutt, stood just outside the car door, feet planted solidly as if to give full purchase for barks, as if the sheer volume of its noise would send it scooting across the ground like a loose cannon if it didn't brace itself. The dog retreated a step when Cooper's head appeared in the window, then held its ground once more and unleashed a fresh volley of yaps.

It took Cooper a moment to realize where he was and what was going on. Last night he had parked the car in the lot behind the Dairy Queen so he would be there as soon as the girl showed up. The dog had found him and taken offense at his presence—they always did. Cooper didn't trust animals and they returned the sentiment, dogs in particular. They howled at him as if he were an invading wolf come for the sheep in their care, following him on the street, snarling and barking, sometimes lunging at his leg. Cooper had seen other people calm strange dogs with a word, watched with amazement as they knelt before the snapping beasts and offered a hand to smell and then petted them as easily as if the preceding frenzy of aversion had just been a charade. Cooper could not believe it, it was as if they had something magic to say to the dogs that Cooper could never hear. People had told him that dogs could hear things that humans couldn't, and he wondered if some people knew how to speak in that language. Whatever the trick, Cooper didn't know it and the dogs knew he didn't know it. He would yell at them to leave him alone if they got too close, and when that didn't work, he would kick at them. Sometimes, when the dogs were large and unusually insistent, he would run from them, but that never worked as it seemed to make them all the more furious at him.

Cooper was hungry and he wanted some breakfast but he was afraid to get out of the car as long as the dog was there. He lay back down on the seat, hiding, but the animal continued to bark and bark. It took a long time for Cooper to realize he could just drive away.

*   *   *

In the late afternoon Cooper returned to the Dairy Queen and parked in the same spot where he had spent the night. The dog started barking as soon as he got out of the car, but this time the sound was distant and Cooper realized the dog was fenced-in now in some neighboring yard.

The girl was working behind the counter, and Cooper waited until she was finished with her customer, standing by the video games and pretending to play. Two animated characters on the screen were kicking and punching each other and although they fell down, neither seemed to get hurt. That did not accord with Cooper's experience of violence. When he hit someone they got hurt, they didn't bounce up again. They stayed down and begged him to stop and sometimes they cried. The characters in the video game wore bandanas on their heads the way a lot of brothers did in Springville, but the characters weren't brothers. Cooper couldn't figure out what they were supposed to be.

When the girl was free, Cooper stepped up to the counter.

She smiled at him, a real friendly smile, showing her gums.

"Can I help you?" she asked.

"I need help," Cooper said. He knew she was just asking about his order, but he hoped she could help him anyway.

"Yes, sir?"

He stood there for a moment, not certain what it was he wanted to say to her.

"I have a car," he said at last.

She blinked but she didn't stop smiling.

"Can I take your order, sir?"

"I want you to come in my car," Cooper said.

"Pardon me?"

"Come in my car."

The girl looked at him curiously, tilting her head to one side like a bird. "Sir, I'm working. Did you want to place an order?"

Cooper did not know how to explain what he needed. He knew he was doing it wrong, but he couldn't think of a better way.

"I want to show you something," he said. "In the car."

The girl turned around, looking for someone. "Dwayne? Could you come out here. This gentleman needs some help."

Cooper shook his head. Now she had it all wrong. He didn't need anything from anyone named Dwayne. He needed help from her. He needed *her*.

"Just come on," he said. He reached over the counter and took hold of her arm and when she started to protest he grabbed her other arm and lifted her over the counter.

"Dwayne! Help!"

Dwayne came running from the kitchen, took one look at the size of the man who had hold of Sybil, and stopped in his tracks. He let them go out the door before he called for the police.

But the police were already there. A cop stood next to Mayvis's Oldsmobile, peering inside. He straightened up when he saw Cooper advancing towards him, half carrying and half dragging a girl.

"Is this your car, sir?" the cop asked, trying to figure out just what was going on between the man and the girl. He was always reluctant to involve himself in domestic disputes, but this one seemed awfully one-sided.

The man kept coming straight at him, not slowing down at all, holding the girl with just one arm now.

"You can't drive around with your rear end like that," the cop said, knowing even as he said it that he was too late to help himself.

Cooper grabbed the cop's neck and pushed his head into the side of the car. He did it twice more until the cop went limp and then he kicked him once for good measure as he fell.

The girl was kneeling over the fallen policeman, making wailing noises and Cooper got into the car and was about to leave when he remembered why he was there in the first place. He grabbed the girl and yanked her into the car and drove off.

Pegeen made the call hoping Deputy Crist would be away from her desk, too busy to talk, out of communication, anything but *there* so that Pegeen would not have to speak to her directly. If she wasn't around, Pegeen could fax the information and be done with it. She remembered the baleful stare which Karen had given her at their last encounter and had no illusions that the other woman would have forgotten who she was. She was the nitwit who had sat around in the motel bedroom while the Deputy Director's man took an unscheduled, spontaneous, and poorly explained shower in the other room. No one believed in the innocence of the occasion and Pegeen didn't blame them, but the men who knew of it were assuming the guilt was Becker's. Karen Crist, however, blamed Pegeen, and she did so because *she* saw the guilt in Pegeen's face. You couldn't hide that from another woman, although men, God knows, were as clueless as stumps about such things. It's not that I actually *did* anything, Pegeen thought defensively, it's not that anything actually *happened*. I didn't even towel him off. He came out of the bathroom fully dressed and we left. But of course the facts were beside the point in Karen Crist's mind—it was what Pegeen *felt* about John Becker that mattered, and Pegeen knew that. And agreed. She was just as guilty in her own mind as she was in Crist's. The difference was that in her own mind being guilty didn't make her bad.

To her dismay, the Bureau in New York put her call straight through.

"Director Crist, this is Special Agent Pegeen Haddad from the Nashville office."

"Yes."

She remembers me all right, Pegeen thought. Thank God it's not a television phone. "There's been a development in the Darnell Cooper case, and we have instructions to keep you posted personally . . ."

"Yes."

Like talking point-blank to a glacier. All that came back was a blast of cold air.

"We have a report of a stolen car. The suspect was working at a fast-food restaurant under the name of Darnell Cooper. He was also wanted for questioning about a purse snatching that took place on the highway three days earlier. He's also suspected of being involved in a robbery and assault with a motor vehicle at a service station."

"Yes?"

"He is also believed to have been involved in an assault on a police officer and the abduction of a young woman just outside of Chattanooga."

"Not exactly covering his tracks. Where is he now?"

"Local and state police are in pursuit, but he has eluded them so far." Pegeen could not remember ever saying "eluded" aloud before. Get any stiffer and you'll be catatonic, kid.

"Kidnapping is a federal offense," Pegeen said, having trouble believing that she was hearing herself correctly. "It falls under our jurisdiction."

She probably didn't know that, Pegeen, you halfwit. Good of you to enlighten her, she'll appreciate it.

"I see," Karen said.

"So we're entering the case directly," Pegeen continued. She could feel the waves of hostility pouring through the phone and straight into her ear.

"Good. Was there anything else?"

"Well . . ." How about if I drive a spike through my head, will that make you happy? Pegeen thought. "No."

Pegeen felt that she should say something more, but she didn't know what it should be. It didn't seem that an agent in her position should be the one to terminate a conversation with an assistant deputy director, however. Surely that prerogative belonged to the the senior agent. Karen did not oblige her, however, and the silence between them grew and expanded uncomfortably and the longer it stretched the more it seemed to fill with the unspoken. Becker. Pegeen had sat silently with a mute telephone to her ear before, but only with boys, only with romantic interests when the silence had been filled with unspeakable longing, never with another woman. An FBI agent, her superior, a tough-assed careerist federal officer. It gave her the creeps.

Pegeen cleared her throat discreetly.

"One thing," Karen said.

"Yes?"

"Watch your ass."

The phone line went dead and Pegeen replaced the receiver as if it were something unclean. *Watch my ass?* Meaning, be careful in your pursuit of Cooper? Or meaning, stay away from my man or I'll feed your giblets to the cats? Was this the way an assistant deputy director normally spoke to other agents? *Watch my ass?* I won't have to, Pegeen thought. She'll be watching it for me.

It was only later, as she replayed the conversation in her mind for the hundredth time while driving towards Chattanooga, that her own thought about driving a spike through her head reminded her of Becker's comment about how to kill a werewolf. Why had he referred to himself like that? Did he really think of himself that way? Why did he perceive himself as a bad man when Pegeen could see so clearly that he wasn't? The man needed help and understanding, and it was obvious he wasn't going to get it from Crist, the frost queen. Some men were salvageable and some were not. She had pretty well come to the conclusion that Eddie, the man she was seeing—sort of—fell into the category of irretrievable junk goods. After six months he had proved to be as receptive to improvements as a shack made of wet cardboard. There was simply very little adjusting the structure could handle. Also, Eddie had broken up with her twice already. She wasn't entirely certain that they weren't broken up right at the moment. With

Eddie, as nonattentive as he was at the best of times, it was hard to tell.

It might be time to give up on Eddie, she thought. There were times when a girl wanted to feel that she was free to explore other opportunities. Karen Crist couldn't hate her that much without *some* good reason.

The girl was worse than useless to him. Every time he took his hand from her mouth she started crying again, and the crying soon built into wailing, no matter how many times he told her to shut up. When Cooper asked her to help him, all she did was wail some more, so he hit her because he didn't know what else to do. He hurt his knuckle on her head, hurt it badly and he had to drive with that hand pressed against his lips while she continued to cry, moaning now along with it. It was driving him crazy.

She made so much noise that he didn't hear the police sirens as soon as he usually would have and he almost didn't make the turn into the woods in time. The police went speeding past the access road, and Cooper drove as far as he could on the rutted path until it seemed to stop of its own accord at the base of a hill where two small streams joined together. Cooper could hear the sirens ululating in the distance as the cop car bounced on the narrow path. He grabbed the girl with his left hand because one knuckle on his right was now hugely swollen and very painful. She clung to the steering wheel, howling, and Cooper was forced to squeeze her throat until she let go. She was still after that and he tossed her over his shoulder and started up the hill. Her silence was such a relief.

The hill was steep and Cooper's knuckle throbbed painfully with every step. Running down the other side was even worse, as each step jolted his legs and ran straight through his arm. The terrain changed on the far side of the hill and the clay soil of the woods gave way to a sandy loam that grew wetter with each step. He had gone only a few hundred yards before his shoes sank up to his ankles in muck, and each stride was accompanied by a loud sucking sound.

Cooper was well into the swamp before he realized that he could no longer hear the sirens behind him. He paused, listening to hear if he was being pursued, but it took him several moments before he could hear anything over his strained breathing. After a time he could discern voices, several people, yelling at each other, but they were too far away for him to make out what they were saying.

He continued, using the voices as a guide, heading away from them.

Otherwise there was nothing to serve as a landmark, no way to tell where to go, just funny-looking trees and weird grass that looked solid but wasn't. Sometimes his legs sunk as deep as his calves and sometimes they barely dipped below the surface at all and there was no way to tell which it would be ahead of time. He sucked on his knuckle as he trudged ahead, trying to remember what someone had told him once about telling direction by the sun. He could find the sun all right, but he didn't understand what it was supposed to be telling him. He decided the best thing would be to just head straight for it. He changed his course, veering towards the sun, and noticed that he was walking straight into the shadows. They were drawn as straight as lines, like arrows showing him the way. Cooper realized he had discovered the secret. He would simply follow the shadows and the sun would take him away from his pursuers and towards safety.

His shoes had been sucked off by the mud long since and when he lifted his knuckle to his mouth he noticed that his entire right hand was blown up to twice its size. It hurt anywhere he touched it and it even pained him when he waved it in the air to aid his balance. He stumbled crossing a small pond and fell to one knee and the girl's body slid off his shoulder and into the water. Cooper was surprised to see her; he had forgotten about her, forgotten the added weight on his back. He studied her for a moment, trying to remember why he had brought her with him. He had wanted her to help him, but he couldn't see how she could help him now.

She wasn't so pretty now with her face and hair wet and muddy and the big, darkening bruise on the side of her forehead. One eye was swollen shut with a lump that reminded Cooper of his own hand. She was the reason he hurt himself, he realized with sudden anger. It was her fault that he couldn't use his hand. It was her fault that the police were chasing him. He ought to kill her, he ought to yank her head right off. He ought to push her under the water and leave her there, stick her head right down into the mud with her feet in the air like a fence post.

He reached for her throat with both hands before he realized what he was doing, and the pain in his right hand was so great that he dropped to his knees again. He cradled his bad hand across his chest and rocked back and forth, moaning. In the distance, but closer than before, he heard the voices calling to each other. Cooper lurched to his feet and marched in the direction the shadows showed him.

The shadows had grown very long when Cooper slumped down at the base of a tree. He was exhausted from fighting against the muck all day and very hungry. He tried to remember the last time he had eaten and he couldn't. The swelling from his hand had increased and the skin looked so tight he was afraid it would just pop open all by itself. Any motion of his arm burned like fire now and he had to walk with his left hand clamping his right arm against his body as if he were holding himself together. As a result, his balance was bad and he fell often. He was covered with mud and his body itched from head to toe.

He was miserable now, but he hadn't been happy since he left prison. He missed his punk, who took care of him whenever he hurt himself or didn't feel well. The punk was as good as a nurse, fluttering around and feeling Cooper's forehead for a fever and giving him rubdowns and making sure he was warm enough, and then telling him stories and talking to him for hours, which was something no nurse would ever do. He never had to worry about his meals in prison, either. He knew when they were and they were always there when they were supposed to be. The servers always made sure that Old Coop got an extra-large helping, too. Everybody took care of him in prison, in one way or another, and everybody knew him. He hated it on the outside, Cooper realized. It wasn't home, it wasn't anything like home. The only good thing he could remember since he got out was the time in the car with the girl but then she even went and spoiled that the second time by acting like she didn't know what to do. The punk always knew what he was supposed to do, and he always did it right or else Cooper kicked his ass. People on the outside never seemed to do anything right, whether he kicked their ass or not.

He thought again of the punk. Swann, that was his name. The punk would be pleased that Cooper remembered. If they sent him back to Springville, he would want to have the punk in his cell again. Those things could be arranged. Cooper knew how to do it. If someone else was living with Swann, Cooper would kick his ass until he gave the punk back to Cooper. The punk belonged with Cooper. He would be happy to see Cooper again, there was no doubt about that, and they would have a lot to tell each other after Cooper's visit to the outside.

He couldn't walk any faster than he was going, but no matter how fast he went, the voices seemed to get closer. He thought he could see higher ground in the distance. Maybe that meant he would get out of this swamp and onto dry ground again. Then he could steal a car and get away from them that way. He didn't understand how they could all walk so much faster than he could, but he didn't think they could drive any faster.

As he got closer he could see that it really was a hill and it looked as dry as he could ever hope for. Cooper drove himself even faster until each breath rasped and tore at his lungs. Just at the base of the hill he tripped, his feet unaccustomed to solid ground. Instinctively he threw his arms out to stop his fall and the impact on his bad hand was so painful he could not keep from screaming. He felt bone grate against bone in his knuckle and heard it, too. It was the sound of it that made him pass out.

When he came to, he heard voices closing in on him, then heard one of them, a woman's voice, calling to the others. Her voice was very close, so close he could reach out and touch her. Cooper kept his eyes squeezed shut, thinking maybe he wouldn't be seen if he just lay where he was.

"Don't move, you sack of shit," the woman's voice said. She sounded really pissed off and scared, too. "I'll blow you fucking away if you move, Cooper."

He was so surprised to hear his name that he opened his eyes. A young woman with funny red hair was standing over him, pointing a gun at him with both hands. She wore a jacket that said FBI in big letters. A radio on her belt crackled and an anxious voice said, "Just hold him there, Haddad. Don't try anything else, just keep him in place."

"I want Swann," Cooper said. He started to shift his weight so he could sit up and he realized that the woman had put handcuffs around his ankles.

The woman kicked his bad hand with her toe and he screamed again and slumped backwards.

"Don't fuck with me," said Pegeen. "Where's the girl?"

Cooper didn't know what she meant so he said nothing.

She nudged his hand again and he yelped like a dog.

"I asked you where's the girl. Unless you want me to do a dance on that paw of yours, tell me where she is."

She didn't look mean, Cooper thought. She looked like a kid trying to pretend she was bigger than she was, but she sure acted mean.

"I'm going to count to three," Pegeen said, "then I'm going to stand on your hand. You understand me, Cooper?"

"Yes," said Cooper.

"Where's the girl?"

"What girl?"

"Sybil Benish. The kid you took into the swamp with you, asshole."

"She left me," Cooper said.

"What did you do to her? Did you hurt her? . . . Answer me! Did you hurt her?"

Cooper stared at Pegeen, uncomprehending. Had he hurt the girl? He didn't think so; he didn't remember hurting her. *He* was the one who was hurt.

"One."

"If I tell you, can I live with Swann?"

"Two."

She lifted one foot and held it over his bad hand. Cooper tried to move it away, but it was like a deadweight at the end of his limb and the entire arm seemed to have stopped working. He put his good hand in the air over the injured one to shield it.

"Where is she?"

"She fell off, I left her back there where I was," Cooper said.

"Three," she said.

"I *told* you," Cooper pleaded, but she stamped her foot onto his hand anyway.

When Cooper came to again there was a swarm of men in FBI jackets running over the hill towards him. The girl still hovered over him, looking enraged and ready to hurt him some more.

As the men converged around him, Cooper was crying, "Get her away from me," and trying to climb up the slope on his ass.

Chapter 24

Hatcher met Quincy Beggs at the Congressman's home, where the politician was hosting an informal dinner for twelve would-be campaign contributors. Ten florid-faced men and two highly lacquered women greeted Hatcher courteously, all professing delight at meeting such a highly placed FBI agent, and with few exceptions feigning an interest they did not have. Hatcher's arrival was unannounced—indeed his invitation to such an event would have been inappropriate both socially and ethically—and after the social amenities had been observed, Beggs wasted no time in escorting Hatcher to his study.

"I would have waited until business hours," Hatcher said, "but I felt you would appreciate hearing right away."

He could in fact have simply told Beggs his news on the telephone, but Hatcher knew the importance of the personal appearance at the right time. Good news delivered over the telephone seems to come from out of the blue. Good news delivered in person comes from the messenger. Hatcher would be there to share in the triumph, Hatcher would be there to modestly deny the credit, Hatcher would be recognized as the source of the blessing, not the telephone, not the impersonal machinery of the Bureau.

"I'm sure you did the right thing," said Beggs. "Just a few of my constituents. Do them good to see that I actually work for a living." Beggs laughed. Hatcher managed a limp smile.

Beggs stuck a cigar the length of a pencil into his mouth and waggled it back and forth with his tongue. He no longer smoked them, but still used them as theatrical props. The Congressman felt they gave him a manly appearance.

"So? What's up?"

Hatcher gestured to a chair. "May I?"

"Good heavens, 'course, man, sit, sit. Don't know where I put my manners."

Hatcher carefully sat and arranged one leg over the other, tending to the crease in his trousers. There was an art to delivering good news, and it took a bit of time and preparation. Just as one did not do it over the telephone, so one did not blurt it out and have done with it. If one was seated, one became a part of the event. The auditors could not dismiss a seated man with a quick handshake and a pat on the back the way they might get rid of a standing courier before rushing off to celebrate with those they cared about. Courtesy demanded that someone seated be treated with deliberation and attention. A standing man was a messenger. A seated man was an equal.

Beggs rolled the cigar impatiently. He didn't like Hatcher, he didn't know anyone who did, but this was Washington and personal tastes were *always* subordinate to other considerations. The quid pro quo was observed, no matter how little personal regard was involved in the transaction, compromise being the currency without which the political process would be bankrupt. No matter how clumsy a performer Hatcher might be, nor how transparent his motives, it had to be granted that he danced the proper steps, honored the rituals, played the game according to the universally recognized rules. Advancement was a matter of accruing favors owed and then cashing them in, and grace and subtlety were ultimately nothing more than frills. What mattered was whether or not you could deliver the goods, and an outright enemy with his arms full of gifts was more welcome than an empty-handed friend. Not that Hatcher was Beggs' enemy, of course. Beggs didn't care that much about him.

"You will recall that we had a conversation some while ago concerning a possible lead in a case that touched you personally?" Hatcher began.

"I do indeed."

"And I undertook to make that investigation a matter for my personal—ah—consideration."

"Which I did appreciate, let me tell you."

"Only too happy to help where I can," said Hatcher.

What a toady, thought Beggs. Obsequious and smug at the same time. He'll go far.

Hatcher continued. "Naturally I couldn't neglect my other duties, but whenever possible I made the case my own. I flew to Nashville to personally debrief the agents, for instance."

"Certainly appreciate your efforts," said Beggs.

"One likes to think one played a part, but of course all credit goes to the Bureau itself. Many dedicated men and women, each doing their bit.''

You made your point—I owe you! Beggs wanted to thunder. *Get the hell on with it.* Instead, he removed the cigar from his mouth and studied the end of it as if it were actually lighted.

''Fantastic organization,'' said Beggs.

''Those of us who are entrusted with the responsibility strive very hard to keep it that way,'' said Hatcher. He, too, studied Beggs' cigar as if to discern the mystery of the nonexistent ash.

''We all owe you a debt of gratitude,'' said Beggs. ''And I, for one, am a man who honors my debts.'' *There, it's said aloud, let's get on with it.*

Hatcher managed a watery smile, casting his eyes to the floor, too modest to speak. Momentarily.

Beggs cleared his throat before replacing the cigar in his mouth, signaling that the preliminaries were over.

''I'm happy to be able to report some good news,'' Hatcher responded on cue. ''Excellent news, most excellent.''

''What?'' Beggs said curtly. The man was more long-winded than an Alabama senator.

''We have apprehended the man who abducted your niece.''

''Good God! You've caught him?''

''Yes, sir.''

''After all these years, you've actually caught him?''

''Yes, sir, I'm happy to be able to say that we have him in custody.''

''Christ, that's wonderful! Do you know how many votes that's worth?''

''I knew you would be gratified.''

''Gratified, shit. I'm as good as reelected, man! Can I announce this? I mean, is it all wrapped up?''

''I thought perhaps a joint announcement. You and I together . . .''

''Of course, of course—but I mean, is it a done deal? You actually have him in custody and you can *keep* him? We're not going to have some civil libertarian lawyer getting him out on a technicality?''

''Naturally he has to be tried in a court of law . . .''

''I'm not going to wait three years for a goddamned verdict and have him get off on insanity or some such shit. Hatcher, I'm asking you, is this wrapped up? Can I go public? We . . . *can we go public?*''

''Yes, sir,'' said Hatcher. ''Not only do we have the perpetrator in custody, the man has confessed.''

"Beautiful," said Beggs.

"Did you wish to contact the girl's parents, or shall we?"

"The girl's parents?"

"The parents of the deceased," said Hatcher. "Your niece."

The dead girl had been the daughter of Beggs' wife's brother, an unemployed mine worker who had deserted the girl and her mother when the girl was six years old. Beggs had played up his relationship at the time of her disappearance because it gave him a vehicle of public sympathy and outrage that he rode all the way to elective office. He had not heard from the girl's mother in years. His wife's brother continued to apply for handouts on a regular basis.

"You do that," Beggs said. "You deserve the credit."

Hatcher launched into another round of modest demurral, but neither man paid much attention to it. Both of them were looking forward to the press conference, and beyond.

Chapter 25

Becker had prepared a cassoulet, a French casserole dish that called for beans, tomatoes, onions, celery, wine, salt pork, duck drippings, lean pork, lamb, garlic or Polish sausage, and either roast duck or canned, preserved goose. Improvising to meet the nature of his larder, Becker omitted the salt pork, duck drippings, pork, lamb and duck or goose and substituted hot Italian sausage. He then doubled up on the beans and threw in a package of spinach because it seemed a thing to do. Having brewed the mess for a couple of hours, he sampled it as Jack entered the kitchen.

"Soccer cleats outside the door, for the hundred thousandth time," Becker said, pulling the wooden spoon gingerly towards him, blowing away the steam.

"Sorry, I forgot," said Jack. The boy sat and removed his soccer shoes and left them directly in the middle of the kitchen door. It was a talent that Becker had noted before. School bags, shoes, clothing—all sloughed off Jack's body when he entered the house as freely as if it were so much dried skin, but somehow the pattern was not random. Things did not just lie where they fell. With an inevitability that promised design, every item ended up where it would be most surely in the way. Shoes were never in the corner, the school bag never behind a chair. Everything was placed, or tossed, or shrugged off, squarely in the middle of the busiest pathway. Doorways seemed to be a favorite, but the hallways got their share of detritus, too. When Jack was home, it was impossible to walk a straight route to anywhere else in the house.

Becker decided the beans were passable if one were just tasting, better if the consumer was hungry. He hoped that Karen was ravenous.

"What's for dinner? I'm starving," Jack announced.

"Jack, old pal, you're in luck. I've got just the meal for you."

"What is it?" Jack asked suspiciously.

"Ask not what it is. Ask what it is not." Becker made a great show of inhaling the aromas from the pot. He knew that the best he could do was lure Jack into one exploratory taste. If the boy didn't like it at first blush, no amount of cajoling or threatening would make him eat more. Becker cooked for himself and Karen. Jack appeared to live on plain spaghetti and peanut butter sandwiches, yet had the energy of ten men and was growing like a patch of kudzu.

"What it is not?"

"The recipe called for duck droppings," Becker said.

"Gah!"

"Well, it's French."

"Gross."

"The problem was, I couldn't find any duck droppings. You don't feel like running over to Scribner's park and getting some, do you?"

"That's disgusting . . . Where's Scribner's park?"

"That's the official name of the town pond where you swim all summer."

Becker and Jack opened their mouths and eyes cartoon wide, stared at each other for a second, then screamed. It was a well-practiced routine that drove Karen crazy but pleased the two of them.

"So I had to be creative," Becker continued. "Since I didn't have any duck droppings, I paid a visit to Emily." Emily was Jack's rabbit. "Bunny droppings make a pretty good substitute. Want to try some, Jack?"

Becker advanced on the boy with the spoon.

Karen entered her house with Gold to find Becker and her son screaming at each other.

"They do that," she explained to Gold.

"A lot?"

"Too much," she said. To Becker she said, "Look what I brought you."

"Ah," said Becker. Karen thought he was suddenly holding the spoon as if it were a weapon.

"Jack, say hello to Dr. Gold," she said and Jack dutifully held out his hand to be shaken and muttered "hello."

The boy waited uncomfortably as Gold made a fuss over him, his size, his age, his grand appearance, then, when the adults had turned their attentions from him, he slipped away.

"You're looking well, John," Gold said.

Becker regarded Karen questioningly.

''I just brought him,'' Karen said. ''I have no comment, no further part in this. I'll leave you two to it,'' Karen said, easing out the door.

''Oh, no,'' Becker said. ''You brought him, you deal with him.''

''I can't,'' Karen said. ''If you don't want to talk to him, fine, but you'll have to drive him to the train station yourself. I'm tired.''

''I can't really talk in front of Karen,'' Gold said.

''Why not? She's with the Bureau, she's got a higher clearance for any classified than I do—if I have any clearance left at all. I don't have any secrets from her.''

''No, but I do,'' Gold said.

Bowing elaborately, Karen withdrew.

''I think it's best that Karen not be involved in this conversation at this point,'' Gold said. ''It's best for her, that is.''

''Are you trying to seduce me with mysteries, Gold? I've got beans to cook.''

''I like beans.''

''Why didn't you just call me if you wanted some *advice?*''

''Because there's some material I want you to look at . . . And it's not a conversation I want anyone to overhear. For that matter, I don't want any mail going back and forth between us that someone might log in. This is just a social visit as far as anyone else is concerned. Including Karen. I just asked her for a ride.''

''But we're not exactly social friends, are we?''

''Would you prefer it as a doctor-patient visit?''

''You make house calls now?''

''Under certain circumstances.''

''Why didn't you just get in your car and drive out here yourself, why bring Karen into it at all?''

''One, I don't have a car. I live in New York—who needs a car?''

''Try again.''

''I was hoping that if I came in under Karen's auspices you'd at least give me a hearing.''

''Well, there you go, finally. Confession is good for the soul, right, Doc?''

''I'm sneaking around like this because Hatcher would have my ass if he knew about it. If he knew what I was about to do, he would probably consider it highly disloyal.''

''I realize I'm being suckered—but I'm all ears,'' said Becker. ''Anyone disloyal to Hatcher has earned my attention.''

"I know that," Gold said, "but I didn't just say it for effect."

Gold placed a pocket tape recorder on the table and positioned two minicassettes beside it.

"You know they caught this man Cooper, the cellmate of the prisoner who wrote to you and warned you about him."

"Yeah."

"The Behavioral Sciences people are having a field day with him. He's told them about killings that go back years. We're going to have local cops cleaning up their records all over the place. The Bureau's national crime statistics are going to go down. I mean, this person is a one-man crime wave. He's stuffed bodies in culverts and tossed them out of moving cars and left them for dead right and left, mostly marginal types, migrant workers, drifters, the kind of people who wind up dead in the parking lot of some roadside tavern in Tennessee and are never investigated very heavily."

"So you've got him—what's the problem?"

"As far as the Behavioral people are concerned, no problem at all. They're delighted to talk to him and to adjust their profile of serial killers. And of course Director Hatcher has been able to deliver the guy who kidnapped and killed the niece of Congressman Beggs. Cooper has become a sort of Golden Boy amongst villains."

"As long as Hatcher is pleased."

"Everybody is pleased. Cooper is talking like a guest on 'Oprah.' He can't say enough bad things about himself. He's a little vague on the details, sometimes, but he's sure as hell willing. Prompt him a bit and he can remember most of it, at least enough to fry himself several dozen times over."

"You've been in on the questioning?"

"John, *everybody's* been in on the questioning. This is the prize bull, they're walking him around the ring for everyone to have a look. I mean, there's a cachet involved in being in on it; if you get a chance to watch it, you take it. Cooper's like tickets to the Super Bowl. You can't pass them up even if you don't like football. I was invited to watch an interrogation session. Somebody thought it would improve my understanding, I guess, give me more insight into what our agents have to deal with, something like that. I was just pleased someone thought I was important enough to invite."

"He confessed to the two girls in the coal mine?"

"Absolutely. Told us where he snatched them and when and how he tortured them with cigarettes and matches until they finally died. That was a revelation in itself. They only found skeletal remains of the girls and no indication of how they died. They found a number of cigarettes and candle wax on the site but assumed they were being used just so the girls, or someone, could see. He had a lot of details like that, stuff that only the killer would have known.''

''So Hatcher has an easy conviction, gets national headlines—and you know that somehow they'll be *his* headlines—and gets in tight with the head of the Oversight Committee, all at the same time. Gosh, I'm glad you paid me this visit, Gold. Just what I need to hear.''

''John, I'm not on the law enforcement side of things, you know that. I spend my time trying to help you agents adjust to what you have to deal with. Once in a while I make a contribution to a psychological profile of some unknown perp. You tell me I'm usually wrong with those.''

''Only in the important details.''

''Thank you. So I'm no expert on the criminal mind, granted. But I'm not an idiot, either. I know a deeply violent, dangerous man when I see one, and Cooper is a deeply violent, dangerous man. A very stupid man, too. Plus he's got a system of values that he picked up from being in and out of penal institutions from the age of fifteen on. He makes my blood run cold. He uses his strength—and the guy's as big as a gorilla—to get his way. He's got a frustration level of practically zero, cross him and he'll throw you through a window because he can't figure out a better way. Of all the guys I've heard about in the years I've been in the Bureau, this one is at the head of my list of people I wouldn't want to be stuck in a blind alley with. His violence quotient is enormous. He even *dreams* about pulling people's heads off. I mean literally pulling their heads off their shoulders.''

Becker sat quietly, listening attentively while keeping his eyes on the tape recorder. He knew that Gold had not yet come to the point. He also knew that when he did, Becker was not going to like it.

''There are a lot of very nasty men I wouldn't put on that dark alley list, by the way. Dyce, the one who took men home and drained their blood because he liked to look at corpses . . .''

''I remember, Dyce,'' Becker said almost inaudibly. He had captured Dyce himself and come within a breath of killing him. Becker's restraint was considered by Gold to be a signal mark of improvement. Becker was far less certain.

''Of course you do. I'm sorry if that's a painful allusion, but my point is, I *wouldn't* be afraid to be in a dark alley with Dyce. I wouldn't feel *comfortable* about it, mind, but I wouldn't feel in immediate danger because Dyce was not *randomly* violent. He was basically a very passive man. When he acted out his awful fantasies, he did it with a purpose, he didn't just lash out at the nearest male. He had something very specific in mind. So do all serial killers . . . Am I right about that?''

Becker nodded slowly.

"If you saw Dyce on the street, you wouldn't even notice him. If you saw Cooper coming, believe me, you'd step aside to get out of his way."

"Just play the tape," Becker said.

"Right. Cut to the chase."

"With respect, Gold, I don't need a primer on serial killers."

"Sorry. I need to convince myself, I think. It helps to hear my arguments aloud. Not that they're arguments. I just don't quite understand."

"Play it."

"Right. Okay, this is what I consider the relevant part of the session I sat in on. He's already told us what and when and where about the girls in the coal mine, very specific as I said. The voice you recognize is mine. I only asked the one question. They looked pretty annoyed that I spoke at all.''

Becker nodded and Gold started the recorder. A deep voice came from the machine. Even in this form and despite the masculine timbre, there was a quality of childishness in the speaker that came through clearly—

"I took her into the cave so we could be alone," Cooper said.

"Why did you want to be alone with her, Darnell?" Becker did not recognize the voice of the interrogator.

"So I could hurt her," Cooper said.

"You could hurt her anywhere. Why did you take her into the cave?''

"So I could hurt her for a long time," Cooper said.

There was a pause, and then Becker recognized Gold's voice.

"What did it feel like when she died?"

"What did it feel like?" Becker could almost see the shrug of shoulders implicit in Cooper's tone. "I didn't care. She didn't mean anything to me.''

"Do you like to hurt people, Darnell?" another voice asked.

"Yeah," said Cooper.

"Does it excite you to hurt other people?"

"Sometimes."

"Tell us how you feel when you hurt someone."

"I feel good."

"Do you feel better when you hurt men, or women?"

"Yeah," said Cooper.

There was a puzzled silence.

"Do you like to hurt men more than you like hurting women?"

"I like it all," said Cooper. "I like to pull their heads off."

"Why do you like to pull their heads off, Darnell?"

"Don't call me Darnell."

"What would you like me to call you?"

"Call me Coop."

"All right, Coop. Why do you like to pull their heads off?"

"You could call me ol' Coop. I like that."

"Tell us about pulling their heads off."

"That's how strong I am."

Becker switched off the machine. Gold let him sit in silence for a time.

"What did he do when he was released?" Becker asked at last.

"He raped a young woman, stole her car. Tried to drive the car over a filling station attendant, kidnapped another young woman, battered a local cop pretty good, hit the young woman in the head a couple of times, tried to strangle her, left her in a swamp."

"Did he kill either one of the women?"

"No. But he thinks he did. He left them for dead, let's put it that way."

"What did they say? Were they conscious or unconscious when he left them?"

"The first one, the one whose car he stole, said she played dead and he lost interest in her. The second one was really unconscious. She had severe bruising on her throat and some damage to her neck. It looks as if he really did try to pull her head off."

Becker rose and turned off the heat under the pot of beans.

"So what do you want from me?" he asked.

"I don't understand the disparity. . . . you heard it, right?"

"Let me get Karen," Becker said. "I don't want to have to go through it twice."

"Are you sure you want her in on it?"

"How else? Do you think I'm the Lone Ranger—I'm going to go riding in by myself? I don't have the authority to do anything on my own, even if I wanted to, which I emphatically do not."

Becker summoned Jack and Karen and the adults ate beans while Jack dined on spaghetti with butter and broccoli. Jack was excused from the table and Becker served coffee.

"We could go into the living room," Karen said.

"We'll stay here," Becker said, closing the kitchen door. "I don't want Jack to hear any of this."

"Meaning I'm to be let in on the big secret?" Karen asked.

"Don't be too happy about it," Becker said. "You're not going to like it."

"Somehow I guessed that. Okay, let's hear it."

Becker looked at Gold, offering him the chance to speak first.

"I'm not the expert," Gold said defensively. "I just thought I noticed something odd and came for advice. I haven't reached any conclusions myself."

"My ball, is it?" Becker asked.

"I'm really just a spectator here," Gold said.

"Could we drop the sports analogy?" Karen asked. "John, just say it."

"Gold tells me that this Cooper is confessing to being responsible for half the national crime statistics. Has any of it checked out yet?"

"Some," Karen said cautiously. "There are a couple of unexplained deaths of migrant workers about ten years ago that match up pretty well with his story. There was a vicious assault on a homosexual in Spartanburg several years ago that was listed as an attempted murder. The man didn't actually die, but we can see why Cooper thought he did—that matches his story. There were the two girls in the coal mine. He had his facts right on those."

"Anything else?"

"We're still checking. Most of them were quite a while ago. He's been in prison for the last five years. Why? Do you think there are more?"

"How did the migrant workers die?"

"One of them was stabbed. Disemboweled, according to the report. The other's head was bashed in with a blunt instrument, probably a rock, the autopsy said."

"And the homosexual who wasn't killed? What happened to him?" John asked.

"He was beaten—kicked and beaten with fists and feet, I gather. He did not volunteer any information, said he didn't remember what happened."

"And where were these things done, the workers and the homosexual?"

"Where were they done?"

"In a mine, in a basement, a closet, an abandoned warehouse?"

Karen paused. "No," she said warily. "The homosexual was in a parking lot behind a bar. One of the migrant workers was apparently killed in an orchard but then dragged to a culvert. The other was found in an open field. There was no suggestion in the report that he had been moved."

"And what's on his sheet? What was he doing time for?"

"Armed robbery, assault with intent. His priors were all violent, if that's what you're after. It is, isn't it?"

"Looking strange, Karen?" John asked her.

"So why would a man whose history is all open violence take two girls to a coal mine and torture them to death? Is that the thrust of all this? It has occurred to us, you know. We are not completely blind just because we're actively involved in law enforcement," she said.

"That inconsistency didn't trouble anybody?"

"Trouble? No. We noticed it. It's unusual for a serial killer to be impulsively violent as well—but it's not unknown. Harris Breitbart killed three police officers in New Jersey."

"Not until they came to arrest him. *After* he had been discovered."

"So? He doesn't fit the mold perfectly. We're constantly changing the profile, you know that."

"What's the average intelligence of a serial killer?"

Karen looked to Gold, deferring.

"Usually higher than average," Gold said.

"It has to be or they wouldn't survive long enough to kill repeatedly. If they kill once and get caught, they're a murderer. If they're smart enough to stay loose and do it repeatedly, they're a serial killer. Ergo, they're smarter. At least that's the assumption, correct?" Becker said.

"Correct," said Karen. "And Cooper is stupid. But you don't have to be a genius to go into an abandoned mine if you're in West Virginia. There are tons of them. If you leave a body there, it's not going to be found for a long time, whether you did it by planning or just dumb luck. It's not as if he did anything clever, he just did it in the right place."

"So then so far he's inconsistent and lucky."

"Apparently. What are you driving at, John? Do you think he couldn't be both?"

"Somebody could be. I'm not sure Cooper could."

"Look, we're not dealing in theory here. If we were, I'd agree, all right. It's not likely that a man who steals cars and drives them around for several days and assaults cops and gets in fights in bars is also going to slip away into the dark with young women and torture them for a week at a time. In theory. But we *know* he stole the car, raped a woman, snatched another in broad daylight with several witnesses, tried to drive the car over a gas station attendant. We *know* those things, they are facts, not theory," Karen said.

"I'm not questioning that side of him—the stupidly violent side has been his whole life."

"You're not questioning the girls in the mine? That's the strongest part of his story. He remembers that better than any of the other things he did. *Those* we can verify a lot more concretely than the migrants or the homosexual or any of the other claims. He's got the details only he could know."

"Except for one."

Karen sighed. "Go ahead."

"He knew what he did and he knew when he did it and he knew how he did it—"

"And he knew *why* he did it," Karen interjected. "He likes to hurt people. You accept that, don't you?"

"Yes, he even knew *why* he did it. What he didn't know was what it felt like."

"Wrong," said Karen. "I've seen the transcripts. He said it felt *good*. Hurting those women made him feel *good*. That's not terribly articulate, I grant you, but it's good enough for me. You have to consider the source."

"I realize it's good enough for you," John said. "It's good enough for practically anybody, I imagine. You've got enough on Cooper that you could get a conviction in any court in the land . . . But Gold played me a tape of Cooper's confession . . . I don't think he did the girls."

"Why are you doing this, John?" She turned to Gold. "Is this what you came for? What's the matter with you two? You think he's a von Munchausen, is that it? You think he's claiming he killed more people than he did? We know that's possible. We'll find out, and maybe he killed only half of what he claims, or maybe a third, or maybe only two. But we know the two he did kill. We *know*."

"You 'know' because he told you," Gold said.

"He didn't make up that confession," Karen said angrily.

"No, he didn't. I agree. But it isn't true, either."

"Why not? Just tell me why in the hell not! What have you two geniuses spotted that nobody else could see?"

Gold put his hands in the air as if submitting. "I didn't spot anything. I just didn't quite understand."

"What? *What* don't you understand?"

"Gold asked Cooper one question," Becker said. "He asked him what he felt when the girls died. Cooper said he didn't care."

"He obviously doesn't."

"No," Becker said. His voice had become sad. "Cooper was answering the question as honestly as he could think to do. He doesn't care when he kills someone—because that's not why he does it. Men who are that violent are not concerned with the death of their victim, they just want to get rid of them because they are thwarting them in some way. Cooper didn't even bother to find out if half his *corpses* were even dead. He claimed the homosexual and the woman he raped and the girl he left in the swamp were all dead, and none of them were. He wasn't concerned about their deaths, he just wanted done with them."

"And that's exactly how he reacted to the girls in the coal mine."

"Yes. But that is not the reaction of a man who dragged them in there and tortured them for days and days. That required planning. He had to have light, he had to have food and water, he had to have the right clothes because it's cold that far underground, he had to have restraints of some kind to keep the girls there while he slept . . . he had to have cigarettes. I'm saying he planned it, kept at it for days, because, as he said, he *liked it*. It made him feel *good*. But the best part of the whole thing for a man who is obsessed enough to do it in the first place is not the torture . . . it's the death. The actual dying is the final payoff, the largest orgasm of all. 'I didn't care' is an impossible response."

Karen looked to Gold for confirmation, but the psychologist kept his eyes on the table. She did not question Becker on his conviction. There were things that he understood that few others did, and she did not want to know the basis of that understanding. She had glimpsed such knowledge and turned away.

"Cooper wasn't lying," Becker continued. "He answered the question the best way he knew how. But he didn't have a better answer because he didn't have the experience."

"Maybe it wasn't a great thing for him. Maybe he thought it would be but it wasn't," Karen said.

"He says he did it twice," Becker said.

"You can't mean he's making it all up."

"He's not making it up," Becker said. "I suspect he believes he actually did it."

"He *believes* it . . . but he didn't do it?"

"That's my guess."

"Why in hell would he *believe* he did it?"

Becker poured himself another cup of coffee.

"I'd just be speculating on that."

"As opposed to what you've been doing? John, with all due respect, you listened to a tape of the confession—and you know that is unauthorized, even *having* such a tape, don't you, Dr. Gold?—you listened to a tape, you thought about it for what, five minutes? And now you want to overturn the best arrest since Ted Bundy because . . . well, because it doesn't sound right to you."

"I'm not overturning the arrest. You can put Cooper away for the rest of his life for what you got. But you won't have the guy who killed the girls in the coal mine . . . But I think we can find him."

"Where? If it's not Cooper, who the hell is it?" Karen asked.

"Cooper got his story from someone. We know he didn't read about it. That means someone told him. Someone who knew the details."

"Who?"

"The guy who's had his ear for the past three years, I would imagine. His cellmate. My friendly correspondent. Swann."

"You're saying Swann told Cooper about it and Cooper thought *he* did it?"

"I imagine it was a bit more complicated, but something like that, yes. Chime in, Gold. Could it be done?"

"I'm not sure what . . . are you talking about hypnosis, something like that?" Gold asked.

"Hypnosis, brainwashing, I don't know what you'd call it. Two men are together in a cell for three years. Could one take on the memories of the other?"

"To the extent that he believes those memories are his own?" Gold paused, looked back and forth from Karen to Becker. Finally he shrugged. "I don't know. If one of them is *trying* to make that happen, if the other is suggestible enough, if the conditions are right . . . I don't know. Why not, sure, yes, *possible*. Things have been done in POW camps by the North Koreans, the Vietnamese, the Chinese—not memory changes, that I know of, but certainly major shifts in value systems, personality makeup, that sort of thing. I mean, it seems to me that some-

thing like what you're suggesting *could* occur, but I'm not saying it
did.''

"A fine professional waffle," Becker said. "Still, it's good enough
for me.''

"Well, it's not nearly good enough for me!" Karen said, anger rising
in her voice. "Hatcher has already delivered this Cooper to Congressman Beggs as a triumph of FBI persistence and overall brilliance—not
to mention Hatcher's own genius, I'm sure—and Beggs has touted it to
his constituents as a personal victory in his war on crime. You want
me—I assume that's why you invited me to join in on your jerk-off
session—you want *me* to waltz in to Hatcher and say, 'Sorry, but you
have to call the whole thing off. Just go tell Congressman Beggs that
you made a mistake—not only *that, not only that,* but tell him the reason I *know* he made a mistake is that former agent John Becker, one of
Hatcher's favorite people, has listened to five minutes' worth of an unauthorized tape that was apparently pirated by a Bureau psychologist—
or worse, a completely *illegal* tape made by the good doctor himself,
and don't tell me which, because right now I'm in no mood to find out,
and he brought this tape to my home, *my home* where he played it in
private to John Becker, who decided that Cooper, who has *already confessed in detail* to killing the two girls, is not really lying because he
does believe he did it, but still isn't telling the truth because he didn't
really do it, he just was talked into thinking he did by his cellmate. Or
so John Becker more or less sort of believes.' Is that what you want me
to do?''

"That's the gist of it," Becker said.

"John, I *like* my job. I worked real hard to get as high as I've gotten
and I was beginning to think I might get even higher, eventually, if I
didn't screw up too badly. You have personal problems with the work. I
understand that, I appreciate that, but I don't. I want to keep the job,
I want to continue to be able to function as efficiently as possible. I have
a son to support, college expenses to prepare for—''

"I give you the information for what it's worth, Karen. What you do
with it is up to you. The morality at the higher reaches of bureaucracy
eludes me, I admit it, I have no experience at that height, I get nose-
bleeds . . .''

"Information? *Information?* You haven't given me any information,
John. You've given me *speculation.* You've given me *imagination.*
Those are fine qualities, John, assuming you want me to get tossed out
on my ass.''

"Maybe I should go into the other room," Gold suggested. He was of the mind that when two people who lived together began calling each other by their first names too frequently, it was time for visitors to depart. Neither of the other two appeared to have heard him.

"I did not want to demean your contribution, Dr. Gold," Karen said. "This is extracurricular work for you and I appreciate very much that you care enough to make the special effort."

"It was my curiosity more than anything," Gold said.

"I understand," she said. "And what you and John have come up with, even though it's only a hypothesis, is troubling to me. Very troubling."

"Not irretrievable, though," Becker said. "Both Cooper and Swann are available as much as we want them. Send the Behavioral Sciences boys to talk to Swann, let them figure it out."

"That's what's troubling," Karen said. "We no longer have Swann."

"He's in Springfield—get him transferred to our custody."

"No, John, that's what I'm saying. He isn't in Springfield anymore. He's gone—he's out—he's been released."

"Released? How?"

"That was his bargain with Hatcher, his price for cooperating in the capture of Cooper."

"He said he wanted safety."

"He would never have been safe in the prison system, we all knew that. So did he. Hatcher got his sentence commuted. He was released from prison the day we caught Cooper."

"Cooperate how?" Becker asked.

"He knew where Cooper was."

"How?"

"Apparently Cooper was sending him postcards. Swann refused to tell us where to look unless Hatcher worked on a commutation of his sentence." Karen shrugged. "Hatcher gets what he goes after. We got the postcards, Swann got his commutation."

"That little shit is *free?*"

"And vanished. He was supposed to meet with a parole officer three days ago and never showed up. We don't have a clue where he is."

"So Hatcher not only caught the wrong man, he let the real killer loose," Becker said gleefully. "I wonder how Congressman Beggs will react to that bit of news?"

Chapter 26

The crowd was so big, so boisterous, so agitated with anticipation that Tommy entertained thoughts of investing in a bigger tent. The whole swing through Kentucky had been like this, the audiences swelling every performance as word of the show spread before them from one town to the next like the bow wave of a ship so that when the Reverend Tommy R. Walker's Gospel and Healing Meeting arrived, the residents had already been buoyed upwards with excitement. Tonight, though, looked like the best ever. The entire audience nearly swooned en masse when Aural did her solo piece—he was going to miss certain things about her, no question, even the Apostolic Choir of the Holy Ghost sounded better when she joined in. Oh, he'd lose a few from the audience when Aural was gone, but he'd keep most of them, he was sure of that. It was still his show, after all. If only just. And soon it would be all his again, only bigger and better.

Tommy whipped into the healing segment with unusual vigor, curing and thrusting with great zest, as if nothing could be more fun. They were lined up with their ailments like he was giving away free money, and he worked his miracles quick as he could shout Hallelujah and Praise Jesus. The deacon and the choir were kept so busy catching cascading bodies that they actually worked up a sweat for a change. It was nice for Tommy not to be the only one bathed in perspiration.

He had cured a gallbladder and healed a kidney stone and pushed a lung tumor clean out of a man like it was nothing more than a chip on his shoulder when one of the overheated supplicants grabbed him. The man seized Tommy by the biceps and pulled him close so that their faces were practically touching. His breath was hot and smelled of mint and Tommy blinked as he puffed it into his eyes with every word.

"I've done terrible things," the man said, his voice low and whispery. "I've done things no man should do."

The man held Tommy so firmly that there was no way the Reverend

could free himself short of kicking the man off him. He was small and
thin, but he clasped Tommy's arms with all the strength of a man in the
grip of conviction. His nose was so close to Tommy's own that the minister had to turn his face and look at him sideways. Tommy thought he
was probably insane, and then he thought of assassination.

"My soul ain't clean," the man said. "I've been places no man
should have to go, and Jesus knows I'm sorry, but I can't help it, I just
can't help it, I get these thoughts, they won't leave me, they force me to
do it."

The deacon had hurried over and was trying to pull the man off
Tommy, but he clung like fury.

"You got to cure my heart," the man was saying. "You got to
cleanse me."

"I'm going to do it, too, if you just let loose," Tommy said.

"Thoughts that would drive a man crazy," the man said, his eyes
widening.

"Let go me, son, and I'll heal that heart in no time," Tommy said,
trying to smile. The man was pushing himself harder into Tommy the
more the deacon tried to pull him off.

"Only Jesus understands," the man was saying.

"I understand you, son. Now let me go and we'll get the holy power
of Jesus working for us."

"You don't understand me," the man said, grasping Tommy even
tighter. "You don't. No one can."

Then the voice of the angel. "I understand you," and a tone so sweet,
so manifestly full of patient understanding, of bone-deep sincerity, that
the man eased up his grip and turned to look Aural in the face.

"Do you?"

She was standing right next to him. She put her fingers on his arm,
that dainty hand coming out of the folds of the robe like soft magic.
That half-smile, that goddamned suggestion of holiness and sainthood
that Tommy couldn't duplicate no matter how he tried, moved her lips
and Tommy watched as it worked its wonders again. The man looked
into her face transfixed, the mania and desperation seeping away like a
long sigh.

"Only a woman can truly understand a man," Aural said, although
Tommy wasn't sure he actually heard the words over the din of the congregation, which was more excited than ever by the new development.
They were shouting at the man to release the Reverend and praying and
praising Jesus and generally talking amongst themselves, every voice

trying to be louder than the other. But the man heard Aural well enough, and when she told him to unloose Tommy, the man did it, and when she told him, sweet as a mother's kiss, to go back to the audience, he did that, too. She said if he was still troubled after the show she'd talk to him some more and he acted like it was pure-D blessing from a saint herself.

Another triumph for the bitch, Tommy thought. Now they think she can calm the berserk and make the insane see reason. Throw away the Thorazine, Aural's here. Meanwhile Tommy looks like a fool, his own self. Can't even get hisself loose from one small loonie. Needs a woman to save him. Might as well give it up right now, change the name to the Aural McKesson Miracle Show, and hand her the business.

Tommy was in a state that night, and even the new variation that Aural had told Rae about, where she did what was called the butterfly, was able to distract him for only so long. Afterwards he was just as riled as ever.

"In the first place, I ain't no priest. You see a collar on me, Rae? I don't do confessions. You got something troubling your conscience? Keep it to yourself, don't go grabbing me in the middle of the show and telling me how bad you are, because I don't care. I'm a *healer,* Rae . . ."

"And the best."

"Damned straight. I'm a healer, not every lunatic's *confidant.* I don't want to hear that shit. I should have been an evangelist, Rae. They don't have to deal with all the whining and carrying on I do. All they have to do is preach."

"Did he come up to her afterwards?"

"There you go again, all the time asking about *her. I'm* the one had the little jerk hanging on me like he was drowning and was going to take me down with him."

" 'Course I'm most concerned about you, honey."

"Yeah. Of course."

"I was just asking in case he hangs around and bothers you again."

"I don't know if he saw her afterwards or not. I went around the other side of the tent so I didn't have to watch her on her goddamned *box.* You'll have to ask her your own self."

He turned away from her roughly, but a moment later he spoke again in the darkness.

"What was that you just done?"

"What you mean?"

"What was that thing you just done to me?"

Rae was quiet for a moment and Tommy knew she was blushing.

"It's called the butterfly," she said. She paused. "Did you like it?"

"Interesting," he said.

At first Rae didn't know how he meant it, but then he put his arms around her when he fell asleep, which was a thing he almost never did.

There was a pounding on the trailer door around three o'clock in the morning and Tommy bolted out of bed to answer it. A long, lean, evil-looking man stood there in cowboy boots and a Stetson that appeared to be as stiff as plywood. Tommy blinked once and waited, but he knew who the man was.

"You Reverend Tommy R. Walker?" the man asked.

Tommy stepped outside and pulled the door shut so that Rae would not overhear. He was wearing silk boxers that Rae had bought for him recently and he sported a sleeper's erection but he was too excited to see his visitor to worry about it.

"I am," Tommy said.

"I'm Harold Kershaw," the man said, removing his hat out of respect.

"God bless you, boy, I know you are. And not a moment too soon, neither."

Chapter 27

Aural awoke from a troubled dream in which a man she had never seen before was showing her his life on film. She was strapped in a chair and whenever the man experienced pain in his life, Aural was administered a shock just as painful. When she awoke, her mind still clouded by the dream, she heard voices outside the trailer that she shared with the female members of the Apostolics. The voices were speaking in the hushed tones of conspirators, the kinds of whispers that seem to carry even louder than regular speech on the night air.

One of the men was the Reverend Tommy, and she wondered what he was doing catting around outside her window in the middle of the night but when she heard the second voice, she knew. The second man didn't even speak, it was more of a prolonged grunt of assent, but she recognized it and it galvanized her into action.

Aural bolted the door, then yanked on her jeans and boots and squirmed out the window on the other side of the trailer. She didn't bother with her purse or any belongings because she knew there wasn't time. Bent over, she scuttled in the darkness towards the cars parked on the strip of asphalt adjoining the vacant lot where they would erect the tent in the morning. She was within a few yards of the cars when she heard the sound of heavy boots kicking at the trailer door.

A body took shape beside one of the cars, stepping towards her. Aural swerved aside but the shape spoke.

"Miss Aural? It's me."

Aural squinted at the man in the darkness. She didn't know him.

"From the meeting tonight?" he continued. "You said you'd talk to me afterwards?"

"Not now, hon. This ain't exactly an appropriate time." Aural tried to step around him but he moved in front of her. Behind her, the Apostolics were sending up a frightened squawk and she could hear the door crashing in. Harold Kershaw was into the chicken coop, but the hen he was after had flown.

"You-all come back when it's light," Aural said, thinking by then she'd be all the way to Maine if she could manage it. "I'll talk to you then."

"I can help you now," the man said, and he opened his car door.

"Bless your heart," she said, dipping into the car, "but we best go right away." She glanced at the trailer and saw Harold Kershaw's ugly face peering out of the window that she had used as an exit.

"That's what I had in mind," the man said. He ran around the car to the driver's side, then fussed with something instead of opening the door.

"Come *on*," Aural said.

"Going as fast as I can," the man said. "I wasn't quite ready for you."

Aural kept her eye on the trailer, expecting Harold to come running at any minute, so she gave only scant attention to the man who was still fussing on the outside of the car. He came around the back to her side again.

"What's taking you so long?" she demanded, still not looking at him fully.

"Ready now. Mustn't go off half-cocked," the man said. "Don't want any mistakes, now, do we?"

Harold came thundering around the side of the trailer, pausing for only half a second to get his bearings, then headed straight for the cars with his heavy-footed lope.

"I can't wait," Aural said, turning to get out, but the man opened her door at the same time and grabbed her hand in his. Distracted as she was, she wasn't aware that he was handcuffing her until the metal clamps were already on her wrists, and when she opened her mouth to speak he slapped a piece of tape across it.

"Fast service, no waiting," he said, giggling. He slammed the door and ran to the driver's side. Aural reached her cuffed hands to open the door but found that there was no handle on the inside. Well, damn, she thought. Who would have dreamed that Harold Kershaw was bright enough to hire an accomplice? She watched Harold pounding inexorably towards them, but then, when he was within a few yards, amazingly, the man started the car and drove away. Harold pounded the car's trunk once with his fist, but that was as close as he got. Aural squirmed to watch him recede in the back window, then turned to take a good look at the driver for the first time.

He glanced at her as he spoke, keeping most of his attention on the road.

"I was wondering how I was going to get you alone," he said. "I knew I didn't dare come into that trailer full of women. You can't be overeager, you have to restrain yourself and be *careful,* no matter what, otherwise . . . well, you just *have* to be careful. But you learn that. You naturally get better as you go along. Anyway, I was thinking and thinking, how am I going to do this *safely* when all of a sudden, there you were. Do you think Jesus sent you to me? I believe maybe he did, I believe he watches over me. Of course, I'm sure he watches over you, too, given your line of work, I mean. I'm certain that you have a good relationship with your Lord, don't you, Miss Aural? Well, that means Jesus wanted us to get together for your sake as well as mine. I think that means we're going to have a *real* good time together, don't you? I know I will. Together, we're going to be fulfilling your destiny. That's a nice thought, isn't it? You're only a part of my destiny, of course, but I *am* yours. I'm what Jesus has in mind for you . . . I'll make it real good for you, I promise you that. Ooh, but it's been a long time. I got such an awful lot to make up for."

He turned away from the road again and smiled broadly at her.

"This going to be *fun,* hon," he said. When he giggled, Aural knew that she was in terrible trouble.

Chapter 28

"Good thing you're so petite," Swann said. "This is a very tight squeeze." He paused to catch his breath. The rope around his waist bit into his skin and he wriggled back towards her to ease up on the tension. Aural was zippered into a leather sack designed to encase golf bags and a full set of clubs for shipping, and the rope was tied around her feet. He had carefully selected the leather because it would slide better than the nylon sacks and it offered a measure of cushioning. Swann had added to the protection by slipping two pillows under her head before beginning to drag her. He didn't want her to get a bump and fall unconscious. The whole point was that she *knew* what was happening to her.

" 'Course, if you was one of those chunky girls, I wouldn't have wanted you in the first place," he said. He knew she could hear him even if she couldn't see. "I like a slim girl, one with a shape, but not pudgy, you know? I believe that a slim girl feels things more intensely, don't you? All that extra padding of fat can seriously decrease your sensations, don't you think?"

Aural made a noise, but the tape over her mouth made her unintelligible and Swann had long since given up trying to decipher her sounds. He knew the general sense of them anyway. He turned to face the way he was going once again. The light on his hard hat illuminated his path for only a few yards before it was swallowed up again by the darkness. Still breathing heavily, he began to crawl forward again, feeling the golf sack catch and then slide after him. The leather had cost more but it was definitely worth it.

Aural could hear him panting and tried to imagine him trudging along, dragging her. It must be uphill, judging by his difficulty, although she had no sense of being tilted. She had no sense of where she was at all, hadn't known since he pushed her into the bag. Disoriented as well as terrified at first, she knew only that she had been dragged for a long time, then lowered with what she assumed was rope around her upper body as well as her feet, then dragged again, this time over considerably bumpier terrain.

He was working hard to get her wherever they were going. Always nice to be wanted, she thought, then realized that her sense of humor was returning. Whatever lay ahead of her, she knew that fear and confusion were not going to help her survive it. Being afraid had never done her any good in her life, but staying calm had saved her neck more than once. The best way she knew to stay calm was to cling to her sense of humor. In this case, that might mean hanging on to it for dear life.

They were still for the longest time, yet and Aural imagined him lying down, panting and wheezing as if he'd run a few miles, but then she realized she couldn't hear him breathing. What if the asshole had died from the exertion? What if she were to be left in this bag, gagged and handcuffed, while her captor lay dead beside her? Where in hell were they? How long before someone found them? *Would* someone find them? .

She wanted to cry out, but a calmer part of her remained in control. She would only waste energy now; she would save her scream until she needed it.

Something fumbled with the sack over her face, then the zipper began its lovely zip. He wasn't dead after all, and Aural felt a confusing flood of relief.

"Boy, am I glad to see you," she said, sitting up as soon as the opening was large enough to allow it.

In truth, she couldn't see much of anything at first; the light was too bright after so long in the total darkness of the bag; but she could make out his shape, kneeling next to her. She squinted while trying to look around to see where she was. There was an odd hissing sound coming from behind him. It sounded like a concert of snakes.

"You like it?" he asked.

"Well, I'm not sure how I feel about it yet," she said. "But whatever it is, it beats the bag."

He giggled, surprised and pleased.

"You a talker, ain't you?"

"There are very few things in life that aren't improved by a little conversation," Aural said, her eyes still scanning the area, trying to figure things out. Shapes were beginning to take form, but they were all odd and unfamiliar.

"You're not afraid?"

"No, I'm not afraid," Aural lied. "Mostly I feel a little cramped from the bag. Say, listen, you're not afraid, are you? Because if you are, I say let's call this whole thing off."

"You're funny," he said. "I like that. You're lying to me, too, but that's all right. I understand that. Before we're through, you'll say anything you can think of."

"Now there's a prospect," said Aural. "The man *wants* me to lie to him. All men do, 'course, but you're the first one who ever admitted it. Don't tell me you're an honest man."

"I'll be very honest with you," he said. "I don't have any reason to lie to you."

Aural looked upwards. She could see no ceiling, only darkness that extended beyond the light.

"So how about I stand and stretch? That be all right with you?"

"Sure," he said. "Why not? You're not going anywhere."

She came to her feet awkwardly because of her handcuffed wrists. She arched her back, rolling her head on her shoulders to loosen the muscles and taking the opportunity to examine even more of her situation.

"Cold in here, isn't it?" She had just noticed the chill. The air felt as if it were above freezing, but not much. "How about turning up the heat?"

"I'll warm you up before long," he said.

"I look forward to that."

"I know you're scared," he said. Aural thought he sounded disappointed, as if being scared were part of the deal. Whatever it was, she wasn't going to give it to him. If she admitted to the fear, she knew it could quickly overwhelm her.

"Why would I be scared?" she asked. "You didn't bring me all this way to hurt me."

He gave that giggle that was colder than the air.

"Yes, I did," he said.

"Uh-oh," she said, grinning at him, right into his face, showing him he didn't bother her. "Sounds like another Danny Leeps."

"Who's that?"

"An old boyfriend. Danny liked to hurt me, too. He wasn't near as cute as you, but otherwise you're just like him."

"I'm not like anybody else!" He was so enraged at the suggestion that Aural thought he might hit her. She readied to duck under the blow and then to push against him and knock him off balance. She could try to run for it—if she had any idea which way to run.

He didn't hit her, though. Instead he bent down to the leather sack and rummaged around, allowing Aural to see the light source for the first time. It was a camper's Coleman lantern, and the hissing sound emanated directly from it. She thought of kicking him while he was bent over, then smashing the lantern and taking her chances in the dark, but she realized that she *had* no chances until she at least figured out where she was and how to get out of there.

He stood up from the sack, holding what looked like a larger, oddly shaped pair of handcuffs.

"I like your hat, by the way," she said.

Swann reached up to touch the hard plastic shell on his head as if just noticing, and at the same time Aural realized with horror what it was, and why. She was underground.

Swann noticed the change in her expression immediately and a slow smile of satisfaction suffused his countenance.

"You just figure it out, honey?"

"Guess you wanted us to be alone," Aural said.

"That's right."

"A motel room would have been easier," she said. She tried to grin but her face felt stiff with fear.

"You remember when Jesus wanted to be alone, where he went? He didn't go to a motel. He went to the wilderness."

"When was this?"

"To the mountains and the desert. And he wrestled with Satan and all? The devil tempted him, remember? Well, you and me have to wrestle with Satan, too. We have our own temptation. 'Course I tend to give in to mine, but Jesus understands and forgives. But there just isn't that much wilderness around anymore, is there? It's not like we have a desert handy. So I came to a place where we could be alone as long as we want."

"How long you figure that is? Just ballpark."

"That depends on you, doesn't it? I can take it as long as you can. Turn around."

Swann slapped the odd-looking handcuffs on her ankles. As she felt the iron tighten on her boot, Aural remembered the knife for the first time. There was nothing to do with it now, not trussed hand and foot, but the time would come. She suddenly felt much better.

"I got other supplies to fetch," he said. "You just stay here and pray.

And think about your Danny Leeps. Think about if he ever went to this much trouble for you."

He snapped on the light on his hat and extinguished the lantern and put it in the golf sack. The headlight beam struck her right in the face.

"You're not going to just leave me here, are you?"

"When I get back we can pray together," he said.

"How long you going to be?"

"Time is relative," he said. "It's going to seem like a very long time to you."

"Well, you hurry on back, then, sugar, 'cause I'm going to miss you."

"I know that," he said. He turned from her and walked away. The beam from his hat had a peculiar yellow color to it and when it struck the wall it reflected back as if from gold. Aural could make out the rock of her prison for the first time.

The light dipped down until it was almost to the floor of the room. She could no longer see Swann himself, only a vague shape interfering with the reflected glow.

"Y'all have a safe trip now," Aural called.

"You better hope," he said and the light disappeared as if it had gone straight into the wall of rock.

His voice continued to echo for a moment or two, and Aural realized that wherever she was, room, or dungeon or cavern, it was vast. For a minute she could hear the scrape of his boots against stone, and then even that sound was gone and she was alone in the darkness.

Not yet—don't scream yet, she told herself. Save it.

Chapter 29

Swann was startled to see how light it had become. It was nearly noon by the time he saw the sun again and it shone with a brightness that he had forgotten while maneuvering with only the feeble light of the headlamp. In fact, he realized he had never really gotten used to the sun, the wind, the scent of fresh air since getting out of Springfield. Prison was like living in a tomb, and no amount of time spent in the exercise yard could dispel the sense of permanent gloom that pervaded the mind of a prisoner. That gloom was not just a matter of light, of course—at times it was entirely too brightly lighted inside. It was a matter of internal vision. If one's eyes could see no farther than the nearest wall, it was not long before the mind could not think past it either. The romantic notion that confinement would release the imagination to soar was nonsense, Swann thought. It cramped and stifled the mind just as it did the body. Most of the men in prison could not hold a sustained thought about anything outside the walls; their minds were mired in the quotidian concerns of survival, cellblock politics, manipulation, fear. Television and radio were not links with the outside world, they were artifacts from a civilization light-years away, one that died when the prisoner entered the walls. Books, with their visions of alternate universes, were as alien as Runic tablets. Decipherable, but irrelevant to the life of those who read them. Life in prison *was* the prison and the role that a man had to play to survive became the man, the man became the role. After a time there was no difference.

Now, however, Swann could shed his role at last. As he walked to the car he realized that he felt truly himself for the first time since getting out. He was no longer anybody's punk, whore, and wife. He was no longer servant, slave, craven. He was in control, *he* was in control. There was no limit to what he could do now, provided he exercised reasonable caution. His only limit was his imagination, and in the real world his imagination flourished. He knew that he was unique in the thoughts that possessed him, he always had been, since childhood, and he had learned early to keep them to himself. They were his treasures that no one else could understand, even though they coveted them. That was the ironic part: they did not approve of his thoughts, he knew that, they thought they were ugly, nasty, shameful, yet they all wanted to take his treasures away. Swann would not let them have his treasures. He clung to them, nurtured them, and kept them carefully hidden from view.

It was at times a burden never to be able to speak of his most prized possessions. There were occasions when he was tempted to share them, when a fantasy had been so real, so enticing, so filled with excitement and pleasure that he wanted to grab a stranger, anyone, and tell them what a joy he had in his own mind. He could not, of course. That is, he could not unless he had a confidant whom he could really trust. The only such people were his girls. He told them all about his thoughts, told them even as he demonstrated to them. He knew they would never betray him. They would never tell another living soul.

Swann drove to town, feeling at last fully and completely himself again. He felt the beast that lived within him stir and stretch its tentacles to clutch his heart and stomach and groin. It tugged, voracious, yearning to be fed, and Swenn felt the old excitement build, the old irresistible joy.

He drove with the window down, smelling the air, loving the scents of the countryside where he had grown up. Everything seemed new again, yet comfortingly familiar. He could not recall ever feeling better. He was in charge, everything was under control and perfectly planned, and there was at least a week's worth of great pleasure ahead of him, perhaps more if she could take it. This one seemed strong and she had a great mental outlook. He liked her spirit, it would help her to stay alive longer.

Swann could not remember when he had ever felt better. After a time he began to sing.

The Reverend Tommy R. Walker met Harold Kershaw in Elmore at a coffee shop named Chat 'n Nibble, where the other customers downed noonday meals of chicken-fried steaks with biscuits and brown gravy. Tommy drank coffee and kept a nervous eye on the front door. He didn't expect anyone from the show to come this far afield—there were several fast-food restaurants between here and the campsite—but it wouldn't hurt to be careful. He sat beside Kershaw at the counter rather than in a booth so that he could disassociate himself from the other man in the unlikely event that Rae or a member of the Apostolics should wander in.

"She didn't have no friends outside the show, not that I was aware of," Tommy said.

"*Some* sumbitch was driving the car," Harold said.

"Well, I can't figure out who it could have been."

"Girl like Aural's got no problem finding friends. Just walk past a bar and get about a dozen sniffing after her."

"I realize that . . . still, I would have heard if it was anybody local. Rae would have told me. Besides, how could she know you were coming? I didn't tell anybody."

"Uh-huh."

"I *didn't*. You think I'm crazy? I want to get everybody back on my side, not turn them against me by doing anything against their little darling."

"Your *little darling* is a dangerous woman."

Tommy glanced at the door, then took in Harold Kershaw's hands and face. He saw no trace of scarring.

"Bitch tried to kill me more than once," Kershaw continued. "Tried to bounce me out the back of my pickup one time. Took a knife to me once."

"I thought she burned you," Tommy said.

"Burned me?"

"That's what she told everybody."

"Oh, yeah. It wasn't me she burned, it was the damned trailer. I was in the pot and she jammed the door shut and packed a bunch of stuff down at the bottom and set them on fire. Mostly my clothes. Bitch burned my favorite boots."

"She didn't burn you, though?"

"I got out the window. Hell, the door was metal, metal don't burn that well."

"Goddamn," said Tommy, feeling strangely disappointed that Aural hadn't actually set the man aflame.

"Watch your language there, preacher," said Kershaw, grinning. "You got to set a good example for the young'uns. Can't go round saying shit and damn. Next thing you know, everybody be talking like that."

"I'm a healer," Tommy said, not knowing exactly what distinction he was trying to draw. He wanted to tell Kershaw to keep his opinions to himself, but the man looked so rawboned and mean that he decided not to. He looked like the kind of man who would hurt you just for practice. It was hard to see how a tiny thing like Aural could have managed to handle a man like that. Or why. For just a moment, Tommy had a flash of understanding that led to an even briefer feeling of sympathy for the plight of women, but it all faded immediately.

Kershaw stripped the cellophane from a toothpick and pushed the tip through a gap between his two lower incisors. He wiggled it up and down with his tongue so that it looked to Tommy like the jerky, exploratory motion of the antenna of an insect. As if Kershaw had just popped a giant bug into his mouth and not yet swallowed it all.

Feeling disgusted, Tommy turned to look through the plate-glass window at the street. A man was passing by with a large bag of groceries on one arm, a pair of nylon blankets still in their plastic wrappings on the other.

"So what's your bright idea, preach?" Kershaw asked but then he stopped so abruptly that Tommy turned back to look at him.

Kershaw was staring at the window, his mouth open, the toothpick drooping. "Fuck me," he said and ran for the door.

Swann heard the running footsteps behind him and was half turned backwards to look when he saw the first blow coming at his head. He ducked enough to take it on the shoulder, but it was still hard enough to knock him off balance and Swann stumbled as the second blow hit him in the chest. The third blow caught him grazingly on the top of his head as he was falling. He landed so hard the wind was knocked out of him and he lay on the ground, gasping for air that he could not seem to capture in his lungs.

A man loomed over him, fists clenched, face in a snarl, but Swann couldn't concentrate on anything else until he finally caught a breath. When he realized he would live, he made no effort to get up. He lay where he had fallen on the sidewalk, canned goods and candles spewed out around his head, the blankets covering his feet as if someone had taken the trouble to tuck him in.

"You don't have to get up," Kershaw said. "I can stomp you even easier laying there."

By now Tommy had joined Kershaw, but he stood apart from him, making just one of the spectators who had gathered around as quickly as if warned in advance of some coming excitement. This was not urban America, where people gave violence involving someone else a wide berth and a studied indifference. In towns like Elmore, men still gathered to see a fight, not worried that it would reach out and kill others at random. They also gave it a chance to play itself out before intervening. There were always the peacemakers, but never in the beginning. Even the peacemakers wanted to see a little action.

"Where is she?" Kershaw asked.

Swann looked puzzled, shaking his head.

Kershaw kicked him on the hip. The crowd gasped, neither approvingly nor disapprovingly. They were withholding judgment until they better understood the conflict. Too much punishment of a downed opponent would have to be stopped eventually, but an exploratory kick seemed tolerable.

"Ain't going to help you to act stupid," Kershaw said. "I'll pound on you till you tell me where she is."

"Who?" Swann asked.

"You know who."

Kershaw drew his foot back again and Swann covered his face with his hands even though his attacker clearly was not aiming there. The boot caught Swann in the side and he cried out.

The crowd murmured again, this time as much in disapproval as sympathy.

"I don't know who you mean," Swann said as soon as he could talk. He rolled his eyes to the crowd, looking for help.

"Aural," Kershaw said. "Where is she, you little peckerwood?"

Kershaw stepped on Swann's shin, holding his foot down until Swann jerked into a sitting position, holding out his arm.

"Least let him get up," said a voice from the back of the crowd of men.

"I ain't keeping him from getting up," Kershaw said, looking angrily around him to locate the protester. "Peckerwood stole my woman."

A collective "ah" escaped from the men as understanding came to them all. Woman stealing, a vague but threatening concept, shifted the sympathy back towards Kershaw.

"I don't know her," Swann said. "I didn't steal her, I didn't steal anybody."

"Shit," said Kershaw in contempt for Swann's story. "You better tell me, 'cause I ain't afraid to kick you to death if I have to."

"You've got the wrong man," Swann said, sounding as pathetic as he could manage. He rolled his eyes towards the crowd again. He knew that eventually some of them would intervene, and he was grateful that Kershaw had not encountered him someplace secluded. Swann knew he would have to wait out the torture—he had done it before more than once—and the only question was whether he would be able to walk when it was over.

"I got no use for your woman," Swann said, playing the only card he had.

The crowd sucked in their collective breath at the seeming insult. Without warning Kershaw stopped and smashed his fist into Swann's face.

Stern murmurings rose from the men. Hitting a man when he was down had its limits and Kershaw was fast approaching them.

"That's about enough," another voice offered, but no one moved forward yet. Moral suasion would be tried first.

Swann spit out some of the blood that dripped into his mouth, then ran his hand under his nose, which was bleeding profusely. He thumbed a tooth as if it were loose although the blow had not hit his mouth. He made no attempt to rise. He would lie there and take it like a punching bag if he had to, but offering resistance or even giving the appearance of being a fair opponent would be disaster.

"I meant I got no use for women at all," Swann said, trying to finish the ploy that Kershaw had thwarted by hitting him so fast. "I'm queer."

That split the crowd about evenly between those who thought he had proven his case and those who thought he deserved the beating on general principles, but the real victory was over Kershaw. It was one thing to stand over a fallen man and kick shit out of him because he stole a woman, quite another to administer punishment to a victim who was so fundamentally weak that he even admitted to the ultimate perversion.

Kershaw hit Swann in the eye, then again for good measure, but the second blow had the halfhearted enthusiasm of a man who knows he has already lost.

The crowd helped Swann to his feet as Harold Kershaw walked away. Tommy Walker deliberately walked in the other direction. After a few minutes Swann managed to convince everyone that he didn't want a doctor, and he was in his car, heading out of Elmore. He watched in his rearview mirror for several miles to be sure he wasn't followed.

When he was sure he was safe at last, Swann pulled over to the side of the road. Now that the adrenaline was leaving his system, he began to feel dizzy from the last two blows to the eye. Vision out of that eye was poor, and when he looked at his reflection in the mirror he saw that it was nearly swollen shut. He had been beaten worse in his time, Cooper had nearly killed him in the first few weeks of breaking him in to his role as compliant concubine. This time no bones were broken; he could move; he could travel. He didn't look very good, but no one was going to see him for a while other than Aural McKesson, and it didn't really matter if he was presentable to her or not, did it?

The only thing that worried him was the dizziness that wouldn't go away. He laid his head back against the seat and closed his eyes. The car seemed to swim about him and he snapped his eyes open again, looking for something to focus on to stop the spinning. The tree he looked at moved and then he was moving, swinging wildly back and forth and the light flickered and went out.

Swann awoke, aware that he had passed out, and panic swept over him. It was not his health that concerned him most, but his security. He had managed to survive all this time, both in prison and before, by being constantly on the alert. He sometimes thought of himself as a mammal in the age of dinosaurs, a small and poorly armed animal that evaded its enemies by its cunning and superior intelligence. Living in the cracks of a world dominated by the huge and stupid, the mammal had persisted, laughing silently at the giants all around as it slipped stealthily between their legs. In time it came into its own destiny, outlasting the monsters, lifted to the top of the heap by its natural superiority. Swann liked the analogy; it pleased and comforted him to think of himself as surviving on guile and craft while the slow-witted ones stumbled about, hunting for him in vain.

The price for such elusiveness was constant awareness, and if he lost that, he was lost. He needed a place to hide now, he needed someone to care for him. A doctor, a hospital, was out of the question. He could not afford to be restrained; his safety depended on a mobility that equated to anonymity. If he was never in the same place twice, he left no impression, there was no one to remember him, no way to connect him to anything, or anyone.

He could not understand how that cracker halfwit had recognized him in the first place. What kind of incalculably bad luck was it to have been shopping in the same place at the same time? The town was twenty miles from the campsite where he had found the girl. What was the man doing there, and how could he have identified Swann? The man could not have gotten more than a glimpse of a shape in the car. It was night, Swann hadn't even been facing the man. Had he? Could he have had that good a look at him? Or was it even bad luck? Had Swann been careless, was his vigilance slipping?

Frightened in a way he had not been since his first few days in prison, frightened for his life, Swann knew he had to find someone to help him until he recovered. There was only one person who could do it and be trusted implicitly.

He forced himself to drive on, struggling for his equilibrium.

Chapter 30

Aural had never known a darkness like this, not on the blackest night of her life, not with her eyes closed, never. Even the blind see more light than this, she thought. This was the darkness of the grave, total and unchanging. It was not a question of her eyes getting used to a lower level of light; there was no light at all, nothing to get used to, no gearing down or gearing up, no widening of the lens would make any difference.

It was not entirely silent as she had thought at first, however. For one thing, there were her own noises, her breath, the rasp of her clothing against rock, the sound of swallowing. Every sound was magnified and the louder ones echoed back and lived on for seconds longer. But beyond herself there was the noise of water. Somewhere in the distance a creek ran over rocks, the familiar splash could be heard as if filtered through hundreds of yards of darkness. And closer at hand, if she remained still herself, Aural could hear water dripping, very softly, with long intervals between drips, but steadily, with the regularity of a clock. She tried to count the interval between drips and determined it to be 180 seconds long, assuming that saying one-thousand-one in your mind actually took a second. Three minutes. She had a drip she could cook an egg by.

How many drips had he been gone? How many before he returned? How many before her real ordeal began? she wondered. She didn't know what this guy had in mind for her, but it seemed a pretty good guess that it wasn't to just leave her alone. Beyond that, she didn't allow her mind to speculate. There was no point in getting scared ahead of time. No point in doing his work for him.

What she had to do was prepare herself as best she could for his return. Since her hands were cuffed in front of her body, getting the knife from her boot was no problem, but she didn't know what to do with it after that. Hobbled as she was, she would not be able to maneuver. She would get one chance at best and even then she didn't know what to do. Say she cut him, so what? She couldn't then run away while he contemplated his wound. All he had to do was step away from her, bind himself up, then attack at his leisure. Or just leave her alone again while he went away to get a weapon. Wounding him, scaring him, would do nothing for her because she couldn't get away. Which meant she had to kill him.

First of all, she told herself, she didn't know if she was up to killing anyone. It was one thing to *threaten* with a knife, which she had done several times, and the threat had always been sufficient to buy her enough time and space to get away, but to *kill* with one was something else again. And suppose she did manage to summon the courage to kill him, what then? Unless she knew where she was, or how to get away, she'd not only still be lost, but she'd have a corpse for company. This place seemed enough like a grave already without adding that touch of realism.

One thing she did know was that she couldn't keep the knife in her boot. Whatever else he had in mind for her, if this guy was like every other man she'd ever known, eventually he was going to want to have her clothes off of her. Which probably included her boots, which meant he'd find the knife unless she already had it in her hand.

On her knees, Aural felt around for a hiding place in the rocks. The rock was moist wherever she touched. And smooth—everywhere she put her fingers it was smooth—as if water had been running over these rocks forever.

With her hands stretched out in front of her, Aural stood and inched slowly to one side. At first she counted her steps so she could return to her starting point, but then she realized that there was nothing to distinguish that point from any other. The only place she needed to mark was the spot where she put the knife.

Walking was awkward on the uneven floor and it was difficult to maintain her balance with her legs so closely constrained. She fell once on the slippery floor and landed hard, unable to break her fall. She started to cry from the shock of the fall, but then wept out of self-pity. She wept a long time, giving full vent to her fright and unhappiness, and her cries filled the vaulted room and reverberated back and forth until she seemed to be in the center of a crowd of moaning, wailing women.

At the end, Aural laughed at herself, pouring some of the same hysteric energy into the laughter so that the stones resounded again. This time it sounded as if she were in a crazy house at the fair, one of a nest of cackling lunatics.

That was okay, she said to herself. Do it once, get it over with, nobody around to hear you make a baby of yourself, except yourself, and you knew that much already. Just do it when you're alone, if you have to, but don't give it to him. That's a reward you must never give him.

She proceeded, half-crouched, feeling the uneven surface first with her hands before inching forward with her feet. When she paused to listen, the running water sounded closer, though still far away, and the drip of her clock was getting harder to detect.

She found a spot at last, her fingers slipping into a recess in the rock that was large enough to hold the knife. Feeling it with both hands, she tried to picture the geometry of the rock. Would it be visible when he brought the light back? She checked each angle of vision in turn, straining to imagine how it would look if someone could see. Even a speck of visibility would be too much—the knife might reflect the light more than the rocks, glint and flash and call out its presence. The hiding place seemed to curl in on itself like the edge of a snail's shell. He would see the opening only if he put his eyes where she had her fingers, which she didn't think was possible, and even then he would see only the hole. The recess itself was behind a curve, the knife completely out of sight. Aural put the knife in the hiding place, took it out again, worried about it, put it back. It was the best she had found. It would have to do, at least until she came up with something better.

She practiced getting her hand into the hiding place while standing up, while sitting down, even while lying on her back. The surfaces of the stone became familiar; she memorized the contours until it was no more difficult than finding a water glass in the bathroom in the middle of the night.

The difference was, she could always find the bathroom. She now had to be sure she could find this spot. Aural removed her boots and placed them so that if she sat with her feet where the boots were, her back would rest in the perfect place to give her immediate access to the knife.

She moved slowly to her right, counting steps, feet and hands feeling ahead of her into the darkness, searching for a different kind of niche in the rock, something big enough to hide herself. After fifty restricted steps she decided to return to her boots and try another direction, but when she came to what should have been the proper spot, her bare feet did not encounter the boots.

An icy panic gripped her. She had lost her way, misplaced her only weapon in a vast cavern of empty darkness. She had given herself over, defenseless, out of her own stupidity. With an involuntary cry of anguish Aural dropped to her knees and groped along the slippery rock with her hands.

Was she too far or too short? Had she already passed the boots in the darkness, slipping past them on her way back? Or had she not yet gone far enough? How far would she have had to be in the pitch black to miss them? An inch? Half an inch? She needed only to have misstepped by the narrowest of margins to have missed them completely, because if she didn't touch them, they were as far away as the moon. How could she have been so stupid? This wasn't like fumbling around in her room with the lights off; there were no landmarks here, no familiar furniture to bump into, no walls to rebound from.

At first she flailed wildly with her bound hands, patting and pawing in all directions, praying for a touch of leather against her fingertips, but when she started to crawl forward, she stopped abruptly. Think, she adjured herself. Think. You can't be that far away now, a few steps in any direction at best, but you must be basically on-line. But if you start to crawl around, you could end up anywhere, pointed in the wrong direction and lost forever with no hope at all. Anchor yourself here in some way. You're not really lost right now, you're just not where you want to be quite yet, but you're not lost if you stay anchored. You need the best way to search the most territory without leaving this spot. Don't be a baby, don't be any more of an idiot than you already have. Think. The farthest you can go in any direction and still stay in place is the length of your body. She lay down on the rock, stretched her hands as far as they would go. There was a particular depression at her fingertips, a hollowed dip that felt like a saucer. She ran her fingers around the saucer, then around the rock immediately surrounding it, trying to establish a context. Her toes were pressed against a slight ridge. Like all the other surfaces, it was smooth and rounded, but it rose up from the floor by several inches. When your toes are there and your fingers are in the saucer, you're back where you started, she said to herself.

Now slowly, carefully. Keep your feet against the ridge and roll. Moving one careful revolution at a time, Aural began to roll in a circle with her toes at the center. Face down, face up, she counted the turns, praying all the while for contact with a boot. Toes against the ridge, heels against the ridge. A slight shift of the body to keep the feet in contact, then roll again. After each half-revolution she probed with her fingers, seeking the saucer.

After sixteen rolls her fingers found the familiar depression. She had done a complete circle. But no boots. She sat up, trying to remember her high school geometry. Something about pi, but what did that tell her? Nothing, which was what she already knew. She remembered protractors and compasses and drawing circles, which she had just done with her body. All right, she had the time, let's continue the geometry lesson. Draw another circle, this time using her hands as the center. With her body as the diameter of the circle—or was it the radius?—she would still come back to this same point with her feet on the ridge and the saucer at her hands. She would not get lost and she would cover more ground. She tried to envision how much more, knowing that some of it would be overlap. Half a circle? Less, more? She couldn't see it clearly in her mind, but she didn't know what difference it made. She had no other plan.

Aural began to roll again, this time keeping her hands always in touch with the saucer-like depression. She counted her revolutions, knowing that sixteen should put her feet back in contact with the ridge, and became so concentrated on finding the ridge again that she almost forgot what her real purpose was. She nearly rolled over the boots with her hips without realizing what they were.

"Oh, you sweet things," she said, hugging the boots to her. "Don't you ever run away from me like that again."

She reached for the niche in the rock and located the knife quickly and easily. She replaced the knife in its secret crevasse, then tried to put her boots on again. It was very difficult to slip the leather uppers beneath the ankle irons and finally she gave it up. She had better use for the boots off than on, anyway, and if he realized she had taken them off, so what? What did it tell him?

Feeling proud of herself for having accomplished something rather than just allowing herself to descend into self-pity, Aural settled herself back against a cushion of rock and began to think of how she was going to deal with her captor. After a moment of silence, she could detect the steady tick of her water clock counting the minutes. Coming from the other direction, the liquid sound of water washing against the rock was soothing. For the first time, she realized that she had not slept in a long time, not since being rousted out of bed by Harold Kershaw's arrival. Blessedly, she fell asleep.

* * *

Aural awoke from a dream of bright sunlight to find herself still in utter darkness. The "brook" still burbled gently in the distance, the water clock ticked on and on, and nothing had changed. And then she heard an alien noise and immediately realized that it was probably what had awakened her. It was a sound of something muted striking stone, a dull thud followed by a scrape, and it came on slowly, very slowly. At first her mind conjured up an image of a large serpent hauling itself dreadfully towards her, its giant tail banging against the rock. It took a while for her to realize it was something being dragged over the rock as she herself had been dragged in the leather golf sack. This time there was something more resonant in the sack than her head and bones, and it sounded clearly if dully from a distance. Whatever he had with him now, he was a long time coming with it. From the moment when she first detected the scrapes that preceded the thuds, Aural noticed long pauses between movements, as if he were resting every few feet. Whatever he was dragging must be very heavy, she thought, or else he's very tired.

It took five ticks of her water clock, fifteen minutes, before she saw the first faint light. It wobbled as if the headlight were planted atop a shaky stalk. Was his head moving that much? She thought he must have palsy to be shaking so badly.

With a slowness that became more frustratingly painful to her the closer it came, the beam of light advanced. Aural realized that as much as she didn't want him to come, she also needed him, and now that he was here, she wanted him to get on with it. She could do nothing by herself, she required his presence, his light, if she were ever to get out of here.

The light was coming from a hole in the wall and very low to the floor. It was a narrowly focused beam, as if shining in a tunnel, and as it made its tedious way towards her, Aural could finally see the outlines of the exit he had used. It must have been the same way she was brought in. There was an opening in the vertical rock no bigger than a man's body—and a small man at that. She wondered if he was crawling through the tunnel—it didn't look big enough to negotiate in any other way.

As the beam moved closer she could hear the man himself. He was panting and moaning. He would advance a short ways—she could hear his boots on the stone now, the tumble of something muted against a hard surface—then the scraping sound of his progress would stop and she would hear his breath, hard and labored. Just before he'd start again he would groan, as if the effort cost him in pain.

Finally the light, wavering, slumping downwards as he rested, wavering again as he crawled forward, reached the opening of the tunnel, and he came into the chamber, moving on his belly with infinite slowness but determination, like a giant garden snail. Trailing behind him, his own sluglike path of mucus, was the leather golf sack, connected by a rope tied around his waist.

When he and the sack were completely clear of the tunnel, he collapsed, his face falling onto the rock.

"Well, numbnuts," Aural said, "You took your own sweet time about it. You think I got nothing better to do than hang around waiting for you?"

He didn't stir. His body was stretched to its full length on the rock, the light on his helmet pointing down at an angle onto the floor. In the diffused beam that shone off the floor, Aural took her first, oriented look at her surroundings. As she had already determined, she was in a cave, a huge chamber hollowed from the rock by the water flow of millennia. The ceiling was so high above her that she could barely make it out in the gloom. The wall from which the man had just crawled was at least thirty yards away from her and appeared to be solid except for the hole which he had just cleared before collapsing. She had thought she was leaning against a wall herself, but now she saw that it was only an outcropping of rock little more than waist high, and the true wall was at least another thirty yards beyond it. To her left, still farther away than the other walls, a narrow trench split the floor and then vanished completely as it hit the rock face behind her. It was probably the source of the running water she had heard, she thought. Whatever underwater river had formed the lake that had once filled this chamber had continued to flow until it worked its way still deeper into the rock and then through the wall, draining the lake with it on its way still farther underground.

To her right Aural could see a series of darker shapes along the wall that looked like waves at their crest, just bending over before crashing back upon themselves, the kind of waves under which photographers loved to capture surfers, surging just below the crest as the top of the wave curled over them—but these waves were rock, and they ran vertically from the floor, some all the way to the ceiling, frozen in time and space when the lake vanished beneath them. The rock appeared to have bent back on itself, as if shaped when molten, and formed scalloped edges reminiscent of the niche where she had stored the knife, only greatly larger, extending towards the roof.

Interspersed oddly along walls were those pointed mounds that Aural knew were stalagtites or stalagmites, she was never certain which was which.

As she studied the huge room that encased her, the light began to move, bouncing crazily off the walls. She looked and saw the man stirring on the floor, trying to lift his head, then falling back to the rock again as if his neck could not support the weight. Again he was still and Aural could hear his hoarse breath gasping from his throat as if even the effort of lifting his head were a great labor.

He rolled over onto his back and the light and shadows went crazy again, leaping about until they settled in a new configuration. The beam now pointed straight up and Aural could see the ceiling of her cage, a huge dome of rock at least three stories above her. If the space stretched that far up and still didn't break through the earth over their heads, how far underground must they be? She was not only buried, she thought with renewed alarm, she was entombed, tucked away as neatly and as far from the living as a pharaoh in his pyramid vault.

"Come here," the man said, and the light wobbled when he spoke, drawing forth new shadows on the ceiling and walls.

Aural watched him without moving, trying to judge the degree of his weariness. She could take the knife with her now, use it on him as he lay there—assuming he obliged her by staying exactly where he was. But if he turned to look at her, there was no way she could hide the knife with her hands cuffed together. Thirty yards was a long distance to cover with the baby steps her leg irons required, and she could betray the existence of her only weapon every step of the way.

"Come here," he repeated. His voice was hoarse and weak. "I need you," he said. And then, bizarrely, he added, "Please."

Aural walked to him slowly, trying to learn as much as she could about the cave as she did so. It was hard to make out anything in detail because each slight move of his head sent shadows winging and lurching about, swallowing each other up as new ones were born to replace them. Nothing ever looked exactly the same way twice because each breath he took caused the cave itself to move in and out of the light as if it had a pulse to match his own.

As she got close to him she realized that she could have brought the knife after all. He had not turned to look at her yet, and she was now within lunging distance, and now closer, now she stood next to him, looking down. She could have cut his throat while he lay there, his eyes closed. For a moment she wondered if he was asleep. She was close to the hole now but the light was pointing up and away from it and she could make out nothing beyond a greater darkness in the rock.

She had seen no other exit. If she were to get out, she would have to go into that hole of blackness. Had she not seen him emerge from it, she wouldn't have thought there was room enough for her shoulders to fit in. The very idea of crawling into such a place filled her with dread. She would sooner have forced herself into a hole in the ground, knowing there was a snake at the other end, but she also knew she had no choice. She would do what she had to, when she had to do it. And if that included slicing his throat open, she would do it. She thought. She hoped. Gazing down at him now as he lay still, breathing shallowly like a dreamer in a troubled sleep, it was hard to hate him enough to kill him.

And then she realized the condition of his face. He looked as if someone had been kicking his head around with cowboy boots. Aural had seen more than one of her boyfriends return from a night in the bar looking that way. One eye was swollen nearly shut; his nose and both cheekbones were puffed and as dark with broken blood vessels as if he had been painting his face with charcoal. Traces of dried blood still clung to his nose and upper lip, and overall he had the look of a man tenuously clinging to health.

He opened his eyes and looked up at her and she realized he had not been asleep, but quietly waiting. Conserving his strength and perhaps waiting to see what she would do.

"Hey, slick, you're looking good," Aural said.

"Where are your boots?"

"I took them off. You go partying with friends?"

"I met a friend of yours," Swann said.

"You should have brought him home."

"Get the lantern," he said. His voice was little more than a whisper, even in the resonating chamber of the cave. Moaning slightly, he rolled to his side, resting his head on his arm so that the light on his hat shone in the direction of the golf sack. Every movement seemed to cost him a great effort. Aural was amazed that he had managed to crawl back through the tunnel. When men administered a beating like the one he had taken, they didn't limit themselves to the face. Not the men she knew. She did not know how long a trip it was, but she knew that it had taken a long time for her to be brought to the cave once she was forced into the sack in the first place. He must have wanted to get back to me very badly, Aural thought, and the thought frightened her.

She unzipped the sack and found that it was crammed with groceries and supplies. What bothered her most was the quantity of canned food. It must have been the cans that caused the thudding noise, she realized, and there were dozens of them, beans and peaches and spinach and baby peas, and dried apricots, too, and dried sausage and a plastic bag full of hard rolls. Four plastic quart bottles of water, two containers of paraffin oil for the lamp. And three cartons of cigarettes. He was planning a long stay, Aural realized with a sinking feeling. There was enough food for weeks.

The lantern was wedged between pillows and wrapped inside a sleeping bag. There was a pack of dinner candles, red and white and blue, and extra bulbs and batteries for the headlamp. Lighter fluid and flints and even extra wicks. He was taking no chances about running short. But there were no matches. Later, when she had time to think about it, that detail frightened Aural most of all. There were no matches despite all the other flammables, she realized, because in the high humidity of the cave, matches would soon become sodden and useless. He knew this from experience. He had been in this situation before. The terrifying deduction from that was that he had not only done this with another girl, but he had gotten away with it or he wouldn't be free now. He had done it, he had learned, he had perfected his method, eliminated his mistakes.

He ignited the lantern with a cigarette lighter which he returned to his front pocket, then placed the lantern in her hand. She thought of swinging it into his face, but his eyes were on her the whole time and she decided to wait. She had to have either her feet or her hands free before she tried to get away; she had no chance without the use of one or the other, even with him as injured as he was. If he could drag the sack all the way, he still had a great deal of strength left in him.

"Take it to a flat spot," he said, "Then come back and get the bag." When she had the lantern in her hands he turned off his headlamp.

Aural carried the lantern back towards her hiding place, studying the details that now sprang up in the increased light. The vertical waves on the wall remained dark, but the rest of the rock took life in a fantastical way. The whole cavern seemed to be tinted a dull yellow, as if it were carved from pure gold. Everywhere she looked, walls, ceiling, or floor, the light reflected back to her with an aureate hue, so that the very light itself seemed composed of the finest translucent golden dust. Under different circumstances it would have seemed a fairy cave rather than a dragon's lair.

"Pretty, isn't it?" he asked, as if reading her mind.

"If you like this kind of thing," she said.

"It's sulfur oxide," he said. "And pyrite, too. Fool's gold."

"Figures. I finally land in a gold mine and it's a fake," she said.

"That's far enough," he said. "Put the lantern down."

Aural continued until she was close to her boots before setting the lantern on the rock floor.

"Now come back."

She hesitated.

With an effort, he rose to one knee.

"Oh, you don't want to make me come after you," he said. "That wouldn't be smart at all."

Leaving the lantern by her boots, Aural returned to the man.

"What friend of mine did you run into?" she asked.

"He didn't tell me his name," he said. "I didn't ask. People like that don't need names, anyway. They're all just the same."

"I wonder if you couldn't say the same for men in general," she said.

"Oh, not me," he said. "I'm not like other men at all. I'm what they would want to be if they had the courage, but they don't. You'll find that I'm quite special." He sounded convinced and proud.

"Not that I've noticed so far."

"But we haven't really gotten to know each other very well yet. You'll think I'm special, I promise you."

"You guys all think you're different."

"I like your courage," he said. "I like that you think you can talk back to me and get away with it. You'll change your mind, but it's nice for now."

He rose to his feet as she approached him. He was unsteady on his legs, as if his balance were off, but Aural realized that she had already waited too long. His strength was returning rapidly. She should have hit him with the lantern when she had the chance; she should have followed her first instinct and gone after him with the knife when he was still supine and had his eyes closed.

"Pull the bag over there," he said, pointing towards the lantern.

When she bent over to grab the rope, he hit her from behind, hammering both hands together into her kidney. Aural fell onto her knees, gasping.

He waited until she could hear him clearly before speaking.

"I apologize for being so crude about it," he said. "I detest that kind of brute violence, but you really must learn to do what I say, exactly when I say to do it. Next time I tell you to put the lantern down and return to me, you do it right then, right that instant, not when it pleases you. Do you understand?"

Aural nodded her head.

"Well, good. Everyone's entitled to a first mistake. Let's not discuss it any further. Pull the bag over to the lantern."

Aural was surprised at how easily she could drag the sack. It seemed to slide across the floor as if it were lubricated. When she got to the lantern she could see that the bottom of the sack was coated with a sort of gray slime.

"What is it?" she asked. He had kept pace with her as she dragged the bag, seemingly unable himself to walk any faster than her six-inch stride would take her.

"Guano," he said.

"What's that?"

"Bat shit, honey."

She noticed now that he had the same slime on his boots, his pant cuffs, some almost as high as his waist. He must have waded through it at some point, dragging the sack.

"It doesn't smell bad," he said. "Isn't that interesting? It's because of their diet."

"I'm glad you told me."

"You don't have to worry. The bats never come in here."

"Might have made a nice change."

"Nothing ever comes in here," he said, giggling.

"Except you. On your belly."

He started to say something, then put up a hand to cover his swollen eye and held his other hand out for balance. He swayed, then stepped back, away from Aural. Now, she thought, take him now, leap on him and pound his head against the rocks. But she did nothing but watch him.

"Kneel," he said when he had recovered himself somewhat. Aural knelt, facing him. Here we go, she thought. Now he unzips his fly and reveals his ambition. She thought of the woman she had spoken about to Rae who had cut off her husband's penis and thrown it out of the car window. I'll bite it off, she thought. That ought to distract him for a while. But he made no gesture towards his fly.

"Now onto your stomach," he said. Aural moved forward as she slid onto her stomach, getting as close as she could to her boots and the knife hiding place without moving the boots. When she was still he knelt on her back, freezing her into position with his weight. His hands fumbled at her waist, undoing her jeans, then struggling to pull them down her legs. She tried to raise up to assist him but he pushed her back down.

"I'll do it," he said brusquely. When her jeans were as far down her legs as the ankle irons would permit, he sat with his full weight on the small of her back and undid her handcuffs. Aural thought of going for the knife then, was about to try to roll him off and lunge forward to the hiding place, but he moved much too quickly for her. With a motion that had the sharp precision of practice, he yanked her onto her side and refastened the cuffs on either side of the ankle-iron chain so that she was now bound with her hands at her feet, forced by her constraints into the fetal position.

"There," he said, obviously pleased with himself.

"Oh, neat," she said.

"Comfortable?"

"Personally, I love this. Wouldn't you like to join me, sugar? We could share these cuffs."

"I have already joined you," he said. "I'll never leave you again."

He knelt in front of her so that he could see her face.

"Will you lead us in prayer?" he asked.

"I tell you what," she said. "Why don't you have the first go at it? I'll catch up with you the second time around."

"I'd think you'd want to pray," he said.

"Sugar, there are lots of things I'd like to do right now, but you know, you just can't do everything all at once. I'm so excited about what you and me are going to be doing together here with me trussed up like a turkey that I can't think of anything else."

"Everyone always wants to pray now," he said, baffled.

"Everyone?"

"The others."

"You mean you've had other girls? Well, now, that does it. You just cut me loose and take me home right this second."

"You'll pray later," Swann decided.

"I'm a professional prayer. Get me an audience and I'll be happy to say a few—"

"Sweet Jesus," he intoned, cutting her off, "give us both the strength to get through the terrible ordeal that is about to come. Give this girl the courage and fortitude to survive for as long as she possibly can. And give me the patience not to rush things, let me proceed with the care and attention that she deserves. In Jesus' name, Amen."

"Nice sentiment," said Aural. She felt a cold chill run down her spine that had nothing to do with the temperature in the cave.

"You're a little frightened now, aren't you? I can tell."

Aural refused to give it to him, but didn't trust herself to speak.

"It's all right to be afraid," he said. "I'm always nervous myself before I begin. It's good, though, it helps to heighten the sensations."

Not a word, Aural vowed to herself. From here on, no matter what he did, she wouldn't cry out, she wouldn't speak, she wouldn't so much as grunt for him. Whatever he had in mind, he would have to do it by himself, she would not help him.

He was rummaging through the leather sack, taking out the candles and a carton of cigarettes. Suddenly he clamped his hand to his swollen eye and bared his teeth as he groaned in pain and confusion. Aural watched him squeeze his good eye shut and sway back and forth on his knees.

He dropped one hand to the ground and continued to moan, hanging his head like a sick dog. When he straightened up at last, Aural could see tears on his face and he looked frightened, but whatever it was, it had passed. He sat back on his heels for a moment, gathering himself, then ripped open the carton of cigarettes.

Swann put a candle at Aural's head and another at her feet and a third behind her, then lit them. Like some kind of altar, she thought. And she was the sacrifice.

He turned off the lantern, and the shadows in the cave went crazy, dancing wildly in the flickering of the candles. The darkness closed in around them and Aural could no longer make out the ceiling or the walls. There was only her, only Swann, only the gyrating shadows to bear witness. Aural's world had shrunk to a little fold of light in the universal blackness and she was at the center of the earth.

Swann lit a cigarette and coughed. "Filthy things," he said. "I don't understand why anybody smokes them. Don't they know cigarettes can kill you?" He giggled as if he had suddenly realized what he had said.

He looked her in the face and grinned. "They do kill, you know. Eventually."

Aural tried to study him, to keep her eyes on his eyes and to ignore whatever else he was doing. She wanted to kill her imagination, to keep it from killing her. Whatever would happen would happen anyway, and anticipation would only make it worse. She stared at the asshole, whose eyes were dancing gleefully. He's insane, she thought. He knows exactly what he's doing, but he's as mad as he can be.

Swann puffed on the cigarette several times until he was contented with the glowing ember.

"Shall we begin?" he asked.

"Shit, yes, let's get on with it," Aural said, forgetting her vow of silence already.

"I usually like to start with the legs," he said, stroking her shin. Aural jerked away but he held her tightly, giving her a stern look of reprimand. When she stopped resisting, he ran his fingers over her calf like an acupuncturist seeking just the right spot.

He found the spot, then held the cigarette over her skin, just close enough so that she could feel the heat.

Fuck you, Aural thought wildly. Fuck you, fuck you, fuck you. You want me to beg, you want me to cry, you want me to piss myself out of fear. Well, fuck you, you get none of it, none of it.

He pressed the cigarette into her flesh and she screamed. She realized very soon that she would give him everything he wanted.

Chapter 31

Hatcher came announced this time, without pretense. He called and asked Becker for an appointment, and when he arrived he was accompanied by Karen and Gold and an agent from the Behavioral Sciences group whose purview included serial killers. Becker vaguely recognized the man.

Becker met them in his front yard, golf club in hand. He'd been hitting plastic golf balls over the roof of the house and into the backyard with a pitching wedge.

As Hatcher and the others stepped out of the car, Becker lofted a perfect shot over the house, then he turned and thrust the golf club into Hatcher's hands before allowing him to speak.

"Try one," Becker said. "Aim just left of the chimney."

Hatcher did not demur. He knew Becker wanted to make him look foolish and he was willing to oblige if that was the price to get what he wanted. He knew he would probably have to debase himself further before he was finished.

Becker toed a ball into position and Hatcher dutifully swiped at it, swinging stiffly in his suit. He missed the ball completely the first time, and tried again immediately as if the first attempt had been just for practice, hoping that his flub was not as obvious to the others as it was to him.

On his second swing, Hatcher buried the head of the club in turf, disconnecting a sizable chunk of sod.

"So sorry," Hatcher said, staring at the clod of dirt and grass that he had just unearthed. It looked like a bad toupee unaccountably dyed green.

He looked at Karen. "So very sorry."

"It's not your game," Becker said in a tone that implied that he was intent on continuing to humiliate Hatcher until he discovered the game that was his.

"I seem to have—" Hatcher bent over, thinking to retrieve and replace the severed turf, then stopped, wondering if calling further attention to it only made matters worse. Gold and the Behavioral Sciences man moved away from the lawn towards the porch, trying to disassociate themselves from the incident entirely.

"Jack does things like that all the time," Becker said. Gold thought he sounded enormously pleased. He removed the club from Hatcher's hands as if taking a dangerous toy from a child. It was not lost on Hatcher that Jack was only ten years old.

They proceeded into the house and arranged themselves in a living room that could comfortably seat only four. As if seeking the supplicant's chair, Hatcher sat on a leather-covered footstool that was a reproduction of a cobbler's seat, a piece of furniture used more for decoration than utility. The footstool forced Hatcher's knees higher than his waist, so that he looked like an adult at parents' night at grade school, sitting uncomfortably at the desk of his child.

"Comfy?" Becker crooned, smiling with a benevolence that fooled no one.

"Fine, yes, fine," Hatcher said.

Gold and the other agent continued to avoid each other's eyes. The psychiatrist glanced at Karen and intercepted a look of cold fury directed at Becker, who seemed oblivious. Gold wondered about the long-term health of their relationship. Certainly the stress of the Cooper case was doing nothing to bolster it.

"So good of you to make time for us like this," Hatcher was saying. "I realize you must be very busy . . . uh . . . with your interests."

"Yes. Today I was trying to learn to cut the ball," Becker said, smiling. "My normal shot is a slight draw, very good for most purposes—better distance, for instance—but there are times when you want to have that high fade available. The kind Nicklaus hits. Faldo and Norman have it when they need it, too."

"Ah, yes." Hatcher nodded. He thought he recognized the name Nicklaus. The others meant nothing to him.

"It's hard, though. Especially with a wedge," Becker said.

"Yes, difficult, I should imagine so," Hatcher said. "Well, now, John, we have come to see you—you do know Special Agent Withers of Behavioral Sciences, don't you?"

Becker nodded. "Withers."

"Of course," said Withers, who knew Becker only by reputation. He returned the nod of greeting.

"We have come on a matter of some urgency which I believe you already know about."

"What's that?" asked Becker.

Hatcher looked at Karen. He hoped not to let Becker drag every bit of the story out of him, inch by painful inch.

"The Cooper business," Karen said briskly. She was in no mood for Becker's antics. Being front man for Hatcher was bad enough for her without jumping through hoops held up by the man she lived with.

"You know about the Cooper business, with the two girls in the coal mine." Her tone allowed no room for disagreement.

"Special Agent Withers raised a few questions about the overall credibility of Cooper's story," Hatcher said. "Nothing crippling to the case, certainly, but an odd question here and there. When these—ah—doubts were brought to my attention, naturally I asked for more opinions. It was then that Assistant Director Crist and Dr. Gold came forward with what they tell me was originally your . . . idea."

Becker smiled confusedly as if he had not yet fully grasped the meaning of the conversation.

"You know what he means," Karen said sharply.

Becker turned his countenance towards her, still looking bemused. She glowered back darkly.

Hatcher continued. "I refer to your—suggestion—that Cooper was somehow coached into confessing the murder of the Beggs girl. While not granting that that is the case at all, not at all, it still raises an interesting line of speculation that one must conscientiously pursue. Dr. Gold has been good enough to do a bit of research into the subject."

Becker turned his attention to Gold. He imagined that Hatcher had given the assignment to Gold for two reasons. The first would be to keep the possibility that Hatcher might be wrong about Cooper's guilt—and that Becker might be right—within as small a group as possible. Since Gold was one of the group that had originated the doubt, Hatcher would be containing the spread of doubts if he had Gold do the work. The second reason, a happy offshoot of the first from Hatcher's point of view, was to punish Gold for having been a party to the doubts in the first place. Becker also imagined that Hatcher's greatest punishment would be reserved for Becker himself. It was Hatcher's way.

Gold cleared his throat. "Well, not to get overly technical, we have done a number of studies on eyewitnesses, as you all know, and the results are not only that they are notoriously unreliable but that they actually 'see' and 'remember' those things which they are preconditioned to see. If they are shown videos of a traffic accident, for instance, and are personally inclined to believe that women are worse drivers than men, given the least bit of ambiguity in what they see, they will identify the driver who has caused the accident as a woman. That's a very simple example, of course. Any skillful questioner can plant suggestions in their minds as to specific details of the scene and they will soon parrot what they were told, convinced that it was what they saw. A rather extensive study of this phenomenon was done at Princeton, where Johnson was able to make her subjects swear they saw and heard things that never happened. They can be shown pictures of people embracing and interpret them as acts of violence, if they have been lead to believe that's what they will see. Most common, of course, is the identification of a perpetrator as being a member of whatever race the spectator identifies with criminal acts. Whites are notorious for believing all black men are dangerous, and consequently 'seeing'' all dangerous men as black.

"Of most interest to us in this case, of course, are those examples in which the questioner can make the witness 'remember' things that did not happen. It is not difficult to do, and the witnesses are by no means stupid or pliable people. It is simply a matter of playing into their preconceptions as to how things are apt to happen, or supplying details that they missed but that their minds tell them should be there. It is easier still if the ideas are planted before the witnesses see the event. If the scene is dark, if details are obscure and the witnesses have been told to watch for a man with a knife, they will 'see' a man with a knife, no matter the facts of the event.

"Now these are ordinary people with no ax to grind beyond ordinary prejudices and preconceptions. Cooper is a very stupid man with a strong desire to believe that he is a killer. Such a notion enhances his self-esteem—and indeed actually gets him the esteem of others within the prison system, where he has spent a good deal of his life. Again, without getting technical, the more people he thinks he killed, the better Cooper feels about himself. To be simplistic about it, we all know high school athletes whose exploits become more and more heroic in the telling the further they get from the event until by the time they're in middle age or beyond they themselves actually believe their stories of past glory. They have convinced themselves through repeated telling.

"With Cooper, we have a man who *could* have been convinced through repeated telling that he did something which in fact he never did. I stress the *could* because right now we really don't know what happened. But given Cooper's need to believe the worst about himself, given his prolonged isolation with Swann, given an apparent cleverness on Swann's part . . ." Gold trailed off, not wanting to reach the danger-ous conclusion aloud.

"Well, hardly the sort of thing to convince a jury," Hatcher said, "but helpful in a speculative way." His fear, of course, was that it was precisely the kind of thing to convince a jury, just exactly the sort of vagary that in the hands of a skillful attorney could turn into a weapon of doubt with which to pry the case wide open. Juries were acquitting people right and left with not much more to justify their verdict than what Gold had just said. There was a predisposition to innocence abroad in the legal system that Hatcher found alarming. He did not dare to risk such an outcome while Beggs stood to lose face.

"What do you think, Withers? This is your line of work," Becker asked.

Withers had been hoping that no one would address him at all. It seemed the sort of conference in which no participant was going to win.

"I'm sure Dr. Gold has done his research well," Withers said non-committally. "There are always some inconsistencies in anyone's con-fession. That's just human nature. All I did was point out a few in Cooper's case. That doesn't necessarily mean anything."

"Oh, good, then there's nothing to worry about," Becker said.

Hatcher improved the crease in his pant leg.

"Actually, John, I must agree with you. There really is nothing to worry about—we have the killer in custody, no question in my mind about that. But there are always naysayers. There are always those who would ruthlessly manipulate the legal system to their own ends. Natu-rally, in the interest of justice, we would like to squelch those voices before they begin. We must have the appearance of justice as well as justice itself. In order to assure that appearance in this case, we feel that it is best to have this man Swann in custody as well."

"Don't you have him in custody now?"

"Actually, he has been released from prison."

"What asshole did that?"

"It was considered the best way to assure his cooperation."

"What stupid son of a bitch gave the order to release Swann?"

"There's really no point in fixing blame in such cases, John. An error seems to have been made; we need to correct it."

"Sure, but what kind of a head-up-his-ass dufuss would let that little shit go in the first place?"

Hatcher adjusted the crease in the other pant leg. The others in the room watched, transfixed, to see if he would avoid the knife poised to take its pound of flesh.

"Decisions of this kind are complicated, but ultimately I must take responsibility for all the actions of my people. It would be cowardly to do otherwise."

Becker was not yet satisfied.

"You're the asshole, then?"

Hatcher lifted his head and forced a smile as wintry as a February night.

"Yes, John, if you want to think of it that way. I am the asshole." Hatcher looked at no one but Becker and his voice had the regulated tone of a metronome.

"I suspected you were," Becker said. He heard Karen's angry exhalation of breath. "But it's nice to hear you confirm it."

He smiled broadly. Withers thought it was the first genuine expression of any kind that he had seen since his arrival. Becker looked, briefly, like a happy man.

"I'm glad you are pleased," said Hatcher. "Now, John, the Bureau needs you to do something. Swann has disappeared completely. We have been unable to get any trace at all on his movements since he left prison. Inasmuch as you have had a rather lengthy interview with the man, and given your great expertise in these matters, and since although you failed to detect the nature of his deception during that interview you did most likely gain some insight into his character, the Bureau hopes— most ardently hopes—that you will assist us in finding him."

Becker had known it was coming from the moment that he heard that Swann had escaped. There seemed no way to avoid the final confrontation that Swann had provoked in the first place by sending his letters to Becker. Having fooled Becker during the interview had only pushed the ultimate outcome to the point of inevitability.

"I will need a few things," Becker said.

Hatcher was surprised at the ease of victory. He had expected much more resistance.

"Of course we will give you whatever you need."

"I want this to be the end of it," Becker said. "I never want to work for you again. I don't want you to forward mail to me, I don't want you to call me, or speak of me, or think of me. I want to be taken off indefinite medical extension and dropped from the Bureau roster as if I were dead. This is the end of it—forever."

Hatcher did not hesitate. He knew he could always renege later. Becker was far too valuable an asset to relinquish forever. Hatcher had built his career in part on Becker's triumphs and had no intention of stopping now, although another triumph in the Beggs case might well put him beyond the need of Becker's heroics. In any event, it was a contingency to deal with in the future. For now, the only thing that mattered was Becker's cooperation.

"As you say, John. It will be as you say."

"You mustn't think I trust you," Becker said.

Hatcher raised his eyebrows and tried to look as if his feelings were hurt. The form had to be observed in these matters.

"I want the tape you made of my interview with Swann," Becker continued. Hatcher raised a finger towards Withers, who made a note.

"When I narrow him to an area, I want to be able to pick and choose from the local agents myself."

Hatcher nodded, again motioning with a finger towards Withers.

"And full cooperation from the national information net, of course."

"Certainly."

"And if I smell you anywhere near me, if I so much as sense your interference, no, hell, even so much as your observation of the case, I'll quit."

Hatcher sat stock-still.

"I have my responsibilities, John."

"My conditions, yes or no. You've fucked up every operation of mine you've ever gotten close to . . . Yes or no?"

Hatcher waited as long as dignity required before finally lifting his finger a fraction. Withers began to write.

Chapter 32

Aural spent the night as if in her coffin. He had put her in the leather golf sack for warmth and zipped it up so that only her face was uncovered. She was still shackled hands to ankles, and he had taken the additional precaution of securing the sack with the length of rope, tying the other end around his leg so that if she moved too far in the night, he would know it. Later, when she was weaker, he could relax his vigilance, but he knew that she still had some resistance left. Eventually she would welcome the end as much as he did, but he wanted to postpone that time as long as possible. When they gave up and lost the will to remain, they slipped away from him much too quickly. Life was a curious thing, Swann thought, capable of withstanding injuries and insults of the worst sort as long as the fiber of the will was intact to hold it together. But if the heat of despair got too high, the will would melt irreversibly, like gelatin oozing between his fingers. He tried to make his girls last longer; he urged them to withstand him and to hold on; but when they decided to go, he could not restrain them. Sometimes they went so quickly that he almost missed the passing, which would have been a terrible waste. He wanted to celebrate the moment, to exult in it, to sanctify it with his great joy and release. It would be an awful thing for them to have suffered so much and then to have slipped away unnoticed, uncelebrated. If he knew that their time had come, he would try to speed them along by intensifying his pleasure, because it was important that *he* should send them, that *he* should be the cause. He would work on them all night, if necessary, never leaving their side when the time had come, ignoring his own need for sleep or food, denying himself comfort for the greater cause. He thought of it as a sacrifice he made for his girls, just as they had made their own for him. It was the least he could do for them; he owed them that much when they had given so much to him.

When their time came he forgave them their spitefulness, he overlooked the horror of their appearance, their mutilated, untouchable bodies, the tears and mucus and excrement with which they soiled themselves. At the end they were all his angels and he in turn was the ministering angel for them, the last sight they saw on this earth, the last human touch they would ever feel. They took him with them into Jesus' embrace and Swann knew that Jesus thanked him for sending them to him. And they thanked him too, or they surely would once they reached the other side. He could detect the light of love in their fading eyes as they eased away. At the end, they understood, he was certain of that. They knew that no hospital emergency team could have tried harder to prolong their life, and that no minister in the world could have given them a more joyful, jubilant valedictory when the inevitable arrived at last.

When he grew weary, when he could take no more pleasure for that day, he had trussed up Aural in her sack and then crept into his sleeping bag with the contentment that came from exhaustion. He turned off the lantern and the insistent hiss died with the light, leaving them in silence except for the sounds of the girl. She moaned when she moved, but he knew that after a few days that would stop. Something happened to them after a few days, and they slept peacefully at night. They still screamed for him when he made them, but they stopped moaning. And this one wasn't a crier, he was glad of that. Sometimes they cried all night long and destroyed his rest, which only made him angry. He regretted that because this was not a business to be done in anger. It had to be done carefully, slowly, with love. If he was angry, he went too fast and hurt them for the wrong reasons. He hadn't gone to all this trouble and taken such risks just to hurt them to punish them. He was ashamed of himself when he allowed his anger to get the better of him and always regretted it later. This girl was not going to anger him, however. She was going to fight him, she was going to hang on as long as she possibly could—and she was not going to cry. She was wonderful and Swann drifted into sleep thinking that he truly loved her already.

Aural was astounded to realize that she had slept. She awoke with a start, not from a nightmare, but *to* it as the realization of what had happened, was happening, flooded back to her consciousness. She heard a noise beside her and realized that he had awakened her with a shout. She could sense him in the dark, twisting about in his sleeping bag, groaning.

"Sweet Jesus," he cried, his voice filled with pain. "Oh, Christ, Jesus."

"What the fuck are you doing?" she asked.

He continued to groan, and although she couldn't see him, Aural could imagine him clasping his head with his hand as he had earlier when he seemed to faint.

"Jesus," he muttered again, then, "Goddamn it."

"I'm trying to sleep over here," she said.

He stopped shouting then, but she could hear him whimpering and rocking back and forth. The noises came rhythmically after a time, as if he were receiving the pain in pulses. She hoped it came like machine gun fire; she hoped it ripped his head off.

"What's the matter?" she asked after several minutes, trying to sound sympathetic.

He did not respond.

"Do you need anything?"

He was silent and she realized that he had stopped rocking. If he continued to whimper, it was so quietly that she couldn't hear it over her own breathing.

Because of the rope tied around the sack, she could not roll over and her back was aching fiercely. Amazingly, the cramped muscles hurt more than the burns, which, at the time they were administered, seared so painfully that she thought they might kill her. She knew now that they wouldn't kill her—at least the pain wouldn't kill her. What effect it would have if he kept at it, if he burned *all* of her . . . she tried not to think about it.

She had been freed once from the contorted fetal position. She had told him she had to go to the bathroom, and to her amazement he had unhooked her hands from her ankles and allowed her to stand. He tied the rope to her handcuffs and secured her wrists in front of her body. He had been strangely courtly throughout the proceedings.

"You will want privacy," he said. He gave her a lighted candle and pointed the direction she should go.

"Keep on until the rope is taut," he said. "You'll find the appropriate spot there." He even handed her a roll of toilet tissue and made a display of turning his back although she felt his eyes on her every step of the way. Aural hoped to get closer to the wave formations on the wall; she thought there might be potential hiding places there if she could ever get to them; but as she veered in that direction, he called out sharply.

"Not that way," he said. "Straight ahead."

"Well, how'm I supposed to know where I'm going?" she demanded.

"Oh, you'll know it when you get there," he said, his voice suddenly amused. "It's well marked."

He was full of these little jokes to himself, giggling at things only he thought were funny. Aural not only hated the bastard in a general, all-encompassing way, but she couldn't find much to like about him, either. He'd be a creep even if his hobby was collecting stamps instead of torturing women.

She walked forward into the wavering candlelight, then stopped and gasped.

He giggled, "Find it?"

A human skeleton lay a few feet from her. The flesh was gone, but long dark hair still curled in a mat under the bony skull. The hands had been crossed over the chest in a mockery of subterranean burial, and the lower torso was covered in patches of cloth that had once been a skirt. The victim's shoes were placed neatly at her feet and her ankles had been crossed, but the bones of the feet had dropped away from each other and lay where they had fallen on the rocky floor.

Aural could not guess how long the girl had been dead, but the shoes looked like new.

She turned away from the skeleton and stepped in the opposite direction. The rope pulled snugly at her waist.

"Anywhere in there will do," Swann called to her. His voice beat back on itself, overlapping the giggle that followed.

Aural moved several steps to the side and squatted. The bones of another skeleton shone dully in the flickering light. This one had been "buried" like the first, her arms crossed over her chest. The ligaments of the hands had disintegrated and the finger bones had fallen in among the ribs.

When she was in control of herself, Aural called, "You been busy, ain't you? You been a real little beaver."

"Oh, you haven't seen them *all*," he said proudly. "These are very early works. I did them *years* ago."

"Well, they say that idle hands are the devil's tool," Aural said, walking back towards him. If there were other bones, she did not want to see them. "It's good to know you've been active so you can't get up to any mischief."

As she approached him she realized she could have grabbed one of the bones, a leg bone, a thighbone, and used it to club him to death. If she had had the presence of mind. If she could have brought herself to pick up the bone in the first place. She cursed herself for another opportunity missed. How many more would she have before she joined the boneyard? Girl, you've got to get in control of yourself, she thought. You've got to take your chance when you get it.

Now, as she lay wide awake, she could hear his steady breathing. The bastard was beginning to snore. He was resting while she was consuming her precious energy in useless rage and anxiety. Damn it, girl, she thought, don't let him sleep. Keep him as bad off as you can, keep him sleepless, get him punchy and careless, force him into making a mistake.

"Hey, shitstick!" she called. "Wake up. Time to be up and doing, we got some business to take care of."

He came awake noisily, spluttering, alarmed.

"What? What is it?"

"Come on, slick, get your ass up. You got things to do. And in the meantime, how about some breakfast? You wasn't planning to *starve* me to death, too, was you?"

"What are you talking about?"

"It's *morning*. Get your ugly ass up. Feed me, then we'll think of something fun to do."

"It's morning?" he asked, puzzled. "How do you know?"

"Let's get at it, slick. Start opening some of them cans. What have we got for breakfast, beans or peaches?"

She heard him fumbling about, then his lighter flared into flame. Aural saw him looking at his wristwatch, trying to figure out what was going on. Baffled by what his timepiece told him, Swann turned to look at her, holding the lighter in front of him like a lantern.

"What are you up to?" he asked.

Swann studied her for a moment in the insufficient glow of the cigarette lighter. He cocked his head to one side, trying to interpret what he saw. Aural's head peeked out from the golf sack, and she was grinning at him.

"Up and at 'em, chief," she said. "Time's awasting."

Swann clicked the lighter shut and the cavern returned to darkness. Aural saw red ghosts dance on her retina while Swann moved out of his sleeping bag. She heard him fumble about for a moment, then the lighter snapped on again and he lit a candle. He walked the few feet to her side and peered down at her for a moment before bending and tugging at the rope that bound the sack to his leg. Satisfied that the rope was still secure around her body, he unzipped the sack far enough to see that her wrists and ankles were still manacled.

He zipped the sack up to her chin once more.

"What are you playing at?" He leaned close to her, peering into her eyes. Aural could smell his breath and feel the heat of the candle.

"Just a little s and m. I'm pretending you've got me tied up and are trying to torture me."

"You'd better be careful," he said. "You'd better be very, very careful. So far I like you."

"I thought you did. I don't know . . . a girl can tell."

"But I know how to be mean," he said, ignoring her.

He moved the candle until it was directly in front of her face, six inches away from her skin. His own face was behind the flame, the features dancing in the flickering light like a jack-o'-lantern. So slowly that it took Aural a moment to realize what was happening, he moved the flame towards her eyes. She watched with fascinated horror as the flame inched closer and closer.

"Tell me when you're sorry that you woke me up at two in the morning," he said softly. Aural did not look at him; she could see only the bright orange flame creeping ever nearer. The fire filled her field of vision, blocking out anything else, and she fought a scream that wanted to tear loose from her chest. Not my eyes, she thought, terrified.

When the warmth of the candle turned to heat, she blew it out.

Swann emitted a grunt of anger, then the cigarette lighter snapped into flame again. He relit the candle and set it on the ground, too far away for her to blow it out again.

He sat with his arms on his knees, studying her as if she were an enigma that he had just stumbled across.

"What *am* I going to do with you?" he asked at last.

"You mean *you* don't know? I was counting on you to have it all figured out."

"Shut up," he said softly.

"If it's up to me, I say let's play another game entirely. How about the one where I stick you in the sack and set you on fire? You'll like that one, I promise. I'm good at it."

"I said be quiet. I'm trying to think."

"While you're thinking, open a can. I'll have the beans."

To Aural's amazement, he smiled at her.

"All right," he said. "Since you're so eager to get at it, I'm up now anyway. Beans do sound good, don't they?"

He released Aural from the sack, undid her handcuffs from the ankle irons so that she could stretch and feed herself, and fed her beans and peaches.

"Eat up," he said. "You're going to need your strength. This will be a longer session than before since we've got more time."

"More time to kill, you mean," Aural said.

"That's good. I like that. More time to kill. That's good."

"I've got hundreds of them," Aural said.

"I like women with a sense of humor," Swann said. "I spent three years living with a gorilla who had the sense of humor of a rock."

"I think I used to date him," Aural said. "Did he have a tattoo on his butt?"

Swann giggled. "You're funny," he said.

"You're a little strange yourself. In a very interesting way. I can see why the girls like you."

"They do, you know," he said soberly. "You're joking, but they do. My girls love me—at the end. You will, too, you'll see."

"Do you get those headaches a lot?" Aural asked abruptly. "I heard you crying last night."

"I wasn't crying."

"You ought to have that looked at."

"Your boyfriend did it to me," he said. "The one who beat me up in town."

"Harold Kershaw? He always was a favorite of mine. He let me set him on fire, he liked it so much he can't let me go. You sure you wouldn't let me try it with you?"

Swann pushed his can of beans from him and took Aural's from her hands.

"How about if I visit the little girls' room before we start again?" she asked.

"All right."

He tied the rope around her waist and gave her a candle. As she walked towards the graveyard, Aural thought of how she might slip a shinbone in her shirt when she squatted. If she kept it hidden long enough, she could pull it out when she got within range and hit him on the head.

Halfway there, the rope grew taut.

"I'm going in the right direction," she complained.

"I know it," Swann said. He was crossing quickly to her, holding the lantern. As she started to turn to face him, he kicked her legs out from under her and rolled her onto her stomach before refastening the handcuffs so that her hands were secured behind her back, making any attempt to get a bone impossible.

Swann grinned at her. "You mustn't ever think I'm stupid," he said. "That would be a serious mistake."

"I sure don't want to get on your bad side," Aural said.

"You're just a little too eager," he said, hauling her to her feet. When she returned, he shackled her hands to her ankles once more.

"Let us pray," he said.

"Praise be to Jesus," said Aural.

He looked at her, pleased.

"Would you like to lead the prayer, sister Aural?"

"Not just yet," Aural said.

"Or sing? Would you sing a hymn for us?"

"I'd rather get burned by cigarettes," she said.

"Very well."

He lit a cigarette and coughed at the smoke.

"I think this relationship is coming along nicely, don't you?" Aural asked. The last words were lost in her involuntary gasp as he touched her.

Chapter 33

Becker lived with the tape of his meeting with Swann, turning it on in the morning after Jack was off to school and turning it off only when the boy had returned home. During the late afternoon and the preparation for the evening meal, Becker acted as if nothing were different, joking and playing with Jack, helping him with his homework, trying to make the mysteries of beginning science and mathematic less arcane. When Karen came home he was still buoyant, almost jolly, but when Jack had gone at last to bed, Becker retired to the office and turned on the tape once more, playing it with the volume low. It was no longer the words he was listening to but the rhythms, the pauses, the stops and starts, the sudden, fleeting fermatas that bespoke lies.

"... You have a rep," Swann's voice said on the tape.

"I'll bet," came his own reply.

"I hear you climb, you climb mountains. You're a rock climber, right?" A pause, no response from Becker, then Swann's voice again, a trace of triumph. "You'd be surprised how much they know about you."

"You a climber, Swann?" Becker could hear the strain in his voice as though it were filtered through the discomfort he felt in the little cell, the unease he experienced in the presence of Swann. I was off balance already, Becker thought, pausing the tape. One minute into the interview and already so skewed by my problems that I wasn't listening right. Swann was telling him what he wanted to know. They always told him; they could not help themselves; they were always so pleased, so proud of their ghastly accomplishments that they could not help but reveal it in some way. The hardest thing for such psychopaths was keeping the secret to themselves; the great trick was to listen. In this interview Becker had listened only to himself. But he could hear it clearly now.

"Well . . . not really. I worked with ropes a little bit, I know what's involved. That's scary work."

He's playing on your ego there, Becker thought. And why? To cover himself.

"Not so scary if you know the safe way," Becker said on the tape. In his own home, Becker squirmed with irritation at his own stupidity. "You ever try it?"

"I believe in gravity," Swann was saying. "If it tells me to go down, I go down."

Becker turned off the tape and glanced at the clock. It was close to four in the morning. He had run through the entire tape dozens of times, trying to filter his own ego out of it. He rewound it and played the same section over.

Karen was asleep, or pretending to be. Becker watched her for a moment from the doorway, then walked through the darkened house to Jack's room. Becker looked lovingly at the boy asleep; innocence, all innocence. He turned away from the door and went outdoors to stand alone in the yard.

He felt like howling. He was giving it up, giving it all up as surely as if he were leaving the earth. When he returned, he would be too vile to live with them again, he thought. His hands would be too bloody, his soul too restless. Innocence deserved to be protected; it could not be entrusted to the ravening beast. Listening to the tapes, Becker had found Swann, but he had lost what he loved.

He was like a junkie with the needle in his arm, Becker thought. He had put it there himself when he had deciphered the first cryptic note from Swann; he had prepared himself for the fix as surely as if he had gone out and bought the narcotic and the syringe that same day. When he performed the actual injection no longer mattered because he was already gone, and he knew it, and anticipation was as much a part of the experience as the act itself. He knew that he had taken the first step down the long, slippery slope and any subsequent flailing of arms or attempts at equilibrium were just posturing for the benefit of others, futile attempts to convince them, and himself, that he was an unwilling victim. In fact he could see ahead of time the terrible fall that awaited him as he gathered speed, and he knew he wouldn't stop until he hit the gutter. He shuddered, looking forward to the trip, his chest fluttering with excitement.

That was what Hatcher knew about him, understood better than Becker would admit to himself, and the real reason he hated Hatcher. In the long run, Becker could not resist the hunt, the chase. He could not ultimately deny himself the kill, which was just the plunging of the syringe.

He was like Swann in that, Becker knew. No, worse, he wasn't *like* Swann. He was the same.

Chapter 34

This time Pegeen Haddad was in acceptable Bureau costume. She met Becker at the airport dressed in a navy blue business suit with a white blouse closed at the collar by a red and blue foulard. Becker thought she looked like an airline stewardess.

"Well, Haddad, there you are," he greeted her.

Pegeen tried to remember any of the witty remarks she had prepared for the meeting.

"Here I am," she said.

Becker nodded several times as if he wanted to say something further and she waited before realizing that he had nothing clever to say, either.

"Okay, then," he said finally. "Let's get at it."

As she led him to the car in the parking lot, Pegeen wondered if it was at all possible that Becker felt as nervous as she did. He was a hard man to read at the best of times, and seeing him again after several weeks was not the best of times. She had not expected to see him again at all, ever. His request to have her assigned to him as an assistant had come as a complete surprise and had raised more than a few eyebrows in the Nashville home office. The story of her presence in the motel room during Becker's unexplained shower had made the rounds of the rumor mill with great celerity, and her continual and increasingly weary explanations of innocence had finally begun to taper off when his sudden request came through, reviving and inflating the previous spate of salacious humor in the office.

He did not speak to her again until they reached the car.

"Got any other clothes with you?" he asked.

"No," she answered, surprised. "Why?"

"Things are going to get kind of grubby," he said. "You'd be better off in a pair of jeans."

"Agents don't wear jeans on duty. This outfit conforms to Bureau dress code."

"It doesn't suit me, though. I'm your boss now, Haddad. They told you that, didn't they?"

"They said I was to assist you."

"That means doing what I tell you to do, all right?" Pegeen did not understand the harshness in his tone. He sounded angry with her. Her first reaction was to get angry herself.

"They didn't tell me why you wanted me to assist you," she said.

"I didn't tell them."

"Want to tell *me?*" she inquired sharply.

Becker studied her for a moment as she maneuvered the car into traffic.

"What do you want to hear—I asked for you because you're the best agent I've ever met?"

"That would be a nice opening, then you could tell me the truth," she said.

"You're not going to like the truth," he said.

Pegeen felt herself blushing. He wanted to be with me, she thought. He wanted to spend time with me, to be with me, he's been thinking about me just as I have been thinking of him. Her ears were on fire, her damned ears were giving her away again.

"What's the truth?" she asked softly.

"Let's go to your place and change your clothes," he said.

She glanced at him for as long as she dared before turning back to the traffic.

"I'm not sure that's a good idea," she said. In fact, she thought it was a splendid idea, if not a very safe one.

"Well, let's try it anyway," Becker said. "Sometimes my ideas are better than they look at first glance."

Pegeen paused for several moments before saying, "I've given it several glances now. I still don't think it's a good idea."

"Do what you're told, Haddad," he said gruffly. "I'm not in a mood to argue with you about everything I say." He laid his head back against the seat. "Wake me when we get there," he said. "I haven't slept for several days."

"I'm glad I have that soothing effect on you," she said, trying to figure out just what was going on.

"It's not you, kid. It's the car." He closed his eyes and by the time Pegeen had swallowed the "kid" and fought back her urge to retaliate with a cutting remark about his age, Becker was asleep.

* * *

When she stopped the car in her driveway, Pegeen had still not decided quite how to handle the situation. Becker made it easy for her. He rolled his head towards her, opened one eye, and said, "Jeans and something old on top, and boots." He then closed his eye and rolled his head away from her.

Racked with confusion and conflicting desires, Pegeen dressed in front of the mirror over her bureau. The jeans were easy enough, but the selection of the blouse took some consideration. She contemplated her reflection as she held a number of possible selections under her chin and against her bra. The brassiere was demure and proper and perfectly appropriate for her business outfit, but not right for the more casual tops she was contemplating. She decided on a purple underwire push-up bra and paused to look at her naked torso. Her breasts were full, almost too large for her body size, she thought, but beautifully formed. She was very proud of the way they looked and regretted at times that her best features were necessarily hidden under her clothes while her face, which she could only tolerate, and her ears, which she loathed, represented her before the world.

As she admired her nakedness, she half wished that Becker would suddenly walk in on her. She imagined him pausing for a moment to admire her beauty, then taking her into his arms and kissing her softly before trailing his tongue down to her breasts.

Christ, she thought, putting on the bra and tugging on a top, you're going to be up on a charge of sexual harassment in the workplace if you don't stop this. The man is asleep in the car, not in here, that ought to tell you something.

As she approached the car, Becker rolled his head towards her once more. "Cover yourself," he said.

Pegeen thought her face would burst into flame. She knew she should not have chosen the tank top.

"I am covered," she said angrily.

"Warmer," he said. He rolled away from her and closed his eyes again.

Fuck you, too, she thought, storming back into the house. She re-emerged with a flannel shirt buttoned at the wrists.

"Good," he said. "It's going to be cold. We're going underground."

"The tank top was less conspicuous for going undercover than this is. I look like a lumberjack."

"Not undercover, Haddad. Underground."

Becker handed her a slip of paper with an address in downtown Nashville written on it.

"Wake me when we get there," he said.

"Is this how it's going to work? You give me orders, then go to sleep? If you'd let me in on what the plan is, I could do a little thinking on my own. My brain does work, you know."

"I thought we got past all this defensive shit the last time around," he said.

"There seems to be some difference of opinion as to what exactly happened last time."

He opened both eyes and studied her.

"What do you mean?" he asked.

"I'll wake you when we get there," she said, throwing the car into gear too abruptly.

"Something wrong, Haddad?"

"What could be wrong?"

"The address is for the headquarters of the speleological society. The guys who crawl around in caves."

"I know what speleology is. They're spelunkers."

"They call themselves cavers these days," he said. "You ever done any caving?"

"No. Have you?"

"Hell no," he said. "I'm scared of places like that." Once more he turned away from her and seemed to sleep.

Erskine Browne was built along the lines of a stiff rope. When he stood behind his desk to greet his visitors, it was easy for Becker to see why he had been nicknamed Weasel by his colleagues. Before arthritis had debilitated his flexibility, Browne had been legendary within caving circles for his ability to squeeze himself into any hole and wriggle through it like a ferret after its dinner. Even now, with his bent and frozen joints, his hands shaped into claws by the arthritis, he looked to Becker as if he could slip through an s-curve if he had to, and his lively eyes seemed to indicate that he wouldn't mind it at all.

"Becker, isn't it?" Browne asked.

"John Becker, that's right. And this is Special Agent Haddad."

Browne offered his gnarled hand to Pegeen.

"Agent Haddad. A pleasure. I didn't realize they made agents so pretty." He winked at Becker.

Pegeen decided that Browne's age allowed him a certain dispensation in the sexism category. Any man over sixty was to be excused for the occasional inappropriate remark because of a deficient early education.

"Only the good ones," Becker said soberly.

Browne winked again and offered such a knowing grin to Pegeen that she changed her mind about dispensation.

"I did the research you were asking for on the phone," Browne was saying. "You wanted me to look for a name in the enrollment roster of the SOA . . ." He turned again to Pegeen. "That's Speleologists of America."

Pegeen did not return the smile.

"I have that," she said.

"Name of Swann, right? The national search was easy, that's all computerized, has been for seven years."

"Any luck?"

"Nope. Of course that doesn't mean too much. There are a lot of amateur cavers—some of them pretty good, too—who aren't members. We only have maybe ten percent of the active cavers in the country, which is a shame because we have a good deal to offer them. The newsletter alone is worth the price of membership."

"I didn't really expect to find him on your list," Becker said. "It was a long shot. People like Swann are not great joiners."

"Well, now, let's not get ahead of ourselves," said Browne. "That wasn't all I did. The FBI calls me, I'm going to put myself out a little bit, right? What did he do, exactly?"

"Exactly, it's hard to say," said Becker. "He may not have done anything at all. He may just be a figment of my imagination."

"Yeah, sure, which is why you go to the trouble of trying to find him in our lists. I figured, it wasn't important, you wouldn't ask. Like I said, the national is all computerized, but it doesn't go back very far. Now *regionally,* we're about halfway through getting all the names into the machine. It takes time, and with these fingers I'm practically worthless myself. But they work when I really need them." He waggled his fingers suggestively in front of Pegeen. She had an urge to take one of the swollen knuckles and bend it backwards.

Browne returned his attention to Becker. "So I looked in the regional records. Now those go back to before we really even organized, just names and telephone numbers on the backs of envelopes in the begin-

ning, people you might call if you were going to be in their area and
wanted to go down. You'd call it a network these days, but you go back
far enough, and hell it was just a friend giving a name of somebody a
friend told *him* about who might know somebody else who was interested. You know what I'm saying. All of that is in that file cabinet over
there.''

''A lot of work,'' Becker said.

Browne shrugged. ''What else have I got to do these days? Anyway,
you were right, your friend Swann isn't a joiner. He never did belong to
the society.''

''Well, I knew it was a long shot . . .''

''I said he didn't *join*—that don't mean he wasn't in the file. I got his
name on a paper napkin, along with the name of Herm Jennings, who
suggested I call him.'' Browne pulled a pale-green paper napkin from
his desk drawer. ''The check mark after his name means I called the
man to see if he was interested in joining. He wasn't, or I would have
put a circle around the check. That's my system. I don't remember ever
talking to him; it must have been twenty years ago or more, so I called
Herm Jennings this morning. Herm can just barely recall him as somebody who went down with him and a couple of others one time. That's
how he knew he was interested in caving. But that's all he remembers;
it's not like he ever really knew the man.''

''Twenty years ago? That would make him about fifteen at the
time.''

''That's right—that's usually when you get started, when you're in
your teens and don't know any better.''

''Did Jennings remember where they went, by any chance?''

''No, I asked him that. But you can be sure of one thing, if he went
with Herm, he went someplace good, someplace tough. That's the only
kind of hole Herm visits. And if Herm passed his name along, the kid
could carry his own weight, fifteen or not.''

''Bingo,'' said Becker.

''That's a bingo? Don't sound like much to me.''

''It shows he knows caves in this region,'' Becker said. ''It shows
he's been at it a long time. And that he's good. That tells me all I need to
know.''

''Well, then, good, glad I can help.''

''You've just started helping, Mr. Browne. What I really need are
your maps.''

Browne turned to Pegeen. "I've got the most thorough maps of all the known caves in my region. They're better than the government maps, better than the geologists' maps, better than anybody's."

"I'm sure they are," said Pegeen.

"No question. I can tell you every hole in West Virginia, Virginia, Tennessee, and Kentucky that's wide enough to squeeze your shoulders through—and I been in most of them myself. I drew more than half the maps personally. You didn't think there was any goddamn surveyors crawling down there, did you?"

"I would think not."

Browne nodded emphatically.

"You got that right. Some of them ain't much bigger than a rabbit run; some of them got more room than a hotel. This whole region is honeycombed with tunnels and caves and caverns and mines—hell, it's a wonder it don't all collapse. It's the limestone substrata, you know. Water just carves that rock like butter. You get any kind of trickle going and pretty soon—a million years or so—the water's cut its way through that limestone like a jigsaw. You ever go caving?"

"Not really," she said.

"Not really or not at all?"

"Not at all."

"You ever want to try, you let me know. I'll take you down personally."

The day I go down in a dark hole with you, old man, she thought. "I'll remember the offer if I ever get the urge," she said, straining for politeness.

"That's right, you get the urge, you think of me," Browne said, winking at Becker.

The old son of a bitch thinks I'm blind as well as stupid, Pegeen thought. She watched Becker absorb Browne's attempts at male conspiracy with just the faintest hint of a smile. He wasn't going along with joke—not that it was really a joke; men always had some faint dream of success, she knew, no matter how pathetically delusional it was; they stoked themselves on fantasies of women overwhelmed by their magnetism and leaping over all bounds of decency, age, decorum, and common revulsion just to get at them—but Becker wasn't telling him to mind his manners, either.

Browne had a sheaf of charts on the side of his desk and he tapped it proudly, as if it were a codex of the classics.

"You tell me what you're looking for, and if it exists, I've got it here."

Becker thought a moment. "It should be somewhere remote, somewhere you could enter and exit unseen. It has to have a sizable chamber in it somewhere, big enough for a man to stand and move around."

"Easy access or difficult?"

"Access to the cave?"

"That's one. Some of these entrances are halfway up a mountain. You got to climb up before you climb down."

"Not too difficult. He's carrying, or dragging, a hundred-pound weight in addition to his gear."

"Okay, that lets out some. How about access to the chamber, you want that easy or hard?"

"He doesn't expect to be found in there," Becker said, "so I guess it's got to be hard. He won't be anyplace where some random caver is going to walk in on him."

"But he's still hauling the hundred-pound weight?"

"Oh, yeah. He'll have that with him—going in."

"Going in?"

"He won't have to bring it back out."

"Well, okay, I won't ask what he's dumping in there, but if I found out he's left his shit in *any* cave I'll kick his ass for him." Browne turned to Pegeen. "Sorry about that."

"What?" Pegeen asked.

"Language," he said.

"Oh, shit. You can't say anything I haven't heard before. Look, if he's got this—weight—with him, that means he can go down easier than he can go up—on the way there. Coming back, I suppose he could go up all right."

Browne lifted his eyebrows at Becker before continuing. "Okay, so we eliminate anything that goes up after entry."

He shuffled through the charts with practiced ease.

"We have them graded according to difficulty," Browne said, but we don't have any code for taking something down that you don't bring back up. That's just not done, at all, period." He muttered to himself for a moment, riffling and shuffling the charts.

"Here's one," he said, marking the plastic coating of the map with a grease pen. "And here, and here. You could probably do it here, but it's a pisser. On the other hand, no one's going to be wandering in by accident. This one's very tough, very difficult. Is this guy an expert?''

"We don't really know," said Becker. "He might be. We have to assume he's good.''

"He'd have to be—at least he'd have to know what he's doing to get into any of these. You do want them tough, right? I mean, no tourists being led in there by a guide.''

"Unless there's some chamber that no one's going to go to, but no, not with guides, I don't think so. Too much of a chance of being seen coming or going.''

"Well, here's ten, twelve, fourteen of them. They're all remote. They all have a big chamber, and the chamber is down or at least level when you're going to it. No one's going to be trying these things on the weekend, or if they do, you could hear them coming a long way away once you're in the chamber. Of course, we don't know if your man even knows they exist—half of these are pretty obscure. Some of them don't show any more on the surface than a breathing hole.''

"A breathing hole?''

"Sure. A cave breathes, you know. If you go down very far you get a constant temperature, year 'round; it's colder than the air aboveground in summer, warmer in the winter. When it's hot, you get this shaft of air sucking down through the hole like a vacuum cleaner. When it's cold aboveground, you get just the opposite, a steady breeze of warmer air. It's damned mysterious if you don't know what you're seeing, but if you find a breathing hole, you've got yourself a major cave at the other end of it.''

"Are they marked in any way or can someone just fall in?'' Pegeen asked.

"Most of them are marked, or boarded over, the ones on public land, anyway. On private land there's usually a damned billboard out by the nearest road so the owner can charge you a few bucks if they're what you call user friendly. But if they aren't big enough to walk into, you're not going to get any tourists, so some of them on private property are pretty much the way God made 'em. They may have had signs or markers once, but if they're out in the woods somewhere, the owner doesn't go there himself, the sign falls over, you know. Out of sight, out of mind. If your man doesn't know where they are, he's not going to find some of these.''

"We have to assume he knows about them,'' Becker said.

"How come?''

"He has an affinity for them. He likes them dark and tight."

Browne laughed. "Lots of us like them that way. Sorry, miss."

"Some of us like them long and hard and pointing up," said Pegeen.

"Huh?"

"Caves, Mr. Browne. We all have our preferences."

Browne looked to Becker uncertainly.

"I'll need copies of these maps," Becker said.

"You're a born diplomat, Haddad," Becker said when they were once more in the car. "You should have gone for the foreign service."

"He's an asshole."

"Probably only because you're around," Becker said.

"Thanks a lot."

"It's not your fault, it's his, but people are going to have a reaction to you, you might as well get used to it."

"Do you find that it works the other way? Do women have a reaction to you?"

Becker grinned. "That would be for you to say."

She turned to him.

"I'll speak for the male point of view," he continued. "You deal with the female."

You know, you bastard, she thought. You know exactly how women react to you. Her ears were blazing.

"There are no mines on that list," she said.

"I don't think he'll try a mine again," Becker said.

"Why not?"

"He got caught. Five years late, but he still got caught. Those were early attempts. He's smart, he'll learn from his mistakes, he'll refine his methods. They always do, they keep adjusting until they find what works best for them."

"Then what?"

"Then they speed up," he said. "When they think they're safe they just keep taking victim after victim."

"What makes you think he's going into caves? Why not anyplace private? An old warehouse, a house in the country . . ."

"For one thing, he told me where he was going."

"He *told* you?"

"In a manner of speaking. He goes where gravity takes him. Down. And he knows the use of ropes. He told me that, too. In some ways going into a cave is just like going down a mountain—plus you need rope work to get back up, if it's steep enough. He'll go for a cave, it's what he needs. Emotionally.''

"He's got an *emotional* need for *caves?*"

"They have fantasies, that's their problem. They have fantasies so strong that they are compelled to enact them. And fantasies have a context, an ambience, if I can say that—they don't take place on Main Street at noon, they exist in a specific environment which is nearly as important as what he does. Your fantasies take place *somewhere,* don't they?''

"Mine?"

"You do have fantasies, don't you, Haddad?''

"No.''

"I see.''

"I don't.'' Unless you count thinking about older FBI agents walking in on me when I'm naked, things like that, she thought.

"Okay. But a lot of us do. And where they happen matters.''

"Do you mean restraints, blindfolds, that kind of thing?'' Pegeen asked after a pause, knowing she ought to let the subject drop but unable to let it go.

"What?''

"I don't have that kind of fantasy.''

"Okay,'' Becker said.

"Do you?''

"What?''

"Never mind.'' Pegeen was blushing again.

"No.''

"Oh.''

Becker watched her drive, Pegeen kept her eyes studiously on the road.

"My fantasies are about people,'' he said finally. ''Not equipment.''

"I see,'' she said. ''That's normal. Probably.''

"I don't know about normal. It's common. I think most of us fantasize about different partners.''

Pegeen nodded and thrust her lower lip forward as if pondering the subject.

"Movie stars, people like that?'' she asked.

"No, just people. Women I meet, women I know.''

Pegeen nodded again in a way that she hoped appeared noncommittal.

"Uh-huh.''

"Not you, though," he said.

"Not me?"

"You don't fantasize like that?" he said.

Pegeen felt herself in such a turmoil she didn't trust herself to speak. She had thought at first that he meant he didn't fantasize about her, and her stomach had seemed to fall away, and then she realized her mistake and was crushed by a sense of her own foolishness. He hadn't meant her, he wasn't thinking about her, the intensity of *her* awareness of *him* wasn't even communicating itself across the width of the front seat.

When she trusted herself to breathe again, she steered the conversation back to business and vowed to herself to keep it there.

"What makes you think Swann is even around here?"

"They always come home, in a general sense. If an escaped con from New York ever had sense enough to hide out in New Mexico, we'd have a hell of a time finding him, but they seldom do. First place to look is their mother's house. He grew up around her, lived less than thirty miles from here when he committed the assault on his landlady."

"What if he did? What if he took off for Portland?"

"Then we'll have a hell of a time finding him. But they usually don't. People stick with what they know. He's comfortable here. He knows how people think, how they talk, the way they do things. Swann's in the region somewhere or he's a rarer breed than I think."

"So what do we do now, go check out all these caves?"

"No, we wait for Swann to tell us which ones to check."

"How does he do that?"

"By his choice of victim. When he takes her, he's going to go to ground pretty close by. He did that with both the girls in the coal mine; he'll do it again. You don't want to have to travel very far with a victim in any event, it's much too dangerous."

"How will we know when he's got a victim, or if he does?"

"Oh, there's no 'if.' He'll take someone soon if he hasn't already, and I'm willing to bet he already has. He was in prison for three years, thinking of little else. He'll take someone fast. He'll need to before he bursts. When he does, we'll get a missing persons report. That's Swann's flaw, you know. He's not like most of them, who specialize in drifters, street urchins, migrant workers, prostitutes, people nobody would miss for a long time. He's so confident of *where* he takes them, so sure that he won't be found there, that he doesn't care if there's a search for the victim. The two girls in the coal mine were connected to solid citizens. A hunt began for them almost immediately. Swann didn't care—he was already underground, doing whatever he does to them and apparently equipped to stay there for a long time. Judging by the amount of melted candle wax and old food tins they found in the mine, I'd say he was down there at least a week.''

Pegeen shuddered at the thought of that week for the girls. ''The bastard.''

'' 'Bastard' hardly does it justice. Our problem is that there's a delay in reporting missing persons. In the case of adults, cops won't even register the report until the person is gone for three days. That means Swann has got that much of a head start whenever he strikes, and my guess is he doesn't need more than an hour or two at the most to cover his tracks.''

''So we wait for the missing persons report to come in that meets our profile? There must be something more we can do while we're waiting.''

''Sure. We go to a sporting goods store and get what we're going to need.''

''Beyond that,'' Pegeen said.

''I'm open to suggestions,'' Becker said.

Pegeen carefully assessed his tone to determine if there was anything suggestive in it. Reluctantly, she decided that there was not.

''I'll let you know if I think of anything,'' she said.

Missing persons reports trickled in with the sluggishness that reflects the degree of importance attached to the matter by most police departments. The simple fact is that most missing persons are not missing— they have simply chosen to depart without telling anyone. Husbands and fathers debunk to avoid responsibility; teens and young adults flee school or their parents; employees quit or go on five-day benders; friends prove not to be friendly enough to say goodbye. For every person reported missing who is actually the victim of foul play, there is a full year's worth of reports on people who simply wandered off in this most transient of countries. Police know this, even though the concerned or distraught friends and relatives cannot imagine the missing departing of his or her own steam. The person has, after all, abandoned *them,* and who could be so fed-up or stressed-out or done-in to want to go to *that* extreme?

Even though the reports dribbled into the Nashville office slowly, they did so in great quantity. They didn't come quickly, but they kept coming, for this is a nation on the move and Becker had pinpointed a sizable portion of it for his search. The reports were fed into a computer which sorted them according to their conformity to Becker's victim profile.

Becker and Pegeen reviewed the most likely cases themselves, adding human perception and intuition to the process.

"Here's a likely one," she said, lifting one of the printout sheets. She and Becker sat at adjoining desks in the Nashville office, isolated and largely ignored by everyone else in the room.

"Mandy Roesch, eighteen years old, Hazard, Kentucky. No problems at home, no boyfriend—probably not pregnant then—sang in the church choir, scheduled to start classes at Memphis State in the fall. Doesn't seem the type to have just taken a hike."

Becker stood at a large map of the Southeastern States that were covered by the Nashville office, atop of which had been placed a clear plastic overlay showing Browne's selection of probable caves.

"She was last seen in Hazard?" he asked.

"Yes. She was supposedly going to choir practice, never showed up."

"Hazard is just a bit too far from either of the closest possible caves. Mark her as marginal."

Pegeen stared at the map.

"What is it?" he asked when she hesitated.

"It seems so . . . hit and miss. This girl sounds exactly like the kind of person he takes. So she's a few miles too far away from one of the caves which we don't know he's going to in the first place. We don't even know that he *is* going to a cave, much less one of those. We don't know how far away from the cave he's willing to drive with someone. We don't even know he's anywhere on that map. It's not even a needle in a haystack. That assumes you've got all your hay in one place. This is like a needle in a whole field of alfalfa—and we're not sure there is a needle in the first place. We don't *know* Swann is doing anything."

"Some fun, eh?"

"Do you always work this way?"

"I've had harder cases."

"Harder? How?"

"You're wrong about one thing. We do know there's a needle that we're looking for. At least I know it. Swann is at work, believe me."

"But how do you know that?"

"How do you know a thirsty man will drink?"

"It can't be as simple as that."

Becker looked at her for a moment. She felt herself squirming under his gaze.

"It's not simple," he said at last. "It's very complicated, but it comes out the same way in the end. The process he goes through before he acts is actually very long and tortured. I'll explain it to you someday if you really want to know."

"We studied it at the academy," Pegeen said. "I know something about it."

Becker smiled ruefully.

"Be grateful that you don't. Not the first thing. You're fortunate that you haven't got a clue."

"What a lucky girl," she said.

"Sometime, when you're got about six hours to kill, I'll tell you about it."

How about tonight, she thought, trying to keep her smile from spreading from the back of her throat to her lips.

"Whenever you feel like talking, I'm happy to listen," she said. She nodded slightly, attempting to convey serious empathy while keeping it all in the framework of business. She wondered how good she was at it; she certainly felt clumsy and obvious, but maybe not obvious for Becker. He had seemed mildly annoyed with her since she met him at the airport a few days ago, sometimes downright angry.

"Thanks," he said, turning back to the map, placing no weight of any kind on his thank-you.

"Do you know what really surprises me?" Pegeen asked, trying to keep the conversation going.

He raised his eyebrows slightly, waiting.

"That it works this way," she said. "I mean the whole process. Look at this: we're after a serial killer, one man in the whole country who has the potential to kill dozens of people. We're a part of a huge, professional, highly organized organization, and what does this manhunt consist of? You and me and a computer and a map. Before I entered the Bureau, even during the academy, for that matter, I had this image of the *FBI,* this massive organization hurling itself into battle all at once. Do you know what I'm talking about?"

"I've been in a while," Becker said. "I'm used to it, but go on."

"Well, I don't know, I just always had this notion that if the Federal Bureau of Investigation was after you, you were in trouble, you were in really deep shit."

"We've got good public relations people," Becker said.

"I don't mean that we're not good," she said.

"Sometimes."

"This is not a disloyal statement, you understand. It's just—it's *us,* isn't it? I mean, I know we can call on agents all over the country if we have to. We can have a lot of people knocking on a lot of doors and we've got all that great scientific stuff, it does amazing things—but really, when you get down to it, this case is just you and me going over a list of names."

"Not quite what you envisioned, is it?"

"No."

"In fact, most of the time it's boring as hell, right?" Becker asked.

"I didn't say that; it's not really boring, it's more—painstaking."

"Tedious, I'd say. But that's the way it works. It's all the nuts and bolts; you've got to sort them by hand. The only intuition comes in knowing what kind of nut you're looking for in the first place."

"At least we know our nut," Pegeen said. "We're lucky in that."

"We know him," Becker said, his attitude suddenly dark. "Know him well. I don't call that lucky."

By the second day of sifting reports, they had a list of manageable size. Pegeen drove the backroads from one small town to the next while Becker lapsed into darker and darker moods. Now that they were actually in the field, interviewing acquaintances of the missing women, Pegeen thought that Becker was sinking somehow, as if the presence of Swann underground with a victim was creating a special gravity that drew him down deeper and deeper into himself, into some black pit of his inner being. He was still crisp and alert when interviewing people, using that curious blend of detached efficiency and sudden knowing intimacy that worked so effectively for him, but afterwards, when he was alone in the car again with Pegeen, Becker would slump into the seat and seem to slump in his spirit as well.

On the second day of driving, she asked him if it was her fault.

"What?"

"Are you mad at me about something? Have I done something to annoy you?"

"What are you talking about?"

"You haven't really spoken to me except to grunt in two days. In fact, you've seem pissed off at me ever since you showed up."

"I'm not mad at you, Haddad. Why would I be?"

"I don't know. That's why I'm asking."

"I'm not. You're doing a fine job."

"I haven't *done* anything yet."

"You're doing it well, though."

"I thought there was something about me that rubbed you the wrong way."

"I'd rather be doing this with you than anyone else I know," Becker said. "Any other agent would be trying to get me to cheer up."

"Fuck you, sorry I asked."

"Would it help if I told you that I'm quiet because I'm thinking?"

"Shouldn't we think together? I might be able to help. My brain works sometimes, too."

"I guess it wouldn't help to tell you that, then. The fact is, I'm not thinking. I'm just depressed."

"What about?"

"What's going to happen," he said.

"What's going to happen? What *is* going to happen?"

Becker scrunched into the passenger seat so far that his knees rested on the dashboard. "We're going to find him," he said.

"How do you know?"

Becker did not answer. He rolled his head to one side and looked at the pine trees moving past the window.

"Are you sure we're going to find him?" Pegeen insisted.

"Yeah."

"Well, that's great, isn't it? That's what we want, isn't it?"

Becker grunted, but she was not certain it was in assent.

"Why does that depress you?"

"Because of what comes after that."

"What? . . . What comes after that? . . . What do you mean?"

"Pegeen, I like you," he said, startling her with the use of her first name. "I like you a lot. One of the things I like most about you is your innocence. You'll lose that eventually, but I'll be sorry to see it go."

"Could you be a little more patronizing, do you think? I've been around a little bit, you know. I just *look* innocent. It's my goddamned complexion."

"I like your complexion."

"Yeah, I'll bet."

"I do. It makes you look innocent."

"Very funny. Look, Becker, I'm an agent, I'm trained, I have a badge, I have a gun, I'm legally authorized to shoot people. I'm not innocent, I'm not a child. You chose me to come along with you on this assignment; you could have had anyone but you chose me. You didn't do it because of my innocence.''

''You haven't figured out why I chose you yet?''

''I have suspicions.''

''What do you think?''

''So you can make fun of me, is what it looks like. Tell me what you're talking about.''

''Let it go.''

''You know what passive-aggressive is, don't you?'' she demanded. ''It's not very becoming.''

''You checked me out, right?'' Becker asked.

''What do you mean?''

''I said you were innocent, not dumb. You asked around to find out about me. If not last time, sure as hell this time.''

''Okay. I just thought . . .''

''Don't apologize. I would have done the same thing.''

''Did you?'' she asked.

Becker laughed. ''Yeah. I checked you out.''

''What did you find out?''

''Not much. You broke up with your boyfriend.''

''Somebody told you that? How the hell does anybody know? I didn't tell anybody. Are they spying on me?''

Becker laughed.

''Welcome to the club, kiddo.''

''It's hardly the same, and don't call me *kiddo,* either.''

''What's hardly the same?''

''Never mind. I'm just shocked that . . . who was it, who told you? Kinnock? He's been trying to get his hand up my skirt since I joined up.''

''You mean there's good reason for people to keep tabs on me but not on you? Because of my history it's all right? But it's not all right for you?''

''I didn't mean anything in particular.''

''So what did they tell you about me, Haddad? What gory stories did they tell you?''

''Just, you know, it's mostly very complimentary. Everyone says you're fantastically good at it.''

''But what?''

"But nothing. Everyone respects you enormously."

"But I'm what, a bit unstable? A bit crazy? A bit dangerous? Or do they go farther?"

"No."

"Do they tell you why they think I'm so good? Do they say why I seem to have such a knack for finding these psychopaths?"

"No."

"Yes, they do, sure they do. Why wouldn't they, they know nothing about it, what better time to speculate?"

"No, honest . . ."

"Christ, let's not be honest with each other, Haddad. Let's keep things just the way they are; we're getting along fine . . . listen, kid, fair warning. Everything they told you is true as far as it goes. If not in specifics, then in spirit. As far as it goes. It's all true . . . It just doesn't go far enough."

Pegeen did not know what to make of his statement, and she got no further help from him. Becker fell into a silence that remained unbroken until she pulled their car into an empty field where a large tent was being erected.

Chapter 35

The Reverend Tommy R. Walker was uncomfortable in the presence of any police authorities, and FBI agents made him doubly ill-at-ease. Authorities had plagued Tommy's life. Cops and sheriffs treated him like he was running a damned carnival instead of a respectable healing and revival meeting, and even after he had paid their bribes and followed their laws Tommy felt guilty whenever they were around. The fact that one of the agents was a girl, probably no older than Aural, didn't help matters, either. She was a kind of goofy-looking creature with her funny ears and all that red hair, but kind of attractive, too, in an unusual way. Still, she had flashed a badge at him, and that meant she had authority. Ceding some sort of power to the man was bad enough, but granting it to a woman was something else, something he didn't like at all. Rae had taken enough control over him since Aural left, haranguing him with questions and accusations and using her body like it was some special treat that she would dole out only if he gave her the proper information. He had become quite dependent on her sexual favors in the past few weeks, he found. The more eager, the more inventive she became, the deeper he fell into her thrall. He didn't know how, exactly, but he seemed to have slipped into a form of vassalage to her body which had given her emotional and intellectual primacy as well. In ways he could not pin down, and by methods he could not adequately name, Rae had become the boss.

She even took charge now, talking freely with the agents while Tommy hung back warily.

"I reported her missing, yes, I did," Rae said.

Tommy noticed that she spoke primarily to the male agent, addressing him with a level of flirtatiousness he had not seen in her before.

"She was a dear friend," Rae continued. "A very dear friend and I was worried about her."

"Did you have any particular reason to worry?" Becker asked. "Couldn't she have run off with a boyfriend, for instance?"

"Aural was off men; she didn't want a boyfriend."

"Why was that?" Pegeen asked.

"Bad experiences," Rae said. "You know how they are."

Pegeen nodded, feeling momentarily sisterly. She did indeed know how they were. Awful at the worst of times, and at the best, still difficult.

"Believe me, if she had wanted any boyfriends, she wouldn't have had to look very far," Rae said. Becker and Pegeen both noticed her glance at the Reverend Tommy that didn't quite take place. The Reverend stirred uneasily. "She set her last boyfriend on fire, that's how fed up she was."

"Set him on fire?"

Rae nodded proudly. "Yes, sir, right on fire."

"Wasn't on fire," Tommy said.

"Certainly was," Rae returned sharply.

"Nope. She tried to burn up the bathroom of the trailer and Kershaw was inside it. He never got burned at all. She's just telling you cow flop."

"No such a thing." Rae was indignant. "She set that man *ablaze,* and he deserved it, too."

"First off, no man deserves that," Tommy said, appealing to Becker as a fellow male.

"I've seen a few," Becker said.

Tommy acted as if he didn't hear the contradiction. "And second, it ain't true."

"Aural told me so her own self," Rae said.

"But Kershaw told *me,*" Tommy said triumphantly, then quickly realized he had said too much.

Becker and Pegeen noticed the change in the relationship between the other two; it happened as palpably as a fifty-degree drop in temperature. The Bureau always wanted agents to interview subjects separately, but Becker had realized long ago that the guideline was often wrong. People who knew each other could send signals to keep the other from saying too much, it was true, but just as often they would react to the presence of an agent as if he were an intermediary in a long-running power struggle. Both would appeal to him to take their side and in the process reveal far more than they might alone. Like a couple before a marriage counselor, each would plead his or her own case in ways never done with the partner.

"So that was Harold Kershaw I heard you talking to outside our trailer," Rae said icily.

"What?" Tommy said. Becker thought his guilt was so obvious he might as well have worn a signboard. Pegeen wondered if all men pretended not to hear whenever a woman asked them the question they didn't want to answer, or if it was just every man she had ever known.

"You gave her over to Harold Kershaw?" Rae protested. "Do you know what that shikepoke'll do to her? How could you do that to that sweet thing?"

"Kershaw ain't got her."

"He might kill her, I can't believe you . . ."

"It ain't Kershaw," Tommy said. "I told you, *he ain't got her.*"

"You know where she is then, don't you? You know how worried I was, why didn't you tell me? You made me go to the police and everything and all the time you knew—"

"Hey, I don't *know.* I don't *know* nothing."

"He knows where Aural is," Rae said to Becker.

"Hey!"

"You might's well arrest him," Rae said. She looked at Pegeen, nodding vigorously. "He's as bad as the man who's got her."

"Rae, Rae, calm down here . . ."

"Take him to the station and beat him with your nightsticks—or I'll do it myself."

"Hey! Rae. Honey. Sugar, what are you talking about?" He turned to the agents, appealing for sympathy. "I don't know where the girl is. I didn't snatch her. Kershaw didn't snatch her. It was this little weasel. Kershaw found him and kicked shit out of him, but Kershaw didn't take Aural, he never got close enough to her, she ran right into this weasel's car, like he was waiting for her. I think she was planning on slipping out on us anyway, Rae, honest to God, she was going away with this little guy, I'm sure of it."

Pegeen pulled a photograph from her purse.

"Was it this man?"

Tommy tried to square the grim-looking still-life of the mug shot with the face of the little man lying on the sidewalk, bleeding, cowering behind his upraised arm.

"Could be, maybe. Sure."

Becker slid an arm around Tommy's shoulders and turned him away from the women. Tommy felt a heat, a sudden urgency in the agent that frightened him. It had not been there before, but seemed to burst into combustion with the showing of the photograph. Tommy knew he was no longer being politely questioned—things had changed with the sudden bewildering fright of a nightmare. Becker smiled at him, but a fire was flashing in his eyes. For a second Tommy remembered the desperate need of the man who had grabbed him in the healing meeting, trying to confess his sins, the desire so strong that it read like a barely sheathed fury. Like something huge and hungry spotting its prey, immediately transformed into a carnivorous concentration so strong that it must act like a form of gravitional attraction, pulling the victim towards it. Tommy realized he would tell this FBI agent everything he wanted to know; he would be afraid not to. He knew that the agent was not after him personally, but he sensed a hunger so great that he might make a mouthful of anything close. Kershaw had frightened him with his potential for violence, but this man, with a single move, terrified him. "Let's you and me talk, Reverend," Becker said.

"You bet," said the Reverend, turning his head to look back longingly at Rae. He realized with a sinking feeling that he would get no help from her.

Chapter 36

Pegeen had never seen Becker excited and she realized he had become a different person. Although he always gave the impression of contained strength, he now seemed as if the strength were breaking its bonds and were within seconds of bursting forth. Through no physical change that she could detect, he now seemed to be coiled and ready to strike.

He spread the charts on the hood of the car at the edge of the field where the revival tent now stood, erected and ready for miracles. He cast a nervous eye at the sky, where the sun was slipping quickly below the trees, then jabbed his finger at a mark on Browne's chart.

"Here, it's got to be here," he said. His finger pointed to a cave called Devil's Den that looked on the map like an old-fashioned hand-weight, two ball-shaped caverns connected by a long tunnel.

"Why?"

"It's the closest. He could have had her there in twenty minutes. The others are at least forty-five-minute drives from where he took her. That one is almost an hour away." His finger danced over the map. Becker was as familiar with its surface as if the marks were dots of Braille and he was blind.

He swept the map off the hood and replaced it with a sheaf of smaller charts, thumbing quickly through them until he found the one he wanted.

"He was waiting for her, right? Maybe he'd even made an arrangement to meet her. The Reverend said she ran right into his car. Maybe that's how he gets them; maybe they go willing at first. I don't know. The point is, he didn't just swoop down and grab her on impulse. He didn't snatch her and run for cover as an afterthought. He had time to plan it, so he would be heading here."

The new chart was much smaller in scale and showed the entrance to the cave in relation to the surrounding area. Browne had gone to considerable pains to locate the entrance accurately, which meant that it must be difficult to reach and hard to locate without the map. Becker glanced at the sky once more, angrily, as if the sun were to blame for setting. Pegeen felt as if he were trying to will the sun back up into the sky.

"Son of a bitch," he said. "It will be dark by the time we get there. We'll have to wait till morning."

"We have flashlights," Pegeen said.

"Look at the terrain. We'd have to be lucky to find it in the dark, and if we go tromping around flashing lights, and he's in any position to see us, he can slip out undetected. If we go now we're inviting him to get away."

"I was thinking about the woman," Pegeen said. "Can she make it through another night?"

Becker looked at her blankly for a moment. "She'll have to make it for another eight hours."

"If we get there tonight, it might save her life."

"If we fuck it up and he gets away, he's going to take a lot more lives, and he'll be a lot more careful next time."

"This woman, this Aural McKesson, is the only life I'm thinking about now. She's the one in danger. God knows what he's doing to her."

Becker swept up his maps and returned to the car.

"We'll find out soon enough what he's doing to her," he said.

"Soon enough for who? How do we know it's going to be soon enough for her?"

Becker tossed the maps into the backseat and grabbed Pegeen's elbow, yanking her around to face him. The muscles in his jaw clenched and unclenched and his eyes were raging.

"Do you think I don't want him *right now?*"

He gripped her arm until she nodded agreement.

"Yes," she said. "I know you do."

"We'll wait," he said, releasing her.

Pegeen put her hands on the steering wheel, borrowing time against her agitation. It was the first time she had been afraid of him. Not that she thought he would harm *her*. But she realized that he was going to harm someone. "All the stories about me are true," he had said. "They just don't go far enough." Having looked into his blazing eyes, she began to believe him.

"Where to?" she asked, starting the car.

"Find us a motel," he said.

"Shall I call Nashville for more agents?"

"What for?"

"For help."

"You need help, Haddad? What do you need help with, me?"

"No, with Swann, of course."

"How many men do you plan to send down into that cave? We don't know if there's room for *us*, yet."

"In case."

"In case of what?"

"In case he's not there, in case he went to one of the other caves, in case he didn't go there at all."

"He's in there," Becker said.

"How do you know that?"

Becker did not bother to respond.

"He's not just yours," she said.

Becker glared at her.

"He isn't?"

"I'm thinking about the woman," she said. She could feel his eyes on her, but she kept her own gaze fixed on the road. Looking directly at him made her more uncomfortable than ever. She was glad it was getting dark so she could avoid his eyes more easily; it seemed to her they had taken on a feral character, as if something wild were hidden within the man and had decided to come out of hiding at last.

"Good. Do that. I'm thinking about *him*."

"He's not our only concern," she said. They had reached the edge of one of the little towns that dotted the Tennessee-Virginia margin.

"He's mine," Becker said. "She's yours. That about covers it, doesn't it? We've got them both taken care of."

"I think I should call Nashville," she insisted.

"No," he said flatly.

After a pause she asked, "Is that an order?"

"Pull in there," he said, pointing at a motel sign that had just come on in the gathering gloom.

When they got out of the car and he put his hand on her arm, it was all Pegeen could do to manage not to push it angrily away.

"Haddad," he said, his voice now soft and calming, "I know what you want. In most cases you'd be right. But we don't need help. And they don't want to send it. Not now, not when we've found him."

She looked at him, puzzled.

"Come on, you get it," he said. "That's why they sent *me*."

He walked into the motel office, leaving Pegeen to interpret his remark. The only translation she could come up with made her shiver.

She was aware of a presence in the darkness outside her door as she
stood in front of the mirror. Pegeen had showered as soon as they
checked into the motel, trying to let the hot water wash off the feeling of
apprehension that clung to her. Things were not right, the whole inexo-
rable flow of events had shifted in its course and was now heading in a
direction she knew was wrong, but she felt powerless to deflect it.
Becker was suddenly a different man and she realized that he was guid-
ing the flow, he was sitting astride the events now, like a man riding an
avalanche, looking to all appearances as if he were controlling it. Perhaps he had been all along and she had been so busy looking at him that
she had not noticed the ground moving underneath her feet. At one
point she had thought this was a Bureau investigation, a search for a
felony suspect being assisted somewhat eccentrically by Becker, true,
but by her as well, plus the power of the FBI, the speed of computers,
the cooperation of countless police, and as with all searches, it took its
own course according to leads and clues and circumstance. Now she
thought it had been a one-man activity all along, and not a search but a
stalk. She had not been assisting, she had been manipulated, just as the
whole massive grid of Bureau procedures had been used to provide
Becker with what he wanted. Had she been wrong about everything
else, too? she wondered. Those qualities of his that had so fascinated
her, his strange moodiness, the sense of great vulnerability that hid beneath the façade of strength like a little boy in a suit of armor, the languid, restrained sexuality that seemed to course from his eyes, his
hands. Was she mistaken about all of it? One of the things that had so
appealed to her was the impression that everything about Becker was
under a tight but temporary control like a coiled spring held in check by
a hair trigger that would release explosively if she could just find the
right spot to touch. She could unleash all that power and passion, she
had thought. Stupidly. Stupidly. Now she feared that he was about to
blow up in her face.

She looked at herself in the mirror, a towel wrapped around her head.
She wore the boxer shorts and tank top she normally slept in, and spots
of moisture from the shower had darkened areas of the tank top. Her
skin seemed even pinker than usual because of the heat of the water and

Pegeen cursed her luck for having inherited none of the olive tone of the original Haddad.

She glanced again at the door with the sense that something was outside. She had heard nothing that she was aware of, but still there was the feeling of something waiting there, something large and dangerous. It frightened her first, and then it angered her. Fuck this, she thought, I'm a special agent of the FBI, I'm not supposed to be afraid of unknown creatures in the dark. She pulled her pistol from its holster atop the dresser and opened the door.

Becker stood several feet away on the concrete porch, leaning against a wooden column, his arms folded across his chest. He was staring at her door, now at her.

"Don't shoot," he said laconically, not moving.

Pegeen moved the gun behind her back, feeling foolish.

"What are you doing?" she demanded.

"Waiting."

"What for?"

Becker said nothing, moved nothing. Even slouching against the column, even in the lanquid pose of a drugstore cowboy, he looked coiled and ready to strike. Pegeen could make out his features only dimly in the light shining from her window, but she thought he was smiling. It's creepy, she thought. What the hell is he up to now? What is he doing, what am I supposed to make of it?

"How long have you been standing there?" she asked.

He still didn't answer and she could feel his eyes boring into her. She was aware suddenly of what she was wearing, of how her heavy breasts would be showing dark against the tank top, of how her legs would look, too pink and speckled by the heat. The anger of a moment before returned, only now it was directed at him. To hell with how I look, she thought. I'm tired of caring, I'm tired of trying to guess what he's thinking and how I should react to it, I'm tired of the whole damned game, the elaborate tease, for that is what she now realized it had been, his holding back, never saying quite enough to be clear but just enough to keep her guessing, or hoping; that was the problem, the meaner he got to her, the more he withheld from her, the more she trailed hopelessly after him. Classic, she thought. Classic dim-witted behavior, chasing someone inaccessible, it was no better than that, however she had tried to dress it up with imagination. Well, fuck it, fuck the game, fuck him.

"What?" he said.

"What what?"

"You should see your face. You look all worked up about something."

Damn his eyes, too, she thought. He never missed anything.

"I'm fine," she said.

"You usually come to the door with a gun in your hand?"

"When I feel like it. Did you want something? Or are you just hanging around outside my door for fun?"

She knew for certain that he was smiling now. He turned his head slightly to indicate the door of the adjoining room.

"I thought I was outside *my* door."

Wrong again, Pegeen thought, but now she was too angry to care. Let him have another victory, let her make a fool of herself, it didn't matter anyway.

Pegeen closed the door and rammed the gun back into its holster. She whipped the towel off her head and glared at her reflection. Sure enough, her ears were fiery red. Well, fuck them, too, she thought.

She flounced onto the bed and stared at the ceiling, trying with all her might to think of something other than Becker. He was an asshole, anyway, and not worthy of her time. He was probably a psycho of some kind—she should have paid attention to the warnings given to her by the agents in the office. Tomorrow she would have to go with him and do God-knew-what under the guise of law enforcement. Think about the woman, Aural McKesson, she told herself.

Pegeen glanced at the clock on the radio-alarm beside her bed. Think about the woman for the next five minutes, she demanded of herself. Think about how you can help her, it's what you're here for, it's why you joined the Bureau. If Becker is right about the way all of this is falling down, you should get to her by tomorrow. If Becker is right, and he seems so confident that he is . . . shit, she was thinking of Becker.

She glanced at the clock again, didn't notice what time it said, and crossed to the door. If he's still slouching against that column, I'll fuck him, she thought, but if he's not there, if he's gone into his room, I'll go to bed and never think of him again.

He was not leaning against the column, he was standing right outside her door, looking as if he were prepared to eat his way through it if necessary.

Those eyes, Christ those eyes, she thought. They were blazing at her, into her, burning through her.

She placed her hand on his face and he jerked back slightly as if surprised by the contact. As she ran her fingers from his cheek to the side of his head he shivered like an animal but made no move towards her. It was like stroking the flank of a tiger or a wolf, something wild and dangerous and unaccustomed to human touch, something that tolerated her, uncertain whether to flee, bite, or give itself over to the pleasure.

She kept her gaze on her hand, watching the fingers as they moved across his flesh, afraid to look directly at him. Afraid to look into those eyes again for fear they might devour her.

When she touched the rim of his ear he jerked again, and gasped. He was quivering all over, his whole body trembling with the effort to hold still.

"Shhh," she said, not realizing what she was saying. It was a sound she would have made to calm an animal.

She ran her hand along his shoulder, feeling the muscles tense under her touch, then slowly trailed her fingers down his arm. She watched her fingers work, saw his bare skin tighten and spring into gooseflesh. When she reached his hand, she caressed the back of his fingers first, seeing him shiver once more, then gently intertwined her fingers with his. Only then, with their joined hands forming a fist, did she look at his face again.

God, the intensity of his eyes. So deep and dark, a tumultuous brown sea of emotion with his whole soul riding on it, begging her, beseeching her, but unable to speak, or unheard over the the tumultuous roar of his passions.

If he didn't touch her now, if he didn't respond, she thought he would surely burst, and so would she. Rising up on her toes, she reached for his mouth with hers, letting her eyelids slide down, searching for him blindly. His lips grazed hers and she heard him make a sound, a whimper, then he pulled his head back.

She looked at him again and saw something change as surely as if something had clicked behind his eyes. Where before he had been all yearning, frightened, vulnerable desire, he was now power. He had taken control of himself. A tiny smile tugged at his lips, knowing, almost mocking.

He touched her neck first and she could feel the sensation ripple through her entire body, tugging at her loins. I'm lost, I may be lost, she thought.

Becker lifted her, carried her into the room, and pressed her against the door. She felt his whole body tremble as he kissed her.

It was all so frantic, so kaleidoscopic in its variety that at times Pegeen was not sure where she was as they moved from the door towards the bed with the haphazard logic of a pinball threatening to burst from the confines of the machine. At one point he sat her on the dresser, her legs locked around him, and at another he was behind her, touching her everywhere with hands of fire. He turned her, twisted her, lifted her, held her against the wall, all the while seeking her mouth, his hands seeming to fly over her and torment her with touches that were never long enough. They stumbled once as she was undressing him, Becker tumbling to the floor, pulling her down with him. Pegeen started to laugh at their desperate need, but then he was atop her, pinning her down at first, then rolling so she was atop him, then rolling again.

He seemed beyond himself, so out-of-control that he did not even know what he wanted from her beyond endless contact, as if he could not get enough of touching her, of kissing her, of holding her, and yet as if each touch and each position deprived him of another and so he went on and on, clutching and shifting with ceaseless abandon, and everything he did felt right and wonderful to Pegeen, so right and exciting that she was close to losing herself along with him.

She panted and moaned and found herself shaking her head from side to side as if she were being tortured, but it was a torture that she embraced and demanded and she cried out, uncertain what she was saying, and he responded, growling something low in his throat as his mouth attacked her face, her lips, her neck, her breasts.

They were nude at last and on the bed and her face was wet with his kisses and her own saliva and her breasts wailed with the pleasure of his mouth and hands and tongue and everything hc did and every move he made seemed to gather in her loins and pull at her as if all the nerves in her body were gathered there and screaming and screaming for more, for release.

Still he didn't enter her but attacked her in a frenzy of hands and mouth, as if he would devour her before he took her. His passion was like a rage and Pegeen was frightened of it as much as she was excited by it. She didn't know what he wanted, what she could give him, and when she tried with her own mouth and hands to give him release he would move away from her, reposition himself and tear at her with pleasure again, too distracted, too delirious to seek relief.

At first Pegeen was too overwhelmed to let herself go completely; she held her innermost self in reserve while joining in his frenzy with her senses, taking all the pleasure he had to give her while protecting her emotions. She wasn't sure that all of this was for *her*, that she could have inspired so much heat and sexual fury, that he even knew who he had in his arms and under his tongue, it seemed *beyond* sex somehow, as if Becker were tormented by a devil who might express himself in sex but could never be fully found there. She did not want to give herself completely to a man who might not even know who he was with and she withheld as long as she could, but finally it was all too much for her, much, much too much and she came to his hand and she came to his mouth and it seemed that she came to his breath alone, screaming and crying out his name and finally cursing and flailing as if her nerves and senses had taken control of her completely and would never stop and never let her go. And even at the height of her pleasure she was frightened because she *had* let herself go and had given herself over to him completely and she knew she was lost, lost and hopelessly gone from safety, in his grip and under his power.

Finally there was nothing for her but to have him and she demanded it, whispering at first that she wanted him, then calling out and pulling him onto her and into her and wrapping her legs to lock him in place. Every thrust made her cry out and seemed to reverberate from her loins to her heart and she heard herself bellowing at him to continue, to do more and more and more and she said he was driving her crazy and she swore at him and cursed him with language of the gutter that astounded her as she heard it, but it was as if someone else were yelling, someone else were writhing on the bed and tearing at his back, someone who had lost her mind completely.

He seemed never to stop, never to tire, and Pegeen thought her body was on fire with sensation and wave after thrilling wave struck her and lifted her and bucketed her and she thought she would surely die and didn't care and finally, finally, with a growl growing low in his throat then building to a final burst that was a gasp as if his heart had ruptured, he shuddered to an end and at that very moment Pegeen was certain she felt everything he was feeling, doubling her own incredible sensation until it was simply too much to bear and she died.

Pegeen came to her senses astounded at herself, but far, far past embarrassment. She had never fainted in her life, but then she had never experienced anything like that in her life either. She did not know how long she had been passed out, or if he had noticed. In fact, she was still not convinced that he knew who she was; his need had seemed so great it was elemental rather than personal, but she had known who *he* was and even as she lay there, hoping he wouldn't speak for fear he might say the wrong thing, she knew she was in love with him.

His body was heavy upon her, his head still facedown next to her neck, where he had collapsed. Pegeen lay quietly, trying to distinguish his heartbeat from her own, his breathing from hers. She realized that all the lights were on in the room and it surprised her because it had seemed that their lovemaking had taken place in the dark, all sensation and with nothing visual at all.

What happens now? she wondered, but before she could think any further she forced herself to stop. Whatever would happen, it would be no good, she knew that much without examining the problem, and there was no point in tormenting herself with it yet. There would be plenty and plenty of time for recrimination and sorrow.

When she touched him he moved, startled, as if she had awakened him, although she knew from his breath that he wasn't asleep. He jumped when touched without warning, she had noticed, even in the most casual of circumstances. It seemed a puzzling trait in a man who was so aware of his surroundings and circumstances. Could a human touch be such a surprise to a man who seemed surprised by nothing?

When she ran her palm down his back she felt the enormous welts she had put there with her fingernails. She had never done that before, either, never been so heedless of her partner that she inflicted pain or damage. All of her previous sexual encounters had been polite, she realized. Which was one of the ways in which they had been inadequate. One of many. After three years with her last boyfriend, it had become so polite as to be downright formal.

Taking her touch for a signal, Becker withdrew and Pegeen realized with amazement that he was still hard.

"Are you all right?" she asked, finding it impossible to think that he wasn't satisfied.

Becker was amused. "It stays that way sometimes," he said, holding himself over her on his hands and knees.

"How long?"

He laughed. "I've never timed it."

He fell back onto the bed on his back, close to Pegeen but no longer touching her. To maintain contact, she put her arm across him, placed her cheek on his chest.

They lay in silence while all the things she might say raced through Pegeen's mind and she edited them and rejected them one after the other. What she *wanted* to say was simple enough, she wanted to tell him that she loved him and she knew he didn't love her but that was all right, at least for the moment, because she was swamped with what she was feeling and didn't *need* to know how he felt, not for this second, at least, maybe longer, maybe for hours, maybe a day. She doubted it could be a day. But for just right now she loved him completely and that was more than enough and she yearned to tell him, just that, she was bursting with the need to tell him that. I don't want to frighten you, she rehearsed silently, and you don't need to respond, but I just want to say that I love you. You don't have to answer, just know it and accept it, it's a gift I want to give you with no strings attached. And that wasn't entirely true, either, she realized, so she rejected that version because there *were* strings, there were hundreds of strings attached. Besides, she already realized that if he didn't say he loved her, too, it would break her heart. So much for the selfless part, she thought. It hadn't lasted very long. She amended what she wanted to say to: I love you and want desperately for you to love me, too, but if you don't, I still love you anyway. But that sounded hopelessly wimpy, as if she were just asking to be taken advantage of, so she rejected that, too. Just say I love you, she thought, and the hell with the qualifiers, and let him respond how he will. But she didn't want to lose control over his response completely, so she didn't say anything even though her tongue was on fire with the need to say it.

Becker spoke first, finally breaking the silence.

"Did you know that chimpanzees eat flesh?" Becker said.

Pegeen couldn't believe the question.

"When they get the chance, chimpanzees in the wild will catch monkeys and tear them apart and eat them," he said. "We think of them as peaceful vegetarians, living off fruit, but they're carnivores if they have the opportunity."

"Why are you telling me this?"

"I was just thinking about it," he said.

"Oh."

Bite your tongue, she said to herself. Bite it off and swallow it before you say anything stupid. She stiffened and rolled away from him, but to her surprise he rolled with her so that he was on top of her again.

She wanted to push him off but he held her arms pinned against the bed with his weight pushing down.

"I had to *stop* thinking about you," he said. "It was driving me crazy."

He kissed her and this time where he had been rough and frantic before he was now gentle and tender. His lips seemed to melt against hers, and then to softly meld into them. When his fingers touched her body they were as soft as his lips, but no longer rudely exploring, now they moved with practiced care, bringing her to him this time with infinite patience.

Pegeen was amazed that she could respond so fully again; she had thought she had given everything she had to give before; but he found new reserves within her and new recesses where she had not known that so much of her lived. She knew from the softness of his touch, the tender patience with which he wooed her that he loved her, too. When he wanted her to, she exploded, and then again and again until she made him stop because it was all too exquisite to bear anymore.

When she had rested he brought her to a soaring peak again. He has but to *think* of me, she said to herself. He doesn't even need to touch me anymore, just *will* it to be so and I am helpless.

He held her the whole night through, never letting her out of his arms—not that she ever wanted to leave them—clinging to her even when she was out of control and heaving insensibly. In the middle of the night she realized that he could not be sated. The fault did not lie with her, because she exhausted him as thoroughly he did her; he could not be satisfied by sex, because sex was not what he craved. He had an appetite for something else and sex was just an available substitute.

An hour before sunrise he released her at last and they rose and dressed and walked to the car in the crepuscular light of the foredawn. Pegeen felt so weak and tired she was surprised that she could even walk, but Becker was as tense as he had been the night before, every muscle seeming to quiver in anticipation. When they reached the spot on the map, he fairly leaped from the car and started off cross-country. Pegeen knew at last what his real appetite was for.

Chapter 37

Aural had begun to believe she was going to die. She had fought him every moment since her abduction, battling him with her will, refusing to give in to her fear or to submit to his power, but she had not slept for two days now, the pain was constant, and worse than the pain was her loss of spirit. It was not total, it came in bouts of despair that would leave her wrung-out and hopeless, making it all the more difficult to rouse herself to withstand Swann's next ordeal. She could still rise up to defy him with her wit and courage, but the episodes of despondency were growing more frequent, lasting longer, and when she rose out of them, she did not rise as high.

She was losing her battle; it was no comfort that Swann seemed to be losing his as well. He seldom went more than an hour or two before succumbing to the torment in his head and eye, clasping his hands over his face and keening. Aural knew it was ironic that the damage had been done to her torturer by the unlamented Harold Kershaw, but she was beyond being buoyed by irony. She hoped that Swann would drop dead, that his head would burst and his brains spill out on the cavern floor, but until he did, his bouts of suffering did nothing for her save offer her a brief respite from his tortures. The rests were never long enough for her to recover, and after each session more of her legs were covered with burns. He would soon start on her trunk, and Aural did not see how she could survive it when he got to her breasts.

She lay awake now, unable to find a position that offered her any relief from the pain. The bravura that had prompted her to rouse him from his sleep and rush back to the torture was gone now. When he moaned in his slumber, she wished him nightmares that would torment him as much as he tormented her, but she let him sleep.

Her resistance would be the strongest when he woke up. She could still taunt and defy him through breakfast, still make him believe that he had not broken her—but the mask would slip now when the day's activities began. Only seldom could she rouse herself to defiance when he worked on her now; it took all of her concentration just to keep from pleading with him. She sensed that would be the end of her, when her spirit broke so completely that she begged him to stop would be the moment when he would triumph. She was still strong enough to deny him that, but she didn't know for how much longer. And in the end, would it make any difference if she went out cursing him or thanking him as he had predicted? It still made a difference to her now, but would it by the end? She was beginning to doubt it.

She felt his eyes on her before he stirred and lit the candle. He would do that, lie there for a time, listening to her breathe, trying to gauge something about her, she did not know what. Or maybe he was just working himself up, savoring the pleasures of the day before they began.

This morning he was bright and cheerful. It was the fifth day. The fuel for the lantern was gone; they burned only candles now.

"I slept really well," he said. He was opening a can of beans.

"Me, too," said Aural. "Slept like a log."

"Did you really? They usually have trouble sleeping."

It always troubled her when he talked about the others. There was no comfort in thinking that she was one of many. He had told her that they usually lasted six or seven days; she was on her fifth. Judging by his cigarette supply, which Aural kept close track of, he didn't expect to be down here much beyond that. One way or another, he'll be gone before long, she thought. He certainly wasn't rationing the food or water; he planned to be out of here.

Swann was feeling chatty. "I'm glad you're well rested," he said. "Today is normally a very tough day, they usually start running out of strength about now, but if you're feeling good, that's wonderful news. We'll be able to work even harder that way."

"You know what would make it even more fun?" Aural asked. He unsnapped her cuffs, repositioning her hands in front of her so that she could eat. "How about if we switch places for a while? This is getting kind of boring this way. I think I'll set you on fire today, and then when it's your turn again, you'll be even better at it because you'll know more about it."

He looked at her for a moment as if considering her proposal.

"You're not as pretty as you were," he said at last.

"How unkind." Some beans dribbled off her chin. She had no appetite and no taste for the food, but she forced herself to eat. It would keep

her strength up and she knew it would delight him to see her failing.
"This is not my best light. You, on the other hand, get more handsome
every day."

"Thank you. My eye didn't bother me at all last night."

"There's good news."

"I think it's healed. Praise be to Jesus."

"Jesus loves a sinner," she said.

"Amen."

More beans dribbled off her chin and fell onto her legs, which made
her wince in pain. She did not seem to be able to control the plastic fork
enough to make it all the way from plate to mouth.

"I don't want to see *that*," he said, annoyed. "Why do you think I
leave your face to last? I want you to look *good*."

He leaned towards her to wipe at her chin, and Aural stabbed at him
with her fork, aiming for his eye. The fork missed and struck him harm-
lessly in the cheek, but the steel of the handcuffs hit the target. It was a
reflex action, totally unpremeditated, and she was unable to follow up
her advantage because she was as shocked as he was. Swann recoiled,
clutching his eye, holding up his other hand to fend off further blows.
By the time Aural thought to strike again he had already scrambled out
of her reach and was on his feet.

"You dirty bitch," he moaned.

Aural looked at the remnant of the plastic fork, which had snapped
off in her hand. A tiny trail of blood was seeping down his cheek from
where the fork had penetrated the skin, and Aural thought that was the
wound which had hurt him. She thought of hitting him again while he
was disoriented, but she realized there was no chance as long as he was
on his feet and she was shackled. She would have had to hop after him;
he could knock her over with the slightest shove.

"You son of a bitch, you dirty fucker," Swann was saying. "You
hurt me."

"Oh, I hope so."

"You *really* hurt me," he said. He kept backing away from her as if
he expected her to leap up and renew the attack.

"It was only a fork," she said. "Don't be such a whiner."

"Oh, Jesus," he said, and he rocked back and forth, holding his
head. "JESUS." He screamed in pain, lashing his head from side to
side, then collapsed abruptly onto the cavern floor.

Aural started to drag herself towards him, moving backwards with
her weight on her heels and hands to keep her blistered legs off the

ground. If she could only get to him while he was passed out, if she could get the key to her chains, she didn't need much of a head start, just give her a minute and he'd never catch her . . .

Swann groaned and rose to his knees. Aural froze, hoping he would be too distracted by his pain to notice how close she was, but he looked at her, snarling.

"Stay away. Stay away."

He lurched to his feet, swaying, and backed away from her again. To her astonishment he held a large chef's knife in his hand. He must have had it concealed on him all the time, she realized, or else it was tucked away in the golf sack and she had not seen it. Whatever the source, he had it now. The long blade glinted brightly in the light.

Aural moved slowly back the way she came, heading towards her boots.

Swann positioned himself with his back against the fat cone base of a stalagmite and sat down, facing Aural across twenty yards of space. He had already shifted his focus away from her, thinking now only of his own pain.

"Help me, Jesus," he said, clasping both hands to his head and rocking slightly. "Help me, sweet Jesus." The knife lay in his lap.

Aural reached her boots and settled back so that her feet were just touching them. She knew her own knife was still in its crevice but had to resist the urge to touch it to reassure herself. It was vital not to do anything too soon. She had to do it absolutely right this time, she told herself. She would not get another chance. The existence of his weapon changed it all.

As Swann moaned and cried out in his pain, Aural leaned her back against the stone and rested. And thought.

Chapter 38

Sunrise was still minutes away when Becker led them by flashlight to a ridge that folded back on itself, forming a crease in the landscape. They were on a steep hillside among the foothills of the Cumberland Mountains, less than twenty miles from where the Cumberland gap pierced the Appalachian massif, tucked into the corner where Kentucky, Virginia, and Tennessee met. Two hundred and fifty miles to the east the underground skein of holes and tubes and tunnels that leached its way under the mountains erupted into one of its more spectacular orifices, the Great Mammoth Cave. Less than fifty yards from where they stood was another opening to the subterranean honeycomb, but Becker knew he had no real hope of finding it in the dark. He was as close as Browne's map could take him.

The land surrounding them was scruffy second-growth forest that had reasserted itself among the rocks—without great enthusiasm—after the original stand had been cut and carted and dragged down the mountain to form the fledgling 19th century settlements in the valley below. The hillside was too steep and stony to farm, the area not yet sufficiently upscale to serve as building sites for overpriced chalets. It was a form of wasteland, belonging to an absentee owner, used occasionally by boys hunting for squirrels. If the entrance to the cave had ever been marked, the marker was too obscure to find in the dark. Light, however, was only minutes away and Becker would be ready for it.

Pegeen regarded him as he squatted just below the crease in the hillside, too agitated to even sit. He reminded her of a cat waiting outside a mouse hole, ready to pounce.

"What now?" she asked.

"We wait until we can see enough to find the entrance—unless we hear it breathing first."

"I can still radio for assistance," she said. She knew he would not allow it, but if things went wrong, Pegeen wanted to be able to say she had tried to do the right thing.

"We'll ask for assistance if we need it," he said. "Right now we don't need it."

She watched him for a moment, then sat on the ground, folding her legs under her. Her body was sore in spots; she could still smell him, taste him, almost feel his hands upon her. She knew it wasn't smart to say anything right now, but she said it anyway.

"Should we talk about last night?"

She thought she caught him trying to stifle a sigh.

"Later," he said.

"I just want to clear up one thing," she said. When he didn't respond, she continued, "Was last night the reason you brought me along on this case?"

Becker turned to her, his brow wrinkled quizzically.

"You said you asked for me to work with you for a special reason," she said. "Was last night it? Was last night the special reason?"

"No," Becker said, surprised. "I didn't expect last night until it happened . . . I love Karen, you know. I didn't mean to mislead you otherwise."

Pegeen gasped inwardly. *Mislead* her?

They experienced it first as a change in air pressure, as if the shock wave of some great cataclysm had swept over them, and then, almost immediately, they heard it—the sound of something enormous coming right at them, swooping down at them with a rush of wings. A great column of moving blackness was overhead, moving very fast, and then it whirled and poured into the ground behind them with a noise unlike anything Pegeen had ever heard. The column assumed a funnel shape as it drained into the earth, accompanied by a cacophony of beating wings and shrieks and pounding air.

"Bats," Becker said, but Pegeen did not need to be told. The swooping, swerving flight of the stragglers on the edges told her what they were; bats, millions of them, flying as if in the vampires' panic to beat the sun to their resting place. As they disgorged into the hillside, vanishing into the solid ridgeline as if by magic, they looked like the ominous whirling wind of a tornado, touching down only yards away from them. Underbrush waved and whipped about in their wake, and the closer trees bent under the pressure created by millions of leathery wings.

It seemed to Pegeen to last for hours, but in reality it was over in a few minutes—the moving cloud thinned to a wispy trail of black smoke tendrils, and then to the few latecomers, each one exposed and vulnerable away from the flock. As if on a signal, the sun's rays hit the sky overhead as the last of the bats vanished into the earth.

"I think we found our breathing hole," Becker said, moving to the spot where the bats had disappeared.

Pegeen realized she had been crouched reflexively into a protective ball, her hands over her head to protect her hair. She was grateful that Becker was more concerned with the hole than he was with her at the moment. She joined him, dragging the two backpacks they had carried from the car.

"You're not planning on going *in* there now," she asked.

"They're insect eaters," Becker said, opening one of the backpacks. "They won't bother us."

"They already bother me," Pegeen said, but Becker wasn't listening.

"He's here," Becker said. His voice was hushed and strained as if holding in excitement. Pegeen thought it sounded almost reverential.

A rope vanished into the hole, barely visible at the lip of the opening but rising slightly above the ground as it approached the tree to which it was tied. Becker sensuously slid his hand back and forth on the rope. "New rope," he said.

In the increasing light Pegeen saw a path leading to the hole, where something large and heavy had been dragged over the weeds and underbrush. The path trailed off down the hillside.

"And he's not alone," she said.

"Not anymore," Becker said, grinning.

He removed a length of synthetic climbing rope that was coiled onto the back of his pack and secured it quickly and efficiently to a tree trunk. Shouldering the pack, he whipped the rope around his body and under his leg. With his left hand on the secured portion of the rope, his right holding the trailing portion, he backed up to the hole. The opening was no more than four feet wide and went into the side of the ridge so that it rode on a plane that was close to vertical before it plunged straight down.

Pegeen surveyed the abyss with her flashlight and saw no bottom.

"Browne's chart says it's thirty-five feet to the bottom," Becker said. "They taught you to rappel in training camp, right?"

"Of course."

"This will be a little different. The chart shows the mouth opening out as it goes down. There won't be anything for your feet to touch after first few feet, so it's more of a free fall, but just take it slow, you'll be fine."

"I know that," she said, angrily. "I can do this."

"If I had any doubts, you wouldn't be here," he said. "Once we're down there, keep quiet. Sound travels a long way."

"I don't plan to sing and dance," she said.

He looked at her for a moment. The sunlight was increasing; Pegeen could make out the shadows under his eyes from lack of sleep. She imagined she looked as bad, or worse. But unlike Becker, she feared that she also looked apprehensive. She certainly felt that way. Becker looked happy; his eyes were shining too much.

"When we get to them, you protect the girl," Becker said. "I'll take care of him."

She nodded. She had no doubt that he would take care of Swann.

"Oh, and, uh—Pegeen," he continued, having trouble saying her first name, "thanks for last night. You kept me sane."

He grinned again—Pegeen was not certain if it was at her or in anticipation of Swann—and backed into the hole. With a little hop, he broke away from the surface and his head dropped out of sight.

Thanks for last night? *Thanks?*

She shone the light into the hole, watching the top of Becker's head recede, spinning slowly as he dropped. There was a small bald spot on the crown of his head which she had not noticed before. Well, why should I? she thought bitterly. I've been blind in general. Thanks for a night that had left her shaken and disbelieving and filled with hope and fear and emotions so raw and basic and mysterious to her that she couldn't even name them? I fucked him to save his mental health, your honor. Never mind what it did to mine—I was happy to make the sacrifice for the good of the Bureau.

When he had reached the bottom of the shaft, Pegeen wrapped the rope around herself and eased her way into oblivion, following a ray of light that he shone up at her. She wasn't frightened, she told herself. She was too fucking angry at the insensitive son of a bitch to be scared of anything, but she kept her eyes fixed on the diminishing patch of sunlight above her. When her feet touched something solid at last, the light had dwindled to a space so small she could cover it with her thumb. So maybe I'm a little scared, she admitted.

Becker awaited her impatiently, turning his flashlight from the rope to the chart in his hand as soon as she released the rope. Without a word to her he motioned with the beam and moved off.

They followed the meandering course of an old riverbed, walking upright most of the time but stopping now and then as the roof curved down. Pegeen could not believe how dark it was. The stone seemed to absorb the light rather than reflect it, and she could see only where her flashlight pointed and nowhere else. She had not been prepared for the cold, either. It felt as if she had stepped into a meat locker, although the sound of water running somewhere told her that the temperature was not below freezing.

Becker slipped suddenly, his feet flying from under him, and he landed on the stone with a squishing sound. She knelt beside him and saw why he had fallen. In front of them, as far as the flashlight would carry, was a spreading mat of bat shit. She played the light up walls and onto the roof, where hung a writhing mass of animals, still settling in for their daylight rest. They hung everywhere she could see, like a million inverted winged mice. Their teeth shone eerily white in her light as they chattered and nipped at each other, and she had the feeling she was being leered at by a madman. The entire mass of them moved and twitched and wriggled like one huge body in torment, as if the cave itself were brought to squirming painful life. The bats were crowded so closely together that Pegeen could not distinguish one from another until an individual one would be knocked loose and it would fly in the characteristic swooping, erratic pattern until it returned to the general body, wedging itself in and vanishing into the whole.

"Holy Christ," she breathed.

"It's bat guano," Becker said, pulling himself to his feet.

"It's bat *shit*," she said, trailing her light from the appalling mass of bats to the equally appalling mass in front of her. The pellets were gray and shaped like grains of rice, and they looked dry and solid but Becker's slip had demonstrated otherwise.

She played the light carefully along the edge of the mat, trying to assess it. "It must be more than three feet thick," she said.

"Closer to four," said Becker. He seemed remarkably unconcerned.

"How do we get around it?" Pegeen asked.

"We don't. We go through it." Becker's flashlight picked out the two-foot-wide trail where something had been recently dragged across the surface of the mat. "He did it. We can."

"Did you know this was here?" she demanded.

"The chamber is on the chart, but Browne didn't bother to indicate what was in it. I guess this sort of thing doesn't bother him."

"Fine, let's get him down here."

"It's only guano," Becker said.

"It's *shit*," insisted Pegeen.

"Only in your mind." Becker stepped directly into it, following the path where Swann had dragged the loaded golf sack.

"I can't believe this," Pegeen said, placing her foot gingerly in the track Becker had created. "I'm walking through shit up to my thighs."

"Sounds like a fair description of life," Becker said.

"Oh, Christ. Oh, Christ."

"Hey, the FBI isn't all paperwork and investigations, you know," Becker said cheerfully. "We got to have some fun sometimes."

Pegeen would gladly have pushed him facefirst into the goo. Just don't let me slip, she prayed silently.

The muck rose above her waist, but the footing underneath seemed dry and solid. She could not imagine the age of the pile, but knew it had to be counted in centuries.

"Oh, Christ. Oh, Christ," she muttered with every step, unaware that her silent mantra was escaping her lips. In front of her, Becker seemed terribly amused and she thought she heard him chuckle once or twice.

"Just think how badly Swann must have wanted to get in here," Becker said in a whisper.

And how badly you want to get in after him, Pegeen finished the thought. Still, she was grateful that he was leading her, taking long, sweeping steps, pushing much of the guano out of her way like the prow of a ship. The stuff didn't appear to be clinging as much as she had feared, only the surface layer was moist, the rest as dry as sunbaked pellets.

When his flashlight picked out the dimensions of a wall in front of them, Becker stopped and turned to Pegeen.

"There's a tunnel ahead of us, according to the chart," he said, his voice hushed. "It looks narrow, we may have to crawl. We'll do it without lights—we don't want anything shining into the main cavern."

"Without lights?"

"You're not afraid of the dark, are you?"

"No more than most sensible people. How do we know where we're going?"

"The chart shows it to be pretty much a straight line. Just keep going forward."

"What if the chart is wrong?" Pegeen hissed. "What if there's a dropoff or something in there that Browne didn't bother to put on the chart?"

"If I fall out of sight, you'll know it's time to stop."

"You won't be *in* sight—we're not using lights."

"Use your imagination, Haddad. You'll be fine."

"Are you going to call me Haddad now? Are we back to that? If we are, would you mind if we just kept going a little further before we continue this discussion?"

"Why?"

"Because I'm standing up to my navel in bat shit and I don't want to be insulted at the same time."

Becker shined his light directly in her face until she pushed the flashlight away.

"You mean last night?" he asked.

"Duh."

"Last night was indescribable. You saved my sanity, I don't think I would have made it until morning."

"Could we not talk about it right here? Could we maybe find a nice sewer to sit in first?"

Becker looked down at the guano rising to his belt as if he had forgotten it entirely.

"It's dry," he said as if he didn't understand her objections.

Pegeen sighed. "Just get me to the tunnel. Please."

"When we get to the chamber, if he hears us he'll probably douse his own light. Don't use your weapon because you'll only pinpoint yourself and he may be armed."

"I won't be able to see and I won't be able to shoot. What am I supposed to do?"

"Whatever I tell you."

"How do we find this son of a bitch in the dark?"

"I'll find him," Becker said.

"Great. How?"

Becker paused. When he spoke, she heard a smile in his voice. It was not a friendly smile.

"I'll find him by his fear," Becker said.

Chapter 39

Swann was moaning now to a methodical rhythm, interspersing little yips like a child's bleats that came with every inward breath. The sound was monotonous and metronomic and Aural wondered if it came now from some source other than pain. It was almost a genteel snore, and in the dim candlelight that illuminated him from a distance she could not see clearly if he was asleep or awake. He hadn't moved in several minutes and both hands were still clasped upon his face. The candle had burned down several inches since he had moved across the cavern, and Aural estimated that it must have been at least an hour. She had tried to time it at first, using the tick of her water clock, but his moans were too loud at first for her to keep track and then it didn't seem to matter anyway. Time had long since lost any meaning. There was no way to measure the length of a torture session—each seemed to last an infinity, and minutes and seconds and hours signified nothing at all. Progress was marked by inches as he burned his way slowly across her flesh, cigarette by cigarette, and by candles that glowed and melted and shrank and guttered into darkness only to be replaced by another. And by pain, endless pain. There was no way to measure the quantity of her agony, but still it was distinguished by a surprising variety. Some things hurt differently than others, some pains lasted so long that she could nearly ignore them and regard them as background, some were so intense she could only scream her way through them.

Aural shivered and huddled her arms against her chest. It was the first time in days that she had had the leisure to notice the cold. Her legs seemed ablaze but her torso was chilled. She had been shaking with the cold for several minutes and hadn't even noticed. Another way to die, she thought. I could freeze to death before he kills me.

The rhythm of his breathing changed and she realized that he was actually falling asleep. When she was sure he was out, she would make her move. She would need at least several minutes to make her way to the tunnel, moving backwards on her hands and heels. Once in the tunnel she had no idea how far or fast she could go, but at least she would be trying. It would be something she could do for herself.

One hand slipped off his face and into his lap, then moments later, the other hand fell away. His head moved back slightly in reaction to finding itself unsupported, then stopped in position. After another few moments the head drooped lower, bounced back up, drooped lower still, bounced again as he nodded deeper and deeper into sleep. Aural waited for his head to come to rest on his chest. One more drop, maybe two.

Swann's head slumped all the way to his chest, then sprang back violently and he woke up crying out in pain as if the final fall had reactivated his injury.

"My eye!" he called, as if he expected someone to respond, as if he expected *her* to help him. "Please, Jesus, please!"

And then Aural realized that she *could* help and she smiled to herself because she felt for the first time as if she had a real weapon. Despite her pain and her condition and her shackles, she realized that he had given her power.

She waited until he was momentarily quiet, and then she spoke to him, keeping her voice low but intense.

"I can help you," she said.

It brought him to silence. He listened for a moment as if he expected her to repeat it.

"What did you say?"

"I can help you," Aural repeated.

She could see him peering at her through the cracks between his fingers.

"How?" he asked cautiously.

"You know how."

He brought his hands to his lap and grasped the knife, suspecting a trick.

"How?" he repeated.

"I can heal you," Aural said. She hoped it was her stage voice but it sounded cracked and wounded to her ear.

Again he was quiet, studying her for deception, then a shiver of pain coursed through him again and he tilted his head and gave a moan like a whinnying horse.

When his spasm passed, Aural said, "You know I can do it. You have seen me heal. You have seen the divine power of Jesus Christ move through me. I have the power."

"Yes," he said. "I've seen you do it."

"God be praised," she said, trying to project strength which she did not feel.

"Amen."

"He works through me." She lifted her hands, already forced into a prayerful attitude by the cuffs, and held them in the air, fingertips touching. "He has given me the hands to do his work."

"I hurt so much," he said.

"Jesus never gives us more than we can bear," she said.

She smiled at him, summoning up the smile of beatitude, the smile that stirred hearts and eased consciences and made miracles seem not only possible but the within the order of things. She smiled at Swann her own sweet promise of love and forgiveness, of redemption and deliverance. It was the reason he had chosen her in the first place—the sign of virginal divinity that he always looked for and then somehow forgot in the vileness of his actions when the beast that dwelled in his chest stirred and took him within its tentacles. But that was not the true Swann, it was the beast. The true Swann loved God and his holy son and yearned for goodness and yearned now most of all for release from his pain.

"Would you do that for me?" he said.

"Only I *can* do it for you. Jesus has not answered your prayers, but he will answer mine on your behalf."

"But I've been—bad—to you," he said.

"It is not for humans to judge," Aural said. She extended her hands toward him, palms up. "Jesus forgave his persecutors, we must do the same."

She had him, she thought, he believed her, he wanted desperately to believe her, and that was always the necessary prerequisite. Their pain, their illness, their unhappiness had to drive them to you, then you had to make them welcome and pull them in the rest of the way. She smiled again, that radiant smile, trying her best to light the cavern with her own illumination. The effort took a lot out of her; she did not know how much longer she could keep it up; she wanted nothing more than to lie back and rest; she needed rest so badly, if only her pain would allow it.

He had risen slowly to his knees, but still he hesitated, cowering back in the shadows so far away.

I've reached them from farther away than this, Aural told herself; I've brought them from the back of the tent when they didn't want to come and didn't even know they needed me; I've summoned up the love of God, the trust of my healing power in souls dark and dead and shut off, those who had come to gape and those who had come to scoff and I've pulled them to me and I can pull this asshole to me, too.

She began to sing, her voice rising with lyric sweetness in the hypnotic melody of "Amazing Grace." She sang it straight to him, straight to his heart, pouring into her voice every ounce of fraud and deceit and practiced cunning that she possessed, transforming it by her art into the irresistible musical locution of the angels.

As her voice filled the cavern with haunting reverberations of the timeless hymn, it was as if she were joined by a heavenly chorus. Holding one hand to his eye, gripping the knife with the other, Swann rose to his feet and crossed the chamber towards her outstretched arms as she sang to him with her face aglow in serenity and her eyes closed with the intensity of her love.

As she heard his faltering step on the stone and saw the glint of the approaching knife blade under her squinted eyelids, Aural thought, Try this one, Tommy R. Walker. You couldn't pull this one off if your life depended on it. And she remembered that hers did and she sang all the sweeter.

The bat chamber was so configured that the guano gave out well before the enclosing wall was reached, and the trail that Becker and Pegeen had followed vanished on the hard stone. They searched for the tunnel indicated on Browne's chart for several minutes, playing their flashlights on the surface where the floor met the vertical wall. When she found it, Pegeen was not certain it was the right trail, the hole seemed so small.

"Could this be it?" she whispered. She knelt in front of the opening, resisting the urge to shine her light directly into the tunnel. She would have to crawl into it on her knees and elbows—there was no other way to fit her body through.

"Must be," said Becker in a voice that made her look at him sharply. She lifted her light so that it spilled from the wall onto his face. Becker wore an expression she had never seen on his features. If she didn't know better, she would say he was frightened.

"It's so small," she said. He nodded with a look on his face that suggested he did not trust himself to speak. Pegeen noticed beads of moisture on his forehead. Sweating in the coolness of the cave seemed so unlikely that she thought he was ill.

She asked if he was sick and Becker shook his head, forcing a very unconvincing grin.

"What's wrong?" she persisted, reaching to touch his forehead. He jerked away angrily.

"You keep asking why I wanted you on this case," Becker said.

She knew immediately that she would not like what he was going to say; she knew he wanted to hurt her because she had seen something that he didn't want her to see.

"Yes?"

Becker pointed towards the entrance hole of the tunnel.

"This is why," he said. "You're small enough to fit."

Pegeen struck back immediately. "You're afraid of it, aren't you?"

Becker avoided her eyes.

"You're claustrophobic?"

"I'm fine," he said. His whole face was now shiny with perspiration.

"I can see how fine you are."

"I'll manage," he said.

"You knew this was here all along," she said. You've been studying the chart on this cave since last night. Why didn't you do something, why didn't we call somebody? Are you so desperate to do this?"

"I'll make it."

"Why didn't you tell *me*, at least?"

"What good would that have done?"

"Maybe I could have helped you," she said.

"I can only help myself," Becker said, but at the moment he looked to Pegeen like someone who couldn't begin to help himself. His whole physical being seemed to have changed, to have softened and weakened, as if the phobia had sapped his very bones.

"You don't have to be brave all the time," Pegeen said softly. "Not with me." She tentatively placed her fingertips on the back of his hand and he jerked as he always seemed to when touched unexpectedly, but when he relaxed he did not pull away and Pegeen gently slipped her hand across the top of his.

After a moment he rolled his hand over so that they were palm to palm and his fingers closed slowly over hers. Pegeen remembered holding his hand in the car before he went into the prison to visit Swann. That was how this had all started for her, this obsession with this powerful, dangerous, complicated man who could be reduced to immobility by his own secret fears, who could rouse such passion in her, in himself, then cloak it again as if it never happened, who could be so vulnerable, then draw such strength from the touch of her hand. He had granted her a power over him on that first day, she realized, and whether he knew it or not, whether he held an equal power over her or not, he had needed her ever since.

"It's all right," she said at last. "I'll go, you can wait here."

He shook his head dully, resignedly, not looking at her, knowing what had to happen.

There would be no easy way out for Becker, Pegeen realized. He would never allow that.

"Shall I go first, then?" she asked.

Becker shivered violently, as if hit suddenly by a frigid wind, but he nodded again and shrugged off his backpack.

"I'll keep in touch with your foot," he said. "But if I don't . . ."

"You will, I know you will."

He was on his hands and knees in front of the hole, his head hanging like a beaten dog's. "If I stop, keep going."

"You'll make it," she said.

"Right."

Pegeen removed her pack and stretched out flat before the opening of the tunnel. She shifted her pistol so that it rode securely in her belt in the middle of her back, reachable but well out of the way.

"No lights, no firing," Becker said. She could hear his voice quavering. Pegeen wanted to hug him but knew that what he wanted most was for her to be gone so that she couldn't see him in the grip of his fears. Pegeen tucked the flashlight into her belt on her back alongside her pistol. She might not use either one, but she was sure as hell going to have them with her.

She took a deep breath as if she were going underwater and went headfirst into the tunnel. Behind her, Becker doused his light and the world became pitch. She moved forward slowly, feeling first with her hands across the surface of the stone that was as smooth as polished marble before pulling herself forward. Sometimes there was room enough on either side for her to slide a knee forward, sometimes the sides narrowed in so that she could propel herself only by pulling with her arms and elbows and the tips of her toes. There were sudden drops of several inches, sometimes a foot or more, as sheer as miniature waterfalls, but everywhere she touched the surface had the burnished feel of ice. It was like crawling into a giant intestine, she thought. Straight up the devil's ass.

Becker crawled behind her, his hand touching her ankle or the sole of her boot when she braced, falling away as she pulled herself forward and then contacting her again as he followed her movements. Pegeen took comfort in knowing he was there and wondered what this exercise was costing him. It was bad enough for her—she felt like screaming at times as the tunnel seemed to stretch forever without end—what damnation must he be suffering? She thought, too, of Swann, following this same course, dragging the girl behind him. He had to drag her, there was no other way. How compelling a need must it be to make a man do that? Becker knew; in some way Becker understood; but Pegeen did not. Nor did she want to.

Swann had advantages, though, she realized. He had been here before. He knew there was an end to the tunnel, and some sort of reward, however sick and twisted, when he got there. And he had light. Pegeen would have given anything for any illumination, even as faint as a spark. Crawling like this was like living without hope.

Her fingers touched a beveled edge and explored it on all sides. The tunnel had reached a cincture, as if a belt had suddenly been tightened. Her hands told her that the walls spread out again on the other side, but at this point the stone narrowed in even farther than before. Her head cleared easily but the gap was too narrow to pass her shoulders straightaway. She twisted her body to one side, squeezing her shoulders towards each other, but then her hips were caught and she hung, helplessly, with gravity pulling her head lower than her waist and her fingers scrabbling for purchase on the ivory-smooth rock.

On Christ, oh shit, oh Christ, oh shit, she thought, repeating the mindless mantra to herself as she wriggled and squirmed. She was caught by the gun and flashlight tucked in her belt and they were on the other side of the opening; she could not reach back to free them; she didn't have enough of a grip on the stone with her hands to push herself up and backwards so she could retreat. She dangled half in, half out, writhing, her fingers scrabbling for a hold.

As she fought her sense of panic it occurred to her that this might be the wrong tunnel, it might be a dead end that narrowed and shrank and came to nothing and she would be trapped within it. They had taken it on faith that this was where Swann had gone, where he had to have gone, and they had trusted Browne's chart, but who knew how thoroughly Browne had searched? Perhaps he had found a different tunnel and had not bothered to mark this cul-de-sac on the map at all.

She felt Becker's hands on her and knew that his fingers were assessing the situation of stone and flesh. He pulled back on her hips and Pegeen rose, her hands now in touch with nothing. As she flailed to make contact with the walls, she felt Becker yank the gun and flashlight from her belt. He put his hand on her ass and shoved. She wanted to tell him to stop, to pull her all the way back, they were heading into nowhere, but she suddenly popped free and had a fleeting image of herself slipping through a birth canal.

Her feet slithered down the three-foot drop-off and her knees thudded against the stone. It took her a moment to realize that she was free and to gather herself before advancing again. Whatever lay ahead, she knew it could not be worse than where she had just been.

The tunnel began to widen and she could get her knees under her and she moved ahead with eagerness, so relieved to be moving at last, until she realized that Becker was no longer with her.

Chapter 40

Swann stood over her, pointing the knife at her, not threatening, just reminding her that he had it, keeping it there for when she looked at him. Aural finished the hymn, keeping her eyes closed until the last sweet note faded and fell to silence. She could see his feet and legs up to his knees through her lashes, but she was careful to keep her visage from pointing directly at him. She didn't want to be forced to look at him, she didn't want to deal with him, until she had to. First she had to summon her concentration onto herself, to focus on creating herself as saint and healer.

She let the silence sink in on him for a few seconds, making him realize what a wonder had been taken from him. She opened her eyes slowly as if recovering from a trance, as if she had not been aware of him at all, standing there with a knife. She took a deep breath and released it with an audible sigh, and then slowly canted her head upwards with a look of mild astonishment as if she could not imagine how she came to be in such a place with such company. Some of her fans had told her she looked reborn when she came out of a song. They thought she must surely have been with the angels while she sang, letting their voices ring through her, which was why she was always disoriented when she finished. They were grateful to her for having come back to *them*, it showed how much she cared for them. Rae said she looked washed clean with the waters of Jordan when she completed a hymn, cleansed and a little shaken by the experience. The Reverend Tommy R. Walker confessed that it was about the neatest trick he'd ever seen.

Aural looked up and fastened her gaze on Swann and realized that he, too, had been fooled. He was gaping at her, not quite sure who, or what, he saw.

"I know why you did it," he said. His voice had changed, grown younger. Aural recognized the childish petulance in it, but there was something else there, something she couldn't identify.

She didn't know what he meant. "Do you?" she asked.

"You hurt me because . . ." He sniffed suddenly, wiping at his nose with the back of his knife hand. Aural realized that he had been weeping. "Because you love me," he finished.

Aural recognized the other quality in his voice now. It was forgiveness. He was absolving her for stabbing him with the fork.

She nodded slowly, not trusting herself to say the right thing, but realizing she didn't need to speak at all, that he had something he wanted to say.

"You only do that because you love me, I know that," he continued.

Aural nodded again, arching her eyebrows slightly, trying to look loving but stern.

"For your own good," she said, suddenly inspired.

Swann's face wrinkled and he whimpered in his throat. He looked at that moment about five years old.

"I know it," he said, crying openly now. "I know I'm bad."

"Sometimes you're bad," Aural said carefully. She was still not quite certain of her role. Was she his mother now? Or was she still the woman he planned to torture to death? He had not put the knife down nor even wavered with it. It continued to point at her as if it were a gun.

"But I do love Jesus, I truly do," he said.

"Do you?"

"Yes, ma'am."

"But you're bad anyway." She thought she had gone too far. Swann stiffened and his lip trembled with defiance.

"Sometimes," he said, agreeing but not giving in.

Aural continued to look at him, not backing down but not knowing what else to do. He had regressed so quickly that she knew there must be something about her that made him think of his mother; something about her; something about pain. For a moment the knife seemed to quiver and she wondered if he was going to stab her. She wondered if he had stabbed his mother.

He stood there for a moment, towering over her as she sat on the floor, waving the blade in front of her face now, closer and closer, looking for all the world like a child with his first taste of power. Aural didn't know what to do, but she knew that she couldn't let him win. If she were to beat him, she had to do it now, when he was five years old and not an adult, when he was not certain he was in control and not happily convinced he was evil.

"Jesus loves you anyway," she said at last.

He had wanted her to plead, to react to his menace; he had not expected calm. For a moment he was startled, as if instead of stepping away in fear she had slapped his face.

"Can I show you something?" he said, and Aural realized that things had changed again. He wasn't fully adult yet, but he wasn't addressing his mother anymore, either. He sounded like an adolescent about to reveal a great truth to a newly discovered friend.

Aural nodded her consent, but he wasn't waiting for permission, he had already sat on the stone and was eagerly stripping off his shoes and socks and then tugging at his pants.

You're not going to show me anything I haven't seen too many times before, she thought, but to her surprise he made no motion to remove his underwear. He thrust a bare leg at her, proudly.

"What?" Aural asked.

"Look." He gestured to his leg, using the knife as a pointer.

It took Aural a moment to realize what she was seeing. Swann looked as if he were wearing the skin of a smaller man, and his entire leg, from foot to thigh, was being shrunken and drawn together as the flesh shriveled and puckered in what Aural finally knew to be the accumulated scar tissue of hundreds of dime-sized burns. His limbs gleamed in the candlelight with the particular sheen of contracted flesh.

He was watching her reaction eagerly, and when she looked at him again with the first glimmer of sympathy he lifted his foot and waggled it to get her attention.

"Look, look," he said, excited by what he had to show her. He placed the point of the knife between his toes where, in the exquisitely sensitive space between the digits, were positioned more scars the size of the tip of her little finger, the flesh still recoiling as if in perpetual horror at the insult of the burning ember placed there years ago and pulling his toes together so that he could barely separate them on his own.

Aural gasped at the unforgiving nature of the traumatized skin. I'll look like that, she realized, and tears of sorrow welled up in her eyes. But there was no self-pity in Swann's face as he pushed forth the other foot to be examined and admired. He looked proud, even smug.

"Your mother?" Aural asked.

"Mother was a Christian," Swann said approvingly. As if she had given her son her own version of the stigmata to prove it.

"I can make it better," she said.

"Can you?"

"I can make it all better," she said. She extended her fingers towards his legs, and then up, towards his head, to indicate his heart, his mind, his past, his memories. "I can heal your very soul."

"God be praised," he said.

"Help me up," she said. He looked at her dully. "On my feet," she said. "I can't do it sitting down."

Swann extended a hand and helped her stand, then delicately traced his finger down her chest to a point just below the sternum, probing gently to find the point where the bone gave way to the soft tissue and muscle of the abdomen. He placed the point of the knife on the precise spot.

"You won't hurt me again, will you?" he asked.

"I'm going to heal you," Aural said. "I am a healer; but you got to trust me."

"I trust you," he said, not moving the knife.

"You got to have faith," she said.

"I do."

"Faith in me, not just Jesus, but faith in me."

"I do," Swann said sincerely. "I surely do." Then his face slowly crinkled into a grin. "But I ain't stupid, neither."

Aural raised her manacled hands. "Let us pray," she said, and her voice took on the reverentially inspiring tone of the show tent. "Sweet Jesus, dear sweet, sweet Jesus, this man is a terrible sinner, this man has the blood of his fellow human beings on his hands, this man has tortured and killed defenseless people, and he will do it again, dear Lord, he will do it again and again because there is no true repentance in his soul. His soul is as black as this hole in the ground, his soul is twisted and warped and unholy, Lord, he is the worst of your children, he is the lost and forsaken and most despised of all your children here on earth. Men have given up on him, men hate and revile him . . . but you love him, Lord."

"Hallelujah," said Swann.

"You love all your children, even the worst of them, even those that crawl and slither like the reptiles are beloved in your sight, Lord, and that's a miracle in itself, that's a blessing that passes all understanding. But you know what we have forgot, sweet Jesus, you remember that even the slimiest of your children has an immortal soul, and that soul can be washed clean, that soul can be washed as clean as if it never was drenched in the blood and the fear and the agony of other human beings' painful dying. You can wash that soul clean, Lord, wash it in the blood of the Lamb until it comes out as sparkling white as snow. Praise be!''

"Praise him!''

"If you can wash this soul clean, sweet, compassionate, Jesus, you can do anything. And we know you can, we know you can. Take his pain, Lord, take away the hurt from his eye and the blisters from his legs and wash away the filth from his spirit and make him like a newborn babe. He loves you, Jesus, he believes in you, and that's all you care about. He believes you are the son of god and you promised us that whosoever believeth in you will be born again in purity and joy forever.''

Aural paused to breath deeply, preparing herself for the moment for which everything else was but a prelude. She could fake belief and feign the fervor, but the courage had to be real.

She edged closer to him, lifting her hands to place them on his head. He winced at the movement, then settled, allowing her to do what he had seen her do before at the healing meeting. She put her hands high on his forehead, avoiding his stricken eye. She didn't want him to make any involuntary movements and stab her in reaction. The knife snuggled up against her abdomen as she moved to him.

"Take the pain away," she said, her voice rising in intensity towards the incantatory peak. His breath smelled of charred rubber.

"Take it away, sweet Jesus, and HEAL!'' She pushed hard against his forehead, at the same time sliding her foot behind his heel. Swann tilted backwards, tried to shift his feet, but was caught by Aural's foot and he fell, instinctively swinging his arms out for balance. The point of the blade sliced across Aural's stomach, barely pinking the skin as it dropped away and clattered on the stone. In three hobbled steps Aural was atop the candle. She hurled it into the cavern and its light blinked out, casting them into darkness.

She had heard his head land on the stone but knew she could not count on his being seriously injured. She was depending on confusion and the darkness. She hobbled and hopped towards the side of the cavern where the vertical wave formations offered her a hiding place. There was no time for anything else, no chance of getting as far as the tunnel. If he was injured in the fall, it was a bonus, but all she really hoped for was a chance to get to hiding before he figured out what to do. She staggered forward as quickly as she could, her hands held in front of her, aching to touch the wall. She knew the way, she had rehearsed it in her mind over and over when she could see, and she knew how long it should take her. If only she had enough time—she had to have enough time. She fell suddenly, crashing forward as her foot hit an outcropping. The burns on her legs raged furiously at the contact with the stone but she scrambled up again, hopping and hobbling and reaching blindly in front of her for salvation.

She heard him moaning, heard him scrabbling around on the stone, wasting his time by feeling for the knife first. She heard the metal scrape against the rock as her own fingers found the edge of the wave shape. She reached around it and her hand groped into empty air. There *was* a space behind it. Aural slipped behind the sheltering rock and tried to quiet her breathing. She knew she couldn't have much more time before Swann was in control of things again.

"Bitch," Swann yelled. "Cunt bitch."

He pulled the lighter from his pocket, snapped it on and held it high, the knife in front of him, half expecting the crazed woman to launch herself at him.

She was gone.

"Cunt," he raged. "Filthy cunt bitch." Then he realized his own noises had betrayed him. If he had been quiet he might have heard where she was going, but he had been too loud, groaning and cursing. He should have gotten the lighter first but he had been afraid she would get the knife and attack him in the dark.

Swann swung in a slow circle, holding the lighter in front of him as if it were a beacon, but it was a pointless exercise. There were too many shadows, too many areas where the light didn't reach. he would have to search for her foot by foot. And when he found her—when he found her. His imagination carried him no further than that. It would depend upon her. If she resisted, he would probably need to kill her right then . . . but he did want to finish, oh, he longed to finish her the right way, the slow way, the only way that would satisfy his demon.

Oddly enough, his eye had stopped hurting him. Maybe she did heal him after all, he thought, no matter how deceitful her intent. He took two candles from the golf sack and lit them both, then used their flames to burn a hole in two empty cigarette packs. He inserted the base of the candles in the holes so that the wax would not drip on his hands, then began his search.

Aural could see the light flickering and jerking off the walls with his movements, but when she looked down at herself her legs and hands were still in darkness. The nook behind the stone was deep and secure from anything but direct light. He would have to be standing behind the recess himself before he could see her. And eventually he would be, she knew that, but she would hear him coming, she would see him coming by the approach of the candle, and she would be ready. She would have surprise and she would . . . she realized with horror that she had forgotten her own knife. It was still tucked away in the niche by her boots, useless, lost to her. A wave of despair washed over her and it was all she could do to keep from crying aloud in anguish.

Chapter 41

Claustrophobia clamped down on Becker and shook him. Uncontrollable tremors racked his body and he shivered as if he were freezing to death. His skin was cold and clammy but sweat sprang out all over it and grunts of panic burbled from his throat despite his efforts to remain quiet. He couldn't move, he could not force his body to take him either forward or back, and he squeezed his eyes closed, trying to escape the encompassing darkness of the tunnel for the safety of his mind. But his mind was no haven. He felt the walls of darkness close in ever more tightly around him, the stone seemed to be growing together, closing over him like a scar, encasing him forever in eternal blackness. Entombed, buried alive, but not alone, for the blackness of his crypt was peopled by the monsters of his youth. The cavern gave way to the lightless cellar where he cowered as a boy, imprisoned for transgressions more imagined than real, awaiting with dread through the interminable night and day for the heavy, drunken tread upon the stair that would signal the beginning of his long, long punishment that ended only with his father exhausted and unable to scourge him any longer. Becker's ears filled with his own youthful cries and fruitless begging, his father's muttered curses and imprecations of damnation, the grunts of exertion that accompanied each swing of fist or belt or shoe; and with his mother's voice assuring him it was for his own betterment, acting as monitor to her husband's severity, never to ameliorate but only to judge and assess the limits of flesh and bone, calling all the while for Becker's repentance and self-improvement, as if a boy of five and six and seven were nothing but obstinacy and willful disobedience.

Afterwards, the sound of his own sobs making barely audible the creaking of the cellar stairs as his parents left him alone in the darkness—the better now to contemplate his behavior—his terror of being left alone in the blackness again surmounting even the pain of his tortured body. Abandoned in the lightless hole while those he loved, those who professed to love him, moved about above him, not indifferent to his fate, worse, the agents of his fate, the architects of his misery. Becker could hear again the sounds of their footfalls over his head, their voices in normal conversation, muted by floorboards and carpet, and occasionally laughter, the cruelest sound of all. They were happy above while he cringed in terror below, waiting interminably for the shaft of light at the head of the stairs that would signal his release, the light that would seem never to come, the light that would be denied him until he screamed and screamed with the horror of his abandonment only to be chastised and punished again for such impertinence. Eventually he learned to bear his torment in silence, listening for the weakness in others.

He heard the voice coming from the radio, filtered and distorted by distance as his mother moved about in the kitchen, turning to music to drown out the sounds of his whimpers, perhaps. Blurred by its passage through the walls and floors, the voice was nonetheless sweet and pure, a voice filled with love and religious serenity . . . and Becker returned to himself and realized that he was not in the cellar of his tormented youth and the singing voice was not from a radio. Someone living, distant but alive, was voicing the old hymn, and the sound beckoned him like a siren's song.

Pegeen saw the light, at first not daring to believe her eyes. The tunnel passage had seemed so long that she had all but abandoned hope of ever getting out of it. Becker had vanished in the hole behind her. She had heard noises from him at times, muffled groans, and she had thought she should return to him, but then she knew that the real crisis lay ahead. Whatever Becker's torments, she knew they would not kill him; she had no such confidence about the woman who was somewhere in front of her. She heard the voice singing, incredibly singing in the blackness of the cave and shortly thereafter Pegeen saw the light, scarcely more than a pinprick at first, but it grew as she hurried towards it.

The singing stopped and Pegeen heard a drone of voices which also ceased abruptly and then the light vanished along with the sound. Pegeen pressed forward, hearing a man's voice calling out to someone, elevated and angry. Then light again, first the flickering light of a flame, then soon something steadier. She could see she was at the end of the tunnel, that the walls gave way and opened out and she hurried even more. Just as she reached the end of the tunnel the lights went out again and the man's voice lapsed into silence.

She paused at the end of the tunnel, not knowing what lay beyond, sensing only the hush of a crowded room that falls into quiet when a newcomer enters and all eyes shift to him.

Swann had put on his miner's hat and switched on the lamp. He left the candles several yards apart so they would illuminate as much of the cavern as possible, then began his search in the section of the cave that served as the latrine, thinking that Aural might have gone that way since it was the only place she had been before the light went out. He scoured that area, then returned to the area lighted by the candles and scanned the walls. He noticed a peculiar pattern of wave-shaped rock formations and started towards them when he heard something and froze in his tracks. There had come a noise from the tunnel and he knew immediately that it was wasn't Aural. Incredibly, someone was there. Someone was coming into the cavern.

Swann doused his headlamp and rushed to blow out the candles. When he stood abruptly from extinguishing the second candle, the pain in his eye struck him so severely that it nearly knocked him off his feet.

Aural heard Swann gasp with pain. He was only a few feet from her, just the other side of the protective formation that shielded her from his view. She would go straight for his eyes, she told herself. If he found her, she would strike at his injured eye with all she had and simply forget about his knife. If she ran into it, what did it matter, she would die anyway if she didn't get away from him. She would lunge before he realized he had found her; if he had the knife in front of him, then she would skewer herself on it, but at least she would be trying, she would be doing her best to ruin him in the process.

His light snapped off abruptly, then the candles went out. Aural could hear him panting with pain, then she heard something else. It sounded like—she knew it couldn't be, it was a cruel trick of her imagination, but still it sounded like someone else entering the cavern . . . but where was the light? No one would come without light.

Blessedly, Pegeen was able to stand. She rose to her feet, stretching her back after the long journey, trying desperately to orient herself. She reached her arms out to her sides and felt nothing. Nothing to either side, nothing above her. The tunnel had been horrible, but at least she knew where she was in relation to her surroundings; now she felt as if she had stepped into the emptiness of outer space. Her feet told her which way was down, but that was all she knew.

She silently cursed Becker. He had abandoned her, sunk into himself, and she had neither light nor weapon. Swann knew where *she* was, he had heard her coming and doused the light, he had had time to prepare, he knew where the tunnel was in relation to his position, he knew what lay between it and himself. Pegeen knew nothing. For all she could tell, he stood within a foot of her. She felt her skin tighten at the thought.

Pegeen bent her knees, sinking into an athletic crouch, elbows out, hands ready. Beyond that, she didn't know what to do but wait.

The silence of the cave seemed enormous as she strained every nerve to hear some human sound. It took several minutes for her mind and heart to quiet enough before she could make out a distant trickle of running water and, somewhere closer, an occasional drip.

Finally, she had no choice but to act. It was why she was here.

"Federal agent," she said. She was surprised by the strength of the echo. "Swann, you're under arrest." She hoped the threat didn't sound as foolish to Swann as it did to her.

She heard a low sound, a moan, then silence. Pegeen moved forward, towards the sound, walking in the crouch, securing one foot before creeping forward tentatively with the next. Her boot slipped out from under her and she fell, catching herself with her hands. He can take me anytime, she thought desperately, anytime. I could walk right onto him and never know it. When she had calmed herself, she started forward again, no longer certain after the fall if she was heading in the right direction or not. But the girl was still alive, she knew that—she had heard her groan. Pegeen used the girl to draw her forward.

"You don't have any light," Swann said incredulously. He couldn't believe it, but hearing the woman stumble about in the dark left him no other conclusion. They had sent a woman to catch him, and she came without light. He could not have asked for more.

He heard her footsteps stop. She would be orienting herself, he thought. She wouldn't know how hard it was to pinpoint the source of a sound because of the echoes; she would need help. Swann smiled to himself. He would help her right onto the tip of his knife. He could hear her coming; she would never know where he was until it was too late.

"Are you afraid of the dark?" he asked. Her steps resumed, heading in the right direction now. She moved quickly at first, then slowed as she lost her bearings.

"Most people are afraid of what they'll find in the dark," Swann said. "I'm not . . . It's me." He tittered, then listened to the steps hurrying towards him again.

Aural could hear Swann edging slowly towards her hiding place, moving when the woman moved. Maybe he wanted his back to a wall when the woman got to him—she didn't know, she only knew that he was coming closer. He was within a few steps now. If only Aural could move silently, if only her slightest movement wouldn't be betrayed by the clink of chains, if only she could help in some way . . . The woman was coming to her death; Aural could hear every step that brought her closer.

Swann felt the rock of the wall with his hand and eased his back against it. He was ready now. The agent was closer, soon she would be within striking distance. He controlled his breathing, keeping it as shallow as he could. She would not hear him unless he wanted her to, and then it would be too late.

Closer she came, only a few steps left, but a little off course. That meant nothing, he would strike her in the side rather than the front, or wait until he heard her go past him, then hit her in the back. She didn't need to come right into his lap, just close enough. She was almost there now . . . but she had stopped.

Pegeen paused. Her nerves were screaming with tension. He had to be close, she was very near him now, must be, but he sent no more clues. The only human sounds were her own. She felt as if every step now was in a minefield, things could explode on her at any time. She wanted to run, to turn and run and hide herself somewhere in the darkness, cowering, pulling her knees to her chest and waiting until someone else did something, someone else took care of it.

She held her breath, straining to hear. Then came the scream.

"He has a knife!" Aural yelled.

Swann turned, startled by the sound, amazed that he had been almost atop the girl the whole time. He reached out, touched only stone, then swung back to face the agent, who came towards him in a rush. Swann struck, hitting up, felt the knife strike bone. Something swished past his face, missing, and he struck again. The agent gasped and fell away from him, landing hard on the stone. Swann lifted the blade to stab again and heard the tinkle of chain just fractionally before he felt Aural's hands grasping at him, locating him, then clawing upwards towards his face.

He turned his head, flew at her with his elbow, then kicked her legs. She cried out in pain but kept after him until he clubbed her with his fist, hitting her several times, then kicking her off balance until she fell. Swann turned back to the agent, feeling for her with his foot on the rocky floor. She tried to scrabble away from him but he had her now. He knelt and lifted the knife.

There was a sound, more of a sense, of something rushing at him very fast, and Swann turned and lashed out wildly with the knife, trying to fend it off. The knife caught flesh, ripped, and he heard a grunt as the momentum of the thing took it roaring past him.

Swann snapped on his headlamp and saw Becker, who had raced several yards past, turn and blink at the light. A gash of blood was welling up across his forehead. In the instant Swann also took in the woman agent who was lying beneath him, her arms crossed to ward off another blow, and Aural, also down, a few feet to one side. For a second, everything seemed frozen in time, then Becker came up on all fours, snarling. Swann screamed and ran towards the tunnel.

In the receding light of Swann's headlamp, Becker knelt beside Pegeen, his hands searching for her wounds.

"Are you all right?" he asked.

"Get him," Pegeen said.

Becker put a flashlight in her hand. Swann had reached the tunnel; the light all but disappeared as it burrowed into the long hole in the right.

"You'll need it," Pegeen said, pushing the flashlight back.

"No, I won't," Becker said and he rose and ran towards the point of light still coming from the tunnel. Pegeen followed him with her flashlight beam and saw him dive into the darkness of the rock before she turned the light back on herself and the young woman next to her.

Aural was sitting up and staring with amazement.

"Damn," she said.

"Are you all right?" Pegeen asked, wondering at the same time if she was all right herself. She had been stabbed in the hip and the armpit, she realized, but neither blow would kill her.

"Honey," Aural said, "I ain't felt this good in weeks. Who was that?"

"A federal agent."

"Is he going to catch him?"

"Oh, yes," Pegeen said. "He'll catch him."

"Will he kill him?"

Pegeen let the question hang although she thought the answer was yes.

"Sure looked like he was going to kill him," Aural continued. "Prettiest sight I ever saw."

Pegeen hitched her way across the surface towards Aural, testing the extent of her injuries.

"You're all right. You're safe now," Pegeen said.

Pegeen played the light down onto Aural's legs and gasped. Aural began to laugh and continued, unable to stop herself, and peal after peal of released hysteria echoed through the cavern.

Swann knew that Becker was behind him, but there was nothing he could do. The tunnel was too narrow to turn around; there was no way to bring the knife into play. Every once in a while Becker would grab at Swann's foot and Swann would gasp and crawl with renewed panic. Becker would laugh.

"Don't look back," Becker taunted. "Something's behind you."

Swann would burst forward with increased effort, and then when he slowed again, giving in to exhaustion, Becker's voice would whisper at him again like a parent teasing a child. "Going to . . . *get* you," he would say, then touch Swann on the foot.

As Swann jerked forward desperately, Becker's laughter filled the tunnel, so loud Swann could feel it pressing on him.

When they finally emerged into the bat chamber, Swann stumbled towards the mat of guano, then turned, slashing with the knife, but Becker was standing well back, out of range of the weapon, mocking Swann's futile attempts with a cruel grin.

"Go away!" Swann cried, his voice cracking with tears. "Go away!"

Becker grinned, waiting.

Swann slashed the air again, lunging forward, and Becker glided away like a gymnast, at ease, enjoying the exercise.

"I'll kill you," Swann said.

"Do you think so?" He sounded calm, genuinely interested. "Or will I kill you?"

The blood from Becker's wound ran down the side of his face, giving his features a ghoulish cast in the yellow light of the lamp.

Swann didn't understand why Becker didn't attack. He could take away the knife in an instant, they both knew it.

"What do you want?" he demanded.

"There's no rush," Becker said. "It will all come clear to you in time."

Swann realized then that Becker would kill him, wanted to kill him, and was savoring the anticipation.

"I surrender," Swann said.

Becker only grinned and shook his head.

"I give up," Swann insisted. He threw the knife into the guano mat.

"Not an option," said Becker.

"You're an FBI agent. I give myself up to you. You have to take me into custody."

Becker's eyes danced with pleasure. Swann began to whimper.

"What do you *want?*" he cried.

"What did *you* want, Swann? What did you come down here for?"

"Please," Swann begged. "Please."

"You said I had a reputation, remember? That's the reason you got in touch with me, that's the reason you pulled me into this in the first place. What did I have a reputation *for,* Swann?"

"They said you were—"

"What? They said I was what? Don't say 'fair,' nobody told you I was fair. What did they really say about me, Swann?"

"They said you were . . . worse."

"Worse?"

"Worse than they were."

"Worse than they were? Worse than the psychos like you? Well, if I were, they wouldn't be able to tell you, would they? They'd be dead. But they weren't all dead, were they?"

Swann inched back towards the path trough the guano.

"WERE THEY?" Becker screamed. The bats roused at the noise and sent forth a squeal of their own. Several clumps and clusters broke loose from their roosts and swooped in panicked flight around the chamber before replanting themselves among the others.

Swann bent, cringing from the bats.

"No, they weren't all dead," he whimpered, trying to placate Becker with his voice.

"No," said Becker. "I didn't kill all of them. Just some of them . . . Some dead; some not dead . . . Which one are you, Swann?"

"Not dead. Not dead."

"I warned you, Swann. I told you I never wanted to hear about you again . . . but here you are." Becker grinned wolfishly. He spoke in a taunting singsong. "Here we are together. Alone at last."

Becker slowly turned his palms upward, flexing his fingers. "Aren't you glad you brought me out of retirement?"

"Sweet Jesus," Swann prayed. "Put mercy in his heart."

Becker stepped towards Swan. "Are you ready?" His voice was a whisper.

Swann turned and ran towards the path in the guano. He was several yards in before Becker hit him, lifting him with the force of the assault and plunging him face first into the shit. Swann struggled but Becker forced him down and down, his weight on Swann's back, his hands pushing his face deeper and deeper into the ooze.

Swann struggled because his body demanded it but his mind knew he was already dead. At the end he thought he was back in his cell with Cooper, the giant's body forcing itself upon him.

Pegeen found Becker sitting on the floor of the bat chamber with Swann's body lying at his feet. Pegeen had seen her cat look like that, a dead bird between its paws, looking to her for approval and feeling proud of itself.

As Aural crawled out of the golf sack in which Pegeen had dragged her through the tunnel, the dead bird twitched—Swann groaned and shifted his leg.

"I thought he was dead," said Pegeen.

"So did he," said Becker.

Aural struggled to her feet and looked down at Swann's prostrate form. "Thought sure you'd kill him," she said to Becker, disappointed.

Becker shrugged. "Thought I would, too. If he would have died a little easier, I guess I would have."

"Are you all right?" Pegeen asked.

Becker grinned and in the light of the flashlight Pegeen could see that his spirits had lifted and his mood had changed completely. Where during the past several days he had been a man sunk into the darkness of his soul, he was now boyish, charming, a man at peace with himself. For how long? she wondered. When will he turn into the werewolf again? What will trigger it? Will there be a warning? Thank God, she thought, surprising herself with the sudden understanding and relief she felt, thank God I won't be with him to find out. He says he loves Deputy Assistant Director Crist? Let her deal with him, and she has my sympathy.

As Pegeen and Becker conferred about the best way to get both Aural and Swann above ground, they heard a sudden *whoosh* of energy behind them. A brilliant light flared up in the cavern and they turned to see Swann ablaze. Aural stood over him, the can of lighter fluid still in one hand, the cigarette lighter in the other.

Pegeen moved forward to extinguish the flames, but Becker grabbed her and held her back.

"You'll only burn yourself," he said, his voice whispering in her ear.

Pegeen struggled until she noticed the look on Aural's face. The tortured woman regarded the fire at her feet with the beatific smile of a saint. Aural's lips moved, and it took Pegeen a moment to realize that she was singing, her voice barely audible over the roar of the flames and the squeals of the bats.

Chapter 42

Karen watched the press conference on television. Both Hatcher and Congressman Beggs were in top form, each deferring to the other, each sharing credit magnanimously with the dedicated men and women of law enforcement in general and the Bureau in particular, yet each managing to make himself appear the true hero of the hour. It was a masterful performance in Washington hypocrisy, simultaneously humble and self-serving. Karen had only a superficial interest in Beggs, but she kept a canny eye on Hatcher's demeanor. He held for her the same disgusted fascination she might have for a snake slithering up a greased flagpole. The man's ability to climb, no matter what the obstacle, was extraordinary. She sensed with suppressed horror that she was looking at the next Deputy Director of the FBI, the man just below the political appointee, the man who ran the show.

The two men gave a compressed and sanitized version of the case. Karen had already read the immediate action reports as well. They had been faxed to her the night before. She knew everything there was to know about the case—except the truth, and she could only get that from Becker.

Becker arrived back in Clamden after a day-long session with Dr. Gold, who had ultimately thrown his hands in the air, despairing of any real progress. "I can't do anything for you by myself, John, you have to cooperate. You have to want get at the root of it yourself."

Becker had grinned in a way that made Gold uncomfortable. "I don't want to root it out," he said. "I've decided to keep it."

"Despite all the pain it causes you?"

"The pain comes from trying to repress it."

"That's not true, John. You know it's not."

Becker had continued to grin at him. "Well, you know best, Doc. It says so right on your diploma."

Gold sighed. Becker had always been difficult, too smart for jargon, too perceptive for banalities, and completely lacking in the respectful awe so necessary in the doctor-patient relationship. They had become, after years of contention, grudging friends, affectionate adversaries. Gold had not cured him and knew he could not and, worse, realized that Becker knew the same. Some conditions were not curable; they could only be contained, and then only at a very high price. Gold feared that Becker was weary of paying the price.

"So what do we do?" Gold asked. "Will you come for more sessions?"

"Do you see any point in it?" Becker asked.

Gold hesitated. There was no point in lying, not to Becker, there was no hope of fooling him.

"I hope you'll keep coming," he said.

"We'll see," Becker said, rising. "Don't look so glum, Doc. There's one good side to this."

"What's that?"

"Hatcher will be so pleased."

Becker and Karen made love before they discussed anything, each trying to rediscover in the other the passion, the magic attraction that had brought them together in the first place. It had never resided just in their bodies, of course, but that is where they looked for it.

"How was it?" Karen asked when they had lain quietly in the dark for several minutes, each lost in his or her own thoughts.

"You read the reports," Becker said.

"But how was it, John? Are you all right?"

"Fine," he said. "No problem."

"How did you . . . was it as bad as you thought it would be?"

Becker was silent.

"I'm out of Serial," Karen said. "Hatcher put me back into Kidnapping this morning."

Becker turned to look at her.

"You okay with that?" he asked.

She touched his cheek. "Thank you," she said.

"For what?"

Karen smiled. "Do you really think I don't know what you're up to or why you do the things you do?"

"You do, do you?"

"I know all about you," Karen said, smiling.

Becker grinned. "You think you know *all* about me?"

"I know what I want to know about," Karen said. "And if I don't want to know, I don't ask."

How wise, Becker thought. How lucky I am.

He took her in his arms again and held her wordlessly, his embrace asking for forgiveness at the same time that it expressed his gratitude.

"I'm coming back to work," he said finally.

"You don't have to," she said.

"Yes, I do. I can't keep fighting it—I'm too tired." But Becker did not feel tired. By giving up his resistance to the pull of his desires, he had unleashed great energy within himself. He felt liberated and invigorated. By submitting to his nature, he had freed himself, he thought. A wolf is a wolf, and cannot be happy as a domestic dog.

"Will you be all right?"

Becker pulled her tighter in his arms, fighting an urge to howl. "I think I can handle it," he said.